The Second Coming

John Niven was born in Irvine, Ayrshire. He read English Literature at Glasgow University and spent the next ten years working in the UK music industry. He has written for the *Sunday Times*, *The Times*, *Scotland on Sunday*, *Esquire* and many other publications. He is the author of six novels including *Kill Your Friends* and *Straight White Male*. He lives in Buckinghamshire.

ALSO BY JOHN NIVEN

The Second Coming

John Niven

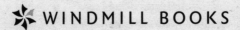
WINDMILL BOOKS

Published by Windmill Books 2014

2 4 6 8 10 9 7 5 3 1

Copyright © John Niven 2011

John Niven has asserted his right under the Copyright, Designs and
Patents Act, 1988, to be identified as the author of this work.

First published in Great Britain in 2011 by William Heinemann

First published in paperback in 2012 by Vintage

Windmill Books
The Random House Group Limited
20 Vauxhall Bridge Road, London SW1V 2SA

Addresses for companies within The Random House Group Limited can be found at:
www.randomhouse.co.uk/offices.htm

The Random House Group Limited Reg. No. 954009

www.randomhouse.co.uk

A CIP catalogue record for this book
is available from the British Library

ISBN 9780099592136

The Random House Group Limited supports the Forest Stewardship
Council® (FSC®), the leading international forest-certification organisation.
Our books carrying the FSC label are printed on FSC®-certified paper. FSC is
the only forest-certification scheme supported by the leading environmental
organisations, including Greenpeace. Our paper procurement policy
can be found at: www.randomhouse.co.uk/environment

Typeset by SX Composing DTP Ltd, Rayleigh, Essex

Printed and bound by CPI Group (UK) Ltd, Croydon, CR0 4YY

For my Mother

'Do you think that when Jesus comes back he's ever gonna want to see a fucking cross again? Kinda like going up to Jackie Onassis with a little sniper's rifle pendant . . .'

Bill Hicks

Part One

eaven

'What they do in Heaven we are ignorant of.
What they do *not* do we are told expressly.'

Jonathan Swift

1

'GOD'S COMING – LOOK BUSY!'

O SAYS THE TATTERED STICKER ON THE METAL FILING cabinet by the water cooler. But today it's no joke: God really is coming and people really are trying to look busy. Raphael and Michael are standing next to the bubbling glass dome, both clutching sheets of paper (that time-honoured office trick, designed to make the wanderer appear purposeful) and their conversation – in contrast to the leisurely banter the two angels have enjoyed around this very water cooler for the past week – is snatched, hurried and delivered *sotto voce* out of the corners of their mouths, accompanied by nervy glances down the main hallway.

'When's the old man getting back?' Raphael says.

'Any time now. Late morning according to Jeannie,' Michael replies without looking at his friend. He's concentrating on the cooler, tugging the lever for the water, a big bubble flubbing up in the crystal tank.

'Shit. Think He's gonna be pissed?'

'Pissed?' Michael considers this, looking out over the main office, sipping his water.

The main office in Heaven is much like any other open-plan office – cubicles, desks with metal filing baskets on them, telephones, waste-paper baskets, photocopiers and shelves full of files – but there are differences too. There is, of course, no strip lighting in Heaven: rather everything is suffused, bathed, washed, whatever you'd like to call it, with pure celestial light, the freshly minted light of a perfect May morning. The atmosphere is generally one of happy, focused, excited work (although today, for the obvious reasons, there is an undercurrent of nervy anticipation), for in the main office in Heaven it is, of course, forever Friday afternoon. Another slight difference – the honeycomb of desks and cubicles extends as far as the eye can see, flattening out towards the horizon and surrounded by cotton wisps of clouds. It may surprise some to learn that people work in Heaven, but it was one of God's most inspired directives. (And God is no stranger to inspired directives.) 'People want to work,' He told Peter. 'Shit, people *need* to work. Look at the long-term unemployed. Look at the idle rich. They look *happy* to you?' Therefore anyone in Heaven who wants a job – and most do – is given one.

Michael tips the paper cup back and closes his eyes in pleasure as the last drops sluice down his throat. The water in Heaven . . . well, you can imagine.

'Pissed?' Michael repeats. 'He's gonna go *fucking nuts*.'

Even Jeannie, God's PA, who is normally unflappable, who, like the chess grandmaster, routinely thinks fifteen or twenty moves ahead, even Jeannie is a little on edge this morning. She's in her early forties, once insanely attractive, now just very. 'No, Seb,' she is saying to one of her two assistants, 'He'll want it chronological. Put those boxes at the front.' In God's outer office Jeannie is putting together a review of the last four hundred or so years on earth. There's a *lot* of stuff: boxes of files, papers and DVDs are piled high on a chain of trolley carts many miles long. There are a couple of miles of carts filled with CDs alone; the entire recorded musical output of earth for four centuries.

Sebastian is bickering with Lance, Jeannie's other assistant. 'No, asshole! Those should go with these, if –'

'Ooh, get her!' Lance says, flattening a hand on his chest. It's hard to tell which of them is camper.

Something Jeannie learned early on when it came to hiring staff for the inner sanctum, and something they seemed to have gotten strangely wrong on earth: God *loves* fags.

'Because, dumb-ass, Jeannie's saying it's to be chronological!'

'Oh, *be nice*!' Lance says, waving him away. 'I was trying to hide it.' He holds up a file marked 'CATHOLIC CHURCH: RECENT HISTORY'. 'You think He's gonna want to read this?'

'Come on, you two,' Jeannie finally snaps as her phone starts ringing. 'Just get on with it. And there's no point trying to hide anything. He'll read it all.' Then into the phone, 'Yep?' Jeannie listens. 'Aha. Yep. OK.' She puts the receiver back down. Seb and Lance look at her expectantly. 'He's on His way up,' Jeannie says.

God, coming through the main office, beaming, slapping backs, exchanging hellos, returning high fives, stopping to talk with people in cubicles. He's now into what people on earth would perceive as his mid-fifties and he's . . . 'handsome' wouldn't quite cover it. God is movie-star handsome, He's a goddamn *heart-throb* is what He is. His hair, once black as motor oil, is now flecked with silver. Silver in His week-old stubble too. And those eyes – pale, pale blue, the blue of the shallow water in a tropical lagoon at midday on a summer afternoon. God picks up His rod and walks on down the hall.

He is dressed in fishing gear: plaid shirt, canvas waistcoat with various bits of paraphernalia stuffed in the pockets. On His head He wears a battered fisherman's hat with brightly coloured flies and lures stuck to it. In one hand He carries his rod and tackle box; in the other hand three fat, perfectly speckled trout dangle from a piece of line tied through the gills.

'Hey, Marcus!' God shouts to the black kid from the mailroom. 'How's it hanging, son?'

'Between ma knees, big guy!' Marcus shouts across. God laughs. God loves spades.

He throws the doors to His outer office open. 'Honeee, I'm home!' He says as he hugs Jeannie with whom He enjoys a healthy flirtation.

'Welcome back, sir!' Jeannie says.

'You miss me?'

'Of course we did.'

'Hey, fellas,' God says to Seb and Lance. 'How's tricks?'

'Great!' Seb beams, nervous.

'Hey,' Lance says, running a hand down God's battered canvas waistcoat, '*nice* outfit. I normally don't care for John Deere but this . . .'

God laughs. 'Get her.'

'And how was your vacation?' Jeannie asks.

'Oh, terrific. Just terrific. You were absolutely right. I will *not* be leaving it so long before I have another one.'

'Mmmm.' Jeannie smiles, thinking about how quickly this view might be changing. It is painful for her to see Him in such a good mood when she knows that the mood will soon be shattered.

'Oh, here . . .' God swings the trout up and passes them to her. 'For you. Just brush 'em with a little butter, salt and pepper, thank you, Seb,' God says, taking the steaming coffee mug that says 'I'M THE BOSS'. 'Stick 'em in the oven at about 350 for fifteen minutes. Squeeze of lemon juice when they're done. Mmmm!' God kisses His bunched fingertips. 'I been eating 'em straight out the river for the past week. So – what did I miss?'

'Well,' Jeannie says as she leads the way towards God's private office. She throws the doors open: the office is the size of a football field and is covered by several city skylines of boxes.

'Shit,' God says, blowing on His coffee. 'They been busy down there, huh?'

'Mmm-hmmm,' Jeannie says, not making eye contact. 'Now, a lot of the older stuff's in these files, but the more recent data's on disks, videotape and on your hard drive.'

'Huh?' God says.

God is a fast learner – the fastest. Under Jeannie's tuition it takes Him maybe one and a half cups of coffee to get to grips with all the technology that has made its way up since he left for vacation: phones, email, computers, CDs, DVDs, television and the like. A brief detour on the fax machine, a now redundant piece of twentieth-century hardware. All this cool stuff that wasn't around when He left. Busy little creatures. He enjoys a playful diversion catching up on video games: stunned that it seemed to take them a quarter of a century to get from *Donkey Kong* to *Halo 3*. (He completes the latter in seven minutes.)

'Jeannie,' God says, standing up, stretching, surveying the miles of boxes, the files glowing on the screen of his new laptop, 'is this going to make me unhappy?'

'Ah, I think that's a fair assessment, sir.'

God moves forward, sits His coffee on a packing crate and

picks up a file at random. It is marked '18th CENTURY: SLAVE TRADE'. Huh? Slavery God was familiar with, unfortunately. Bastard Pharaohs had been mental for it. But slave *trade?* 'The fuck is the "slave trade"?' God asks, opening the file, frowning.

'I think it's best if we give you some time to go through all this,' Jeannie says.

2

WORD HERE ABOUT THE DIFFERENCE BETWEEN celestial time and time as it is experienced on earth. Time still passes in eternity but *slower*. Much, much slower. A day in heaven passes by at about the same rate as approximately fifty-seven earth years. When God took His first – until this past week His only – vacation four point six billion years ago it was the Hadean aeon. There was no oxygen and the earth was basically still a molten ball, fresh and smoking from the Big Bang some ten billion years before. (That had been a total accident, of course. God enjoys the occasional morning toke, but sometimes rues the results. Hammerhead sharks? Platypuses? The baboon's ass? Come on. You'd cut back, wouldn't you?) It would be thousands of years before there were even oceans. A guy could take a little time out, right?

When He took this week off it had been the year 1609 on earth, the height of the Renaissance, which God had been enjoying enormously. Copernicus, Michelangelo, da Vinci. What's not to like? When He left, tackle box tucked under His arm, fishing hat jauntily perched on his head, *King Lear* was being performed on the London stage while, across town, Bacon worked on *De Sapientia Veterum Liber*. El Greco – tongue pressed into his upper lip in concentration, brush trembling – was painting *The Opening of the Fifth Seal*. Galileo was squinting through his prototype telescope, his eyes alighting for the first time on Jupiter's four satellite moons. Monteverdi had recently finished composing *L'Orfeo*. A good time to go fishing, God thought.

When He returned from the far-flung countryside of Heaven, refreshed and bearing trout, almost exactly four hundred years had passed. It was the year 2011 on earth. As we know, it had not been an uneventful four centuries . . .

God is a fast reader. The fastest. He is capable of digesting thousands of dense documents near simultaneously while watching the videotapes and DVDs and clicking through the computer files that make up His briefing on the latter part of the time He has missed. It takes God the whole morning and a little of the lunch hour to get up to speed. He quickly learns a torrent of geography: Auschwitz, Buchenwald, Belsen, Guantánamo, Belfast, Cambodia, Vietnam, Flanders, Ypres, Nagasaki, Hiroshima, Rwanda, Bosnia. From time to time Jeannie, Lance and Seb jump at their desks as they hear the muffled screams and cries.

As He works through the twentieth century – pausing regularly to throw up – God learns about strange, incredible new concepts, about capitalism and communism. About nuclear deterrence and mutually assured destruction. About the military-industrial complex. About pro-life and zero tolerance. About junk bonds and short-selling. Gazumping and negative equity. Fatwa and jihad. Ethnic cleansing and repatriation. Photos, taken in hot, dusty squares in Arabic countries: two gay kids being hanged. A woman, an adulteress, crying, buried up to her shoulders in sand, a crowd of men hefting stones visible a few yards away. He turns to the computer and clicks on a file on the desktop marked 'Islamic Fundamentalism: Beliefs and Practices'. Mmm, something called the Taliban. Right, what was going on with these dudes? Busting some bad-assed beards from the looks of things . . .

A few minutes later Jeannie can hear muffled screams and swearing coming through those heavy, cathedral-sized doors. Stuff being kicked over.

God reads about the burqa and the hijab. The deal according to these dudes seemed to be something like this: all men are barely contained rapists who can be provoked by even a glimpse of an ankle. So chicks have to march about in head-to-toe black sacks. But all women are basically temptress whores who want to fuck all men all the time. So if one of them somehow breaks a good, honest married man down by wantonly flashing, say, a kneecap at him, and he gives in and fucks her, then it is suitable for her to be literally stoned to death – a big circle of men hurling rocks at her fucking head – while the guy gets a parking ticket. He reads on – a list of stuff the Taliban guys were resolutely not having: 'pork, pig, pig oil, human hair products, satellite dishes, cinematography, music and equipment that produces the joy of music, pool tables, chess, masks, alcohol, tapes, computers, VCRs, television, anything that propagates sex, wine, lobster, nail polish, firecrackers, statues, sewing catalogues, pictures and Christmas cards'.

Sewing catalogues?

He reads about the execution of homosexuals. The stoning and whipping of people for . . . well, for not very much really. About a sixteen-year-old schoolgirl getting hanged for something called 'crimes against chastity'.

Then, for balance you understand, He watches a quick

compendium of the most popular American TV shows – a gang bang of reality buffoonery, get-rich-quick, get-famous-quick nonsense – and, just for a brief moment, He gets a flash of how those Taliban dudes must be feeling, sat there in your cave, with your AK-47 and your bowl of mung, thinking about fucking a goat while you're watching *America's Newest Top Whore Meets the Kardashians*. God experiences an urge to ban television Himself.

A couple of fingers of malt whisky and a big, tightly packed joint constitute lunch and help get Him through more of the recent past: Deforestation. Globalisation. Collateral damage. Brand awareness. Marketing. Product placement. Corporate sponsorship. Inbuilt obsolescence. *Republicans.*

For the remainder of His lunch hour, God weeps.

In the outer office Jeannie has sent the boys off to lunch. She bites her lip as she listens to Him sobbing, a sound she has never heard before. Because, despite His chummy, friendly demeanour, God is old school: a tough guy. A man's man. After a while it is quiet for a long time.

When He throws the doors open He has composed himself. Only the slightest rawness in the voice would give away what has just happened. Jeannie looks up and swallows. He is no longer heartbroken, He simply looks very, very angry. This is actually a good sign, Jeannie thinks.

'Jeannie,' God says softly, His throat raw, His fury quiet and controlled, 'where is the little bastard?'

3

T'S LIKE, UH, LIKE A DIP TYPE OF THING, YOU know? Kinda like baba ganoush? I think there's chickpeas in there, maybe a little cumin, lemon juice, onion, and, uh, here . . .'

Jesus takes a heroic toke on the blunt and passes it back. The reefer in Heaven – well, you can imagine. You know what He left down here, right? Shit, even Thai stick doesn't cut it in Heaven.

'. . . and, uh, garlic. But it's not like one of those garlicky things where you're like "uh, there's a lot of garlic in this, man". It's just like a *hint*. They spread it on this really thin, toasted pitta bread and it's like . . . ohhh, mama!'

'Shit, man,' Jimi says, drawing heavily on the blunt himself now, 'shut the fuck up! You're making me hungry.'

'I'm telling you, baby, I had it down there a couple of times. The Middle East, it, it's like a really underrated food region. I, fuck, I'm . . .' He gazes off into the thick blue skeins of marijuana smoke, his train of thought tumbling off the tracks and barrelling down a hillside.

Stoned? Wrecked? Blitzed? Totalled? Wasted? Trashed? No.

Jesus is *cunted*.

They're stretched out with the usual paraphernalia scattered around – a cooler full of beers, ashtrays, pipes and bongs, roaches, torn cigarette packets, pizza boxes, amplifiers and leads. Jimi is cradling his white Fender Stratocaster. Jesus' rosewood Gibson SG lies on a cushion beside him. Jesus has inherited many features from his dad: he's tall too, a little over six foot, and undeniably good-looking, with those liquid blue eyes. (Admittedly, they're flecked with red right now.) The hair is blond though, thick and long, hanging down to his shoulders. Absent-mindedly, Jimi flicks off a little riff high up on the fretboard, the last note echoing off into the clouds around them.

'Wow,' Jesus says. 'How d'ya do that?'

'It's just a little blues thing, man.'

Jesus picks up his guitar and Jimi begins showing him the lick. Jesus likes fooling around with Jimi best. There were some other great players up here, no question – Roy Buchanan can really make that Telecaster cry, but Roy can be, well, cranky. Jimi, on the other hand, is such a nice dude. Hendrix, in his turn, has found Jesus to be a very promising pupil, a more than capable rhythm player who has some talent for chunky, ringing bursts of lead. Guy had a great voice too, no denying that. A few passes and Jesus has the little riff down cold. 'And if you're in, like, a minor key,' Hendrix says, 'you can just . . .'

They're just getting it together, each playing the same riff in a slightly different place on the neck, the two guitars locking and chiming together, when Lance materialises. He takes in the cloud of sweet smoke, the detritus of another dope-fuelled jam session and the misty-eyed pair in the centre of it. 'Oh my,'

Lance says. 'Looks like a couple of teenage potheads threw up in here.'

'Hey, Lance,' Jesus says. 'You want a beer?'

'Oh, beer! How macho!' Lance says, clapping his hands together. 'I'll pass, a little early for cocktails for me. Your dad wants to see you.'

'Shit, I forgot. He's back today, huh?' Hendrix says.

'He's back and he's bad, sweetheart.'

'OK, tell him I'll be right up.'

'Uh, no offence, but I think He meant now. As in *right now*.'

'Ah shit.' Jesus unstraps the Gibson and takes a last hit. He gets up, his tall, gangly frame unfolding languidly from the beanbag. 'Later, Jimi.'

'Be nice,' Hendrix says.

'Always.'

God looks up to see Jesus strolling in, Jeannie closing the doors behind him. 'Dad!' Jesus says, arms outstretched. 'How was it? Fish biting?'

Father and son embrace, the son smelling trout, sweat and stale plaid – for God has not had time to change since his return – and the father, in His turn, smelling beer and pepperoni sausage and the sweet fragrance of very good grass. 'Son,' He says brightly, 'take a seat! How you been?'

'Oh, great, just great.'

Jesus takes the seat closest to his father's desk and swings his bare feet up onto the edge. God perches on the edge of the desk.

'Good, good,' God says, beaming. 'What you been up to?'

'Ah, you know, just chillaxing.'

'Taking it easy, huh? That's great.'

'Yeah, playing a little guitar, a little golf. Blowing some grass?'

'Yeah? You look a little parched, son, you want something to drink? Nice glass of water or something?'

'Uh, yeah, that'd be cool, thanks. You know, you look good, Dad.' God, His back to Jesus, pours a glass of water from a pitcher. The water is rust-orange in colour, with thick sediment in the bottom. God brings it over, His hand covering the glass as Jesus goes on. 'Look like you got some sun.'

'Yeah?' God says.

'Yeah, Jeannie was right. You should get away more often.'

'You think?' God says, handing Jesus the water.

'Shit, yeah. You gotta take some time for, for yourself now and then, right? Gotta –'

'Mmmm.' God watches, smiling as Jesus breaks off to take a long drink.

'Krrooooo-aghhhh!' Jesus, spraying the water all over the place, retching. 'What the fuck is –'

'THAT IS A WATER SAMPLE TAKEN FROM THE GANGES RIVER THIS AFTERNOON!'

'It's . . . uh, what?'

'THEY ARE USING THAT PLACE AS A HUMAN FUCKING TOILET WHILE YOU'RE LYING ON YOUR ASS, YOU LAZY LITTLE BASTARD!'

God in a good mood? The kindliest uncle you ever dreamed of. Jack Lemmon or Jimmy Stewart on Ambien. God pissed? A Hollywood studio chairman with a lousy opening weekend on his hands. Joel Silver or David Geffen on crack.

In the outer office people bury their heads in paperwork. This is tough. Everyone loves Jesus.

'I . . . I . . .'

'Come here. Come here.' God grabs Jesus by the ear – *'Ow! Ow! Ow! Ow!'* – and pulls him towards a huge white Nobo board where He has written various headlines from his briefing. 'They are using the rainforests as a goddamn lumber yard. There is a hole – A FUCKING HOLE – in the ozone layer the size of my dick. The oceans . . . what fish are left in the oceans are living on a diet of turds, crude oil and old refrigerators.' God lets go and Jesus goes stumbling back, rubbing his ear. 'I, Dad –'

God holds up a finger. Jesus shuts up as God brings this finger close to His son's face. 'That's just the eco crap. Morally, I . . . have you any idea where those people are at morally nowadays? You'd find more common decency at a rapists and usurers convention.'

'I, you know, I haven't been back that long myself, Dad!' (This is kind of true. A couple of thousand years: just a month or so in celestial terms.)

'You couldn't stick your head in and see how things were going? You know what your trouble is? You're feckless, lazy and unfocused. You seem to think you can bowl through life with kind words and a goofy smile. You never –'

God went on with the parent speech. Oh boy, He thought as He listened to Himself, hearing Himself saying things like 'responsibility', 'self-discipline' and 'attitude', did this speech sound old. Even in Heaven – were we ever going to evolve to the point where you could stop having to say stuff like this to your children? Everyone else loved the kid. Was it just that you expected so much more from your own?

Finally, sensing Jesus is on the verge of tears, God takes a deep breath and reels it in, His tone softening as He comes around to perch on the desk closer to His son. 'Look – don't get me wrong – you'd earned a vacation, no question. But I thought you'd, you know . . . mind the store a bit while the old man was out of town?'

'It's just . . . the ones I've been meeting from the twentieth century have all seemed so cool.'

God sighs. 'You're in Heaven, numbnuts. Of course they're gonna be cool. And you always think the best of people anyway.'

Father and son gaze at the board in silence for a moment or two: at the terrible facts and figures, the names and the various photos God has stuck up there: the piles of naked, skeletal corpses behind barbed wire, the children on pipe-cleaner legs with swollen bellies clutching empty bowls, an enormous nuclear submarine.

'Shit,' Jesus says quietly. 'What happened to "be nice"?'

'Be nice'. Whenever He reflected on the wonderful simplicity of this, His original and only commandment, He automatically flashed onto the following thought – *fucking Moses*. What kind of arrogant fuckstick bins the one commandment they're given and rocks up with ten of their own? Moses, that's who. Whole bunch of shit about coveting thy neighbour's goddamn ox. (Moses, it was well known around the place, had always been a little nuts. A little nuts? The dude was off of his freaking teats.) Why? Why'd he have to go and sex it up? Power. Ambition. Ego. The usual reasons stuff got done.

'That's what we're gonna find out,' God says, swinging into getting-stuff-done mode, thumbing the intercom on His desk. 'Jeannie? All the Head Saints please, in the boardroom now.' God sighs again as He says this. Because God *hates* meetings. You spend all your time in meetings, you're just firefighting, dealing with problems.

'Already done, sir. They're in there waiting for you.'

'Good girl. And Jeannie?'

'Yes, sir?'

'Sandwiches, coffee and doughnuts. We're gonna be a while . . .'

OUR VERY NERVOUS SAINTS – PETER, MATTHEW, Andrew and John – sitting around the conference table, smoking and chugging coffee. The conference table is enormous, made of glass, and has a map of the world finely etched upon its surface. Each of the saints has a pile of papers in front of him.

Peter's pile is an overview prepared by all departments. As General Manager of Heaven the buck theoretically stops with Peter. However, as God's consigliere – and the only person who told Him a holiday might not be a great idea (Peter had an inkling as to how religion was taking hold down there) – Peter is a little less nervous than his colleagues.

Matthew's pile, as befits a former tax attorney, deals with statistics, facts and figures. Matthew is bespectacled, balding and drinks from his water glass with a trembling hand. He is also the proud possessor of one of the most boring voices known to man or angel: a monotone purr capable of reducing the finest prose to the phone book.

Andrew's pile is small and relates mainly to the twentieth

century. The patron saint of Scotland would be best described on earth as God's spin doctor. Andrew is good at his job, but he knows it's going to be hard work to put any kind of positive gloss on what's in front of him today.

John's pile contains radical ideas and future projections. Fittingly for someone whose father was named Zebedee, John is something of a 'blue-sky' man. An 'outside-the-box' thinker. (But God help you if God heard you using expressions like that.)

'Oh God, oh God, oh God,' Matthew is saying as he pores over his briefing.

'Give it to Him straight,' Peter says. 'Just paint a clear picture.'

'A clear fucken picture, ya fucken wide-o ye?' Andrew says. 'Like a picture o' a fucken giant turd that some cunt's pished on and then stamped intae the fucken ground with a size ten Doc Martens boot? Would that aboot sum it up, dae ye think?'

Matthew sighs. 'Does everything have to be turds and piss with you?'

'I think we'll be OK,' John says, looking up from the joint he is building. 'I mean, down there, yeah, it's a bit like, uh, Dad went away and the kids had a party, you know, the carpet got stained, a few glasses got broken, maybe like, uh, a window got smashed, but, at the end of the day, the house didn't get *burned down*, right? No one *died*.'

Andrew snorts a derisive laugh.

'Er, actually, statistically speaking –' Matthew says, looking up from his charts, graphs and lists.

'John?' Peter interrupts.

'Mmmm?' John is putting the finished joint in his mouth, patting his robe for a lighter.

'Shut the fuck up.' Peter snatches the joint from his lips and lights it himself. John shrugs as they hear voices and footsteps approaching. 'Oh God, oh God, oh God,' Matthew says again, and then, suddenly, the doors are flying open and God is entering, Jesus trailing behind Him.

John is closest and first on his feet. 'Hey! Welcome back! Looking good.'

Matthew gets as far as, 'I hear the fishing was excell—'

'You two,' God says, cutting them off, 'can the fucking bullshit right now and sit your asses down or, I swear, I will rip off your fucking cocks and wear them as earrings for the rest of this fucking meeting.'

'Sorry,' Matthew says.

'No problemo,' John says as they both sit back down.

'Hey,' Peter says softly as he and God embrace. 'I'm not one for "I told you so", but –'

God holds up an index finger, silencing him.

'A'right, chief?' Andrew says simply, nodding across the table.

'Hey, guys,' Jesus says, grabbing a doughnut from the buffet and sliding into a chair beside Matthew.

'Right,' God says, rapping his notes on the table and settling himself down at the head. 'Seeing as they seem to be throwing themselves into a genocide or a famine every ten to fifteen minutes, let's get to it. So . . .' God plants his elbows on the table, clasps His hands together and leans in towards them. 'What the fuck is going on down there?'

OURS LATER. SHIRTSLEEVES ROLLED UP. THE ashtrays full. Coffee mugs and dirty plates strewn everywhere. Papers spilling over the table and onto the floor and the air thick with dope smoke from the many joints being passed around to aid concentration and radical creative thinking. God sighs, exhaling herby, woody smoke as He finally asks the obvious question.

'What the fuck,' God asks, 'happened with the Christians? There are fucking Christians *everywhere*.'

'It, uh, it got convoluted,' Peter says.

'Convoluted? What the fuck is there to get convoluted about "Be nice"?'

'If I may, sir,' Matthew says, standing up. God gestures, indicating that he has the floor. 'There's been a lot of splintering going on. You have the Catholics obviously.'

'Right, so that's one,' God says.

'Not exactly one, sir, no. There's various, um, subgroups within the Catholics. You've got the Maronite Church, the

Melkites, the Ruthenian – or Byzantine – Catholic Church, the Chaldeans, the –'

'Look, what's the difference?' God asks.

'Well, they mainly believe that the Pope is your representative on earth –'

'Fuck me,' God says.

'But,' Matthew continues, 'there are differences of theological emphasis concerning, er, things like, say, the Latin depiction of purgatory.'

'Who,' God says, pouring more coffee, 'gives a drop of fucking piss about the Latin depiction of purgatory?'

'A fine point, sir. However, some seem to. Then there's things like the Patriarchal Exarchate for Orthodox Parishes of Russian Tradition in Western Europe, there's Oriental Orthodox Churches – as you'll remember they *didn't* accept the Council of Chalcedon back in 451 – the Coptic Orthodox Church of Alexandria, Jacobite Syrian Christian Church, the Malankara Orthodox Syrian Church, Eritrean Orthodox Tewahedo Church, Assyrian Church of the East . . . Mariavite Church, Palmarian Catholic Church, True Catholic Church, Liberal Catholic Church, Chinese Patriotic Catholic Association, Catholic Charismatic Church of Canada, Communion of Christ the Redeemer, the –'

'These are all still the Catholics?'

'Yes, sir.'

'Skip forward,' God says. Matthew's voice, literally driving everyone insane.

'Well . . . then there's the Protestants. Within that you have Presbyterians, Baptists, Anabaptists, Methodists, Pentecostalists, Episcopalians, Charismatics, Neo-Charismatics and the, um, Lutherans.'

'Right. Thank y—'

'And within those groups there's the likes of the Apostolic Lutheran Church of America, the Confessional Evangelical Lutheran Conference, the Remonstrant Brotherhood, the Confederation of Reformed Evangelical Churches, the Upper Cumberland Presbyterian Church – this list is by no means exhaustive by the way –'

God disagreed. He was already exhausted.

'Then there's the Amish – you've got Swartzentruber Amish, Old Order Amish, Nebraska Amish, Beachy Amish, then the Hutterites, the Bruderhof Communities, Abecedarians, no, hang on, they're extinct, sorry, the Mennonites, and, within that, the Chortitzer Mennonite Conference, Holdeman Mennonites, Evangelical Mennonites. The Methodists – Christian Methodist Episcopal Church, Free Methodists, United Methodists, Primitive Methodists. The Baptists – Old Time Missionary Baptists, Regular Baptists, Old Regular Baptists, Progressive Baptists, Separate Baptists, Separate Baptists in Christ, Seventh-Day Baptists, Southeast Baptist Convention, Southern Baptists of Texas, Free Will Baptists, Bible Baptists, Conservative Baptist Association of America, Primitive Baptists, Black Primitive Baptists, the Norwegian Baptist Union and, um . . . the Interstate and Foreign Landmark Missionary Baptist Association.'

'That's it?'

'For the Baptists. Then there's the Brethren – United Brethren, Free Evangelical Brethren, Plymouth Brethren, the Pentecostals – Church of the Little Children of Jesus Christ, Fire Baptized Holiness Church of God of the Americas –'

'Hang on,' God says, stubbing a joint out. '*The Fire Baptized Holiness Church of God of the Americas?* Are you making this fucking shit up?'

'No, sir. The God is Love Pentecostal Church, Church of

God Jerusalem Acres, Church of God with Signs Following . . .'

Jesus – asleep now.

'. . . Church of God of the Original Mountain Assembly, Potter's House of Christian Fellowship. The Charismatics – Calvary Chapel, Charismatic Church of God, City Harvest Church, Jesus Army, Ministries of His Glory, New Frontiers, True Jesus Church, New Birth Movement, New Life Fellowship, uh, sorry, the last few were actually *Neo-*Charismatic. The Quakers, the Stone-Campbell Movement, the Millerites, Southcottites, Seventh-Day Adventists, the Mormons, they believe your son visited Salt Lake City in Utah at some point where he ministered to –'

'Hey, dufus,' God says to Jesus, who is snoring lightly. God throws a pencil at him, getting him on the forehead and causing him to snap awake.

'Uh, what?'

'Were you ever in Salt Lake City?'

'Is, is, this about that girl? Look, she said she was eighteen. I –'

'Forget it,' God says, waving a hand for Matthew to continue.

'. . . ministered to the, uh, Nephites. Then there's the Latter-Day Saints, the Prairie Saint denominations – Hedrickites, Bickertonites, Cutlerites, Strangites and so on. Then there's the more out there stuff like the Christadelphians, Christian Scientists, Spirit-Wrestlers, Subbotniks, Molokans, Jehovah's Witnesses, the Swedenborgians, the –'

'OK, OK,' God holds up a hand. 'Matthew, please, shut the fuck up. Cut to the chase, OK? How many of these sons of bitches in total?'

'Different Christian denominations? Um . . .' Matthew consults his notes, 'a little over 38,000.'

A long silence before God says 'Fuck me' once again.

No one's arguing with that and, after another long moment of silence, God asks, 'How did they get so caught up in the worshipping thing? I mean, do they think I care if they believe in me or not?'

'They all got really hung up on biblical interpretation,' Peter says.

'Man, the fucking Bible?' Jesus says.

The fucking Bible. What a lemon. They'd got hold of a few stories – anecdotes, gossip – and they'd appended, annotated, amended, extrapolated and embellished until folk could extract a rubber stamp for just about anything they wanted to do out of that shit. (The feeding of the five thousand, yeah, right. Jesus remembered that meal: you were lucky if there were fifty of them there. But it was like Lenny Bruce at the hungry i, or the Sex Pistols at the 100 Club: if every fucker who claimed they'd been there had actually attended those gigs then they wouldn't have fitted into Yankee Stadium. And, aside from the loaves and fishes, they'd used a lot of fucking couscous that night, man. A *lot* of fucking couscous. Stretching that food dollar.) Not that the Bible had a monopoly on this kind of generous interpretation of course. A beardy German economist knocks out a little theoretical number on the nature of capitalism. Half a century later here comes Stalin, Mao and Pol Pot, and before you can say 'means of production' some poor Cambodian motherfucker's lying there bleeding into the ground, watching his liver getting carried down the street on a stick because he owned, like, a *fork* and there's something like fifty million Russians queuing up at the Pearly Gates.

'Oh, haud oan a minute,' Andrew says, pointing at Matthew. 'You left oot the Creationists, ya fanny.'

'Well, actually, Andrew,' Matthew replies, 'I think you'll find that Creationism is a belief that's spread across many different sub-branches of Christianity rather than an actual distinct branch in and of itself.'

'Creationism?' God says. 'What's that?

'Right,' Andrew says, already laughing, 'there's these bams doon there, mostly in America, right, they're aff their fucken heeds, so they are, Boss, but check this oot, ye'll no believe it, these cunts believe that the earth is aboot ten thousand years old.'

God looking at him, not understanding. 'What do you mean "believe"?'

'Ah mean,' Andrew says, 'they *believe* it. They took the ages of every cunt in the fucking Bible and added them up back to Adam and Eve and that's how they reckon the age o' the fucking earth. Ten thoosand years.'

Another long pause before God *explodes* with laughter.

God's laugh – you really have to hear it. It's the most infectious, throaty cackle ever. After a minute *everyone* is howling so hard that Jeannie pops her head around the door to check everything's OK. Fuelled by the spliffs, soon God is on His knees on the carpet with tears of mirth streaming down his face. 'Oh, no, oh, I . . . I . . .' God is saying, gasping for breath, 'oxygen, need oxygen.'

Ten thousand years!' Jesus repeats. 'Oh man.'

'No, stop it!' Peter says.

'But . . . but . . . what about the rocks?' God asks, fighting to speak. 'The fossils? Haven't they figured out carbon dating yet?'

'They have, they have,' Matthew says. Even Matthew is crying with laughter.

'But,' Andrew says, 'check this oot – the Creationists say you created the earth with *the appearance of age*, so people would think it was older than it was!'

'AHHHHAHHHAAHHH!' God is helpless with mirth

now, banging the desk with His fist. 'You, you mean I gave it a
. . . a nice antique-y feel?'

Everyone screaming with laughter.

Finally God pulls Himself up into His chair. 'Oh dear, oh
man. That . . . that's priceless.'

'I know!' Matthew says. 'You wouldn't believe so many of
them would go for it, eh?'

'How do you mean?' God says, still chuckling, wiping a tear
away.

'Well, some estimates put the number of Americans who
believe Creationism has some validity at between 40 and 45 per
cent of the population.'

God stops laughing. 'What?' He says, very quietly.

'Yes,' Matthew says. 'They teach it in schools.'

'They teach this shit,' God says slowly, biting His lip, '*to kids*?'

'Umm, yes.'

'*ARE YOU FUCKING KIDDING ME?*'

God smashes the place up.

Files going flying, a heavy ashtray shattering off the back
wall, a coffee mug following it, a chair getting upended.
Everyone stares at their notes, waits for it to blow over. Finally,
breathing hard, He sits back down. 'But what,' He says, 'what
about this kid Darwin? He pretty much figured it all out bang
on.'

'Aye,' Andrew says. 'They say he's the devil.'

'Are these people literally fucking morons?'

'Ah, it would appear so, sir, yes.'

'I mean –' God takes an unlit joint from the ashtray and holds
it up – 'aren't they smoking enough grass?'

'Well, not really, sir, no,' Peter says.

'Uh, Dad,' Jesus says, 'hello? Grass is, like, illegal in most
places down there.'

'*It's what?*'

'It's against the law to sell or possess marijuana in –' Matthew checks his notes – 'America, the United Kingdom, France, Australia, Japan, Canada . . .' he goes on.

'Why?' God says leaning towards Peter, ignoring Matthew's drone. 'Why would they make something I put there for their pleasure illegal? Don't they like to get high?'

'They largely use alcohol and tobacco,' Peter says.

'. . . Italy, Spain, Argentina, Ireland . . .'

'But –' God takes a quick, deep toke – 'why one and not the other?'

'Money,' Peter says simply. 'They –'

'. . . Belgium, Thailand, Finland, Iceland, Norway –'

'OK, thank you, Matthew,' God says.

'They tax the sale of booze and cigarettes. It's –'

'. . . Russia, Germany, Singa—'

'WILL YOU SHUT THE FUCK UP?' God throws a doughnut at Matthew who shuts up.

'It's a big money-spinner.' Peter says.

'Is there anything,' God asks the table, 'they won't do down there for a fucking buck?'

Silence. God rubs His temples, twists His neck, working out some tension before He says, 'And we haven't even gotten onto what the Muslims are up to yet. Have you been keeping tabs on all this?' A few sad nods around the table. 'I mean, obviously not all the Muslims. But some of these guys they . . . like these Taliban guys? Or in Iran? The shit they're up to? I . . .' Running out of words, God hits the speakerphone button on the telephone. 'Jeannie, did you get hold of Muhammad yet?'

'He's holding for you, sir, I'll put him through. He's in the car.'

'Hello there!' Muhammad's voice comes crackly and cheerful through the speaker. 'How was holiday?'

'Great, great thanks, Muhammad. You're on speaker. I'm here with Peter, John, uh, Matthew and Andrew and my son.'

'Hello, my friends!'

'Hey, Muhammad!' everyone choruses. Everyone likes Muhammad. A nice dude.

'Jesus, my man!' Muhammad continues. 'How you liking being back?'

'Ah, it's all good, buddy.'

'The fuck it's all good,' God cuts in. 'Listen, Muhammad, down there, on earth, what the fuck's going on with some of your guys?'

'Ah, look, I know what you mean –'

'These Taliban dudes, I mean, these fucking guys, man.'

'Ah yes. Bad men. Very bad men. I agree. I – Pick a lane, dipshit!' They can hear Muhammad getting on the horn. 'Sorry.'

'Yes, but what are we going to do about it?'

'It is very difficult. They read something, they have their own ideas . . . next thing you know, is all very bad.'

'No shit,' God sighs. He'd only been back half a day and He was already heartily sick of textual interpretation. Fine for an undergraduate lit course. If all you're gonna do with your interpretation is sit in the student union bar and argue about Joyce's symbolism then go, as they say, with God. But these guys – these *fucking* guys – were taking their textual interpretation and going out and telling folk they had to walk around in a sack their whole lives. Stoning people.

'Look, God, my friend, I hate to say this, but you –'

'Muhammad, I promise you, this is *not* the time to start in on me about free will.'

'OK, OK. Hey, what does Muhammad know? I only work here. I –' A jarring burst of static, crackling radio waves. 'We . . . should . . . perhaps . . . when . . .'

'Muhammad? You're breaking up.'

'Listen – I am . . . tunnel . . . you back later?' The line goes dead. God jabs the phone off and sits back.

'Well, gentlemen,' He says finally. 'What are we going to do about all this?'

'It may be a moot point, sir,' Peter says. 'We've run some projections. At the current rate they're using up natural resources – the melting of the polar ice caps, ozone depletion, greenhouse gases and so forth – they'll render the planet uninhabitable within, oh, three to five thousand years. I mean, if you look at something like this . . .' Peter thumbs a remote control and the centre of the great glass desk lights up, showing an image of an ocean. He zooms in further and an enormous dark grey swirling pattern becomes visible. Peter zooms again and they see that it is a series of gyres, an enormous vortex of chemical blackness.

'What the fuck is that and what's it doing in my fucking ocean?' God asks.

'It's what they're calling the "Great Pacific Garbage Patch",' Peter says. They see now that much of the expanse is made up of plastic waste, chemicals and sludge, all trapped in a frothing cross-hatching of currents. It looks enormous. 'A black hole of man-made non-biodegradable waste.'

'How, like, how big is that?' Jesus says.

'It's hundreds of thousands of square miles,' Matthew says. 'Approximately six times the size of mainland Britain. Or twice the size of Texas.'

God stuffs a fist in His mouth and stifles a scream.

'And it just wasn't there a couple of days ago,' Peter says. 'I mean, a couple of days our time. They've done that in sixty or seventy years their time. It's contained to a degree by the currents of the North Pacific Gyre, but unchecked, within another century, it'll basically be a continent of shit.' He hits the remote again and the table goes blank. Everyone stares at the blank table in silence.

God gets up and walks over to the window. He looks out over the endless springs, meadows and beaches of Heaven. At the perfect sunshine. 'Fuck me,' He says for what feels like the umpteenth time this morning.

'I don't think we should let it get to that,' John says. Everyone at the table turns to look at him.

'Go on, John,' God says, His back still to them.

'We need to make a statement. Why let those animals just gradually trash the place on their own? Fuck all that.' John stands up, takes the floor. 'What we need to do is remind them who's boss. Out with a bang, not a whimper. I say we take them all out now while we've got the muscle. I'm talking Revelations-type shit, I'm talking fire-and-motherfucking-brimstone. Floods. Locusts. Tsunamis. Armageddon. Asteroid collision. The Four Horsemen riding in, Gabriel's trumpet right up the ass. The earth splitting open like a goddamn piñata. Judgement Day and SAY HELLO TO MY LEETLE FUCKING FREN!'

'Wipe them out and start again?' Matthew says.

'Yeah, fuck them.' John is breathing hard and he has flecks of saliva at the corners of his mouth.

'Boy might have something,' Andrew concedes. 'Whit dae ye think, sir?'

God picks up a small rock from the windowsill and turns it over in His hand. On the bottom is the fossilised impression of a tiny trilobite, a kind of woodlouse that lived over 500 million years ago and one of the first organisms to develop something resembling eyes. God runs a finger tenderly over the impression. 'Precious little creature,' He whispers to Himself.

'Sir?' Peter says.

God turns to face them and speaks quietly. 'Are you guys out of your fucking minds? "Start again"? What do you think this is, a jigsaw puzzle? A batch of chocolate cookies? Have you any idea how much work went into that place? It took me a couple of billion years to get to this.' He holds up the trilobite. 'You guys have been up here for about five fucking minutes. I had to sit through the Archaean and Proterozoic periods on my own. You try having a conversation with a eukaryote. Then there was the Palaeozoic – that was a bunch of fun. Three hundred million years with nothing but bugs and lizards? Oh yeah, that was party-hearty. Even when Man arrived,' God, moving around the conference table now, His hands behind His back, His voice gradually rising as He addresses each of them in turn – 'you think that was a blast? I mean, have you any idea how boring the Bronze Age was?' He asks, stopping behind John, leaning close to him. 'The main form of entertainment *WAS FUCKING BRONZE!*'

Everyone looks at the floor.

'Then, finally, the Greeks – literature, drama, fags. It was all happening. The Romans –'

'Hey, hey, hang on, they crucified the shit out of us!' Jesus says, gesturing around the table.

'Aye, you hud it easy,' Andrew says. 'Try getting crucified oan a fucking X-shaped cross. That'll wake ye up in the morning, son!'

'Get bent,' Peter says. 'They did me upside down.'

They begin arguing about who had the worst crucifixion.

'Come on,' God says, 'crucifixion's a doddle.' The saints and

Jesus burst out laughing. God had found time to bone up on some of the better aspects of the twentieth century too. Comedy and rock and roll. It wasn't all genocide and famine. They found time to invent the electric guitar too, didn't they?

Andrew points at God. 'Aye, good wan!'

'It is a deceased parrot!' Matthew says.

'They're my juniper bushes!' John chips in, everyone laughing now, grateful for a little light relief.

'Hey, Dad, you got to meet Chapman,' Jesus says.

'OK, shut the fuck up,' God says. 'Like a bunch of fucking students. Where was I? Oh yeah, Romans. Granted we had our differences and yeah they went a bit off their tits towards the end, but they could build the shit out of a road, couldn't they?'

Everyone nods.

'Obviously we had a bit of an, um, energy dip in the Middle Ages, but then – bam – the Renaissance.' God sighs. 'Art up the wazoo, continents getting discovered like it's going out of fashion. I mean, yeah, you could already see that we were gonna have to watch the fucking Catholics, but on the whole it was looking promising. Then what? I go off and pull a few trout out the river and the place gets fucking trashed. That's what.'

God sits down heavily in His chair at the top of the table. 'What I really want to know,' he says, 'is how did the son of a bitch get so far ahead?'

'He puts the hours in, you gotta give him that,' Peter says.

'Aye, the boy's nae dummy,' Andrew agrees.

'Shit,' God says, thumbing the intercom. 'He's gonna be unbearable.'

'Yes, sir?' Jeannie says.

'Jeannie, can you arrange a meeting with . . . him?'

'I'd anticipated that a meeting might be in order, sir,' Jeannie says. 'So I took the liberty of making sure he was free for dinner tonight.'

'Dinner?' God groans. 'Oh well, I suppose so.'

'Do you want him to come here?'

'No, no. Down there. I want to have a look around.'

'Very good, sir. Eight o'clock?'

'Fine.' God clicks off and looks across the table to Jesus. 'You, laughing boy, you're coming too. Suited and booted.'

'Aww, Dad. I was gonna –'

God looks at him.

Jesus shuts up.

6

OD AND JESUS IN THE GLASS-WALLED ELEVATOR TO Hell, going down. A muzak version of 'I Believe I Can Fly' by R. Kelly plays softly in the background, the melody picked out on pan pipes. God is wearing a beautiful bespoke suit; it's light grey with a fine chalk pinstripe and notched lapels. Crisp pale blue shirt and striped silk tie furled in a perfectly knotted half Windsor. God scrubs up well.

Jesus fidgets with his collar, trying to loosen his tie. His suit is black, skinny-legged, with narrow lapels. His white shirt is untucked, his thin black tie askew, his long blond hair spilling down over his collar. It's kind of a new-wave look.

'For goodness' sake, c'mere . . .' God says as He begins retying His son's tie. 'Thirty-three years old and you still can't put on a goddamn necktie. I blame myself.'

'I hate wearing a tie.'

'Of course you do. You're a bum,' God sighs.

Jesus looks up at the descending numbers as God tucks and folds, the circles of Hell flashing by: –2, –3, –4.

Dante had been nearer the mark than many thought. He'd been right on the money about the avaricious; here they are in the fourth circle, those whose life pursuit had simply been the making of money, slithering around Jesus and God as the elevator glides smoothly and noiselessly through the flames. Floating by the glass windows, writhing in agony, we see the investment bankers, junk-bond and currency traders, financiers, corporate raiders, estate agents, moneylenders, loan sharks and the proprietors of certain types of all-night convenience stores.

The temperature rising, the muzak a little louder now as the sixth and seventh circles go by: rapists, murderers, wife-beaters and paedophiles – all covered in burning, scourging demons, sinking their molten teeth into smoking flesh. Contrary to what Dante – and many organised religions – thought, there were no suicides in the seventh circle. God understood it just got too much for some folk. He got that. Man, he'd nearly topped Himself after that asteroid took out the fucking dinosaurs. A couple of billion years of work up the shitter. Back to the bastard drawing board. There were no blasphemers or heretics here either. God, as we know, doesn't give a shit if people believe in Him or not. Also no sodomites. (God loves fags.)

Jesus rests his head against the warm glass and looks down into the well of flames a million miles deep, at the uncountable burning souls.

'Dad?'

'Mmmm?'

'I'm sorry things got so fucked up.'

God regards his son: a thirty-three-year-old teenager fidgeting in a suit and tie. Thirty-three. Used to be you had better be damned sure you were grown up by then. Not now, God thinks. People didn't grow up like they used to. The boy had much to learn, about responsibility, about hard work, about putting the hours in. Still, there was a fundamental core of decency there. It was what had got him through the last time. He sighs and pats Jesus gently on the shoulder. 'You're a good kid,' He says.

The muzak changing, the pan pipes essaying 'Land Down Under' by Men At Work as the elevator glides into the ninth circle: the pyre blazing with the souls of millions of corrupt politicians and CEOs, the demons down here really working overtime, eternally stuffing fistfuls of burning money into orifices, slicing off penises, gouging out eyes, administering Chinese burns and twisting nipples, the screams almost audible through the thick plate glass. They briefly glimpse Kenny Lay, former Chief Executive Officer of Enron. He is almost invisible below several excited demons who are in the process of attaching jump leads to various extremities and snipping things off with garden shears. One squats over Lay's red, sweating, screaming face, preparing to defecate.

Suddenly it's quieter as the ninth circle vanishes into darkness above them. God shoots His cuffs, makes a minute adjustment to His tie. 'OK. Heads up. Behave yourself.'

A bright 'PING' as the number 10 lights up.

Another mistake of Dante's.

The elevator doors opening: God and Jesus strolling into the lobby of the tenth circle of Hell where a huge neon sign proclaims 'BIG ROCK MOVIE DINER'. Glass cases with musical instruments and movie paraphernalia adorn the walls: there are gold and platinum discs from Genesis, Debbie Gibson and the Jonas Brothers. There is a golf club from the movie *Uncle Buck,* a uniform from *Police Academy: Mission to Moscow* and a lightsabre from *The Phantom Menace*. MC Hammer's pants are proudly displayed above the reception desk.

'Hi there,' the girl in the chic black catsuit behind the desk says to them. She's gorgeous, tall, all catwalk legs. 'Please, let me show you to your table.'

God and Jesus follow her through the busy restaurant where a pan pipe version of 'Hip to Be Square' by Huey Lewis and the News plays loudly. 'And here we are,' the girl says as she seats them at a good table – a large banquette against the back wall overlooking the main dining area. 'He'll be with you in a moment, gentlemen. Can I get you something from the bar?' she asks as she hands them their menus.

'Uh, can I get a Michelob?' Jesus asks.

'We have Carling or Budweiser.'

'Shit. A Heineken?'

She smiles tightly.

'We'll order some wine in a minute,' God says.

'Very good, sir. I'll have the waiter bring you the wine list.' She gives them a little bow and ticks off on her heels.

'Carling or Bud?' Jesus says.

'You're in Hell, retard,' God says, not looking up from His menu. 'Anyway, we're having dinner here. Have some wine. What are you, sixteen?'

A commotion breaks out across the room and they turn to look. A large, rowdy table of rabbis is trying to place a complex order with their waiter, a short man with a small black moustache whose fringe is plastered to his forehead with sweat. 'Ja, ja,' he says, holding up a hand, trying to quieten them. 'So – drei gefilte fish, ein pastrami sandwich, zwei brisket, ein lox and zwei matzo ball soups, Ja?'

'No, two pastrami sandwiches, one brisket!' one of the rabbis says.

'And some more latkes!' one of them shouts.

'And a side of onion rolls.'

'You know what, I'll have a soup too.'

'So das ist – drei matzo ball soups?' the waiter asks, crossing something out on his pad.

'No, the soup *instead* of the fish.'

'Ja. So that's one fish?'

'No, *two* fish, moron!'

'And some pickled herring!'

Someone throws a bread roll and it smacks off the back of Hitler's head as he trudges off towards the kitchens, crossing something out on his pad. 'Hip to Be Square' finishes playing. And immediately begins again.

God turns to Jesus, smiling. 'You can't deny the little bastard's got a sense of humour.'

'Literally, speak of the devil,' Jesus says, nodding.

God looks around to see Satan coming towards them. He is *beaming*. Satan is a short, fat, balding man – two hundred plus pounds and a little over five two. What remains of his black hair is pulled back into a tight ponytail. Under his black suit he wears a lurid Hawaiian shirt and an unlit cigar is clamped between his teeth. He takes it out as he reaches their table, God and Jesus standing to greet him.

'BIG GUY!' Satan says, pumping God's hand, throwing his other arm around God's shoulder. 'Looking good! Damn, look at those arms. You been working out?'

'Lucifer,' God says. 'Been a while.'

'You're telling me! And you brought the kid! Hey, kid, how you been?'

'Yeah, good,' Jesus says, shaking hands.

'You're back all this time and you don't come say hi?'

'Well, you know, I –'

'I'm fucking with you, kid. Sit, sit.'

They sit back down and Satan slides into the booth beside them. 'Hey, you got no drinks. The service in this fucking place, huh? Let's have a drink. Lemme grab a waiter. Ronnie!' Satan yells.

Ronald Reagan in waiter's uniform appears. 'Uh, Ronnie, bring us a bottle of champagne. The good stuff, OK?'

'Very good, sir.' Reagan bows and heads off.

'Sorry I'm late,' Satan says, settling back and lighting his cigar. 'It's just been . . .'

'Mayhem?' God says.

'Exactly! Mayhem down here.'

'I'm not surprised.'

'You been getting up to speed on recent developments, huh?' Satan asks.

God nods.

'What can I tell you?' Satan spreads his hands, gesturing at the packed restaurant. 'Business is good.'

Reagan reappears. 'Ah, would you like to order some drinks?'

Satan sighs. 'We just did this, Ronnie.'

'I . . . uh,' Reagan looks confused.

'A . . . bottle . . . of . . . champagne,' Satan says, spacing the words out slowly.

'Uh . . . I . . . unnn,' Reagan says. His face is colouring, his jaw set. He's straining.

'You OK, Ronnie?' Satan asks.

'UUUGHH!' Reagan says. Suddenly there is a dreadful stench. Reagan slides his hand round to the small of his back and pushes it down his pants. When he pulls the hand out again it is covered in excrement. Reagan looks at it, surprised. Everyone looks at Reagan. Finally he speaks. 'Mummy,' he says.

'Holy shit,' Jesus says. God edges a little further back in the booth.

'Fuck,' Satan says. 'OK, Ronnie, get . . . just go.'

Reagan stumbles off in a slow, bandy-legged stride, still staring at his shit-covered fist.

'Sorry,' Satan chuckles. 'Old Ronnie, he's . . . y'know.' Satan twirls his index finger in a circle next to his temple. 'Ironical punishment. What can you do, huh?'

'Well,' God says, 'that isn't even ironic. On any level.'

'Anyway, you know what's good tonight?' Satan says, ignoring Him. 'The steak, have the steak.'

'I'll have the chopped salad,' God says.

'Yeah, me too.' Jesus.

'Come on, guys. Live a little.'

'Funnily enough, I'm not that hungry,' God says.

7

OD AND JESUS PICK AT THEIR SALADS. SATAN EATS FOR three, attacking two portions of ribs then a forearm-sized strip steak with fries, slaw and a side of refried beans. Somewhere into Satan's steak, the small talk out of the way, God eases into the big talk. He looks around the packed restaurant and, having to raise His voice to be heard above 'Hip to Be Square', which is starting again now, says, 'Well, I have to hand it to you, you're doing well.'

Satan smiles benevolently. 'Just kicking ass and taking numbers, baby.'

'But, down there, up there I mean, on earth, it . . . it's insane. How did you –'

'Well,' Satan leans back, still chewing, 'I hate to say I told you so, but that old free will. That turned out to be a motherfucker, didn't it?'

'No other way to go,' God says.

'Check it out,' Satan says. 'I think no one did me more good than the hard-line Christians.'

'How so?' God says.

'Conception of sin. You got people, they will fuck anyone and everyone in the ass for a buck, but they think that by going to church every Sunday and saying they believe in you they're going upstairs. Meanwhile they think someone who smokes a few jays or snorts a little Bolivian is coming here! You got these anti-abortion motherfuckers –'

'Pro-life sons of bitches,' God says. 'You must have a few of them down here?'

'Oh yeah,' Satan says. 'We got James Kopp, Eric Rudolph. I got them chained up downstairs performing abortions 24/7. Anyway, you got people like that telling penniless, uneducated kids they have to have their babies and then thinking they're the ones going upstairs and not the single moms who – surprise, surprise – can't cope with their kids. They seem to think that as long as they believe in you, they can do whatever the fuck they want.'

'But the . . . hatred,' God says. 'These people hating gays, hating blacks, hating whatever. How, why, would anyone –'

As his father and Satan talk on, Jesus turns his cool, blue gaze over the restaurant, gradually getting a sense of the scale of the place, the thousands of banquettes, the sea of tables stretching off into the baking horizon. *Man*, he thinks. *We really fucked up*.

A busboy appears to clear the plates away. His name tag says 'JESSE'. 'Hang on,' Satan says, interrupting God, placing a hand on the busboy's arm, 'Let's ask old Jesse here. Jesse, why did you hate fags and niggers and feminists and dykes and all that stuff?'

'Bible said,' Jesse Helms says quietly, gathering plates and cutlery, not making eye contact. Satan laughs. 'But Jesse, look, I got God right here. He says it ain't so.'

It is difficult, if not impossible, for someone as wretched as

Helms to meet the gaze of God. His eyes flicker around the table, down to his shoes. 'Why weren't you just nice to people?' God asks gently.

'Bible said,' Helms repeats, but with less certainty now.

'But didn't you understand?' God speaks slowly and softly, as though to a child or an idiot. 'Didn't you understand that you would wind up down here if you said all those things you said?'

'Bible said . . . I . . .' Helms looks up and catches God's eye. It is also impossible to look God in the face and lie to him. Suddenly Helms looks panic-stricken. 'I . . . I LIKE BIG DICKS!' He erupts, all of it suddenly coming out, Jesus and God reeling back. 'COCKS! GIANT BLACK FUCKING COCKS! GOD. PLEASE PUT IT IN ME! I . . .'

'Sorry, guys,' Satan says, picking up his steak knife. He slashes Helms's throat and the former Senator from North Carolina topples over in a spray of blood. A few diners look over. 'Lemme just turn that off, so to speak.'

'Right,' Jesus says after a beat, recovering. 'If what he really wanted was to have sex with a bunch of black guys, why didn't he just go ahead and do it instead of –'

'Bible said,' God says, beginning to understand.

They skip dessert. 'Come on, guys,' Satan says. 'I'll walk you to the elevator. I got a couple of things to do on the way.' As they leave Helms sits up on the floor rubbing his neck, looking confused. The wound is gone, ready to be re-inflicted for eternity. God and Jesus step around him. Satan kicks him in the face and skips merrily down the stairs towards the kitchens. 'Short cut,' Satan explains.

In the kitchens in the restaurant in the tenth circle of Hell a terrible scene is taking place as they come through the swinging doors. There is screaming and shouting and searing heat and the floor is awash with blood. There, on the table in the middle of the room – the table where one imagines food is prepared – Reagan is beating a screaming Hitler over the head with a severed arm; the glistening nub of white bone smashing hard off Hitler's face. They are shouting at each other in a mixture of German and English, an argument over tips.

'Holy shit –' God and Jesus begin together.

Jerry Falwell, dressed in the rags of a dishwasher, lies slumped in the corner, bleeding profusely from the stump where his arm used to be. Falwell shrieks when he sees them enter. 'God, Jesus!' he says. 'I'm not meant to be here! Help me!' He tries to crawl across the bloody floor towards them, JC and God stepping back, palms outwards, their jaws dropping.

'Come on, Jerry,' Satan says, not missing a beat, as though this were just another day in Hell's Kitchen (which, of course, it is). 'Those dishes ain't gonna dry themselves.'

I've only got one arm!' Falwell screams.

'Improvise, Jerry,' Satan says as he steps through another set of swinging doors, holding them open for God and Jesus to follow him.

'Fun never stops, huh?' God says.

'You know it,' Satan replies, the door swinging shut behind them, drowning out the screaming and cursing.

It's quieter and cooler as they take a flight of stairs down another level. Level eleven of Hell leads onto a bleak stone corridor with cells all along one wall. Bare bulbs hang from the low ceiling spreading weak, murky light. On the other wall a huge picture window overlooks an endless, burning canyon filled with row upon row of men – there are *millions* of them – pedalling what appear to be exercise bikes. They are all screaming (noiselessly, the glass is a foot thick) because the pedalling motion is causing a ten-foot-long, cast-iron, barbed-wire-spiked dildo attached to each bike to pound relentlessly in and out of their anuses. 'False prophets, religious hypocrites,' Satan says by way of explanation.

'Don't you get tired of all the anal violation?' God asks. 'Does everything have to be up the ass with you?'

'Hey, if it ain't broke . . .' Satan says.

Jesus hangs behind, taking in the brass nameplates on the long row of cell doors – MENGELE, J., POT, P., JACKSON, M. – while God and Satan walk on ahead.

'In all honesty?' Satan says. 'I thought you'd be sorely tempted to flush the whole thing down the fucking toilet and start over.'

'Not the first time I've heard that today,' God says.

'John?'

God nods. They pass a demon in work overalls who is standing on a stepladder in front of the open door to an empty cell. He is stencilling a name onto the brass plate – 'LIMBA—' – while, inside, a couple of demon maids are preparing the bed for a new arrival, carefully strewing broken glass and razor blades. Busy, busy, busy.

'And I'll tell you something,' Satan goes on, 'the way it is up there right now, it's all good for me. All those reality-TV shows? You got kids whose only ambition is –' here Satan puts on a mall-rat voice – ' "to be, like, totally, *totally* famous!" I mean, just a planet full of pumped-up egos running about screaming "Look at me!" No one interested in learning anything. No one interested in being good at something for its own sake.'

'Come on,' God says, 'they've done some good stuff. Poetry, cinema, rock and roll. Not the shit you have down here obviously –'

'Obviously.' Satan gestures towards the faintly audible

muzak version of Bowie's 'The Laughing Gnome'. 'I mean, can we talk?'

'But there's some real good stuff.'

'It's history, baby. Over. No one gives a shit about quality any more. It's "where's the money and I want my picture on the cover and fuck you very much". It's my shot now. Seriously, you think you got any kind of a way back in up there?'

God is looking back down the corridor, watching His son ambling along. Jesus playfully hits a dangling light bulb and it sways back and forth above, casting crazy shadows on the walls. He is absent-mindedly singing 'Rockaway Beach' by the Ramones, the simple melody echoing along the corridor. God smiles, watching His son. Satan looks at God, then along the corridor at Jesus. Then back to God. 'Oh, oh, hang on a minute. You're not? No way . . .'

'Lucifer?' God says, pulling Himself up to His full height. 'Thank you for your time.'

They shake hands formally. 'Yeah,' Satan says, changing tone as Jesus arrives to join them, 'any time.'

'S'up, dawgs?' Jesus says.

They have stopped in front of a cell with the name 'GORDON, G.W.' on it. At the end of the corridor the freight elevator doors rattle open. 'Right on time. We run a tight ship down here.' The three of them watch as what looks like an entire basketball team emerges from the elevator and pounds down the hall towards them. Fourteen big black guys. Big black guys? No. The biggest black guys. Ever. The shortest, weediest of them is six five and maybe two hundred and twenty pounds. They gather round Satan, towering over him.

'OK, fellas, who's the monster? Which one of you guys is King Dong?'

One of the biggest, baddest-looking guys in this big, bad-looking bunch grabs the front of his trousers and says 'I got thirteen motherfucking inches down here, motherfucker.'

'Ooh, baby,' Satan says. 'Unlucky thirteen? My kinda number. OK, you're up first.' He opens the cell door and begins ushering them in. One of them is fingering a pack of condoms. Satan snatches them from him. 'What the fuck? Condoms? Are you shitting me? We go bareback down here, son.' A white man, naked, hanging in a harness of some sort, can just be glimpsed inside the cell. Satan turns back to God and Jesus. 'Sorry, guys, gotta work here. You have a nice trip back up.'

'No, no! Not again! Nooooooo!' the figure in the cell begins howling.

'Uh, thanks for dinner,' Jesus says.

'No problem, kid. You . . .' He looks at God. 'You look after yourself, huh?'

A shrill, agonised scream comes from inside the cell. It is cut off as Satan slips inside, closing the door behind him.

'Dad?' Jesus says a moment later as God thumbs the button for the penthouse.

'Mmmm?'

'Who's G.W. Gordon?'

'George Washington Gordon. He helped found the Ku Klux Klan.'

'Ah.'

The elevator begins to rise skyward as the pan pipes version of 'My Heart Will Go On' by Celine Dion plays softly.

8

T'S LATE NOW.

God alone in His office, a single banker's lamp with a glass shade casting a pool of green light over His desk, the long shadows thrown by the stacks of boxes towering around Him – the twentieth century in full, terrible detail.

A heavy heart. God knows that you are dealing with truly terrible decisions, with full-force main-event stuff, when clichés hit you with all of their original oomph. Yes, His heart felt heavy. Forget lead, it felt like it was made of plutonium, with its atomic weight of 244, its density more than tenfold that of platinum. In fact, forget plutonium, His heart was made of francium, the heaviest of all the alkali metals, a mineral so dense that God had ensured there was never any more than thirty grams of it in the earth's crust at any one time.

And it wasn't just His heart that was heavy – everything was heavy. His legs, arms, organs, they all felt like they were hand-crafted from francium. He could barely lift the Scotch to his mouth. God rests His francium chin on a francium palm and

His eyes, teary from the whisky fumes, drift over to the five-foot-high stack of files nearest to his desk, the top one marked 'BOSNIA–HERZEGOVINA CONFLICT'. He feels His blood give a sick lurch of rage, feels His thoughts turn crude and savage: some clowns, some fucking retards, decided they believed some bunch of total shit and here's what you got.

Flush it down the toilet and start again.

Easily done. Up the sun's temperature by just a handful of degrees, nudge its orbit just a fraction closer, and it was all over down there in a few years. Throw another meteorite their way. Something just the size of Belgium – of fucking *Manchester* – would probably do the trick. Boom. Say hello to my leetle fren. A virus. He had samples in the lab He'd been scared to even get out the Petri dish: stuff that made Aids look like a head cold, made Ebola look about as infectious as an indie B-side. A few grams of that into the water supply and mainland Europe would look like the third reel of a fucking zombie movie inside a month.

And then, and then . . . He turns and looks at the new shelves filling the wall behind Him, groaning with books, records, CDs and DVDs. Scanning from left to right, reading chronologically, he goes from Daniel Defoe to Irvine Welsh, from a scratchy gramophone recording of 'The Blue Danube' to the Chemical Brothers. From *Battleship Potemkin* to a box set of *The Wire*. From one to the other in each medium in such a very short space of time . . .

Where did it all start to go tits? Moses, you'd probably have to say. That faker. One of the first to fall to ego. When he'd got up there on Sinai and clapped eyes on that one, pristine, immaculately chiselled tablet – the words 'BE NICE' engraved in God's beautiful ever-so-slightly slanting copperplate – he'd freaked out. All that build-up and he was gonna, what? Come back down and say 'Hey, be nice, folks! And, well, that's all. Have a nice life'? The fuck he was. Son of a bitch got busy with the chisels and slate. Spent forty days knocking out all that mad crap. The whole 'Thou shalt not covet thine uncle's graven ass on a Thursday' bullshit? All pure Moses. (Jeez did he get an ass-kicking when he got up here. God started the ass-kicking when the fucker walked in the door and stopped some time during the Dark Ages: a good few hundred years. His cheeks looked like a pair of boiled beetroots.) And what followed from all that crap? Interpretation. The whole 'I-think-what-God-meant-to-say' industry. Bam – a millennium later some burly motherfucker is cutting babies' throats and tossing them over his shoulder cos he reckons God is on his side.

What the fuck was there to interpret about 'BE NICE'?

As God had repeatedly screamed during Moses' centuries-long ass-kicking.

Anyway, we're past all that now, God thinks, sighing as He realises where His thoughts are taking Him. Someone had to re-teach the meaning of 'Be nice'.

He loosens His tie further and pours more Scotch into His glass. He lifts the smouldering Cuban from the ashtray and leans back in His chair, hand-tooled leather brogues up on the desk. He uses the remote to turn up the music, a compilation CD His son made for Him. ('Burned' the kid called it.) God listens to Townes Van Zandt singing 'Tecumseh Valley', enthralled at the way the little, circular acoustic patterns chase the singer's voice around, at the way the two sounds – raw voice and woody instrument – overlap, merge, separate, rise and fall.

God is enchanted.

A creator first and foremost, He is never more pleased with

His creations than when they perform the most godly of acts – that of calling something into being from nothingness. This song: a few chords and a handful of words and yet how eternal the pleasure from something so simple. His eyes drift over to the screen of a laptop glowing on the corner of the desk – a collection of quotations from so-called religious leaders: basically a compendium of bile, invective, hatred and fear-mongering, this last act the most baffling and enraging. But they had sold it. Sold this fucking lemon: millions of humans believed that homosexuals would never see the face of God. Or those who indulged in multiple sexual partners. Drug addicts. Gamblers. The unbaptised. Blasphemers. Non-believers.

And where was the laughter with these guys? It was the sound you heard everywhere in Heaven. People were always cracking up. Out in the big office, where it was forever Friday afternoon, the newest, funniest gag was always doing the rounds. It was one of the first things decent, but humourless, souls were issued with when they arrived here – a sense of humour. That great moment when the scales fell away from their eyes and the world exploded into Technicolor, when those who had been used to frowning and saying 'I don't get it' finally got it. Priceless.

He drifts back into the music, John Coltrane doing 'A Love Supreme' now. The simplest of riffs, just three notes really, but, man. The stereo, the fine brogues, the aromatic cigar, the fragrant malt whisky, the laptop . . . so much cool stuff here that wasn't around when He left. Yes, busy little creatures.

A soft knocking. 'Come,' God says and Peter's head appears round the door.

'Burning the midnight oil, huh?'

'Yeah. Come on in, Pete. Have a drink.'

Peter pours himself a stiff belt, they chink glasses, the noise seeming to chime with the music, and Peter flops down into a huge, soft leather beanbag at the Boss's feet. God has His eyes closed, nodding along to the riff Coltrane is playing. Peter can read God's moods better than most and he knows this is not the right moment for a 'what-are-we-going-to-do' conversation. Peter drifts into the track himself, closing his eyes and nodding along, enjoying God enjoying the music as much as he's enjoying the music itself. It's been a while since they did one of these late-night-in-God's-office-putting-the-world-to-rights-over-a-bottle numbers.

'It's good, isn't it?' God says.

'Mmmm,' Peter says. A pause, exactly the right length, before he adds, 'Worth saving.' There is no question mark.

He opens his eyes and looks at the Boss. God gets slowly to His feet, holding His whisky glass downwards by His fingertips, swirling the amber liquor around. He drains it, sets the empty glass down and picks up a framed photograph of Jesus. It was taken at his tenth birthday party. Jesus is laughing hard at something happening off-camera, his eyes are crinkled tightly and there is such pleasure on his face, the face of the man not yet properly visible, still hidden behind the chubby skin and too-big teeth of the child. God tenderly runs a hand over the photograph, over His son's face.

'Yes, it is,' God says quietly.

Peter sees that tears are not far from God's eyes now. 'Oh no,' he says, realising. 'You're not gonna –'

'No other way,' God says, very softly.

'B-but, they're animals down there. They'll tear the kid apart. It was bad enough the last time. These days? I mean, they make the Romans look like fucking social workers.'

'You think I don't know all this?' God says.

Peter shuts up. They both stare silently at the photo of Jesus for a long time. When God makes up His mind, that's that. Peter is already concerning himself with practicalities.

'He's gonna need a new name,' Peter says.

'What's wrong with Jesus?' God asks.

'No offence, Boss,' Peter says, topping up their glasses, 'but everyone's gonna think he's a fucking busboy.'

'Jesus is fine,' God says. God is old school.

9

HE FOLLOWING MORNING, JESUS SAYING 'YOU'RE kidding?' as he looks away from his father, over towards Peter. 'He's kidding, right? I . . . Dad, what do you expect me to do down there?' They are in the meadow that lies off the French windows behind God's desk, the place where the souls of toddlers and babies play.

'Lead. Inspire. Help people.'

'But . . . how?'

'You did it before.'

'It was a lot simpler then. Now their heads are full of so much crap. I mean . . . miracles! They believe I performed miracles! What am I meant to do about that?'

God places a hand on His son's shoulder and looks him square in the eye. 'You are the Son of God. Speak the truth and people will listen. Roam the land. Gather disciples. Favour the underdog. Show them the error of their ways. Bring hope unto the hopeless and the wretched. Preach love, tolerance, justice, mercy – all the crap they've flushed down the shitter. Remind them of the value of community. *Be nice.* Teach them the importance of "be nice".'

'There's gotta be another way.'

God shakes His head, slides His arm around Jesus' shoulder and together they walk the meadow.

'I remember the day you were born, son,' God says. 'They held you up to me, all covered in crap. Shit – you looked like a tray of lasagne. You had one eye screwed up shut, the other one looking right at me. I mean, right at me from across the room. Doctor said babies can't see anything beyond a few feet. Doctors. Fuck do they know? Until about fifteen minutes ago they thought leeches were a good idea. Anyway, we made this eye contact, you're hanging there, all bloody as a blue steak, and I felt this connection like I'd never felt before.' God stops, takes Jesus gently by the shoulders and turns him to look him in the eye. 'You are my treasure, son. A hair breaking on your head is like a sabre in my fucking heart –'

'Oh Dad,' Jesus says, looking away, off into the blue horizon, beginning to resign himself, beginning to say goodbye to the endless comfort and pleasure that surrounds him here, beginning to remember how it went the last time down there. How much they can hate.

'And, make no mistake, they *will* hurt you down there.' God cannot sugar-coat it. He embraces His son and whispers close to his ear. 'But I will always be watching over you. And I will bring you back to me . . .'

Man, it is hard to leave this place.

On earth, thirty-two years ago, somewhere in the American Midwest, the first week of April 1979, a virgin – God *is* old school – is just getting worried about what happened to her last period, wondering about why she's been throwing up the past few mornings. Jesus can feel his body beginning to dissolve as his father hugs him harder, all the billions of atoms within him coming apart, every single atom a tiny him, all the tiny hims beginning to reconstitute themselves in that tiny knot growing in that Midwestern virgin's belly.

April 1979 – so she'll be due late December that year. God wants the boy to have gone through enough shit in time to be ready for the right opportunity to come along.

Timing will be everything.

Jesus is disappearing from his father's embrace now, disintegrating, vanishing back across time and space, coming together as a bubble in that soft, warm belly three decades before. God, who has been catching up with the great novelists of the twentieth century, finds Himself thinking of Nabokov's expression: *'the tiny madman in his padded cell . . .'*

Part Two

ew York City

'Robinson Crusoe, the self-sufficient man,
could not have lived in New York City.'

Walter Lippman

1

EATWAVE.

You could griddle a goddamn egg on the sidewalk and there is little mercy for the poor. In the winter the accidental mercy comes gusting up warm through the grates and vents of the subway system. But in the summer – nothing, save for loitering in one of the fast-food joints off Times Square where, Jesus knows, you can enjoy the A/C for as long as you can spin out your soda.

Shit, Jesus thinks, it's already *this* hot? He can pretty much tell the time from the noise of the traffic flow on Broadway, but he looks at his plastic Casio anyway – 5.48 in the a.m.

Jesus swings his legs down off the narrow cot and his heels come down to touch the worn linoleum. At the last moment he swivels the ball of his left foot to avoid bringing it down onto the mashed corpse of a roach next to the bed. Morgs must have killed it when he turned in last night. Jesus smiles as he looks at Morgan's sleeping form in the bed across the room from him, the bed underneath the Arcade Fire poster Kris tore off a wall near the Bowery Ballroom a few years back. Morgs is his drummer ('Yeah, right. Drummer,' Morgs would say. 'When did we last do *anything*?') and he works as a busboy at a diner in midtown, often not getting back until three, four o'clock in the morning.

There are three of them sharing the two-room hundred-square-foot top-floor apartment. Kris – bass – works nights too and sleeps in Jesus' bed during the daytime. There is, obviously, no A/C. Jesus opens the little icebox in the corner, enjoying even the feeble ripple of cold air, and takes out the McDonald's cup he filled with tap water before he went to bed. He takes a tiny sip and puts the cup back on the shelf – Morgan will be thirsty when he wakes up. Jesus opens the drapes just a crack. Their room looks straight out onto the fire escape of another building just a couple of yards away, but, if you crane your neck, you can see a strip of sky between the two buildings.

He dresses quickly, shorts and sneakers, no socks, and an ancient, frayed T-shirt that says 'TRUCKERS DO IT BETTER'. Some guy gave it to him, down in New Orleans, after a show. Jesus checks his pockets before he leaves and finds he has two one-dollar bills and eighty-two cents in change – more than he expected. He leaves the two bucks on the bedside cabinet for the guys and heads on out the door.

Out of the relative cool of the building, along the alleyway and onto Broadway. Few of the stores are open yet and the only traffic is a couple of delivery trucks and the odd cab nosing its way downtown.

In days gone by he'd have been heading across to Washington Square Park, or on further south to Wall Street to stand on that upturned crate and try and speak to people, get them to listen. Not any more. Man, did that get old quickly. A guy standing on a street corner speaking his mind was no longer a viable look here in the West early in the twenty-first century. The

Christians had fucked that one up too. Not just the Christians: here in New York it seemed like *everyone* had a story to babble, some mad take on events that needed to be heard. Jesus hadn't minded the odd beating that had come his way back when he was doing that, or the nights in the cells when the cops were bored and looking to up the arrest numbers with a few vagrants and panhandlers. But he had minded people thinking he was a Christian.

He hurries across Broadway. The weekly shopping to do. Mouths to feed.

Relief in the supermarket, cool air for the produce at least, Jesus drinking Poland Spring as he walks the aisle, marvelling at the goods as he always does. Man, the shelves of America: green beans from Kenya, starfruit from Papua New Guinea, iridescent sides of salmon fresh from the Highlands of Scotland and the mountain rivers of Canada, legs of lamb from New Zealand, tomatoes and basil from Tuscany, Spanish olives and South African oranges. There is almost nothing from the many miles of farmland that surround New York City. Another thing: it is high summer and yet the vegetable aisles still groan with swedes, parsnips, cauliflowers, sprouts and squash. Jesus reflects, not for the first time, on the expense and grief caused by going against nature, by fucking the seasons in the ass for a buck. The insane way they do business down here.

The true insanity of man was not to be found on the shelves, however, but in the trolleys and on the faces of the customers. Man, the shoppers of America. Jesus watches them as he lounges against a chest freezer filled with fourteen different kinds of frozen French fries, feeling cold air sparkling against the small of his back. In this supermarket, in one of the less salubrious corners of Manhattan, during working hours on a weekday, you looked at the faces and into the trolleys of the stay-at-home moms, the unemployed and the simply very greedy. Ignoring the tumbling shelves of fresh fruit and vegetables they wheel by Jesus into the freezer aisles. They fill their trolleys with frozen pizza. With microwavable instant dinners, with the many varieties of French fries, potato croquettes, hash browns, toaster pockets. Pints of ice cream, cheesecakes and pies. Jesus watches one woman – whose trolley is already bursting with plastic gallon bottles of fluorescent sugary drinks, with sliced loaves of white plastic bread, with huge silver sacks of potato chips, glass jars of hot dogs and pickles, cakes, biscuits and catering-sized packs of candy bars – trying to decide between two boxes of Popsicles. The woman weighs 250 pounds easy. Even in the iced air of the freezer aisle sweat is beading along her nose and soaking through her shapeless purple T-shirt.

And she is by no means the most obese of these shoppers. Two other browsers within Jesus' eyeline have long since abandoned the use of their own legs. They propel themselves through the aisles on motorised electric carts, stuffing their food into baskets mounted on the handlebars of the vehicles. Two hundred and fifty pounds would be a *target* for them. And no one is stopping them. No one is helping them. Jesus looks around the supermarket and he thinks – whoa!

He'd given up on trying to help these people. You'd be surprised what you got for your trouble when you leaned in, smiling, and said 'Excuse me, ma'am? Sir? Should you really be eating all that food? You know you're going to kill yourself, right?'

You got told to go get fucked.

You got your face spat in.

You got, on one occasion, your nuts whacked with a walking stick.

He checks the Casio as he makes his way to the bakery area. *Right on cue*, Jesus thinks as he sees the manager and a younger kid coming pushing a big cart along. They trundle it through the hanging plastic strips and into the darkness of the warehouse in back. Jesus hurries on out of the store.

Down the alley and along the fence that overlooks the delivery area out back of the supermarket. They're already there: about a dozen people waiting in the alley, hunkered down against the wooden fence, trying to stay in the shade. There's Becky and her two little boys, Danny who is seven, and his little brother Miles who is five. There's old Gus, a wino in his sixties, and Dotty, his girlfriend. There's Al and Frankie and Meg, the junkies, and Big Bob and a couple of others whose names Jesus doesn't know yet, who probably heard about this deal from one of the others.

'Hey, JC,' Becky says. 'Hey, JC,' Becky's kids chorus.

'Hi, guys,' Jesus says, ruffling Miles's hair.

'Frag,' Bob says softly as they shake hands. Big Bob is, well, big. Over two hundred pounds but lean and muscled for a guy in his late fifties. The others are saying hello too, smiling, coughing. Most of them don't look too good. They're dirty and sick and hungry. 'OK, everyone,' Jesus, speaking in a whisper, 'Any minute now. Everyone keep quiet, OK? You all brought your bags?' Everyone holds up their plastic bags. 'Good.'

Jesus climbs softly onto a trash can and peeps over the top of the fence. It's all real quiet for a minute and then the metal doors at the back of the supermarket crash open and the manager comes out with three kids in supermarket uniforms, wheeling two big carts. The kids begin emptying the carts into an orange dumpster while the manager watches them, yawning in the early-morning light. Jesus crouches back down and gives the thumbs up to everyone. He has them gather round and speaks in a whisper. 'OK, looks good. Now, same as usual, let's form a chain. Bob? You and me on the dumpster.'

'Frag,' Bob nods, twitching.

'Throwing to Frankie and Meg in the middle of the yard. Can you handle that, guys?'

They nod, Frankie giving Jesus a weak, shaky thumbs up. He's sweating, probably hasn't shot up since yesterday afternoon.

'OK, good,' Jesus says. 'And Frankie and Meg throwing them over to Al and Becky at the fence who'll throw them down to Gus, Dotty and the boys in the alley, yeah, kids?'

'Yeah!' Miles says. 'I'll catch 'em good.'

'You always drop 'em, dumb-ass!' Danny says.

'No – you do!'

You can just about live in New York City on the poverty line. If you get free food and someone covers your rent you can just about live.

'Guys?' Jesus claps his hands together at the boys. 'Come on, stay focused here. We're in and out of there fast.'

He pops his head back over the fence a fraction. The kids are swinging the last of the bags into the dumpster. They all head back into the store, the manager scraping the metal door shut behind him. ' OK,' Jesus says, 'let's go.'

Jesus over the fence, hitting the ground running, followed by Bob, then Frankie and Meg, then Al and Becky. Jesus and Bob reach the big dumpster and Bob gives Jesus a leg-up. He swings his legs over and looks down on a mountain of food: whole chickens and dented cans of tomatoes and soup, bags of rice and pasta, heads of lettuce, ears of corn, boxes of cakes and cartons of OJ. All expired, all part of the hundreds of millions of dollars' worth of food the USA flushes down the toilet every day. Jesus grabs the nearest chicken and begins swinging it over to Bob when the smell hits him. It's not the smell of rotting food – Jesus knows most of this stuff will still be good for days after the supermarket throws it out – it's a sharp, chemical smell. Jesus holds the bird to his face, the tang of ammonia making his eyes water.

'*Frag!*' Bob grunts, beckoning him to hurry up and throw the goddamn thing.

'Hang on, man,' Jesus says, 'there's something . . .'

A metallic creak – the back doors to the supermarket swinging open and the manager is standing there, two of the bigger kids coming out behind him.

'Shit,' Frankie says as he and Meg start running for the fence, Al and Becky already scrambling over. Bob and Jesus are caught – Bob shuffling embarrassed, Jesus waist-deep in the reeking dumpster. The manager is laughing.

'You like that, asshole?' The manager says. He's a young guy, around JC's age, maybe thirty? With a clip-on tie and a wispy moustache. 'You got a taste for Clorox?'

'OK, guys,' Jesus says, climbing out, 'we don't want any trouble.'

'Then get the fuck out of here,' the guy says.

'What's with this?' Jesus says, dropping down onto the hot asphalt. 'Why's there bleach on the food?' Jesus' manner – friendly, authoritative even. You'd never guess he'd just been busted scavenging food from a dumpster.

'New policy,' the manager says. 'Some low-life fucks in Indiana tried to sue the store after they got sick from eating expired products. All food gets bleached now before we throw it out.' The manager moves towards them, eyeing Big Bob, twitchy in his dirty combat jacket.

'But that . . . that's nuts,' Jesus says. 'Come on, man, I got hungry people here.' He gestures towards the fence where the others are huddled, peering over. 'Little kids. Folks down on their luck. Nobody's gonna sue you.'

The manager spits on the ground. 'New policy,' he shrugs. The sun beats down.

'Listen,' Jesus says, smiling, 'sorry, what's your name?'

'My name? I'm the fuckin' Fuck You Man. That's my name you fuckin' bum.'

Bob growls. The two big employees stand up behind the manager.

'Easy, Bob, easy,' Jesus says. 'Listen, Mr Fuck You Man. You've got a chance to do something wonderful here. These people are real hungry. Your company made, what, however many billion dollars in profits last year, right? You can throw us some food, can't you? Forget policy. You got a chance right here to make a difference in the world. To do a good thing. To, you know, be nice.'

The manager looks at Jesus, looks into his liquid blue eyes, shining bright in the early-morning sun, standing here on the asphalt lot. The balls on this guy, the manager thinks. 'Yeah,' the manager says, 'you know what? Fuck all that. Get the fuck outta here before I call the cops.' He turns away and starts walking back towards the loading bay.

Jesus swallows, controlling his anger. People, especially people like this hard-assed proto-Republican son of a bitch right here, often assumed that liberalism was easy. That 'Be nice' was a passive, default position. Man, Jesus thinks, how wrong can you be? Some days, days like today, it took every ounce of strength and discipline he had to love those who hated. Took all his self-control not to run amok on an ass-kicking frenzy of righteous fury. Like when he sometimes tuned into what was going down over in the Middle East, with the fundamentalist dudes. These dudes, man, what did they want? What were they after? (And what did they *do*? Where was their fundamentalist music? Their books? Their art? What happened to all that shit?) When you saw pictures of chicks with a hole in the middle of their face because some guy had cut their nose off because she ran away from home, when you saw women getting their backs turned to mush from a hundred lashes because they looked at a guy the wrong way, when you saw teenagers getting strung up and hanged in public squares because they were gay, or 'honour killings' . . . it took all he had to stay focused on 'they know not what they do'. Sometimes it took every bit of strength, courage and love not to give into John's way of thinking – *Say hello to my leetle fren. Bomb these motherfuckers back to the goddamn Stone Age, Dad. Flush them down the fucking toilet and start again. Come, Armageddon, come.*

Jesus takes a deep breath, reins it in, and says, 'May God forgive you.'

'What's that?' the manager says, turning round.

'I said –' Jesus speaks clearly this time – 'may God forgive you.'

'You think I got nothing better to do than stand here being bad-mouthed by a fucking bum?' the manager says, striding back towards them.

'I didn't mean to insult you. I apologise,' Jesus says, backing away, palms spread towards the man in deference.

'You're goddamn right you apologise,' the manager says. 'Now get the fuck off the property, asshole. Before I –' Here he jabs two fingers hard into Jesus' chest, sending him stumbling back.

That does it.

Bob howls as he flails in with a haymaker, smashing it straight into the manager's jaw, the guy's knees buckling as he hits the ground. 'No, Bob!' Jesus shouts as suddenly more staff come piling out of the store, jumping down from the loading bay, heading towards them. '*Run, Bob*,' Jesus says. Bob has a bunch of outstanding warrants.

'Frag.' Bob's for staying, squaring up.

'Come on, run!' Jesus shouts, tearing for the fence. Bob gets there first and vaults it easily just as the first punch connects with Jesus' temple.

He folds himself down onto the dusty ground and feels the fists and kicks rain down, hears the sirens drawing nearer through the heat.

2

HE TANK.

Again.

And the tank is packed: maybe thirty guys in a space meant for half that. Ceramic brick walls and metal bars. The tank never smells too good, but today, with the heat and all, it's indescribable. But we have to try: it's like someone got hold of a big old fish, stuffed the fish with dirty gym socks, anchovy paste and a hot human log, tucked that sucker inside a radiator, and then left the radiator on full blast for a couple of months.

It's the weekend – not the best time to be in here with the growlers, the yelpers and the mutants; the people who can't seem to get along with the codes that are needed outside. But Jesus, lacking the capacity for fear, knowing only love, is not afraid. He crouches quietly in the corner, knowing that this moment too will pass, that something will happen next and his story will move along. A huge, tattooed guy is eyeing him from across the packed tank, nudging his buddy, who is, if anything, even bigger, with a shaved head glistening in the half-light.

Man, Jesus thinks to himself, *we've been in a few of these.*

It's true. In his thirty-one years down here he's seen holding pens in Frisco, Vegas and New Orleans. He's sweated in cells in California and shivered in tanks in Colorado. Affray, breach of the peace, resisting arrest . . . all the channels they have down here for people who dare to put their hands up now and again and say '*this ain't right* . . .'

He looks up at the tiny, grilled window. He can't see any stars, just sodium-orange street light burning hard outside, but he knows there are stars up there. *Shit, Dad*, he thinks. '*Lead*' . . . '*Inspire*'? They're cool words and all, real cool, but do you know how resistant to inspiration many of these people are? Yet, funnily enough, they are easily led. They just got lousy taste in leaders for the most part. That time in Denver when he was talking to that crowd and that anti-abortionist lady spat in his face and then her husband, or boyfriend or whatever, started beating on him. It wasn't them who wound up in the tank. 'I would have kicked your ass myself,' the cop who locked him up told him.

'But why?' Jesus asked him.

The cop had shrugged. 'I'm a Christian,' he said.

Hardest part of the job, loving those who hated.

Jesus sighs and rests his head against the warm, ceramic brickwork. Kris's birthday tonight. Surprise party up on the roof. They still needed to get some things: hamburger buns, hot-dog sausages, cheese. All the stuff he'd been hoping to get from the supermarket. It didn't matter – he had some cash squirrelled away, he could cover it. And Morgan was getting the liquor, he had the dough for that, so that would be cool.

Kris and Morgan. His band. His guys.

They'd been playing together in various line-ups since they were teenagers, back in the late nineties in Cozad. (Yeah, Cozad.

Cozad, fucking Nebraska. Pop: 4,000. Thanks a bunch, Dad. Forget LA or New York, or Seattle. He didn't even land him in Omaha, where they might have lucked into the whole Saddle Creek, Bright Eyes thing.) Various guitar players had come and gone until they'd settled into being a three-piece in the classic Hüsker Dü/Dinosaur Jr/Nirvana fashion. (*'Favour the underdog.'* Of course Jesus was an indie kid.) There had been the tiny record deal about seven years ago: their relocation to New York and a brief flowering of hope. Then the zero radio play, the album that sank without trace, the endless touring, playing to fifteen people at the Silver Dollar in Arizona, the Bottom Line in Delaware, the Mission in Castle Falls, the slow dawning that the full extent to which the general public did not give a fuck about their music could not be measured. Then came the McJobs, washing dishes and bussing tables in their late twenties, the downgrade to the tiny two-room apartment, the new material they were working on when they could afford rehearsal space. JC had thought it would all be simple down here: form a cool band, sell lots of records and then use your platform to tell people how badly they were fucking shit up. You know, kinda like Bono did. But way cooler.

Yeah, right, he thought now.

Gradually, these past few years, with his music career, um, stalled you might say, he'd decided, well, if you couldn't reach the world to change it, then you tried to change the world within your reach. God bless the guys, Morgan and Kris had stuck by Jesus as these extra-curricular activities started to overtake those of their band. It'd started with Becky and the boys, a few years back. He'd helped her get clean, off junk. Like they were trying to do now with Meg. They helped Becky and some of her friends with their social security forms. Helped a few others getting into a hostel. They started taking hot leftovers from the kitchens they worked in down to the dark places below the elevated tracks of the subway line. They got to know a few of the people they were feeding and JC found himself helping them with their welfare claims, trying to get them into shelters and stuff. Making sure they had food in the most expensive city in the world, a place where it often came down to this: eat, or have some place to sleep. It had evolved into a kind of self-funded, DIY outreach programme and they'd wound up taking care of a kind of menagerie of waifs and strays: Becky, Meg, Bob and Gus and Dotty, the old winos who would surely have died this past winter if it hadn't been for Jesus and the guys.

Big Bob they met when he was burned out of the dumpster he was living in with two buddies. Three old vets – guys who'd bled into the Vietnamese dirt – who wound up living in a dumpster over in Chelsea. And someone torched it. Bob's buddies both died, burned alive. Another buddy of Bob's had told them all this, of course. Bob hadn't spoken properly since 1973 because –

'Hey, fucko.' A kick against his leg and Jesus looks up. The two guys – Mr Shaved Head and Mr Tattoos – are standing over him, others already clearing out of the way.

'Evening, guys,' Jesus says, smiling. 'Hot, huh?'

Tattoos crouches down next to Jesus. His wife-beater smells like it was used to wrap the log/fish package. One of his tats, a big one on the forearm, shows a naked woman on all fours. She has breasts growing out of her back as well as dangling from her front and the inscription above the tattoo reads 'MY DREAM'. *Wow*, Jesus thinks. *What the fuck is this dude selling?* Although he is not old, the guy has few teeth and his voice comes in a sibilant whisper through the gaps in his dentistry.

'Son,' the guy whispers, 'it's 'bout to get a lot fucken hotter.'

'How so?' Jesus asks, looking directly at the guy. This is a tough son of a bitch, but even he is momentarily unsettled by Jesus' gaze, by its cool, blue purity. His eyes dart skittishly around the cell while he speaks through those bad old teeth.

'Here's how it's gonna be. You're gonna bend over in that fucking corner and me . . .' He lowers his voice even further at the sound of footsteps approaching. 'Hey, man, where my fucking lawyer at?' someone shouts out. 'Shut the fuck up,' the guard shouts back and walks on by. '. . . and me and my boy here are gonna do what we need to do.'

'Really?' Jesus says. 'That's what you . . . you wanna sodomise me?'

'Sodda-what now?' Shaved Head says, leaning down too now.

'It means have sex with me,' Jesus says.

'Listen, you smart-mouthed motherfucker,' 'MY DREAM' says, 'you make a fucking peep and I'll do you in the fucking kidneys.' He pulls his vest up to show he's got a small, nasty-looking home-made shiv stuck in his waistband; it looks like a plastic toothbrush handle with a razor blade melted into it. There's another tattoo – a bullet hole – above it. It reminds Jesus of a statistic he read about, how every single male executed in America in modern times had a tattoo of some kind. Execution. Man, they still did that shit down here.

'In front of all these people?' Jesus says. 'Look, I know a lot of terrible things probably happened to you when you were growing up to make you think something like this would be a good idea but, I mean, will it really be any kind of fun? Think about it. Cos I'm willing to bet that as soon as you ejaculate you're gonna feel just dreadful. Like, ashamed and guilty and all that? I was with this girl once, in, uh, Florida? And –'

The shiv is suddenly in his face, wavering near his eyeball.

'Shut the fuck up and take your fucking pants down,' Mr Tats hisses through gritted, broken teeth.

Jesus sighs as he does so. Yeah, that girl in Florida, after a show. She'd been hot, man. There'd been a bunch of chicks but nothing serious. Why not? Well, a part him of sensed that, given what he was trying to do, trying to get the whole 'Be nice' thing back in circulation, things probably weren't gonna work out too well down here. Like now for instance – Shaved Head forming a kind of protective barrier, screening them off from the rest of the tank, while Tats gets into position, fumbling hurriedly at his zipper. People look the other way. No one says anything of course. Had Jesus been one of these people he'd have said something. Yeah, and wound up in the infirmary no doubt. He can sense stuff going on behind him, someone getting into position. Come on then, get this over with. Forgive them for they know not what they do and all that stuff.

What had he been thinking about a minute ago? Oh yeah, Bob.

Bob, Corporal Bob in 1973, was just twenty-one then. The village was thousands of years old. Near the Cambodian border, pockmarked by artillery, dusted with napalm, the treetops still burning, that toasted petrol smell in your lungs, the roar of the F-4s still washing back across the jungle, and then Bob and the guys coming in, capping off in all directions, Bob getting told to frag a tunnel, VC all over the fucking place. He dropped three of those high-impact bad boys down the hatch, felt the ground all rippling up beneath him and then swung down in there, his M16 hot as a griddle, burning his fingers on the frame as he slammed another mag home, pulled back the bolt and got ready to rock and roll. The smoke cleared and he saw the enemy up close and personal.

Two little kids.

One flat on its back, screaming with no legs. The other one hopping around – not screaming, glazed – with one leg and one arm, trying to balance against the wall, trying to pick up the severed arm with the good one, the mud floor of the tunnel an abattoir. A woman – their mom, Bob guessed – trying to crawl towards them, holding her stomach in but long strands of intestine trailing along behind her.

A baby's head and shoulders were just lying there, the rest of it atomised, gone, all gone.

The kid with no legs juddering and banging her fists on the floor – he saw now it was a girl – fitting, going into shock; the one with one leg hopping around, trying to clutch the leg stump, trying to get that one hand over the jagged bone, trying to stop the blood gouting out, the femoral artery sheared open, that arterial blood thick as molasses. Pots of rice still bubbling on a little stove set into the mud wall (Bob could draw you those pots today in total detail) and Bob realising that they were many, many klicks from the nearest conceivable evac point. Bob doing what he had to do, the first time he'd used his .45 in combat, pressing it oh-so gently to those temples, using up the last of his sanity. Bob's CO finding him in the tunnel later, covered in blood, surrounded by the dead family, just saying, 'Frag, frag, frag.' The only word Big Bob had spoken since that morning. Psyche discharge and fast-forward thirty-eight years to a dumpster in New York City was all she wrote.

He feels spit dribbling onto his buttocks now, an exploratory jab with a thumb down there. One of those guys getting ready to . . . Jesus tenses, tries to relax, but he's tensing as he feels it, hard as Bakelite, twanging against his cheeks, probing for his, pressing right against his . . . forgive them, Lord, they –

The footfall of the guards and then a voice saying 'Jesus? Jesus Christ?' The guy's laughing as he says it, as folk often do.

'Here,' Jesus says, holding his hand up.

'Get your ass out here. You made bail.'

The (not totally unpleasant it has to be admitted) sensation of that half-inch of cock popping back out of him and Jesus is pulling his pants up as Shaved Head and Tats rearrange themselves, scrambling away from him. Timing, JC thinks, is everything.

'Another time, pretty boy,' Tats whispers.

'You are forgiven,' Jesus replies.

The guy punches Jesus square in the face, mashing his nose up, blood streaming down his chin and onto his T-shirt. 'Forgive that, you fucking faggot,' the guy says.

'I'm the faggot?' Jesus manages nasally, through blood.

3

ORGAN, STANDING THERE GRINNING IN THE SUN-
shine on the jailhouse steps. He's a tall, kinda
goofy-looking black kid, with a lazy smile, sleepy
eyes and a frizzed-out, mid-length Afro. About
Jesus' age, but he could pass for five years younger. Terrific
drummer. He's wearing knee-length Bermuda shorts, battered
sneakers and a loose white tee. Morgan watches Jesus coming
shakily down the steps, a bloody paper towel pressed into his nose.
'Shit,' he says, 'what the fuck you gone and gotten into now?'

'Ah . . .' Tell Morgan? Neh. Most people had more trouble
than JC with forgiving stuff. 'I got into an argument with a
couple of guys. No biggie. I left a couple of bucks on the
nightstand man. Did you get some breakfast?'

'Hot dog.'

'A hot dog?' Jesus says. 'You should have some fruit in the
mornings, Morgs. A little melon. Grapefruit. Something like
that. You gotta take better care of yourself.'

'Yeah, yeah. I ain't the one standing here with ma damn nose
looking like a fucking horror movie.'

'Hey,' Jesus stops and turns round, lifting the paper towel off his nose. 'Look at that. Stopped bleeding already.' They're on a busy street corner in midtown, New York City rush hour, no one paying any attention to the tall blond white guy with the busted face talking with the skinny black kid.

'Yeah, real slick. You're looking good.'

'Anyway,' Jesus says, 'how'd you get the bail money?'

'Uh.' Morgan looks down, kicking his heels.

'Morgs?' Jesus says slowly.

'I pawned Daisy down at Harvey's.'

'You fucking what?'

'What else was I gonna do? Leave you in there so everyone could have their turn beating on you?'

'Oh man,' Jesus says, striding off.

Harvey's – the pawnshop they favoured on the Lower East Side. Glass cases of jewellery – bracelets, earrings and necklaces – and watches; the Rolexes, Cartiers and Pateks that once belonged to those who had risen fast in this fast city but who had fallen even quicker and harder. You can find anything from an amethyst-encrusted snuffbox to a .357 Magnum in Harvey's.

Jesus, moving quickly through the aisles, heading towards the musical instruments section at the back of the place, Morgan following. They can see Harvey leaning on the counter reading the sports pages, a cup of coffee steaming beside him. Harvey looks up as they come up the three stairs that separate this section from the rest of the store. 'Hey, JC!' he says. 'Had a feeling I'd be seeing you before too long. Your boy here told me you were in a jam, so I cut him a real sweet deal.'

'How much, Harvey?'

'Five fifty.'

Jesus' jaw drops as he turns to Morgan. *'You pawned Daisy for five hundred and fifty dollars?!'*

'Come on, man,' Harvey says, 'I wouldn't get more than a thou for her if I put her up for sale. Market's dead right now.'

'Bail was only five hundred. I still got fifty bucks left!' Morgan says, pulling out some bills.

'Oh great,' Jesus says flatly.

Harvey laughs. 'Hey, seeing as it's you guys, I'll hold her a few days past when the ticket's due. Give you a little more time to get the dough together.'

'No,' Jesus sighs. 'Hang on.' He starts unlacing his sneaker. 'You know, Harvey, usury and all that. You're gonna have a hard time getting in upstairs.'

'Yeah, you're killing me,' Harvey says.

Jesus pulls the sneaker off: a battered Converse with the words 'Modest Mouse' written in black felt tip along the white edging of the soles. His feet don't smell too good.

'You know, JC, the man don't retail second-hand sports-wear,' Morgan says.

'Funny,' Jesus says, feeling inside the sneaker. He pulls out the filthy, crumpled roll of bills.

'Ben!' Harvey shouts. Almost immediately a kid's head pops around the door leading to the private part of the pawnshop. 'Go get the man's guitar. It's the Gibson. The '68 SG.'

'Where the hell you get that?' Morgan asks.

'I been saving it. For tonight.'

'See, son?' Harvey says to Morgan, nodding towards the roll of bills. 'These are the benefits of hanging out with Our Lord. Always carrying.' Harvey, like most folk they hung around, knew JC's story and routinely mocked it. Not that it bothered JC in the slightest.

'Yeah, right,' Morgan says. 'That's why we living the good

life. Standing here in a goddamn pawn store.' Morgan also thought his friend's claim to be the Son of God was a total crock. But the guy never preached about it. Just routinely did the right thing, which was way harder than it sounded. Motherfucker was cool though. Un-fucking-flappable. Hell of a singer and guitar player too. Morgan had an uncle who'd been convinced he was Alexander Graham Bell in a previous life. Always talking 'bout when he came up with the telephone. So Morgan figured – shit, whatever gets you to sleep at night, man. Dude ain't hurting no one.

'Now listen,' Jesus says, turning back to face Harvey, 'help me out here, Harv. We got stuff we gotta get for Kris's party tonight. Guy's turning thirty and all . . .'

'Yeah, yeah . . .' Harvey says, counting out that greasy money.

4

IKE THE SONG SAYS, IT IS INDEED A PITY THAT THE days can't be like the nights in the summer in the city. It's late evening, cooler, and a crowd is gathered on the rooftop of their apartment building, seven floors up looking out over downtown Manhattan; the white frizz of headlights coming along Broadway, the uptown people coming downtown, people with restaurant reservations, parties to go to.

It's been quite a party up here too. Little Miles and Danny are asleep, stretched out on a blanket over by the wall. Kris is grilling up the last of the burgers and shish kebabs on the makeshift barbecue, Becky's singing a Carpenters tune while Morgs strums on an old acoustic, Gus and Dotty, listening, drunk, Al, Frankie, nodding out in the corner, Meg sitting a few feet away from them, a little twitchy, finding it real hard, these first few days clean. There's a few others they don't know so well here too. Bob sits quietly on the ledge, still feeling bad about getting away while Jesus took the rap no doubt. (But, as Jesus told him, if they'd grabbed Bob and got a look at his sheet they'd have had to pawn a lot more than a vintage guitar to cover that bail.) It's been a feast. Harvey cut them a deal – JC can be hard to say no to – and Jesus and Morgan hit the FoodWay: hamburger meat, buns, a birthday cake, a shitload of candy for the kids, a couple of cases of beer. Some tequila. Beautiful, man.

A couple of strings of cheap Chinese lanterns criss-cross the roof; Pozlowski the super bought them for a Halloween party a couple of years back and they still work – they're casting pools of yellow, green and orange light on the people sitting around smoking, drinking, laughing and talking.

Jesus looks over the scene, takes a hit on the joint (man, it took him a while to adjust to the weed down here) and smiles. Yeah, the whole miracle bullshit and the way the goddamn Christians got hold of it *was* bullshit. But, at moments like this, he realises that sometimes it *is* nothing less than a fucking miracle that these people have somehow gotten through another day in a city like this. And not only gotten through – they're sitting here with full bellies and cold drinks, singing and talking and laughing. He turns, hooking an arm over the ledge of the rooftop, and looks out across Broadway. There are men in overalls, working even at this hour, high up on a scaffold, taking down an enormous billboard advertising underwear, getting ready to put a new advert up overnight. Because God forbid, Jesus thinks, people should be allowed to go a single goddamn day without having some piece of shit product forced down their throat.

'Want one?'

Jesus looks up – Fat Kris, standing over him, smiling, with a fistful of hamburgers wrapped in paper towels. Jesus smiles, shakes his head. 'No, man, I'm good.'

'Ah, come on. These onions are, like, melting, dude.'

'Really, man. You go ahead.'

Kris shrugs happily, sits down beside him and starts eating. He's a big guy, Kris, pushing two hundred, his wrinkled, ancient Mudhoney T-shirt stained with sweat from working the grill on this hot night. They made an unlikely pair, Kris and Morgan, the rhythm section: the fat, white cheerful bass player and the skinny, mocking drummer. Morgs was the more aggressive of the two, with a weary cynicism about most things; a nice balance to Kris's puppyish enthusiasm. Kris said nearly everything with an exclamation mark. He was trusting, practical and keen. Morgan more caustic and cautious. JC took counsel from both. Keep a range of views around you. Dad had taught him that, with his mewling Matthews, his mincing Lances and his militant Andrews.

Across the rooftop Al and Morgs are singing 'Visions of Johanna' now. Kris steals a sideways glance at JC, enjoying watching him enjoying the scene.

'Hey, JC,' Becky shouts over, 'get off your ass and give us a number.' The others join in, calling on him. Al holds the guitar out towards him.

'Neh, I'm tired. You guys are sounding great.'

'Come on!'

'Later.'

They boo and the guitar gets passed on to someone else. JC smiles at Becky and she lifts her middle finger to him. Man, Becks was looking good these days: her long black hair clean and shining under the lanterns. Her freckled skin clean and shining too. JC watches as she stretches her shapely, bare legs out on the blanket in front of her, casting a glance every few minutes over to where her boys lie sleeping. The girl had come on a ways since they met her a couple of years back, through a friend of hers who worked washing dishes with Morgan.

Originally from Ohio, she was real pretty and a real mess: just getting off crack, still drinking too much. She had, they knew, made a few bucks from time to time working for an escort service. Always on the verge of having the boys taken away from her, she'd been about to get evicted from the one-bedroom shithole she rented on the Lower East Side. They scraped some money together to cover a little of the outstanding rent and JC went and talked to her landlord. The guy had relented and Becky got to keep her place. It turned out to be a turning point and it was really something to see this girl clean and sober now. Taking care of her kids and looking to find some sort of job, although that was gonna be tough for a twenty-six-year-old girl with no qualifications and two boys aged five and seven. Shit, what wasn't tough in New York? One thing, though – since she'd gotten clean Becky was an instinctive, natural-born organiser. It pained JC to see all this potential being told to go get fucked on a daily basis, usually for minimum-wage jobs the girl could do in her sleep.

Kris leans forward under a yellow lantern to take a good look at JC's face. 'Wow! Look at that nose. Is it sore?'

'Ah, you know. A lot worse things have happened tonight than a bust nose.' He gestures across the rooftops, out at the hot, wailing city.

Kris looks over at the group of waifs and strays, the menagerie, and sighs. 'The thing is, we're just firefighting, you know, JC? It's all day-to-day stuff. Helping people out with this or that, getting someone a little food here, a little medicine there, a little money sometimes.

'I know, man. We're –'

'I mean, don't get me wrong, I love you and all, but . . . we ain't played a gig in months. Gig? Shit, we ain't even *rehearsed* in months.'

'I know, dude. We've kinda had our hands full. We're just, you know, doing the best we can until . . .'

'Until?'

'Until we get the opportunity to do something more, I guess.'

'Like what? We waiting for, like, a sign or something?' Kris looks at him innocently, hopeful.

'Maybe,' Jesus says. 'Something'll happen.'

Kris nods. Sometimes – he'd never say anything like this to Morgan of course – but sometimes, when he looked into JC's eyes, when he was saying something, or, more often, when he was playing, he thought maybe there was something in this Son of God business. Or maybe it was just that he thought JC deserved to be a star. Best fucking frontman Kris had ever played with at any rate. Like back when they were kids, if Kurt Cobain had said he was the Son of God Kris would have bought that. No problem, man.

'Come on!' someone shouts. Jesus looks over. Bob is shuffling towards him, bringing the guitar, holding it out to him.

'Come on, guys,' Jesus says, 'who else wants to sing?'

'Shut your humble ass up and play the motherfucking gee-tar,' Morgan tells him.

'Ah shit, one song,' Jesus says, relenting, taking the guitar. 'What you kids wanna hear?'

'Something old!' Gus shouts.

'Something old . . . something old . . .' Jesus says to himself, tuning up. Al's guitar is a beaten-up piece of old crap. You can never get it properly in tune. He hits a few harmonics, tunes the B string up a notch. 'Close enough for country,' he says and starts in on 'May You Never', by John Martyn, working up a little intro by picking the melody out on the G and B strings among a rhythmic flurry of chords.

Jesus plays great, with a real talent for dropping unexpected little phrases in between lines, snapping them off for punctuation and emphasis. Everyone sits a little closer and really starts listening. In the middle he brings it right down and takes a solo – his thumb still picking out a bass line on the bottom strings while his middle and index fingers trill on the lead notes.

'Love is a lesson to learn in our time . . .'

His guitar playing is great, but his voice is really something else – clear and sweet on this song, but with that edge, that hurt and desperation every great singer from Hank to Kurt has. People know it too. Terrible thing, Kris thinks, watching the people listening to JC, but most people go their whole lives without ever getting close to someone who can really cut it playing and singing a song. They'll see it on TV here and there, coming through two-inch plastic speakers, or, maybe, see a real good concert once or twice, but, nowadays, almost no one gets to sit in a small room with someone who can really let go, where you can feel their breath on your face, feel the soundbox on that beat-up old acoustic moving the air. It's a hell of a thing – even people who don't know anything about music know they're experiencing something of a different order. They don't know why those little pimples are puckering up on their forearms and the backs of their necks, but they sure as shit know they don't get this feeling from the car radio too often. The poverty of most people's experience only gets real to them when you put something great in front of them. The rest of the time they figure it's all good.

Jesus finishes dramatically – his fingers running up the neck in a flourish, coming together into the final chord which he then bends up a semitone and lets fall back down into place. He looks up into their faces – everyone, from little Miles, who has woken up, to Gus and Dotty, everyone watching him, utterly enraptured. They burst into applause.

Morgs slaps him across the back of the head. 'You a show-off sonofabitch, ain't you?'

'Shit, son,' Jesus says, comically Southern, cracking open another beer, 'you got it, flaunt it.'

They call for another tune. He obliges. There's still plenty of beers left and their singing carries across the rooftops, getting lost in the traffic blare somewhere over Broadway in the night; the sirens that rip the air, the blue lights circling by down below sending strobing flashes up the walls of the tenements, reminding you that for many in this city, this evening will continue outside the reach of any helping arm.

5

HE SIGN APPEARS TO THEM THE NEXT MORNING. And, appropriately enough, it is Kris who sees it first. The sign is a hundred feet tall, fifty feet wide, towering over Broadway, as though God has indeed put it there just for them. Kris shakes Jesus awake excitedly, not troubling much over the fact that he has a girl from the party – Carol something, Kris thinks – in bed with him. She's real pretty. Jesus always got laid when he sang. 'You gotta come and see this,' Kris says, like a kid on Christmas morning, tugging the bed sheets off JC.

'What the fuck, man? What . . . what time is it?'

'Early. Here.' Kris throws pants at him. Carol gives a soft moan, buries her face into Jesus' long blond hair. 'Come on. You gotta see this . . .'

'Shit, it's Sunday morning,' Morgan moans from the other bed.

'You too,' Kris says.

The four of them stumble barefoot out onto the street, the

pavement already warm beneath their feet, and look up, following Kris's trembling finger. 'Look,' he says.

The workmen, high on their scaffold in the night, had put it there. Block capitals thirty feet high say:

AMERICAN POP STAR!

They read on, squinting into the early-morning sun. There is a picture of a black girl, her head thrown back as she wails into a microphone, and, in slightly smaller type, the words:

SEASON 3: THE SEARCH BEGINS . . .

Kris watches them reading, Jesus, Carol and Morgs, their lips moving slightly.

ON ABN THIS FALL.

'Yeah?' Jesus says, looking at Kris uncertainly.

MILLION DOLLAR RECORDING CONTRACT!

'Read on. The bottom.'

Auditions begin nationwide July 10.

'So?' Jesus says.

'Lissen,' Kris says, taking him by the shoulders. 'You are going to go on that show and you are going to *win* it. Huh? Huh?' Kris is beaming now as he steps back from them and starts doing a little jig on the sidewalk. Carol laughs.

'Damn,' Morgan says, watching Kris, speaking to Jesus.

'And I thought you were the one who was supposed to be crazy . . .'

'You're outta your mind,' JC tells Kris over coffee in the diner at the end of their block. 'Those shows suck, man. Just all these spineless, wet, suck-o, ballad-singing, corporate rock bitches. They never have anyone who rocks on these things.'

'So?' Kris says. 'Show 'em someone who does.'

'Hey,' Jesus says, 'do you guys wanna split some waffles?'

'No, lissen, lissen –' Kris says, closing the menu.

'Kris,' Morgan cuts in, 'he's right. Come on, man – that show's a piece of shit.'

'So? You go on and you kick ass and people feel it and then, well, we'll take it from there.' Kris says. 'This is it. This is the sign.'

'It's *a* sign,' Jesus says. 'Anyway, they'd never let you use your own group. I bet you that. Right? You'd have to use the house band.'

'So?' Kris says.

'So it'll suck.'

'It won't suck completely,' Kris says. 'You're good. You telling me that Jimi Hendrix would've *completely* sucked playing with the house band?'

'Well, no.' Jesus allows himself a smile, remembering swapping riffs with Jimi, wondering what he was up to right now. Getting laid no doubt. 'I just, I wanted you guys to, you know, get in there too.'

'Fuck that shit,' Morgan says. 'Maybe fat boy here's got something. I could go for this, you know? Sitting at home – pissing ma goddamn pants laughing at your scared white ass on TV.'

'I'm not scared,' Jesus says.

'Then what's the problem?'

'I'm not scared of singing on some lame TV show.'

'Prove it then.' Kris.

'Yeah, prove it, motherfucker.' Morgan.

'I . . .' Jesus laughs. 'OK. Fine. Shit. Fuck. I'll prove it. I'll go to the goddamn audition. OK? You douchebags happy now?'

'Awesome,' Kris says. 'I am awesomely happy.'

'OK. Then we're all happy. Great. Can we please order some breakfast now, huh?'

'Get what the fuck you want,' Morgan says. 'We ain't stopping you.'

'Good. Right. I'm gonna have some waffles.' He snaps the laminated menu back open. A rare sight – Jesus a little flustered. Morgs and Kris settle back to enjoy it, nudging each other.

'I'm having waffles,' Jesus repeats.

6

HE ABN BUILDING ON TIMES SQUARE: ALL THE freaks are out today, the queue snaking along the west side of the square, coiling around the corner onto 42nd Street and continuing on for several blocks, reaching halfway to Eighth Avenue. The big Jumbotron above the Coca-Cola sign proclaims '*AMERICAN POP STAR* – THE SEARCH STARTS HERE!' Cops on foot and horseback mill around, keeping the people off the street, keeping the crossings clear. Hot-dog vendors and cold-soda merchants have gathered too, working the line, knowing the freaks are going to have a long, hot wait. Many have been here since the night before, spending the hot summer evening on the warm sidewalk. Tourists with their cameras stop at the most extreme examples in the line and snap away – what a story to tell the guys back in Omaha/Idaho/Toledo!

And they are not short of extreme examples to photograph: the seven-and-a-half-foot-tall pair of goths, their Mohicans dyed candyfloss pink and electric blue, the platform soles of their industrial spaceboots two feet tall alone. The trio of identical sisters dressed as sex pixies: puffball skirts with stockings and suspenders, cleavages straining against taut ivory basques, their hair all matching lilac bobs. There are he-men, she-men, robots, superheroes, the near-naked, the heavily made up and the God-knows-what. Some are children, some are senior citizens, some appear sane enough and some are clearly as mad as a bottle of fries. Many of them are singing, practising snatches of songs, arias, scales, vocal exercises. They stop and break off to perform for the cameras of the TV crews that roam the line, some of them from the show itself, getting audition footage to cut into the programme, some of them from the New York City news stations. As another camera car glides down 42nd Street, filming out of the window, a girl bends over and lifts her skirt, flashing them plump white buttocks quivering atop black stockings. A man falls to his knees and starts screaming the intro to a song. Another pair, a giant and a midget – some kind of double act – throw themselves into action; the midget scampering rapidly up onto the giant's shoulders and both of them bursting into song. All of them – midgets, giants, old, young, beautiful, ugly – all of them have the same disease: fame as birth right.

'Oh man,' Jesus says, turning his face away as yet another camera wagon trundles by. 'This is fucking embarrassing.'

'Easy money, JC,' Kris tells him for the umpteenth time. 'Easy money.'

Jesus has his Gibson slung over his back and a little Pignose amplifier strapped to his belt. He has tried several times this morning to leave, only to be cajoled back by Kris.

Hours pass, the line shuffles forward inch by inch, with Times Square itself seemingly never getting any closer. A reporter on foot, microphone in hand, camera crew following, is roaming the queue conducting random interviews with likely subjects. He swings abruptly round and thrusts the mike towards the two attractive girls standing in front of Jesus and Kris.

'Hi there,' he says. 'Tom Barker with ABN Breakfast. How long you been here, girls?'

'Oh God! Since about five or six this morning, Tom? We got the bus over from Jersey. I'm Debbie, she's Tammy, we're the Foxes!' They chorus the last words.

'Do you think you'll get on the show?'

'Sure!' Debbie says. 'Look out, America,' Tammy cuts in, ignoring Tom, playing straight to camera, 'we're comin' atcha!' The two of them start singing a Britney Spears number very, very badly.

'Oh man,' Jesus mutters as he looks up to the sky. 'God, why hast thou forsaken me?'

Samantha Jansen, Executive Producer of *American Pop Star*, freshly flown in from Los Angeles that very morning, presses her forehead against the tinted glass of the office window and looks down fifteen floors onto the corner of Times Square and 42nd Street, where the crowd looks peaceful and harmless. 'How many?' she asks.

'Um, we think,' her assistant Roger says from the edge of the desk where he is reading a sheaf of memos attached to a clipboard, 'close on ten thousand. Up over 20 per cent on last year's NYC auditions.'

'And elsewhere?' Jansen says, turning round, folding her arms, leaning back against the window, the afternoon sun behind her low over Manhattan, making her just an outline to Roger.

'All good. Huge numbers in LA, Chicago, Seattle. Seems to be down a little in Houston. Probably the heat.'

'Mmmm. Probably.'

Jansen is concerned.

For a while, during the first season, *American Pop Star* had been the biggest – the only – fun in town. The show came out of nowhere and smashed all known ratings records. Right now they were still the country's top-rated show; if they could hold onto that position for three years running it would be a feat not achieved since the great days of *The Cosby Show* back in the eighties. Then, last year, *Talent USA*, launched on NBC. The show took the same format as *American Pop Star* but focused more on the freaks, maniacs and crackpots, on the hard-luck backstories of the contestants. No one thought the show would last but, like the boss is fond of saying, there's no bottom to where people will go with this kind of shit (or 'shite' as the boss would say) and, sure enough, *TUSA* was back for a second season and looking to make a steady climb up the Nielsen ratings. It seemed that, while America was interested in talent, what it really liked was salivating, lock-'em-up-and-pump-'em-full-of-Thorazine, honest-to-goodness, off-their-titties maniacs. And plenty of 'em. *TUSA* hadn't made enough of a climb yet to really challenge Jansen's position as Exec Producer of America's number one show, but enough of a climb to make the boss nervous. And when the boss was nervous you had better be more than just a little concerned.

She turns back to the window and looks down at the milling line. 'Here we go again,' she says, to herself more than Roger.

7

'K,' ONE OF THE FLOOR MANAGERS IS SAYING TO Jesus as he manhandles him towards the side of the auditorium, 'can I have you over here with this guy and –' Jesus has a number pinned to his T-shirt – 'you and you as well.' Four of them are herded into a small group and are taken down a short hallway to wait outside one of the many audition rooms. Jesus greets his fellow contestants: 'Hey, guys, how you all doing?'

The guy nearest to him, a nervy dude in some sort of spandex catsuit, just giggles and slides away down the wall, glancing nervously from side to side.

Right, Jesus thinks.

'How many times, sweetheart?' another one asks. He is a tall Puerto Rican kid, dressed in a white tuxedo.

'Uh?'

'How many times you auditioned?'

'Oh, never,' Jesus says. 'Just this. This is my first time. How about you?'

'Third,' the kid says, wrinkling his nose, taking in Jesus'

filthy sneakers, stained shorts, sweat-ringed Folk Implosion T-shirt. 'Nice to see you made an effort,' he says and turns away and starts practising some vocal scale.

'Don't mind him,' a girl says. 'He's an asshole. I'm Clare. It's my third time.' They shake hands. Clare is a big girl. She's dressed in a pink leotard, like a giant psychedelic seal. 'Hey, you play guitar too?' she says, noticing the Gibson strapped across his back. 'Neat. What you gonna sing?'

'Uh, I dunno. Hadn't really thought –'

'OK!' someone shouts and the four of them are being ushered into the room. Sam Jansen and a couple of underlings sit at a long table. There is a video camera set up on a tripod and two bulky security guards lounging at the back of the room. 'What's with the heavies?' Jesus whispers to Clare.

'Oh, they get some total maniacs in here. You know?' she says, snapping her thumbs out of the shoulder straps of her leotard, her enormous bulk rippling and bobbing.

'OK,' Jansen says, '4,410 . . . Lord Alfonso?' Her voice modulates into a sigh as she says his name.

The Puerto Rican kid twirls into the centre of the room. 'We meet again, darling!' he says.

'Yes. What do you have for us this year?'

'I will be singing "Anything Goes".'

'Right, sure. When you're ready.'

The embarrassment Jesus feels watching the kid strut back and forth in his tuxedo while hammily butchering Cole Porter cannot be measured. After exactly fifty seconds of the song he is about to go into a tap routine when Jansen looks up and says, 'Thank you, Alfonso! 4,411 please!'

He bows and says, 'That's *Lord* Alfonso.' And turns and stalks to the back of the room. 'Fucking dyke,' he mutters under his breath as he passes Jesus.

Clare gets up and begins a nerve-racked a cappella rendition of 'Lucky Star' by Madonna while attempting a dance routine that looks like a five-year-old trying not to go to the bathroom in their pants.

A few seconds into it and Jesus is thinking – *God damn*.

You get a sense, when you walk the streets of a city like New York, of a lot of madness just held in check: the babblers and howlers and the waiters and the cabbies and the buskers: a million tons of thwarted dreams and ambitions zinging and shimmering around the hot streets. But here, here it was all brought so close together that it felt like there was enough crazed energy to power the entire city, the fucking nation.

'Thank you, Clare,' Jansen was soon saying, holding a hand up. '4,412 please.'

The twitchy guy in the spandex walks into the centre of the room and bows deeply.

'Hi, um, Moonchild?' Jansen says reading from her clipboard. 'And what –'

Before she can finish the sentence Moonchild turns round and bends over. He grips his buttocks and tugs them apart and there is a crinkle of Velcro as a seam running down his ass comes apart. He looks up, facing now towards Jesus and the others standing at the back of the room, his ass pointing towards the producers, and grunts, his face turning red. A split-second pause and then a filthy torrent of liquid shit sprays out of his ass, spattering onto the floor in front of the table.

'Fuck!' Jansen says, scrambling backwards as the security guys charge in, each taking an arm as they carry Moonchild out of there. He is giggling and gibbering 'I showed you . . . I showed you my trick' over and over.

'See?' Clare says to Jesus.

It takes a while to get going again. They have to move rooms while guys come in with mops, buckets and disinfectant. From the corridor where they wait Jesus can hear the muffled wailing and caterwauling coming from other rooms where duos of producers sit through 'My Heart Will Go On' and 'The Greatest Love of All' and 'Don't Wanna Miss a Thing'. Scraps and fragments of American melodrama; the auditionees knowing that ballads are very popular on the show. (The boss's influence.)

Settled now in a fresh, un-excremented room, Samantha Jansen scans down the sheet with a 'where-were-we?' sigh. '4,413' she reads. 'Jesus Christ.' Her sigh modulates into one of exhaustion. 'Another wack job,' she says to Roger. 'Let's get this done and call it a day.' She motions to the security guards and they usher Jesus in. 'OK,' Jansen says, 'uh, Jesus?'

'Yeah. Um, hi.'

'Go ahead.' *Handsome*, she thinks. *A bum, but handsome.*

He blinks up into the harsh fizz of the single spotlight as he swings the Gibson round from his back, clicking on the Pignose on his belt as he does so. A brief squawk of feedback as the body of the guitar passes too close to the tiny amp. Jansen winces.

'Sorry. Right, ah. OK . . .' He thinks for a second. Jansen checks her watch.

'Uh, OK, OK.' He holds up a finger, nodding to himself, takes a breath, then snaps off a fluid run of notes, starting high on the neck and cascading down to finish on an open G, which he starts strumming softly, cranking the volume pot down a notch with his pinkie. He starts singing, gentle, clear and calm, head nodding and eyes closed.

As soon as the first line has been sung Jansen and Roger look at each other. By the time he is singing the first chorus they are only looking at him – his head moving gently side to side, a little half-smile on his face, eyes still closed in concentration as he hits the chords gently, almost whispering the lines in a voice like crystal.

'The only living boy in New York . . .'

Clare and the security guards, who are standing behind him, are transfixed now too.

He reels off a melodic, economic solo after the second chorus and then comes up big for the finish, swelling the volume on the guitar, throwing his head back as he lets himself go full voice into the climactic line of the song.

'Hey – let your honesty shine, shine, shine . . .'

Jansen feels the skin on her forearms and the back of her neck puckering up. Under the harsh single spotlight his limpid blue eyes are shining like the song, his blond hair glinting. She is aware that her mouth is open. He finishes with a flourish of notes and leaves the harmonic G at the twelfth fret ringing open.

Silence. Then a sound Jansen has only heard on a handful of occasions on many thousands of *APS* auditions – applause, from Roger, Clare, even the heavies.

'Right,' she says, gathering herself, tilting her Mont Blanc at Jesus. 'Handsome. Take a seat. Tell us a bit about yourself.'

Jesus starts telling them his story.

8

UCH LATER, SAMANTHA JANSEN IS FINISHING UP A conference call with the boss and the head producers from the other audition centres. As the others ring off in Chicago, in North Carolina, in California – 'Bye, Bob. Later, Trish. OK, Ted' – she says 'Uh, can I get a minute, boss?' and stays on the line.

'I got this one guy today – I've just emailed the audition clip to you – who's really got something.'

'Mmmm?' The boss sounds bored, rich, far away. The usual.

'Yeah. Now, don't say what I know you're gonna say, he sang a Simon and Garfunkel number, played electric guitar –

'Jesus, Sam, don't be giving me that fucking nonsense. I don't need to be hearing some fucking cunt scratching away on a guitar on the fucking show for fuck sa—'

'I know, I know. Hear me out. He'll never make it all the way. But he's good, he's a looker, great voice and – get this – he's called Jesus. He literally thinks he's Jesus Christ. I mean, he really believes he's been sent to earth on a mission to help mankind or something like that.'

'He's properly fucking mental?' the boss says, a little more interested now.

'Off his tits, as you'd say,' Jansen says, the British expression sounding comic in her accent. 'Well, he's not *insane* insane – I mean, I had one who took a goddamn shit on the floor today –'

The boss cackles. 'Send me that tape,' he says.

'But he's definitely worth bringing out.'

'OK, well, your call at this stage. Keep me posted.'

'Will do. Bye, Steven.'

'Yeah, laters.'

Click.

9

HE FOLLOWING DAY — JESUS AMBLING BLEARY-EYED into the reception area at ABN with his signed and completed forms stuffed into his back pocket. The forms are stained with wine and coffee and the ash from spliffs and cigarettes and had been the subject of a two-hour, three-way argument between him, Kris and Morgan in the early hours of that morning.

Jesus and Kris had been completing the forms, filling in the biographical details, elaborating, embellishing, when Morgan began reading the small print.

'Holy shit,' he said. 'You can't sign this!'

'How come?' Jesus said.

'Have you pair of retards read this thing? The slaves putting the fucking Pyramids together got a better deal. Look . . .'

They went through it.

It turned out that in addition to giving the producers of the show exclusive rights to his recording career, Jesus was not allowed to perform live, record material, or to appear on any similar TV shows without their permission for twelve months after the final episode of *American Pop Star* aired. In addition he granted them permission to exploit his likeness and image in any way they saw fit. He assigned the show's producers his merchandising rights and granted them the exclusive option to become his managers and to sign his songwriting publishing if they saw fit. He agreed to take part in commercials for any sponsors tied into the show at this point – including, but not limited to, Ingrams Soft Drinks Company, Cable and Wire Telephone, the Powell Motor Corporation, Sentinel Computers, Grain Whole Cereal, APS Computer Games and Bell Jeans – or who became affiliated with the show at any point in the future. He was required to undertake any 'reasonable' promotional duties requested by the producers (the definition of 'reasonable', for the avoidance of doubt, was to reside solely with the producers) and was forbidden from entering into any other product endorsements or commercial services without their written consent.

'I mean,' Morgan said, 'they could have you drinking their fucking cola while dressed up in some crazy outfit, singing some song that you wrote but they own, while you're driving a car made by some motherfuckers who sell machine guns to African dictators, while you're playing some lame-ass computer game on one of their motherfucking cellphones. Meantime they're collecting every goddamn penny and you're getting maybe five cents in the dollar. Shit – who wrote this fucking contract? Satan?'

'Yeah, but if he doesn't sign it,' Kris says, 'then he won't, like, get on the show. Right?'

'Fuck the show, Kris. I'm a *musician*, man, this kinda shit makes me sick to the pit of my motherfucking stomach.'

'Look,' Kris says, 'I hear you, man, but let's get a foothold then –'

'You can't get a little bit pregnant, motherfucker.'

'Guys, guys,' Jesus said.

Round they went for a long, long time – pragmatism versus idealism, realpolitik versus taking a stand, Trojan Horse versus Storming the Gates, means-justifying-the-ends versus fuck-those-slimy-record-company-motherfuckers – until finally, around three in the morning, Jesus leaned in, swooped the forms off the little coffee table and just signed them lying down on the carpet.

'There you go,' Kris said.

'What the fuck?' Morgan said. 'Man, I thought you were against all that soulless, life-sucking corporate sponsorship, exploitation bullshit?'

'Morgan,' Jesus said, 'calm down, dude. There's nothing to worry about.'

'You just agreed to –'

'I'm not gonna do shit. I'm just gonna sing a few songs.'

'They're gonna tell you it's in your contract.'

'So? What are they gonna do?'

'Sue your fucking ass,' Morgs said.

'So?' Jesus said, relighting the spliff, grinning.

Morgan realised, started smiling too.

'Huh?' Kris said.

'What do you get if you sue someone, man?' Jesus said.

'Money.'

'Exactly,' Jesus said. 'If there is any, they can have it all. Who gives a fucking shit about that?'

'You brought your completed forms?' the girl in reception is saying to Jesus now.

'Yes, ma'am,' he says, handing them over.

'Great. We'll see you in LA. Congratulations.'

'LA?' Jesus says. 'What's in LA?'

10

A?' Becky says.

'Wow, that's great,' Meg coughs.

'I can't go to LA,' Jesus says. 'I thought it was gonna be here. In the city. There's stuff to take care of. We got responsibilities.'

They're all hanging out in Union Square, trying to get some shade under the trees, the boys playing on the swings nearby, the sun beating down, the pigeons sweltering as they clockwork by. Meg is shivering even in the heat though. Her dirty blond hair is pulled up into her beanie and she wipes at her streaming nose with her sleeve. Heroin-sick and waxy, she's a few days into kicking junk, trying to get through what Becky went through before her.

'Like what?' Morgan says.

'Who's gonna look out for Gus and Dotty?' Jesus gestures to them, lying on a bench in the shade a few yards away, brown-bagging. 'Huh? Or Bob? Or Meg here . . .'

'I'll be OK,' Meg says. 'I'm through the worst of it.'

'We can handle all that while you're gone,' Morgan says, nodding to Kris.

'Ah,' Kris says.

'What?' Morgan says.

'I kinda wanted to go to LA too.' Kris says this more than a little shamefully, eyes on the ground, toeing the gravel with a battered sneaker.

'Oh yeah,' Morgan says, raising an eyebrow. 'To do what exactly?'

'Help out with . . . stuff?'

'Hey, fucko, there's shit to be "helping out" with here. Real shit. Like paying the rent kind of shit.'

'Man, it's hot,' Jesus says.

'How are you getting out there?' Kris says to Jesus.

'Show gave me this,' he says, digging in his pockets and pulling out a crumpled silver-and-blue paper wallet. He hands it to Kris.

'Shit, man,' Kris says after a moment. 'You know what you got here?'

Jesus, Morgan and Becky look at him. 'Uh, a plane ticket, I guess,' Jesus says.

'This,' Kris says, holding it up, 'is an open-ended, round-trip, first-class air ticket to Los Angeles. You know how much this thing is worth?'

'Uh,' Jesus says, clueless, 'like five hundred bucks?'

'Try five thousand, my friend.'

'So?' Morgan says.

'When you got to be in LA?'

'Day before Labor Day. Couple of weeks?'

Kris is grinning. 'You don't want to leave all the guys to fend for themselves while you're in LA, right?'

'Right.'

'Then how about the mountain comes with Muhammad?'

'What you talking about, fat man?' Morgs says.

'I'm talking about a road trip . . .'

Kris lays it out for them: they cash in the plane ticket and buy a minibus, some old piece of shit for a thousand bucks. He knows a lot out in Brooklyn. They pile everyone in there and drive cross-country. Two weeks would be plenty of time to get there. That'll still leave around four grand – enough to pay the rent on their place for another month *and* pay for gas, motels and food and stuff en route. The show, it turns out, is putting JC up at somewhere called the Chateau Marmont in Los Angeles. 'It'll be like a vacation,' Kris says, beginning to do his little hopping from one foot to the other routine. 'Get out of the city, summertime in LA. Hit the beach. What's not to like, man?'

'Hell, we probably won't even be there that long,' JC says. 'I'll be kicked off the show soon enough.'

'Hey, kids,' Becky shouts excitedly over towards the swings, 'we're going on vacation!'

'Yayyy!' the boys cheer.

'Oh man,' Morgan says.

Part Three

Road Trip

'When you're born you get a ticket to the freak show. When you're born in America you get a front row seat.'

George Carlin

1

HE HISS OF BRAKES AND A SQUEAL OF FAT TYRES AS the bus pulls up in front of their building. Morgan, sitting on the baking stoop, lowers his shades and says, 'You gotta be shitting me . . .' Another hiss, and a slight delay as the old-style concertina doors judder open and Fat Kris comes bounding down the steps looking like he's won the lottery.

'You will not believe what I picked this up for, man.'

'JC,' Morgan shouts over his shoulder into the darkened stairwell where Jesus is humping the last of his gear down, 'you gotta see this.'

Jesus comes out, hand shielding his face from the blinding glare of the noon sun beating off the silver panels of the bus, and takes in the scene: Morgan starting to laugh now, Kris standing proudly in front of a huge, filthy, ancient, decommissioned Greyhound bus which is still, half a minute after he turned the ignition off, gurgling and rattling and farting itself into silence. Cabs and cars are honking angrily around them as they try and make it through the narrow gap on the other side of the rusting, hulking bus.

'Shit, Kris . . .' Jesus begins, stepping into the shade cast by the enormous vehicle, 'there's only, like, ten of us.'

Morgan is blunter. 'Fat man,' he says, 'are you out of your fucking mind? How old is this piece of shit?'

'Hey, lissen, these babies are built like aircraft carriers, dude. There's only 230,000 miles on her and she'll go twice round the clock no sweat.'

'Only?' Morgan says.

'And I know what you're thinking,' Kris continues, excited, ushering them onto the bus, 'it'll be heavy on gas, right?'

'That is *not* what I was thinking,' Morgan says. 'I was thinking more like, "What the fuck happened to the minibus idea?" You know – *mini*? Because this shit right here, this is most definitely maxi motherfucker.'

'But check it out, I got it all figured – we can rip a bunch of seats out, put some mattresses in back, we'll save more on motels than we'll spend on gas. Come on, I'll give you the tour.'

The smell hits them when they climb on board. 'Whoa,' Morgan says.

'Yeah, I know, she could use a little spring cleaning, but lissen, the guy who sold her to me said – You guys listening? You won't believe this – he said Black fucking Sabbath used her once back in the day!'

'Yeah?' Morgs says. 'As what, man, a toilet?'

'Do you have to be so negative?' Kris says.

Jesus walks down the aisle between the rows of seats. 'Will it get us to LA?' he asks.

'And back, dude,' Kris says. Morgan lets out a short laugh.

'She's got air con, right?' Jesus asks.

'Oh yeah, we'll be nice and frosty.'

'You know, I think I kinda like it,' Jesus says.

'I knew you would,' Kris says, heading back down the passageway. 'I'm just gonna go get some water. The guy said I should keep the radiator topped up when it's this hot.'

'What's wrong with the radiator?' Morgan shouts after him, but there's no answer, just Kris's back as he bounds up into the building.

Jesus smiles. 'Hey, look at the big guy go, huh?'

Morgan sighs and slides into the row of seats across from Jesus. 'Look at you. That motherfucker turns up with a handful of magic beans and you're acting like he's brought home the fattest cow in town. Lying there just smiling your ass off. You coulda been sitting in a first-class seat for a few hours with a cold drink in your hand and a hot stewardess smiling at you. I'm talking right in the nose cone of a big old jet. Some broad with a fine ass plumping up your pillows and handing you a hot towel while you're deciding between the beef and the chicken and flipping through nine different movies. Ice sculptures and lobsters and real cutlery and shit. Instead you're gonna spend a week roasting your nuts off in a tin can with a bunch of goddamn maniacs. I mean – why you always gotta do things the hard way, man?'

Community, Jesus is thinking, lying back on the ripped button cloth seats, looking up at the buckled, discoloured cream ceiling, smelling the stale reek of the thousands of farts that have been pumped into these seats over the last forty years. That was what was all fucked up down here. There was no sense of it. Well, they had their own little community here. A deranged, fucked-up one composed of winos, misfits and junkies to be sure, but a little community was what it was. It was the world within his reach at the moment and it was fragile. Damned if he was going to just go and fuck off to the other side of the country for maybe months and let whatever happens to it happen.

'You know, Morgs,' Jesus says, yawning, 'sometimes the hard way is the hard way for a reason, you know?'

'The hard way is the hard way for a reason?' Morgan repeats slowly.

'Yup.'

'Should I be writing that down? Add it to your pile of wondrous sayings so I can pass your teachings and shit on when you're gone?'

'Be my guest.'

'Shit, we'll see how cool you be acting when we're in the middle of nowhere with that sun beating down on us and the A/C on this worthless piece of crap goes bye-bye. And if you even think this pile of junk is gonna make it to –'

'Mmmm,' Jesus is saying, his baseball cap pulled down over his eyes now, the heat lulling him, Morgan's voice becoming a pleasant burr, his monologue of complaint fading, just a soothing babble as Jesus drifts off for a lovely nap.

2

HEY LEAVE TOWN THE LAST WEEK OF AUGUST, THE great silver bus choking and rattling and shuddering across town, along Columbus Avenue, then Ninth Avenue, West 41st Street and then they're taking their place in the queue for the Lincoln Tunnel, millions of tons of Hudson River roaring above them, little Miles and Danny running up and down the aisle whooping and shrieking because they've never left Manhattan before, except for that trip out to the beach at Fire Island last summer, and then, suddenly, they're out of the city and the greenery of Jersey is flashing by, Jesus noticing 'FOR SALE' signs on the houses – *lots* of them – before he turns round to survey the bus.

There's Bob, twitching and muttering and staring out the window at the back; Gus and Dotty, singing and uncapping the T-Bird at 10 a.m.; Meg sniffing and sweating and strewing dirty Kleenexes all over the place; Becky yelling and laughing and chasing her boys around; Fat Kris in the driver's seat, serious in his mirrored sunglasses as he ignores the honks and stares of the late rush-hour traffic; Morgan sitting up front, ragging on Kris about what lane they should be in. And Jesus, smiling his little smile and strumming his unplugged electric, the huge tyres sizzling on hot macadam beneath him as he watches the highway delivering them from Manhattan, that island off the coast of America, into America itself.

Kris had christened the old girl *The Orca* and he'd spent the last few days decking her out pretty good too. There was a little fridge up behind the driver's compartment. Bob had helped them wire it into the generator that ran off the engine and they'd bolted it to the floor so it didn't slide around. It was filled with cold drinks and cold cuts and the little bit of methadone Meg had scraped together to get her over the next few days. Up back, screened off by a curtain, were two double mattresses, one on each side of the bus. They'd taken out some seats and, like Kris had said, they fitted in real nice. There was another mattress about halfway down, on the right-hand side as you looked towards the front of the bus. Gus and Dotty slept like they always did: sitting up in their seats cradling their bottles. Bob never seemed to sleep. So, between seven of them including two kids, three doubles would be about right. There was even an old TV and VCR wired in. Morgan reckoned you could pick up VHS tapes for a buck or so at truck stops now that everyone was switched to DVD. Kris had been right, Jesus thought as Morgan came swaying down the aisle, handing Jesus a thick joint as he passed, it was nice having all the space.

So what if their top speed wasn't much more than sixty? *American Pop Star* started going out live the day after Labor Day, which gave them nearly ten days to get to LA. They just had to cover roughly 250 miles every day, which with traffic and rest stops and general snafus meant about six or seven solid hours driving per day. No sweat.

(Well, actually, lots of sweat. The one thing even Bob hadn't been able to coax into working was the bus's ancient air-conditioning system. But, hell, Jesus had experienced worse. It was nothing like the dry heat back in Israel. Now that was a motherfucker, like sticking your face in a hot oven every morning.)

'Hey there.' Jesus looks up. Becky is standing over him holding a videotape. She taps it against his knee. 'Let's do it.'

Jesus groans. 'Shit, do we have to? I mean, now?'

'Come on, you gotta get an idea of what you're getting into.'

He sighs and puts the guitar down on the seat next to him, allowing Becky to help pull him with her outstretched hand. They stagger down the rocky aisle, holding onto the metal seat rims for support, passing Morgan stretched out sleeping.

'Sit.' Becky guides him onto the row of seats right in front of the TV and VCR and slips the cassette in. Becky was about the only one out of all of them who watched TV regularly. She knew all about *American Pop Star*, about the first two seasons, about the stars it had created and the elimination process and how it worked. It seemed simple enough to Jesus: you went up there every week and did your number and if enough of the folks back home liked you then you stayed on the show till the next week. I mean – did he really need to watch the fucking thing?

'Come on, Becks, do I really need to –'

She presses a finger against his lips and settles in beside him. A crackling snowstorm of static then it cuts right into the middle of an episode – a black girl, and this was a *big* black girl, singing 'Respect' by Aretha Franklin. Now, if you looked at her – whole load of junk in the trunk, huge moon face, eyes closed in passion – Jesus figured you'd probably have said, 'Yeah, man, I bet that chick's got some pipes.' You'd be wrong. She was *butchering* Aretha: wrong key, wrong words. It was like she was singing a song she'd only heard once – being whistled by a man passing her on the street about fifteen years ago. She reaches the chorus, screeching, 'ARRR EEE PEE TEE ESS EEE SEEE!'

'R-E-P-T-S-E-C?' Jesus says.

Now the camera pans to a woman Jesus guesses is one of the judges. She's black too, middle-aged, clearly once beautiful, and she's fighting giggles, stuffing a knuckle into her mouth and glancing nervously to her left and right. 'That's Darcy DeAngelo,' Becky says. 'She's real nice.'

As the girl starts the next verse the camera pans to Darcy DeAngelo's left, to a white guy, late middle-age, bearded, heavy-set. He has a hand over his face and is peering at the girl through a gap in his splayed fingers. 'That's Herb Stutz,' Becky continues. 'He's, like, a big-time rock manager. He can be a bit mean sometimes.'

'Right,' Jesus says, nodding. 'Mean. I get it.'

The shot cuts back to the girl singing just as the song finishes abruptly on a shouted 'RESPECT!' The girl stands there, head thrown back in the silver and blue spotlights, basking in triumph and applause, the applause hearty and surely heavily ironic. Now the camera cuts to a third judge, the only one they haven't seen yet. He's younger, in his late thirties maybe, tanned and handsome in a crisp white shirt, with dark slicked-back hair that glistens under the studio lights. His expression cannot be read. 'That's Steven.' Becky almost whispers it with awe, the fact that no surname seems to be necessary perhaps an indicator of the kind of power this man has.

'Is he nice or mean?' Jesus asks. Becky just looks at him and shakes her head.

First the camera goes to Herb Stutz, who speaks with a heavy New York accent, so heavy that Jesus figures Herb probably comes from somewhere in the Midwest. 'Well, listen, sweetheart, Simone? You had a good time tonight, right?' Simone giggles, nods enthusiastically, still on a performance high. 'Well, that's good, you take those happy memories home with ya, cos I think this is as far as you're gonna go on the show.'

Simone looking crestfallen as Darcy DeAngelo starts to speak. 'Simone, sorry, you know I hate to agree with Herb, but I don't think you're ready for this yet, baby. But you keep on singing, you hear me? You got to work on your voice, but your performance? My God, girl! You really gave it all you got!' The audience cheering and clapping this sop of kindness as Simone smiles, mouthing 'thank you' and wiping sweat from her forehead as the camera pans finally to the guy called Steven, who surprises Jesus with the darkness of his eyes – noticeable even on this crappy videotape, on this crappy TV – and the chilled formality of his British accent.

'Yes, thank you, Darcy,' he says. 'Unfortunately there's no point in "giving it all you've got" if what you've got is a steaming pile of crap.' Darcy DeAngelo shaking her head, the audience booing softly, Simone starting to say something but the Steven guy holding his hand up. 'Please, Simone is it? Please let me speak. I had to listen to you, the least you can do is listen to me for a minute don't you think? I mean, I'd like to speak if that's OK with you.'

'Go ahead. I ain't stopping you,' Simone says, defiance bristling in her now. Arms folded.

'It's actually an insult,' he continues, 'for us to have to sit here and be put through this, you know that, don't you? I mean, what do you do? For a living?'

'I work at the In and Out Burger in –'

'Right, so if I came down there and ordered fifteen burgers and I stood and watched you make them all and then I said, "Actually I don't eat hamburgers," you'd be pretty pissed off at me for wasting your time, wouldn't you?'

'Lissen,' Simone says, a ghetto edge in her voice now, 'I know I can –'

'You don't know anything, love. Zero. You're a waste of space.' The audience gasps. 'Get off. Stop wasting my time.'

Simone close to tears now.

'Right,' Darcy says, turning to him angrily, 'fine, you didn't like the girl's singing. You don't need to –'

'Oh, get back in your box, Darcy,' Steven says. 'I'm doing her a favour. There's no point in encouraging her.'

'Don't you listen to him,' Darcy tells Simone.

'No, *do* listen to me, Simone,' Steven goes on. 'Enjoy singing to those burgers as you flip them because that's the most appreciative audience you're ever going to get.'

Simone crying now.

'I ain't listening to this,' Darcy says, getting up.

'Come on, guys,' Herb says.

'Oh yeah, here we go,' Steven sighs. 'Darcy's big walk-off. Boring. Bye, Darcy. Bye, Simone.' He waves at the crying girl as she's led off, a little wave, just waggling the fingers, the booing of the audience getting louder.

'You're a jerk,' Simone shouts through her tears as she leaves the stage.

'That's right,' Steven says. 'I'm a jerk. Next!'

'Can you stop it there?' Jesus says.

Becky leans forward and hits the pause button, stopping it on a grainy shot of this guy Steven's face, his smile savage and laconic at once.

'I don't understand,' Jesus says.

'What?' Becky asks.

'That girl, she was . . . awful, right?'

'Yeah.'

'I mean, when I auditioned in New York they were rejecting people who could sing better than that.'

'So?'

'So, I'm guessing these people –' he gestures towards the blurred, pixelated still of the guy Steven's face – 'or someone who worked for them had heard her before she walked on to the show that night, yeah?'

'Of course.'

'So . . . why would they have her on the show if she's that bad?'

Becky looks at Jesus for a long time, looking into those clear blue eyes – not completely clear, a little pink in the whites from all the joints going around the bus – the blond hair tumbling down like sunshine, real sunshine pouring through the window behind him, exploding off the hair, making him seem to glow. Yeah, Becky thinks, not for the first time, what you have here is a true *innocent*. Does Becky think Jesus is Jesus? Not for a second. He is someone who helped her for no reason. He's never even made a pass at her, even though she's seen him hit on (or, more usually, get hit on by) other girls. Becky often wonders why that is.

'Uh, for entertainment. To humiliate her, I guess,' Becky says, feeling bad that she even understands what he cannot.

'Wow. So when that guy, the British guy, Steven?'

'Steven Stelfox.'

'When he got angry that she was wasting his time, he already *knew* that she was going to waste his time?'

'Yeah, I guess so.'

'Right,' Jesus says. 'So he was just pretending to be angry? So it's all like a big . . . act?'

'Yeah. Entertainment.' Becky gets up and starts ejecting the tape.

'But –' he isn't done – 'that girl, she really thought she could sing, didn't she?'

'A lot of them do. Do you wanna soda?'

'I mean, it's possible she wasn't quite right in the head . . .'

'A lot of them aren't.'

'So, what you're saying, if I'm getting all this right, is that what people really seem to like for entertainment these days is *watching mentally unbalanced people getting bullied and humiliated on TV*?'

'Uh, it would, um, appear so, JC. I guess we're pretty uniquely fucked up, huh?' Becky heads down the aisle towards the fridge.

No, Jesus thinks, watching her go, not unique.

He remembers a story one of his boys told him way back – Matthew? Or was it John or Luke? Shit, his memory. Well, it was more than a couple of thousand years ago, and they used to drink a *lot* of fucking wine back then. Anyway, one of them had been travelling through some Roman province and he got dragged along to these games they were having in this little makeshift arena. The Romans loved that shit. They had a bunch of prisoners – criminals, politicals, the usual stuff – who they were making fight in these games, making little weedy guys fight big, tooled-up motherfuckers, lions, wild animals, shit like that. And a couple of them, these prisoners, were handicapped guys. Retards, they used to call them. And they made a couple of these retarded guys fight a fucking *bear*. He said the guys didn't know what the fuck was going on, just stumbling around drooling and gibbering and this bear came in and just ripped the two of them to fucking pieces, man. Just ate them up right in front of these people. And the people were laughing their asses off.

So here we go again, Jesus thinks.

3

UT I DON'T SEE THE PROBLEM. IT'S TWO WEEKS TO the opening show and we've already got fifteen-second idents going out every half-hour in selected areas and full thirty-second spots going out every hour on the hour all across the network, syndicated to every market. I don't see what else we need to –'

Without turning from the window, everyone in the room just seeing his black silhouette against the trees and rooftops of Burbank, Steven Stelfox simply holds up his right hand with forefinger extended, like a man hailing a cab he is certain he is going to get, and the speaker, Danni Plessman, ABN's new Vice President of Marketing, immediately falls silent along with the rest of the room. Stelfox turns, smiling, looks Plessman pleasantly in the eye, and says softly, with no hint of rancour (a very bad sign indeed), 'Why are you calling me a cunt?'

Silence for a moment. Plessman, confused, saying 'I, uh, excuse me?'

'A cunt, Danni. Danni is it? Yes, you seem to be calling me a cunt. I'm simply asking you for a little more help in marketing this show properly and your reaction is to call me a cunt and tell me to go and fuck myself in front of all these people.' A few of the boss's inner circle are fighting smiles now.

'I certainly didn't mean to –'

'What have I ever done to you, Danni? Except make your poxy fucking network billions of dollars in advertising revenue, I mean.'

'Steven, please, all I'm saying is that I, we, the network feels we're doing enough to ensure –'

'Here's what's going to happen,' Stelfox says, resuming his seat at the head of the huge oval conference table. 'We're going to increase those fifteen-second idents to full ads and I don't want to hear this "selected areas" fucking nonsense ever again. Everything goes out everywhere.'

'How do you mean every—'

'I mean EVERY-FUCKING-WHERE!' Stelfox screams.

Plessman jerks back in her chair.

'I mean that next week I'm going to fly out to the tiny hamlet of Anal fucking Sex, Arizona, and I'm going to find the most arse-backwards street in that shithouse town and I'm going to get hold of the most ancient, dried-up cunt of a granny on that street, the one who watches maybe five hours of fucking TV a year, and I'm going to ask her when the show starts and what channel it's on and if she can't answer me instantly and to the exact minute I'm going to fly back here and I'm going to come into your office and I'm going to cut out your ovaries with a rusted fucking Stanley knife and eat them in front of you so that you'll never spawn a fucking kid who can one day grow up to call me a cunt in a marketing meeting.'

Plessman goes to say something, thinks better of it. She's looking around the table in a 'can-this-be-happening?' way, looking for support. She finds none and it really is happening.

'And if anyone upstairs has a fucking problem with that then tell them to call James Trellick at Trellick & Co. and we can start having a chat about my contract which is – and it's frankly incredible that I need to remind anyone of this – up for renewal after *this fucking season*.'

Pause. Silence. People shuffle papers, play with their pens. Stelfox reaches for a pastry, bites into it and says through a mouth of flaky dough, 'With me?'

'I'll pass that along,' Plessman says, managing a defiant smile.

'Thank you, love,' Stelfox smiles back, still chewing. 'What's next?'

'This lawsuit,' says Evan Litt, ABN's Vice President of Legal and Business Affairs, 'the girl from last season who's in an institution. Her family says you mentally unbalanced her on the show.'

'Oh fuck me,' Stelfox sighs.

It's going to be a long day.

4

HEY MADE IT ALL THE WAY THROUGH OHIO THAT first night, the highway almost empty save for the big silver bus slicing through the warm blackness. Morgan wakes up first, scratching his head, digging his nails deep down through that crinkly Afro and into the scalp, yawning and already thinking about strong black coffee. He sits up – he's stretched out along the back row of seats – and looks out through the rear window of the bus. Dawn is already well along; the sun just fully over the horizon, picking out the great shapes of long-haul trucks parked around them.

For the first time in his life, Morgan is waking up in Indiana. Beyond the pitted gravel parking lot he can see the highway with its slow trickle of early-morning traffic, beyond the highway yellow fields of Midwestern wheat rippling like a cereal commercial. Coffee nearby. Those styrofoam cups.

Padding down the aisle he hears voices coming from near the front – little Miles and Danny, hunched up over a comic book on the mattress. 'Hey, kids,' Morgan says, 'it's early. How long you boys been up for?'

'Just now. We're hungry,' Danny says.

'Hold that thought. I'm gonna get the team together and then we're gonna go across the way and score us some big-assed trucker breakfast.'

'Can we get pancakes?' Miles says.

'You bet your skinny white ass, son. Uncle Morgan gonna show you how to eat pancakes.'

He finds Jesus stretched out on his back across a row of three seats, fully clothed, his Converse dangling over the end, his beanie pulled down over his eyes, still sleeping. Guy can fall asleep at the drop of a dime. Sleeps like a goddamn baby too. The sleep of the innocent, Morgan knows. He shakes him. 'Hey, cocheeze.'

'Mmmm, morning, man.' Those blue eyes opening slowly. 'How we doing?'

'All good, buddy. The kids are hungry. Front me and I'll take them over the way and bring back the bacon.'

'Oh, sounds good.' Jesus sits up, yawning, and starts fumbling in his pockets. 'Howd'ya sleep, man?'

'All right. You hear the goddamn rain last night?'

'No.'

'Shit, motherfucker, you'd sleep through a fucking Sonic Youth soundcheck.'

'I think I did once. In, uh, Washington?' He's still fumbling in his pockets, a look of confusion coming over his face.

'That was Tortoise.'

'Oh yeah. Shit, toss me that jacket, man.'

Morgan throws JC his coat, other voices coming from the back of the bus now, everyone waking up. Jesus is going through his jacket, getting faster now, almost scrabbling at the pockets. Morgan feels his blood give a seasick lurch. 'Uh, you're kidding, right?'

'I . . . where'd I put the fucking money?'

'Oh shit, man, you didn't drop it in that diner yesterday, did you?'

'I, no, most definitely not. I remember having it in my hand when me and Meg were walking toward the bus last night. Fact, she told me to put it away.'

'Check your pants again. Shit, maybe Meg knows wh—' Morgan turns round straight into Becky, who's all sleepy-eyed in just knickers and a faded Beastie Boys T-shirt.

'Hey, have you seen Meg?' Morgan begins. 'JC can't –'

'We saw her going out last night, when it was raining,' Danny volunteers.

'She had her bag too,' Miles adds.

'Ah fuck,' Morgan says.

'Oh Meg,' Jesus sighs as he stops fumbling in his empty pockets. He sits back in the seat and notices that someone – one of the kids? maybe Meg? – has drawn a lopsided smiling face in the condensation misting the window beside his head.

5

'HAT FUCKING JUNKIE BITCH SLUT WHORE.' BOB
has taken the boys out for a walk so Morgan is
free to use whatever language he needs to.

'I can't believe she did this to us,' Becky
sniffs, still crying.

'Goddamn it, Meg,' Kris says softly.

'Fucking thieving lying cunt –'

'OK, Morgs,' Jesus says, having heard about enough of this.
'Cut that shit out. Meg's our friend and let's hope she doesn't
get into no trouble with all that money on her.'

Morgan just looks at him. This guy, man. 'Trouble?' Morgan
says. 'What, like the kinda trouble we're in now?'

'Look, she's junk-sick. She gave into temptation, took the
money and probably hitched a ride outta here at the truck stop.
Let's just hope she's safe.'

Kris bangs his head on the table.

'Oh God,' Becky says. 'What are we gonna do now?'

'Shit, guys, it's only a little money. Come on, pull yourselves
together.'

'A little money?' Morgan says. 'Dude, have you got like a platinum fucking Amex tucked away somewhere we don't know about? That was *all* our money! We are in the middle of nowhere without a fucking dime!'

'Bullshit,' Jesus says, reaching into his pockets and turning them out. A hanky, some plectrums, keys, a few crumpled bills. 'I got, look, twelve, fourteen, a twenty! Forty-six bucks and change. Kris, what you got left from the money I gave you for gas?'

'Ah, maybe thirty or forty bucks?'

'And what you guys packing?'

Morgan and Becky turn out their pockets, producing a few grubby ones and fives and some change.

'Right, so that's another fifteen, sixteen. Dotty, Gus?' He calls over their heads, looking up. Dotty and Gus: passed out, her head slumped against his chest, a long strand of drool connecting her mouth to one of the buttons of his coat. 'Uh, I reckon those guys probably can't contribute too much,' Jesus says. 'Anyway, look, that's – what? – over a hundred dollars!'

'Motherfucker,' Morgan says. 'How you gonna feed and transport nine people all the way to LA from Indiana on a hundred bucks?'

'It's enough to get us to, um, what's the next decent-sized town Kris?'

'Indianapolis, I guess.'

'Indianapolis,' Jesus says, beaming. 'We got it made in the goddamn shade, man!'

'What's going to happen in Indianapolis?' Becky asks.

'Oh, something or other'll happen,' Jesus says, happily folding all the bills together while Morgan looks at him with a level of incomprehension previously unknown to man.

6

OWNTOWN INDIANAPOLIS IN THE MIDDAY HEAT. They've taken care of the basics; parking the bus up and settling Gus and Dotty down in a nearby park with the fifth of off-brand vodka that represents just about the last of their booze stash. JC, his acoustic guitar slung over his shoulder, turns to face the gang. They're all sitting around a little fountain in a plaza surrounded by office buildings and shops, the lunchtime foot traffic starting to increase, the Chase Tower looming over them a couple of blocks away. 'Right, guys, everyone do what they can to bring home a few bucks and we'll meet back here at four.'

No one moves. 'What?' Jesus says.

'We're hungry,' Danny says, staring sadly at a man who is unloading trays of sandwiches onto a trolley from a small van, food for the office workers who are all packed into those little grey cubicles stacked up into the sky. Jesus once worked in an office for a short while. Man, that was rough. *Cut off my hair, and send me to work in tall buildings*, Jesus thinks.

'OK,' Jesus says, looking around the mutinous, breakfastless group. 'I think we still got some money, I guess I could eat too.' He fishes into his pocket and comes up with four dollars and a plectrum.

'How we gonna feed everyone on four dollars, man?' Morgan says. 'What's that, sixty cents each?'

'Goddamn you, Meg,' Becky says again.

'All right,' Jesus says. 'Calm down. Let's just . . .' He looks over to where the guy is still unloading the sandwiches. The side of the van says 'SANDWICH KING! INDIANAPOLIS'S FINEST!' Then, below that, 'CATERING, OFFICES, EVENTS', and a phone number. The trays are labelled 'McDonnell Howells Board Meeting' and the Sandwich King's sandwiches do look very fine and royal. All surrounded by frosty-looking Cokes, juices and bottles of water. It is hot, man. Jesus licks his lips.

He looks over to the building the sandwiches are rolling into. A big brass nameplate announces 'MCDONNELL HOWELLS: MORTGAGE BROKERS'. Jesus, thinking.

'Kris, you got any credit on your cellphone?' he asks.

'Maybe a couple of bucks left.'

'Toss that bad boy here.'

Jesus takes his guitar off and stretches out on the marble ledge surrounding the fountain, cradling the cellphone, watching the building.

'What the hell are you doing now?' Morgan says.

'Just hang on. Everyone, uh, enjoy the sunshine.'

A couple of minutes later the sandwich guy comes out wheeling his empty trolley, loads it up in the van and drives off. Jesus watches the van go – everyone else watching Jesus – and punches in a number. 'Hi, Sandwich King? Yeah, this is McDonnell Howells down on, uh –' he looks up at a street sign – 'Indiana Square. You just delivered the food for our meeting? No, no problem, it's just that we've, ah, had a lot more people turn up than we expected and we're gonna need another delivery. Lemme see, oh, maybe if you just bring the same again that'd be great. But they need it in there, like, right away or I'm gonna get my ass kicked. Hungry stockholders, you know? Can you help me out here? Yeah, just put it on our account. Twenty minutes? That's great, thanks a lot. I really appreciate it.' He hangs up, triumphant.

'Great,' Morgan says. 'Now what you gonna do? Mug the guy when he comes back?'

'Oh Father,' JC says, dialling again. 'You gave them eyes but they cannot see.' Then, into the phone, 'Hi, can I have the number for McDonnell Howells, mortgage brokers in Indianapolis? It's on Indiana Square. Aha . . .' He writes it on the back of his hand. 'Great, thanks.' Jesus, dialling again, everyone watching him. 'Hi, McDonnell Howells? Can I speak to someone about a mortgage? Yeah, I'll hold.' He smiles at Danny, ruffles the kid's hair. 'Hi, yes, I'm looking to obtain a new mortgage, a friend of mine recommended you and I wondered if someone there could help me out. Well, it's pretty large, there's this building I'm looking to buy. I'd rather not discuss the details on the phone, could I make an appointment to come in and see someone? Great. No, sorry, I have to catch a plane later this afternoon. As a matter of fact I'm downtown right now, could we say fifteen minutes? Great, I'll see you then. Oh, my name? It's Mitch, Mitch Mitchell. And you are? Ray Kroll? With a "K"? Thanks, see you soon, Ray.'

Ten minutes later Mitch Mitchell signs the book in the lobby, snaps on a name tag, and is very politely directed to take the elevator to the fourteenth floor, which he does. Jesus walks through the oatmeal-carpeted corridor of McDonnell Howells, catching glimpses into the tiny offices on either side: folks talking on the phone, or hunched over computer screens, doing the stuff they have to do. He slides quickly by the door marked 'R. KROLL', walks past a door labelled 'BOARDROOM' and rolls on down to the end of the hallway where he sees the green sign and the little white stick man walking down a flight of stairs. Exit route. He ducks into a bathroom, slicks back his hair with some water, tucks in his shirt, and waits a few minutes before he comes out and begins walking back towards the elevators. There is a cheerful 'PING' and the doors open to reveal one of the Sandwich King's minions pushing a trolley bearing a huge platter of sandwiches.

'These for the boardroom?' Jesus says.

'Yup,' the guys says. 'You people sure are hungry today. Twice I've had to drag my ass here.'

'Yeah, sorry about that, man,' Jesus says, slipping the guy two of the four bucks he has left as he lifts the heavy platter. 'Here, lemme take it from here . . .'

'Anyone want the last crayfish salad?' Kris is asking a half-hour later, everyone stretched out on the grass. A few weary, stuffed groans answer him.

'Now, you sure that this constitutes a victimless crime?' Morgan asks.

'Sure,' Jesus says, picking a shred of lettuce from his teeth. 'Well, probably. I mean, so we stiffed a mortgage company for a few sandwiches. These guys have been giving it to working people since forever, Morgs.'

They gather up their stuff, saving some of the leftover sandwiches for later, giving away some to the bums they encounter on their way back out of the park.

'OK, people,' Jesus says, hoisting his guitar across his back as they come out of the park gates onto the hot sidewalk. 'Meet back here at six?'

7

IX O'CLOCK AND JESUS COMES WHISTLING AROUND the corner to find Kris sitting on a low wall with Miles and Danny. The boys look exhausted, Danny's head resting sideways on Kris's great gut. 'Hey, guys. Howd'ya all make out?' Jesus asks.

Kris is rubbing his bare feet. 'Becky asked me to watch the boys, said she had an idea but wanted to go off on her own. We found this tyre place that wanted people to, like, give out leaflets. Five bucks an hour for me and two fifty for the kids the guy said. I said, "How about minimum wage?" The guy laughs and says, "Take it or leave it, fat man." Can you believe that? Man, and they say there ain't no slave labour nowadays. We worked three hours, all over town. Beat.' With some effort Kris sits forward and reaches into his back pocket. 'Here.' He hands Jesus twenty-five bucks and some change. 'I bought us some sodas and candy bars. Sorry.'

'Hey, well done, guys!' Jesus says, bending down. The kids smile. 'You really did good.'

'Twenty-five bucks,' Kris says. 'You any idea how much gas

it takes to fill that clunker? Maybe we should just call it quits, JC. Sell the bus, try and get the money together for tickets back to –'

But Jesus isn't listening, he's standing up clapping his hands together as Bob approaches, shuffling wearily. 'Hey, the Bob Machine! Zero defects! How was your day, big guy?'

'Frag,' Bob says, slumping down beside Kris. 'Fragged.' He reaches into the pocket of his combat jacket, the edges of the pocket frayed and greasy, and takes out his cardboard 'VIETNAM VET, HUNGRY AND HOMELESS, PLEASE HELP' sign. He piles some small bills and change on top of it. Jesus sifts through, counting. 'Twelve, thirteen, nearly fourteen bucks. Way to go, Bob! You did better than me!'

Kris and Bob look at him. 'Yeah,' Jesus says. 'I mean, I played everything from Dylan to goddamn show tunes out there today and got eleven bucks. I guess the folks around here don't care for music too much.'

Morgan has fared better. A stint washing dishes in a burger joint downtown has netted him fifty-two dollars. 'That's, ah, just over a hundred bucks and some change plus whatever Becky brings back,' Jesus says. 'That's gotta get us down the road a ways, huh, Kris?'

'Yeah, we're getting all of fourteen miles to the gallon in that piece of shit,' Morgan says.

'Hey, Morgan,' Kris cuts in. 'When I bought the bus gas money wasn't going to be an issue. I thought we'd –'

'Hey, come on, guys, cut it out,' Jesus says. 'We're in the shit and we're all doing the best we can, huh?'

'Mom!' Miles cries, hopping up and running towards Becky who is coming down the street now. She's late, it's nearly seven. Becky scoops the boy up and flops down onto the wall, her head flopping down onto Bob's shoulder. She looks wiped out. 'We made thirty dollars, Mom!' Miles tells her excitedly.

'Did you, baby? Good boy. Did you have fun with Uncky Kris?'

'Yeah. We met lots of people. Here.' He hands her a leaflet for a lube job. Becky smiles.

'Mom did OK too.' She hands a roll of bills to Jesus.

'Thanks, Becks,' he says, counting, 'you look b— Holy shit.' He realises he is counting twenties, fifties, a single hundred. 'There's, like, four hundred bucks here.'

'Nearly five,' Becky says.

'Mommy!' Miles exclaims. 'You got more than everyone!'

'I got a shift waitressing,' Becky says, looking only at the boys, not at any of the guys. 'At this real fancy place. They were busy and I got a full share of the tips.'

Jesus swallows, looks down. Kris and Morgs and Bob not looking at each other either.

'Wow, Mom,' Danny says.

'Come on,' Becky says. 'Let's go get Gus and Dotty and get back to the bus. I'm beat.'

They man up and head off into the gathering dusk, Becky walking on ahead, one of her boys' hands in each of hers, Jesus and Morgan walking a little way behind. 'Shit, JC,' Morgan says softly. 'Girl having to do that shit.'

Jesus sighs, stuffing the six hundred or so dollars into his pocket. 'God damn you, Meg,' he says for the first time.

They fill the tank and leave town in the middle of the night, after Kris has napped for a few hours, looking to take advantage of those empty roads, trying to make up some time. It's quiet on the bus, everyone sleeping, stretched out on the mattresses or across the empty rows of seats, just Kris awake at the wheel and Jesus sat up back, smoking and thinking about sacrifice as he watches the lights of Indianapolis glow fainter behind them in the dark.

8

'YNERGY,' Trellick is saying. 'Branding,' Trellick is saying. 'Tie-ins,' Trellick is saying in their booth out on the patio at the Polo Lounge of the Beverly Hills Hotel. People – producers, agents, actresses – drop by every few minutes to say 'hi', to press a little flesh, to feel the heat.

'Yeah,' Stelfox says. 'I'm thinking mugs, T-shirts, pens, iPhone apps, fucking . . . dolls. I mean, we are *not* making enough fucking money. Am I wrong? It's a joke.'

'Correctos,' Trellick says. 'Understand this – last year the Warner Brothers merchandising stores turned over more fucking cash than every studio picture *combined*. The show needs to become a feeder for all this other stuff. Because, at the end of the day –'

'We're still working for a living, aren't we?' Stelfox says.

'Exactly. Which is fucking depressing any way you slice it.'

They sigh and lift gin and tonics. The two friends are both into early middle-age now; a little thickening around Stelfox's waistline, flecks of grey peppered through Trellick's stubble. Rich beyond any sane boundary of avarice – and wanting to get much, much richer – together they have done an awful lot of cocaine and black, black business deals over the years. They don't do the cocaine any more, but they still drink. As Trellick is fond of saying of the many mutual friends who have found their way to rehab in the last decade or so, 'If you *have* to stop drinking, you're a fucking loser.'

As they wrestle with the ever-present question of how to make money while they sleep, a producer from Fox who Stelfox vaguely knows – Adam something – stops by their table with a girl in tow. She's young, fourteen or fifteen, full make-up, pointlessly beautiful in the Beverly Hills manner.

'Hey, Steven, how's tricks?'

'Ah, all good, uh, Adam, all good. You know James, my lawyer?'

'Sure, we met at that ICM thing.'

'Hi.' Trellick offers a limp handshake, clearly not knowing Adam from Adam.

'Sorry to interrupt, guys, Chloe here, my niece –' he indicates the teenage girl who is looking embarrassed and bored simultaneously – 'wondered if you could score her some tickets for the opening show.'

'Yeah, sure,' Stelfox says, smiling at her. 'I'll get Naomi to send them over to the lot.'

'Thanks,' Chloe says, smiling too, flashing tens of thousands of dollars' worth of dentistry.

'Great,' Adam whoever says. 'See you Friday.'

'Sure.'

The pair head off, Stelfox and Trellick watching them go. 'What's on Friday?' Trellick asks.

'Fuck knows.'

Trellick yawns, still watching Chloe's teenage ass as it swishes off across the patio. 'I'd do her,' he says. 'And I wouldn't even feel that guilty about it.'

'Yep,' Stelfox says, signalling for the check.

9

THUNDERING DOWN A DUSTY COUNTRY ROAD, A sandstorm trailing up behind the bus, fields of corn shining endless on either side, no road signs for miles, and Jesus' *GREATEST NEW YORK BANDS EVER!* compilation CD loud from the sound system, The Voidoids doing 'Love Comes in Spurts'. Morgan and Becky are arguing over the map, Jesus is sitting up front, keeping Kris company, when they see a guy up ahead by the side of the road, a few hundred yards away, one hand held up shielding his face from the sun, the other arm extended wearily, the thumb held out here in the middle of nowhere. The first hitchhiker they've come across since they left NYC. 'No way,' Morgan says, anticipating.

'Pull over, Kris,' Jesus shouts.

'Aw, come on,' Morgan protests. 'Some guy way out here on his own? He's probably just killed a bunch of people.'

'Don't be stupid. Pull over.'

Kris starts braking and there's a piercing squeak of hydraulics as the bus quivers to a halt, the clouds of sandy gravel

that had been trailing it now overtaking it, blowing over the
hitcher as he steps towards the bus. Jesus hops down the three
steps and smacks the button so the concertina doors judder
open.

'Afternoon,' Jesus says pleasantly, the others crowding round
behind him.

'Sir,' the kid says, nervous, clearing his throat. And he is a
kid – maybe twenty, wearing an old plaid shirt and tattered
work pants. Fine, sandy-brown hair falls in his eyes and he's
freckled, with a teenage rash of acne still scarring his forehead.
A faded blue canvas knapsack hangs over his shoulder. 'How
much would the fare be from here to Nashville?'

'I hate to break it you, kid,' Jesus says, 'but this isn't like, uh,
regularly scheduled programming or anything.' He waves a
hand at the others, at Fat Kris, stripped to the waist and smiling
in his mirrored Aviators, Morgan, his shades pushed up onto
his forehead to better squint at the newcomer, a fat jay dangling
from his lips, sweet clouds of it drifting out of the bus, Becky in
her underwear, rock and roll blaring, the New York Dolls
singing 'Trash' now.

'Sir?' the kid says, not understanding.

'Son, where the fuck are we?' Morgan asks.

The boy eyes Morgan briefly, averting his gaze from Becky's
bare legs. 'You're in Hogg County, sir. North Kentucky.'

'I knew it!' Morgan says. 'We been going south since
Indianapolis, you fat fuck!'

'Fuck you, gimme . . . gimme that fucking thing.' Kris
wrenches the crumpled map from Morgan and begins frowning
at it.

'Guys, guys!' Jesus says. They shut up and he turns back to
the kid. 'You're headed for Nashville? Are you a guitar player?'

The kid looks at Jesus oddly. 'Ah, no, sir. Ah'm trying to get to New Mexico. To Santa Fe? I hear I can get the bus there from Nashville.'

'Shit, New Mexico?' Jesus says, turning to the others. 'Kid's going our way.'

Morgan sighs.

'Lissen, buddy,' Kris says, leaning forward from the cab behind Jesus and Morgan, 'do you know the way from wherever-the-hell-we-are-now to the Missouri border?'

The kid nods.

'Then welcome aboard,' Kris says, crunching her into gear as Jesus reaches out a hand to help the kid up. 'What's your name, son?' he asks.

'Claude.'

'Good to meet you, Claude. I'm Jesus.'

'Like from the Bible?'

'Just like that.'

'So, Claude,' Jesus says as they settle down around one of the metal tables up front, Claude nervously clutching his knapsack as he takes in all the faces: Miles and Danny smiling up at him, Big Bob scowling down, Gus and Dotty grinning, benign, that gallon of Mad Dog 20/20 they scored back the way slipping down nicely, Morgan already rolling another joint, Becky opening a Coke. 'You from round here?'

'Yessir,'

'JC. JC is fine.'

'We got a farm a couple miles back.'

'You a farmer?' Becky asks.

Claude nods, maybe embarrassed, hiding behind that fringe. You get the sense the kid hasn't met too many people, that sitting here he feels like an unusual object on display.

'Wow, I never met a real-life farmer before!' Becky says, crossing her long, bare legs, getting him blushing, causing him to smile for the first time, revealing bad teeth and a cute little dimple.

'So what's in New Mexico, baby?' Morgan asks, lighting the joint, blowing on the end of it, making it flame, sending curlicues of black ash breaking off and trembling towards the ceiling.

'Cousin of mine's gonna get me a job. In them oilfields.'

'The farm not doing too good, huh?' JC asks.

Claude shakes his head and looks at the table. 'No, sir, my momma said, says, we might as well sell up the land but there ain't no one wants to buy land out here these days.' Jesus nods, thinking about all those 'FOR SALE' signs, all those people in foreclosure, all those folks who kept hearing buy, buy, buy. You can't lose. Get in the race. Gotta be in it to win it. Where's your piece? Everybody wanting in until they wind up paying hundreds of thousands of dollars they don't have for a bit of timber and drywall in the middle of nowhere and then, when the whole shithouse comes tumbling down, these same guys on TV saying, 'Well, that's what the market did. We didn't expect that. Sorry.' Jesus, remembering that elevator ride down to Hell. Morgan offers Claude the joint. The kid looks at it for a moment before shaking his head.

'What does your mom think about you going to work in those oilfields?' Jesus asks him.

'Long as I can send some money home . . .'

'How about your dad?' Becky says.

Claude just keeps looking at the table. 'Ain't seen him in years.'

It's quiet for a moment before Miles says, real serious, 'Do you have a tractor?'

Everyone laughs as the Velvet Underground comes blowing out the speakers above their heads.

'You like rock-and-roll music, Claude?' Jesus asks, not waiting for an answer, already reaching up and turning the volume up, Lou Reed asking *Who loves the sun?* as they drive right into it at sixty-five miles an hour, the Kentucky fields silently eating their dust, Jesus picking up an acoustic and playing, him and Morgan singing along with the track.

'Excuse me, ma'am,' Claude says, getting up.

'Becky.'

'Ah, Becky. I just need to use the bathroom.'

'Remember,' Becky calls after him, 'no number twos on the bus.'

Claude hurries off, embarrassed, clutching the knapsack and Becky giggles. 'Sweet kid,' she says to herself as her youngest son appears.

'Who is?' Miles says.

'You are, baby!' she says, picking him up and tickling him.

Claude locks the door of the tiny bathroom at the back of the bus and sits down on the ox-collar of the toilet seat. He opens his knapsack and roots through it, squinting in the murky, feeble fluorescent light. His spare shirt, two pairs of socks, a T-shirt, the rusted tobacco tin containing his net worth of eighty-six dollars and change, a photograph of his mother. He pauses at this, frowning at the faded colour shot of her sitting on their porch, half smiling, a chipped enamel coffee mug in one hand and a cigarette in the other. He puts it aside and roots on down to the bottom of the knapsack.

Claude lifts out the gun. It's an old army-issue Colt .45 automatic, just like the one Bob used in that spider hole back in the day. It's flecked with orange rust, big and heavy, his small hand just fitting around the chequered-wood grip. The gun is older than Claude, older than his daddy even. Family legend has it that Claude's grandpa, his mom's dad, brought it back from Korea, where he killed a bunch of gooks with it. He clumsily pops the catch, releases the magazine and runs a finger over the fat brass slug that nestles at the top, his six buddies crouched beneath him.

The gun is old but the bullets are brand new. It all works. Claude has made sure of that, practising in the woods. He slips the magazine back into the butt of the pistol, snicks the safety on and carefully begins to repack his things.

10

OWN THROUGH MISSOURI, LIKE THE SONG SAYS. State highway most of the way, passing the towns of Sikeston, Willow Springs and Mountain Grove until they pick up the interstate, Highway 44, just east of Springfield, Kris gratefully turning onto the wide, brightly lit macadam in the middle of the night, getting the foot down, making time but being careful not to push that big old bus *too* hard, the Burritos ringing out, Gram, Merle Haggard and Waylon Jennings, everyone on a country kick as they follow that grey ribbon through into Kansas, crossing the state line near Pittsburgh, passing Wichita in the dawn's early light, the city sparkling in the cool of morning and JC and Morgan up back with the acoustic guitars singing *'I am a lineman for the county'* over and over again.

They stop at supermarkets and grocery stores, sleeping on the bus, buying bread, baloney and American cheese and dried pasta that they can boil on the little hotplate when they stop, Becky and Morgan taking turns cooking, making simple sauces, stretching that food dollar. And everywhere they stop they start to see the billboards screaming:

AMERICAN POP STAR!
THE NEW SEASON BEGINS!
LABOR DAY, 8PM ON ABN!

Some of the billboards are huge and have the smiling faces of the three judges emblazoned across them, the Stelfox guy, Jesus notices, standing off to the side, arms folded, and even though he's smiling he's still terrifying, with eyes that his smile never reaches. Some of the billboards are smaller and just read:

APS!
LABOR DAY, 8PM, ABN

But all of them are reminding them of the same thing: they have to be in LA in four days' time, September 5 at 10 a.m. Failure to be at the ABN lot at this time may, as Jesus' contract confirms, *'lead to instant dismissal from the show'* with the network enthusiastically retaining the right to *'sue the party or parties for any expenses occurred and any or all loss of earnings and income resulting from the contestant's non-appearance at the contractually stipulated time'*.

Like Morgan said: Life. With an option.

Kansas boiling, the late August heat continuing right into this first week of September as they go through Greensburg, Bucklin and Meade; little towns as they hug near the southern border, heading towards the corner of the state, for the tight intersection formed by Oklahoma and Colorado until, finally, just as they get to the town of Democracy in Brig County, a little over a hundred miles from the state line, the Indianapolis money runs out.

*

Conference time at a rest stop off the interstate, Becky chairing the meeting while the kids play on the grass, next to where Gus and Dotty are stretched out in the sun splitting a plastic jug of strong cider. 'OK,' Becky says. 'Kris. Gas situation?'

'Ah, kind of fucked?' Kris says. 'We're running on fumes right now.'

'OK. Morgan. Food?'

'Fucked. We got a couple of cans of tuna, some rice, maybe a can of tomatoes. I mean, we can eat tonight, but that's it.'

'Oh man,' Kris says. 'If I have to eat rice or pasta again I am going to hurl. I need a steak, some chicken or something. Some protein, man. I'm gonna get rickets or some shit like that.'

'Dope?' Jesus asks.

'Fragged,' Bob says, not in a good way, holding up an empty plastic baggie that has just a few of those beautiful dark green strands left in it from the wad of bud they left NYC with.

This is serious, Jesus thinks.

'How far you reckon we got to LA, Kris?' Becky asks.

'Shit, thirteen hundred miles easy. Two or three days. We're gonna need something like five, six hundred dollars for gas alone, Becks.'

'Right, right.' Becky rubs her chin, thinking, looking off towards the highway. 'How big is this town coming up? Democracy?'

Morgan flips through the Kansas tour guide they picked up a while back and reads out: '"Democracy, Brig Co. Pop: 28,000. Industries include meat processing, energy and tourism, blah, blah . . ."' he reads on.

'OK, nearly thirty thousand people, it's big enough to have a pawn store,' Becky says, standing up. 'Looks like we're gonna have to part with some stuff temporarily. We'll have to lose the good acoustic.'

'Your Martin?' Kris gasps to Jesus.

'Afraid so,' Becky says.

'Shit, she's right,' Jesus says. 'We'll get a month. We'll come back and get it. That should fetch four or five hundred easy. The little Pignose amp should be good for maybe another hundred. Anything else?' He looks around the table without much hope, his friends grimy, tired and poor.

'There's the CD player,' Kris says.

'Uh-uh,' JC says. 'Three days? No tunes? No way.'

Claude clears his throat. 'When we get to Santa Fe I'll be able to help you out with a couple of hundred.' They all look at him. He shrugs. 'My cousin's making good money.'

'Are you sure, man?' Jesus asks. Claude doesn't look like he knows the kind of people who have a couple of hundred bucks to spare.

'Yeah. You folks been good to me.'

'We'll pay you back,' Jesus says, smiling.

Claude looks at him and knows for absolute certain that this man is not lying. 'I believe you will,' he says.

'So how far to Santa Fe?' Becky asks Kris.

'*They say, that Santa Fe,*' Jesus sings, '*is less than ninety miles away . . .*'

'Actually, it's like five or six hundred,' Kris says.

'*So there's still time,*' Jesus sings on, '*to roll a number and rent a car . . .*'

'Obviously,' Becky says, 'Neil Young weren't starting from where we are . . .'

'Shit,' Morgan says, suddenly looking back up from the guidebook. 'Listen to this. "Kansas," ' he reads, ' "is famous for not having elected a Democratic president since the early 1930s.

It controversially removed evolution from the State Teaching Standards in 1999, banned same-sex marriages in 2005 and has placed restrictions on abortion."'

'Wow. Democracy here we come,' Jesus says.

11

HE American Broadcasting Network Studios, Burbank, Los Angeles.

The eye of the storm. T minus four days. Great noise as last-minute adjustments are made to the *APS* set, carpenters hammering and electricians soldering, production managers and heads of department shouting at one another about deadlines, budget overruns and the like. There is great heat too as the massive lighting rigs suspended from the ceiling are given a full run-through while the heavy cameras glide back and forth silently, panning, zooming at the empty stage.

Serene through this chaos comes Steven Stelfox. He is trailed at a respectful distance by his entourage: Naomi his personal assistant, Harry the show's director and Sherry the line producer, with Trellick bringing up the rear, talking on his cellphone. With the show now into its third season, what might be called its 'imperial' phase, the protocol when Mr Stelfox is on the set is well established. Heads dip respectfully as he passes. There is nothing written down but the basics are known to all:

no one is allowed to make eye contact and God help anyone below the level of Head of Department who comes up and tries to initiate a conversation. Like the lighting cameraman of last season who made the mistake of falling into step with the Chief as he walked the corridor from his dressing room to the studio, taking the opportunity en route to give his opinion on a better way to shoot the judge's reaction-to-performance shots. It was to be his last creative contribution to *APS*. He was fired the next day.

No one fucks with the Chief.

There are many benefits to being the creator, mastermind and single most recognisable face attached to the biggest TV show in America, but one of the most pleasurable is that Stelfox does not have to do anything he does not want to do. Which certainly includes conversing with technical staff.

No. One. Fucks. With. The. Chief.

'Is this it?' Stelfox says, clearly puzzled. They are standing on set now, in front of the long desk that the three judges sit behind.

'How do you mean?' Sherry the line producer replies, already, always, nervous.

'I mean, Sherry, how many logos can you see here?'

Sherry surveys the desk carefully. There are the judges' water glasses, now emblazoned with the ice-blue logo of Vibe Cola. There is the top panelling on the front of the desk, which has the wording 'American-Pacific Airlines' running all the way across it. There are the laptops that now sit in front of the judges, each opened at a specific angle so as to best position the manufacturer's logo towards the cameras. 'Um, three?' she says finally, looking at him like an uncertain pupil in front of the class, praying she has got the answer right.

'Well done, love,' Stelfox says. 'Now, how many official sponsors do we have involved with the show?'

'Ah . . . um . . .' She flips through her clipboard.

'Fourteen,' Trellick says automatically from somewhere behind her.

'Thank you, James,' Stelfox says. 'So why am I only looking at three logos in shot?'

'Well . . .' She looks towards Harry the director. 'I don't see where else we could –'

'What about this?' He points to an area of studio wall, behind and to the right of the desk. 'We could stick a fucking car or a hamburger or something here, couldn't we? It wouldn't be in shot all the time, but still. Or how about the backs of the chairs. We swivel about a fair bit. Or –'

'You don't think,' Harry says, 'it might look a bit, ah, tacky?'

Stelfox turns to face the director. 'Tacky?' he says.

'Well, if we fill every other inch with product placement –'

'Product *integration*,' Trellick corrects him.

'Sorry, product integration. I mean, if we overload the frame like that, won't it –'

'*Overload the frame?*' Stelfox says. 'Fuck me. Listen Orson, I don't give a fuck if you can't even *see* the fucking desk for the amount of shite we're trying to flog. If it brings in one solitary fucking penny more what's the fucking downside?'

'Some people might think it's, um, distasteful,' Sherry says, trying to side with the director.

'What people?' Stelfox asks, genuinely interested.

'Just, you know, the public.'

'Oh, *them*,' Stelfox sighs, relieved. 'Naomi –' he turns to Naomi, lithe, gorgeous twenty-three years old and devoid of heart or conscience – 'get a list of the sponsors and get Terry in advertising to make a few last-minute calls. See who comes up with the best offer for that wall at least. Tell you what, Sherry, why don't you email "the public" a copy of my last bank statement? Let's see how fucking "distasteful" they find that. The fucking losers . . .'

With that he's off to the next problem.

12

RIS STAYS BEHIND TO DO SOME WORK ON THE ENGINE, Big Bob helping him. Dotty and Gus are sleeping, or more accurately passed out (that cider packed more of a punch than they reckoned), and the kids are off exploring the woodland by the rest area. So that leaves Jesus, Morgs, Becky and Claude for the expedition into town.

Along Main Street they come, Becky in her tiny denim miniskirt, cork platforms and thin cotton vest, turning heads here in this hick burg. JC and Morgan, having many tours of the indie circuit of the United States under their belts, are old hands at getting around the country with very little in their pockets. They know that if they find the courthouse then a pawn store will not be too far away: folks handing over those watches, wedding bands and geetars, trying to pay those fines and make that bail money. Sure enough, hard left by the courthouse, down a couple of side streets and there they are, three golden balls hanging in the sunlight. Claude and Becky park themselves on a bench while Jesus and Morgan go in with the Martin and the Pignose.

Three minutes or so later they're coming back out the door, Jesus counting money.

'Sonofabitch,' Morgan is saying as they approach the bench. 'I can't believe you took that.'

'No good?' Becky asks.

'It's fine,' Jesus says.

'Three hundred and fifty dollars for an early-eighties Martin worth at least a thousand bucks? Seventy for the amp?' Morgan says.

'Hey,' Jesus says brightly, 'it's enough to get us all fed and watered and down the road apiece! Huh, buddy?' He punches Claude affectionately on the arm. Claude smiles. 'Come on, let's go find some sandwiches or something to take back for the guys. Couple of bottles of T-Bird for the oldsters. Hey, look at this.' He gestures to the sunshine and leafy trees of Main Street. 'Ain't this a helluva day!'

Rounding a corner, looking for a deli or something, they see a crowd, maybe thirty or forty people, gathered outside a building across the street. They're chanting, waving placards. 'Wow,' Becky says, 'check it out. A protest.'

As they get closer they can make out some of the stuff on the placards. 'NOT HERE!' reads one. 'AIDS: GOD'S JUDGEMENT!' another. The crowd is mixed, some old folks, some well-heeled middle-aged ladies, some younger moms with their kids in tow. A pretty teenage girl is wearing a red T-shirt with 'GODHATESFAGS.COM' emblazoned on it. Just as they reach the edge of the crowd the door they're all gathered around opens and a guy comes out. They get a glimpse of him – he's in his twenties, scruffy and frightened-looking, harried – before the jostling starts and the crowd presses in, shouting stuff – 'Faggot', 'Aids' – as the guy tries to pass through them. Someone nudges him, sending him toppling forward as he reaches the edge of the crowd.

'Hey!' Jesus shouts as Morgan catches the guy's arm, keeping him upright, the guy flinching, as though he's about to be hit. 'Shit,' Morgan says, 'you OK, man?' The guy nods, looking embarrassed. Up close Morgs can see that the dude is filthy, he's wearing too many clothes for this heat, his corduroy jacket is greasy at the collar, matted with dandruff. He smells bad and his teeth are green. His face is bruised and cut too, but not from just now; they're old wounds, a faded ruby under both eyes, which must have been very black at one point, a lime-and-yellow iridescence from the right temple down into the cheek. A front tooth missing too. Morgs knows homeless when he sees it. The crowd are still shouting stuff at the guy as Jesus steps in front of him.

'What's the problem here?' Jesus says to the nearest person in the crowd, a well-dressed lady in a pastel summer frock. She's wearing sunglasses. With one hand she holds onto a little girl, about four or five, dressed similarly to her, while with the other she wields a home-made placard, a piece of card stapled to a short pole that has 'QUEERS BURN IN HELL!' written on it.

'This clinic,' the lady says.

'Clinic? Sorry –' he waves an arm at Morgan, Claude and Becky – 'we're from out of town.'

'The city council have allocated funds to open a . . . a drop-in centre –' she says these words as though they were the filthiest expression ever invented – 'for people with Aids. Right here! Off Main Street!'

More shouting from the crowd.

'And you're saying there *shouldn't* be a clinic?' Jesus asks.

'That's right.'

'But . . . what's the problem?'

'The problem?' The woman seems disarmed by this, as

though the problem was so obvious that this part of the conversation was something she never planned on having. The little girl looks up at her quizzically. The whole crowd draws up behind the woman. 'We don't want these people here.' She nods to the guy who came out of the place, who is sheltering behind Morgan and Becky now. 'We don't want them infesting our town.'

'What people?' JC asks, all innocence.

'The Aids people. The heroin addicts, the homosexuals and the prostitutes and the like.'

'We're good Christian folk here,' a bearded guy cuts in.

'No you're not,' Jesus says pleasantly, no anger, no scorn in his voice.

'Excuse me?' the summer-dress lady says.

'You're not Christians,' Jesus says.

'How do you figure that, buddy?' the bearded guy says.

'Ah, well, sir, you seem to be holding a placard that says –' JC tilts his head to read, ' "WHORES AND JUNKIES GO TO HELL".'

'And they surely will,' someone shouts out.

Jesus looks around at the faces of this sorry crowd, most of their lips twisted, angry, hating. He looks down at the little girl who smiles up at him. A couple of the men in the crowd are moving closer in. 'These people have *forfeited* God's love,' someone says.

'Let me tell you something,' the woman is continuing, indignant. *Let me tell you something* usually being a pretty good indicator that you're about to hear a bunch of nonsense. 'I pray to the Lord every night and –'

'You know, lady,' Jesus sighs, 'you can dress a dog up as Superman every night. The sonofabitch still ain't gonna fly around saving the world.'

There's a gasp at this and the woman actually flattens a hand across her breast. 'Are you calling m—' she begins, but a big man steps in between her and Jesus. 'It's OK, Annie,' he says to the lady, taking over. 'Listen friend, where are you folks from anyway?'

'New York City.'

The man smiles and shakes his head, looking balefully over the long hair, the black guy and the trampy girl. 'Well, that would explain it. See, we don't want our town turning into a cesspit like you live in. Understand? So why don't you and your friends take this queer with you and just get the hell out of here and leave us decent, God-fearing folk in peace?'

'Well,' Jesus says, 'you're right about one thing, sir.'

'What's that, *friend*?' The guy is pretty close to Jesus now. He's breathing a little hard. Jesus looks him dead in the eye.

'You are absolutely right to fear God,' Jesus says.

Jesus turns and takes the guy's arm and they walk away with shouts of 'Go back to New York' and 'Jesus died for your sins' being thrown after them.

'Oh, be nice!' Morgan shouts back at them.

'Yep – welcome to Democracy,' Becky says.

'What's your name?' Jesus says to the guy.

'P-Pete,' the guy says.

'You eaten today, Pete?'

'Sorry?' Pete says.

'Eat? Food?' Jesus says, miming a knife and fork. 'You wanna come eat with us, buddy?'

The guy looks at JC, confused, unable after the last few moments to quite believe that kindness still exists in this world. His face starts working as he blinks the tears back.

'Hey,' Jesus says, 'that's all . . . you're OK, man. Yeah, you'll be all right.'

13

HERE JUST WASN'T ANY WORK AROUND, YOU know? All these houses they'd been building, it all just stopped. My boyfriend died, he was older than me, he'd had it for a long time. I went a little nuts for a while there and pretty soon I got through my savings, I got kicked out of my apartment, my Medicare ran out, so I couldn't afford all the drugs, all the antiretrovirals and stuff? They're expensive. The only place I could get free treatment was a clinic over in Torrance, but that was like an hour bus ride away. There used to be a place closer but it got closed down a few years back – fucking Bush, you know? – and it was getting to the point where I couldn't even afford the fare every few weeks, so when I heard they were opening a place right here in Democracy I thought "thank God", but, the way it's gone, it looks like they might shut it down pretty soon, all the pressure they're getting from the "community". There's those church groups outside all the time, you get abuse shouted at you. Today was only the second time I'd gone in. A few weeks back, the first time, I swear, I cried for half an hour. Little kids, you know, junior high kids, calling you a faggot and saying God wants you dead and stuff like that. The parents right there with them. It's like, like you're a goddamn . . .' Pete tails off, on the verge of tears again, here at the picnic table in the shadow of the great bus. Becky reaches out and places her hand on top of his.

Leper, Jesus thinks, finishing the thought for him. *Like you're a goddamn leper*. Pete snuffles, picks a piece of bread from the gap where his tooth was.

'What happened to your face?' Becky asks.

'Oh, some guys worked me over a few months back.'

'What for?' Morgan.

'I guess cos they were drunk and I was sleeping on the sidewalk.'

They all take this in. Jesus, Becky notices, crushes the aluminium soda can he is holding a little harder than he had been and takes a deep breath before asking, 'Exactly what line of work were you in, Pete?'

'Construction. I was a carpenter.'

'Is that a fact?' JC says, smiling. 'So, Pete,' Jesus says, standing up and stretching in the sunshine, 'you wanna come with us to LA?'

Pete looks at this guy who he met all of an hour ago. 'Excuse me?' he says.

'Listen,' JC continues, 'if you come with us you'll have food to eat, a place to sleep, we'll get your medication sorted out and, down the line, we'll get you working again. I promise you.'

Pete looks up, having to squint into the sunshine, JC's blond hair tumbling down and gleaming, his blue eyes calm and serene. 'Now how you gonna do all that?' he asks.

'Ah, we'll figure it out,' JC says.

Pete turns to the table and asks, 'Is he for real?'

'Motherfucker's crazier than a shithouse rat,' Morgan says.

14

VER THE BORDER AND, BRIEFLY, INTO COLORADO before Kris points the bus south and they're cutting across the top corner of Oklahoma, passing through the state just north-west of Boise City, before crossing their third state line in just a few hours and suddenly the desert of New Mexico is endless all around them.

Claude sits up front, staring through the windshield to Kris's right, watching the dust and cacti blow by, like he can will Santa Fe to appear over the horizon just by staring long enough. He's been quiet since Kansas. Well, even quieter than usual. Just looking out the window, clutching that little knapsack that goes everywhere with him, when Jesus swings into the seat beside him. 'Hey, kid,' he says, holding out two beers as he sits down, but Claude shakes his head. JC shrugs and pops one open anyway. He chugs it down, burping happily, and joins Claude in staring out the windshield, where the sun is sinking ahead of them, the day finally beginning to cool. 'Pretty, huh?' JC says.

'Yeah.'

'Everything OK, kid?'

'Sure.'

'Looking forward to meeting your cousin? What's his name?'

'Uh, Sam.'

'And you figure he'll get you a start out here?' JC says, sipping his beer.

'Reckons he can. Good money, he says.'

'Dangerous work.'

'Can be, I guess.'

Silence again. Just the diesel blare, the black asphalt getting swallowed up beneath them, the barren sand spilling out all around them. JC cranes his neck and looks down the bus, to where a bit of a party atmosphere is breaking out up the back. They picked up a couple of cases before they left Democracy and now Pete is standing in the aisle, his back to Jesus as he talks to Morgan, Becks and Big Bob, gesturing with a beer in his hand. He's wearing a pair of Jesus' jeans and a clean Veruca Salt T-shirt that belongs to Kris and is way too big for him. He's scrubbed up well: they paid for him to use the shower facilities at the truck stop before they set off, Pete emerging all clean and pink with the dumpster grime off him. Amazing how a hot shower and some fresh clothes were the difference between someone you partied with and something most folk stepped over.

'And how's your mom?' JC asks, turning back to Claude. 'You been calling her?'

'Yeah. She's good.'

'Good,' Jesus says, draining that beer. 'And I bet she feels better knowing you're going to be with family out here, huh? Good old cousin Dan.'

'Yeah. I believe she does.'

'Sorry,' Jesus says, his brow furrowing, 'I meant Sam.' He looks at Claude. 'Didn't I?'

'Yeah,' Claude says, his eyes darting quickly towards JC's then away again. 'Sam.'

'Right. Cousin Sam. Just wanted to get that straight. You sure you don't want this?' He picks up the second beer and waggles it. Claude shakes his head again. 'Come to Papa,' JC says, popping it open and putting his feet up on the partition in front of them, just bringing that cold can up to his lips when Kris shouts, *'Hey! Will one of you guys please bring me a fucking beer?'* and Jesus is sighing and getting to his feet again.

15

ANTA FE, NEW MEXICO. THE CITY'S NAME, AS Morgan points out from his guidebook, actually means 'holy faith', but after Democracy, Kansas, nobody's putting too much faith in names any more.

Early September is pretty much the best time of the year to be in Santa Fe: cooler than the desert heat of August, the aspens of the Santa de Cristo mountains turning bright yellow. They're all having dinner in a funky little Mexican cantina, Claude's farewell meal, and spirits are high because, as Kris points out, they are now only eight hundred miles from LA. Get there easy with a day to spare. Claude keeps borrowing Kris's cell to call and check if his cousin's home yet, but no answer. The place is cheap, the fish tacos are good, and Jesus and Morgan lean happily on the bar, getting another round of beers in, a few more tequilas.

JC and Morgs clink their little shot glasses together and toss that burning spirit back. 'Eee-ha!' Morgan says, reaching for a lemon.

'Hey, look at them,' Jesus says fondly, gazing across the restaurant in a tequila haze to where their party sits under a big ornamental cactus plant; Big Bob is pulling his canvas jacket up over his face, just his eyes peeking out as he makes monster faces and chases Miles and Danny around the table, the boys shrieking with delight. Pete is talking to Kris and Becky. Claude is heading outside again, dialling once more on Kris's cell. 'Been quite a few thousand miles, huh?' Jesus says.

'Sure has,' Morgan says.

'Listen, Morgs, you notice anything about Claude?'

'Like what?'

'Kid seems distracted, like . . .'

'Well, probably nervous about being in a new town, you know? Meeting his cousin, trying to get work and all that. Shit,' Morgan says, 'he's just a kid. He's not much on conversa—'

'Shh, heads up,' JC says, spotting Claude approaching them. 'Naw, I reckon it sounds better in F sharp,' he says.

'Uh, that was my cousin. He's back home now.'

'Great,' Morgan says.

'Look,' JC says, 'I don't feel right about this, Claude. Having you turn up and ask your family for money straight off the bat just so you can give it to us? I reckon we can at least get to Phoenix with what we got and then –'

'It's no problem,' Claude says. 'You folks been real good to me. I'll be 'bout an hour or so, I guess.'

'If you're sure, man.'

He nods.

'See you soon then, kid,' Morgan says.

Claude checks the big old grid of buzzers and doorbells. The old Spanish-style adobe building has been subdivided many times over the years, apartments multiplying, splintering like cells in a living, growing organism, and it takes him a moment before he finds the name he's looking for. It's handwritten under a clear piece of yellowing Scotch tape, writing he recognises immediately although he hasn't seen it in many years. Apartment 215. He retreats to the shadows near the door of the apartment building and waits, five minutes, ten, until he sees the door opening and he hurries on up the steps, looking purposeful as a middle-aged Hispanic woman comes out. It doesn't look like the kind of place where people ask too many questions and, sure enough, she leaves the door swinging open for him to enter.

Up the stairs to the second floor, apartment 209 on his left, reaching into his already open knapsack, passing 211, his hand curling around the chequered-wood grip, apartment 213, sliding the safety off with his thumb, his hand still deep in the bag outside 215, his breathing short, swallowing, as he knocks on the door quickly, not giving himself time to think this through any more. A moment passes, there's the sound of glass breaking, a bottle being knocked over, and then suddenly the door is being flung open and a middle-aged man stands there, balding, a big gut hanging over the waistband of stained grey sweatpants, a grubby white vest above that. The man's face is unshaven and he's red-eyed, half in the bag, just as Claude hoped.

'Yeah?' the man says in a Kentucky accent, surly, irritated, just the way Claude remembered. For a moment Claude can't speak, he just looks at him. 'Look, what the fuck you want, ki—' the man begins, glancing behind Claude and along the corridor, a flash of worry that something's up, that Claude, whoever he is, is not alone. But he doesn't finish the sentence – Claude whips the .45 out of his knapsack and smashes it hard into the guy's face and he falls backwards, his nose breaking, blood spraying out of his nostrils as Claude steps quickly into the apartment and pulls the door shut behind him.

'Been a while, huh?' Claude says, pointing the gun at the sprawling, bleeding figure on the carpet.

HE FUCK –' THE GUY SAYS, CLUTCHING HIS NOSE, blood soaking his vest as he starts to get up. He thinks better of it when he hears the icy, metallic 'schlock' – Claude ratcheting back the slide on that big old .45.

The two men eye each other for the first time in five or so years: one breathing hard, raging, staring up at the other through stinging pain and streaming eyes. Claude in his turn is trembling, the enormity dawning on him – this moment he has so long dreamt of finally having arrived.

'This is for Momma,' Claude says as he levels the pistol and starts to pull the trigger.

The guy's eyes widening.

Then the door is swinging open, Jesus saying, 'Hey there. Problem, buddy?'

A stunned pause, Claude's eyes briefly shifting to Jesus, the gun staying on the man on the floor. 'This ain't none of your business, mister,' Claude says to Jesus.

'I hear you, man.' JC closes the door softly behind him and

moves into the centre of the room, taking it all in. 'Sorry I followed you and all, I just had the feeling, you know . . .'

'You can stay if you wanna see him die,' Claude says, all his focus back on the bloody mess on the floor.

'Uh, O-Kayyy. Mind if I ask why you're gonna kill your cousin, Claude?'

'Ain't no cousin,' Claude says.

'Claude?' the man says nasally, a blood bubble forming and popping on his nose.

'He's my daddy.'

A pause while everyone takes this in. The man moans.

'That so?' Jesus says, quite close to Claude now.

'You try and take this gun off me I'll kill you too,' Claude says.

'I believe you,' Jesus says.

'Listen, son,' Claude's father begins.

'You shut your fucken mouth, you piece of shit!' Claude snaps, pointing the gun right at him, the hammer cocked, his finger trembling, hovering over the trigger.

'Claude,' Jesus says, calmly, quietly. 'I'm just wondering, what you gonna do after you kill him?'

'Huh? Kill myself.' Claude says this as though Jesus were a moron for not realising it. Might as well have added 'of course'.

'Right, right.' Jesus says. 'Now why would you go and do that? Think about your mom. The farm.'

'Ain't no mom. Ain't no farm. Cos of this fucker here.' He's addressing his father now.

'What happened to your mom, Claude?' Jesus asks gently.

'Died last month. Drank herself to death after he left us. Took her five years . . . with the Vicodin and the whiskey, and I tried to get her to stop but she . . . and the corn went bad. The bank put us in foreclosure. She just, I . . .' The kid's losing it now, fighting tears, trying to keep his rage on the boil. 'I couldn't manage it on my own, we couldn't afford no help. This fucker never sent us a dime. It . . . it's all gone. You hear me, you fucking bastard?' His finger tightening again, his father flattening himself further into the wall, remembering well the hair trigger on that old gun. 'She . . . she wouldn't eat. She just stopped eating. Up in her room, crying. Drinking. I tried, I . . . weren't nothing left of her in the end. Sk-skin and b-bone.' The tears coming. 'My poor Momma. What am I gonna do now?'

The room very quiet now except for Claude's sobbing.

'Claude?' Jesus says softly. 'Look at me, Claude.'

Claude turns and meets JC's gaze through his tears, the quavering gun staying on his father. 'Would your momma read to you when you were little?'

'Read?'

'Yeah. Stories and things.'

'S-sometimes.'

'Remember sitting in her lap? Her chin resting on the top of your head? Your hair smelling so good to her. Remember that? It was maybe bedtime, or you'd just had your bath? You were just perfect to your momma, you know?' JC's voice slow and hypnotic as he gets closer, Claude getting lost in that Pacific gaze. 'You think she'd want to see you putting a bullet through that beautiful head? All your brains and everything all blowing out through a hole? She only wants you to be happy.'

'She's gone.'

'Just for a while. You'll see her soon enough. But not yet, man. Not like this.'

'You don't know that.'

'Oh man. You gotta trust me on this one.'

'I . . . I ain't no good for nothing.'

'You're a farmer, Claude. That's about the best thing you can be.'

'Ain't no farm no more.' He's really crying.

'Well, we're gonna take care of that too somewhere down the road.'

Claude, looking into the eyes of this guy he's only known a few days, this guy sounding so calm, so certain. 'You . . . you promise?' Claude sounding five years old as he says this.

'Come here, son.'

The kid collapses sobbing into Jesus' arms, burying his face in his chest, the gun dropping down by his side. Claude's father sees his chance and springs forward. Before he's even on his feet JC has whipped the gun up and is pointing it straight at him again.

'Sorry, sir, if you could just sit back down.' He speaks to the man while still cradling Claude, the boy's tears hot against JC's neck. 'I understand this has been a traumatic evening for you but it's nearly over. Now, embarrassingly we find ourselves short of gas money so I'm going to have to ask you to lend me the contents of that wallet I can see on top of the TV set there. I've got your address memorised so I'll be happy to reimburse you once we're on our feet again. Or, in light of recent events, you could take the view that you're perhaps long past due in sending your son here some maintenance. In which case we could consider the money Claude's and I'll make sure he gets it back. What do you reckon?'

'Just take it,' Claude senior says through blood and shame.

'Much obliged, sir.' Jesus says.

They pawn the gun too and there's enough to fill that big tank. Claude crying for a long time in the back seat between Jesus and Becky as they drive across Arizona all through the night, just one rest stop somewhere past Phoenix, Kris gunning the engine into the home stretch and then, all at once, they're taking the 1-10 West into Santa Monica, the ocean appearing out of nowhere, looking sudden and beautiful in the morning light, like it has to millions of tired pilgrims before them.

Part Four

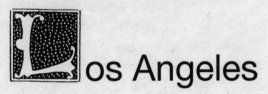os Angeles

'Every country gets the circus it deserves. Spain gets bullfights. Italy gets the Catholic Church. America gets Hollywood.'

Erica Jong

1

'HAT'S GREAT, THANK YOU. OH, ONE MORE THING.' Jesus, turning back and tapping his room key on the marble counter, casual. 'Can you tell me where we might be able to buy some inflatable mattresses?'

'Inflatable?' The receptionist's eyebrows are arching up again, as they have done many times during this long, complex check-in.

'Mattresses. You know, for sleeping on?'

'Ah, I really . . . maybe you could try back along Sunset? I think there are a couple of hardware stores. If you turn left out of the hotel entrance . . .'

'Right,' Jesus says, turning to look across the lobby of the famous Chateau Marmont, to where Kris lies slumped on a sofa, his huge, red face beaded with sweat, his eyes closed. Spent, all gone, the last hour of wrestling the overheating bus through the LA morning rush hour having done for him. It was pleasant in here, cool and dark and all wicker and tapestries and stained wood and soft amber light. The others were scattered around in various states of exhaustion and curiosity, the lobby echoing to the odd delighted shriek from Becky and the kids, or the occasional surprised 'Frag!' from Bob, as they discovered some new wonder somewhere among the opulence. 'Hey, man,' Kris shouts over, suddenly excited. 'Did you know Led Zeppelin stayed here?' Regular guests rubbernecked by, movie stars and agents and producers and whatnot.

'You know what, ma'am, I think we'll go freshen up and maybe take a stroll along there later.'

'No problem,' the girl says, smiling. Jesus was already getting the sense that *nothing* was a problem here at the Chateau. 'And would you like anything sent to your room?'

'Uh, anything like?'

'Refreshments. Drinks? Food?'

'To tell you the truth, Miss,' JC says, leaning in conspiratorially, 'we don't have too much money.' The receptionist, a pro, did a very good job of managing to look surprised and saddened by this information. 'And I'm guessing it ain't exactly discount prices here.'

She leans fractionally forward across the cool marble counter, her voice dropping slightly, as she says, 'Your bill is to be sent directly to the studio, sir.'

'Well then. I guess we could use a little breakfast . . .'

The show was springing for a bungalow. And a very nice bungalow it was too – over a thousand square feet, lounge, bedroom, two bathrooms and sliding doors leading out to a patio and, beyond that, the blue, egg-shaped swimming pool – for about the two and a half minutes it took the menagerie to settle in. Yep, two and a half minutes to go from the front cover of *Vanity Fair* to the kind of photograph that might accompany a heartbreaking article on a refugee camp. Jesus smiles, relighting a joint as he surveys the scene from the comfortable vantage of a lounger on the patio – Gus and Dotty on the floor methodically emptying the minibar, Miles and Danny mid-pillow fight, thundering water audible from the nearest bathroom as Becky fills the tub, Claude and Pete on a sofa together, the latter explaining the plot of *Beaches* to the former as the near life-sized image of Bette Midler fills the titanic plasma screen in front of them, Big Bob on the far side of the room transferring the contents of the fruit bowl to his many pockets, snatches of music coming from further off as Morgs and Kris get to grips with the sound system in the bedroom – wiggling his bare toes in a square of sunlight, and thinks to himself: *well, we did this at least.*

'Shit, this'll work,' Morgan says, taking in the scene as he comes out from the bedroom and flops down on the lounger opposite Jesus, Jesus handing him the joint.

'You think?' Jesus laughs.

'The bed's like a goddamn football field. We'll get four in that easy. One on each sofa in there, drag these bad boys in at night –' Morgs slaps the lounger he's lying on – 'and we're good for another two. Bob prefers the floor anyhow. I mean, man, what kind of lunatic would need all this space on their own?'

'Look at them in there,' Jesus says. 'Helluva thing to give folks a good time, ain't it?' Morgan nods, grinning too. 'Rock-bottom minimum? I get kicked off the show the first time I'm up? At least these guys are gonna have a no-shit vacation.'

They watch as across the room Bob opens the door and four waiters begin wheeling in the piled trolleys, silver salvers glinting in the afternoon sun, everyone moving in, lifting lids, grabbing glasses and cutlery. The waiters are pros too, Jesus thinks. They act as if all this – half a dozen ravenous misfits descending like gannets, a couple of fetid alcoholics stretched out on the floor, sweet dope smoke filling the air – is business as usual. Bob is pointing uncertainly through the sliding doors towards Jesus and Morgan and one of the waiters detaches himself from the chaos, threading his way across the suite and out onto the patio, smiling as he hands Jesus the check.

'Thanks, man,' Jesus says, signing, adding 30 per cent, 'and sorry about, you know, all the . . .' He gestures with the joint towards the menagerie.

'Please, sir,' the waiter says. 'We had Metallica here for a week. Back when they were still partying? Oh my.'

'Whoa,' says Morgan. 'What were those guys like?'

'Lovely gentlemen. *Thank you*, sir,' he says, inclining his head towards Jesus as he takes the check back. 'And this came for you at the desk.' He hands JC an envelope embossed with the ABN logo. 'And, if I may say so, good luck on the show.'

'Thanks, bro,' Jesus says, flashing that smile.

Jesus works his thumb into the seal and cracks it open: a laminated pass and a letter, confirming that a limo will collect him at 9 a.m. the following morning to take him to the ABN lot in Burbank.

'Hey, how much was it?' Morgs asks.

'Huh?'

'The tab, numbnuts. How much?'

'Oh. Like, four hundred?'

'Four hundred dollars for breakfast?'

'Including tip, Morgan.'

'Get you,' Morgan says, grinding the joint out in a heavy crystal ashtray. 'Last week we were stealing sandwiches, motherfucker. Man, we are gonna get kicked out of here so fast.'

'No, we're not,' Jesus says, still studying the letter. 'And if we are – so what?'

'Dude, does anything worry you?'

Jesus thinks. 'Neh,' he says finally. 'Not so much.'

2

IRST DAY ON THE SET, STEVEN STELFOX STRIDES down the corridor leading from the dressing rooms to Studio 4, a phalanx of assistants, producers and make-up artists forming a praetorian guard around and behind him. Darcy DeAngelo and Herb Stutz bring up the rear with their own, smaller, entourages. First day on the set, but much good material from those regional auditions already in the can, America's freaks already edited together, concisely shamed. Nerves high, as they always are among the production crew when Stelfox is on deck, but nothing like as high as they would be from next week onwards, when the show started going out live, 'when the contestants have been chosen' but, of course, the contestants have already been chosen. Narrative, Stelfox is always thinking. What, who, will help to build a compelling narrative? One that can be sustained until Christmas, when it's time to drop the bomb.

'Yep, on our way,' a girl is saying into a headset.

'Naomi darling,' Stelfox says, handing his half-drunk bottle of Evian to her, 'make sure that fat fucking retard working camera three knows that if he shoots me from low down on the left-hand profile again he's going to be filming inserts on a Mexican soap opera for the next twenty years.'

'He knows, SS.'

The studio doors swinging open, Stelfox rearranging his features into a pleasant, benevolent smile, and it was time for the general to meet the troops.

It works like this. The opening show would be composed largely of footage from the regional auditions; basically a continent-sized net containing much of the American population that should, by rights, have been scratching with their toes at the soft walls of padded cells: the fifty-year-old faggot capering in a leotard and yowling Madonna songs; the twitchy, nervy child molester mumbling an Eagles number; the three-hundred-pound yodelling housewives. Then, gradually, they would focus on specific characters from three groups. 1) The few with actual talent *and* looks who were definitely going through. 2) Those with talent counterpointed with weight problems, boss eyes, wardrobe-sized buck teeth and fluorescent acne. The ones who *might* be going through if their backstories were deemed to hold enough heartbreak and drama. (Dialysis machines and poverty. Broken homes and orphanages. Missing parents and lost childhoods. And that 'might' only functioned for the audience who watched the show – the *cunts* to use the industry term employed by Stelfox – the production team had, of course, long since decided who was going through.) Then there was 3), the smaller, more rarefied group that Jesus belonged to, those who were attractive and talented and clearly *completely off their fucking tits*.

In the big dressing room, more of a holding area really, Jesus can hear the laughter coming from the studio audience as the audition tapes are played back for them. He absent-mindedly plucks a few notes on his unplugged Gibson and looks around the room. There are maybe twenty of them herded in here: all of them nervous, pacing, trilling out scales, warm-up exercises, all of them dressed in their best clothes, all of them eyeing one another cagily, some blatantly hatefully.

All bar Jesus of course, whose beatific grin and tattered jeans and sneakers are topped off with the fresh but faded Mogwai T-shirt he borrowed that morning from Becky, who had been the only one of them with the sense to do some laundry at the hotel. A big black kid squeezes past Jesus and lodges himself in the corner, sweating, trembling. It looks like he's trying to position himself close to the sink, like maybe he's going to throw up. He's huge, maybe 250. 'Hey, you OK?' Jesus asks.

The kid shakes his head. 'Man, I can't wait for this to be done.'

'How come you're doing it?' Jesus asks, not unkindly.

'Want to help my family,' the kid shrugs.

'What's your name?'

'Garry.'

'Jesus.' They shake: JC's hand cool and dry, Garry's like a vibrating dishrag.

'Like in the Bible?'

'Like in the Bible. Look, don't worry, kid. What's the worst can happen?'

'They don't like me.'

'So fuck them. I like you.'

A young woman with headset and clipboard bursts in. 'Jesus?' she says. 'Jesus Christ?'

'That's me.' As he stands, swinging the guitar round behind his back, there is the ripple of laughter that usually greets his full name being said publicly.

'You're up next.'

From the side of the stage Jesus watches the previous singer being questioned by the panel of judges.

'I've known since I was a little girl,' she is saying, cameras creeping all around her, 'that I was going to be famous. I've always felt different to other people. I –'

'Yes, love,' Stelfox is interrupting, 'I'm sure you are *different*. The problem is you're not *talented*.'

Boos and catcalls from the audience as the girl's lip starts to tremble.

'Come on, Steven,' Darcy says. 'We've heard a lot worse than Carrie right here in this room.'

'Oh, so that's a reason to put her through, Darcy? "We've heard worse!" I mean –'

Laughter mingling with the boos.

'I'm just saying there's no need to –'

'Yes, and I'm just saying "Next". Thank you, Carrie.'

'You're making a big mistake,' Carrie says defiantly.

'Oh, I'll live with it,' Stelfox says. 'Next!'

Jesus comes out, blinking in the chrome spotlight, and, as scripted, Herb Stutz asks him, 'What's your name, son?'

'Jesus Christ.'

Laughter as Stelfox does a (scripted) double take. Jesus smiles. Thirty-one years of this. Fucking Dad.

'Sorry?' Stelfox says.

'Jesus. Christ.'

Darcy puts her hands over her face to stifle a giggle. The audience laugh harder.

'Well, not much to live up to, is there?' Stelfox says.

'Where you from, son?' Stutz asks him.

'Ah, New York City.'

'Off you go then,' Stelfox says, before adding, 'umm, Jesus.'

The audience laughing again, still laughing as Jesus goes into his agreed number, the same song he did at his audition, 'The Only Living Boy in New York', just him and his electric guitar.

The laughter dies down pretty quick. Stutz and DeAngelo are enraptured, the former grudgingly, the latter unreservedly. Stelfox unreadable. There are spontaneous whoops and cheers as he takes a short fluid solo in the middle. As the last chord rings out the audience bursts into sustained, genuine applause.

'Ohmigod!' Darcy says. 'That was *so* amazing!'

'How long you been playing that guitar, son?' Herb Stutz asks.

'Since I can remember.'

'You can play, kid. Lemme tell ya. And I've worked with some of the best guitar players in the business.' He looks along the desk to Stelfox, who is writing something down, and asks, 'Steven?'

'Right,' Stelfox says, looking up now, like he hasn't been paying attention. 'Unlike my colleagues here I'm not wetting myself because you can play the bloody guitar – I could throw a stick down Hollywood Boulevard right now and hit ten people who can play the guitar like that. Playing an instrument doesn't necessarily make you a star. And that's what this show is about, finding a *star*. And look at you . . .' He stops, expecting some resistance at this point. But no, Jesus is standing there, just nodding, looking a little distracted. Dead air. Nervous laughter from the audience. 'Sorry,' Stelfox says, 'am I boring you, *Jesus*?' More laughter at the name, already becoming a running gag.

'Uh, kind of.' Jesus laughs, completely relaxed. The audience gasps and laughs harder.

'I'm boring *you*?' Stelfox says. 'Well, this is a first. Let's see if this bores you – yes, you can play the guitar, well done, yes, you can carry a tune and, yes, you're a good-looking guy, but I don't sense any star quality from you and I think your choice of material is lame in the extreme. Simon and Garfunkel? Please. So obvious.'

'Yeah? You know, I thought about maybe doing a little Hendrix? But the guys said –'

'Jimi Hendrix?' Stelfox says. 'Please, buskerville.'

'Ah, that's enough of that,' Jesus says, quietly but firmly.

'Excuse me?' Stelfox says.

'You heard me, big guy. Don't you be dissing Jimi now.'

Whoops and cheers from the audience, for they have never seen this before in the previous two seasons. People do stand up to Stelfox, but usually in a jaw-trembling, fists balled 'you're wrong about me' kind of way. Occasionally in a shouty, bitchy way, but never like this. Calm. Collected. The audience are not the only ones sensing something different.

Stelfox leans across the desk, eyeing Jesus. 'Some people might think I know a little something about finding talent,' he says. 'And, for me, it's a pass. Guys?'

'You're kidding, right?' Herb Stutz says. 'This has to be one of the most talented kids we've seen here.'

'Kids?' Stelfox says. 'Sorry, what age are you Jesus? I think you're . . .' He scrabbles at his notes.

'Thirty-one.'

'Hardly a kid then.'

'Who cares?' Stutz says. 'I'm sold. Darcy? Looks like you have the casting vote here.'

DeAngelo, who has been listening to this exchange while watching Jesus with a little smile on her face, looks from Stelfox to Stutz and shakes her head. 'I just it love when the boys argue. Jesus, you're working for me, baby. I say you're in!'

A huge cheer and applause going up, applause before the red 'APPLAUSE' signs have even lit up. From Jesus, no punching the air, no 'YES!', no leaping or crying. Just another barely perceptible nod.

'Dearie me,' Stelfox says, shaking his head. 'Well, which one of you is going to mentor the Good Lord here?'

Stutz and DeAngelo look at each other and she leans in whispering something in his ear, him nodding. 'Honestly, Steven?' Darcy says. 'The kind of music I think this boy's going to be doing? I think Herb's the best fit.'

'Herb?' Stelfox says. 'Your funeral.'

'Man,' Herb laughs, 'I'm gonna love proving you wrong on this one.'

'OK,' Stelfox says. 'Herb's going to mentor you. See you next week.'

'Right . . .' Jesus says uncertainly, nodding, cradling his Gibson.

As the audience continues to whoop and cheer and whistle, Jesus makes his way along the judges' table, shaking hands with each of them in turn. He comes to Stelfox last. The two men shake – Stelfox's grip cold, sub-zero, inhuman – and lock eyes for just a second: Stelfox looking into irises blue as cornflowers floating on the Pacific, Jesus in his turn looking into eyes as dark as space, a fathomless pit of nothingness, bats circling in the black wells of the pupils, falling down towards the vacuum of the soul.

Jesus shudders.

Stelfox feels something unusual too . . .

The general arc of the 'debate' about having Jesus on the show had, of course, been scripted. But something had not. Something Steven Stelfox is struggling to place as Jesus walks off and he runs a thumb under the collar of his black cashmere V-neck, feeling the release of some heat, feeling something he hasn't felt in a while, not since he'd been creator and ruler of the number-one-rated television show in America. The realisation was simultaneously exhilarating and unsettling.

He felt the presence of an adversary.

'And what the fuck is mentoring?' Jesus finally remembers to ask Becky later that day as they sit sipping daiquiris by the pool.

'You never watched the tapes?' Becky says.

Jesus shrugs helplessly. 'I tried, it's just, it's . . . so fucking horrible, man.'

'It's . . . Who's your mentor?'

'Uh, the big fat white guy? I have to meet him tomorrow.'

'Herb Stutz? Euch! Darcy's nicer. Anyway, they, like, help you pick songs and work out arrangements and stuff.'

'Why would I want some old douchebag picking songs for me?'

'It's what happens on the show.'

'Yeah, well, the show can kiss my ass.'

'Try and play nice, sweetie,' Becky says, standing up, looking good in her bikini, already getting a nice, even tan out here.

'It's just . . . why's it all have to be so competitive?' Jesus says sadly. Becky looks down at him. 'You're so sweet,' she says, kissing him on the forehead. She hovers there, close to his face, their eyelashes almost touching. He can feel her breath. If he stuck his tongue out it would touch her lips. Jesus reaches up and strokes her cheek. 'Look, Becky, I just . . . I'm not really in a commitment kind of place right now.'

'Ha,' she laughs, getting up, slapping him lightly. 'As if. Get over yourself, Mr TV Star.' He watches her swish off towards the pool, then a splash as Becky makes a neat dive into the deep end.

*

Later they all gather in the bungalow to watch the opening episode: beers, candy and popcorn piled high on the coffee table, even Gus and Dotty stretched out front and centre. Miles and Danny are excited, pumped up – 'You're gonna be on TV! – like none of it's been real for them until tonight. Everyone watches as *American Pop Star* sets out its stall: the twelve acts who had made the final cut, one of whom would be eliminated each week until only two remained for the finale in December.

Among the 'lowlights', as Morgan says, there is Ryan Crane: a chiselled white kid in white vest, also mentored by Herb Stutz.

There is Harmonix: a hard-dancing boy band composed of what appear to be four Ryan Cranes of slightly varying ethnic origin who perform hip-hop-tinged pop.

There is Laydeez Night: an all-girl trio who wear tiny costumes of fishnet and hot pants while they belt out raunchy R&B.

There is Garry MacDonald: the big, sweet black kid Jesus met at the taping, his huge voice thundering out of his huge frame. ('Filling out the freak quota,' Morgan whispers to Kris.)

Then there is Jennifer Benz: the tiny *Playboy* centrefold mentored by Stelfox himself, an all-American sweetheart possessed of a cut-glass voice with which she wrings every ounce of nuance out of a seemingly endless power ballad.

And then, suddenly, last of all, there is Jesus: huge on the plasma screen, eyes closed, blond hair falling over his face as he sings in front of the judges. They all scream and clap as Jesus groans and pulls his sweater up over his head.

Pete gasps and flattens a hand dramatically on his chest. 'The camera loves, loves, loves you!' he says.

'Yeah, looking good, man!' Kris says.

Then footage switches to Jesus' audition interview. 'Why do I want to be on the show? Uh, well, when I say I'm the son of

God –' laughter dubbed over this from the studio audience – 'I, um, I know how that sounds . . .'

'Uh-oh,' Morgan says.

'. . . but, unfortunately, it's true.' More laughter. 'You know, I came back here to try and help people, to try and inspire you guys to, you know, be nice. You all seem to have forgotten about that, which God, you know, God isn't too happy about. I think –'

He goes on, saying more, and then it cuts to a commercial.

'Well, you set your stall out,' Pete says.

'Do you think the guitar was a little out of tune?' JC asks Kris.

'You had to go and say all that, huh?' Morgan says. 'You know what you are now, don't you?'

'Morgs,' Becky says.

'You're the mental case who thinks he's the son of God.'

'Shut the fuck up, Morgs,' Kris says.

'It's OK, guys,' Jesus says. 'So?'

'You were the one who said he didn't want to go on this because it was just a freak show. You just became the biggest fucking freak on it. You're comedy relief.'

'We were talking for a while. I didn't know they'd use that bit.'

'You know,' Morgan says, getting up, 'for the son of fucking God you ain't that smart sometimes.' He walks through to the other room.

'Shit,' Jesus says. 'What's his problem?'

'He doesn't want people laughing at you,' Becky says.

'Oh, who cares?' Jesus says. 'It's only a TV show. Anyway, look I got my per diem from the studio today. Kids, you wanna go get some ice cream?'

About a half-hour later, standing in line at a Baskin Robbins on Melrose with Big Bob, Miles and Danny, Jesus found out who cared. Cars slowed, people shouting out nice things – 'Hey, Jesus! You rock!' – and mean things – 'Hey! Save me, you fucking freak!' 'Be nice!' Passers-by gasped and gawped. There were three autograph hunters, two photo requests and one threat of violence that terminated when the angry Christian realised Bob was part of the entourage.

'Shit,' Jesus says as they wait for a cab back to the hotel, Miles and Danny deep into their chocolate cones. 'People really do watch this shit, don't they?'

'Frag,' Bob says plaintively.

Steven Stelfox turns from the window of his living room thinking, tapping the snub black remote control against his teeth. Behind him, through the softly tinted glass that takes up the entire wall of the room, a stretch of Malibu sand, his personal stretch of Malibu sand, sparkles golden in the sun and, beyond it, the Pacific Ocean. Steven Spielberg is his closest neighbour, a half-mile along the beach.

He presses 'PLAY' and watches the interview again. The good-looking, though decidedly stoned, blond guy talking to an off-camera Samantha Jansen. 'I don't expect anyone to believe me really,' he's saying, 'I've just been getting on with things and trying to, uh, to help people in my own small way. Me and my buddies, Kris and Morgan? People seem to think Dad – God – is like this vengeful, wrathful guy who's gonna destroy them if they don't, like, totally worship him. And that's so wrong. I mean, He's definitely got a short fuse, but –'

Stelfox hits 'PAUSE': Jesus' face filling the sixty-inch plasma screen. Handsome motherfucker for sure. Good voice too, though Stelfox could really do without him scratching away at that electric fucking guitar. But, here was the thing: he seemed to completely believe what he was saying. So clearly he was utterly fucking mental. Could definitely be good for the freak quota, for adding viewers for a few weeks. The ideal contestant, Stelfox had come to believe, would probably be an attractive but crazed maniacal freak with the ultimate hard-luck story who actually had some talent. But it never worked out that way; they were usually nuts for a reason. The hard-luck story was usually well earned.

He walks through to his kitchen. It takes some time, this walk, and he passes modern art on the walls – a Warhol, a Damien Hirst, a Banksy. (Just a lowlife vandal the last one if you asked Steven. And a fucking lefty to boot. But the prices were going up and his dealer assured him it was 'a good thing'.)

In the kitchen – a seemingly endless expanse of Italian marble and vintage, reclaimed wood that had, according to the decorator (a triple-bent, simpering San-Fran fag, but the guy who was doing *everyone's* places right now), come from a nineteenth-century Quaker church somewhere in Massachusetts or some fucking place – it takes him a good minute to find one of the fridges (houseboy's day off) where he takes out a bottle of ice-cold Grey Goose, the vodka thick and viscous, right on the point of freezing as he pours it over ice and adds a strip of lime rind which the maid has already pre-sliced.

The good life. Here it was then.

The result of many years of, well, not sweat and tears. Blood certainly. Knives plunged in backs and fronts. False rumours propagated and stoked. Misinformation and dissembling and cover versions and making sure you could hear all the fucking words. Well on his way now towards being a billionaire, he sips his drink and looks at the glittering sea, at the pacific Pacific. *Everyone is going to pay*, he'd once said to himself, meaning it too. And now everyone was paying. The fucking *world* was paying. In ballads. He'd bump into some of the clowns from the old days now and then, when he was over in London. At the Groucho, at Mark Hix or Nobu. Derek, clinging on by his fingernails to the managing directorship of some filthy piece-of-shit indie back-catalogue label. Sweating about his fifteen-pence marketing spend on some reissued Stiff Little Fingers live album. Dunn, still – just – a plugger at what, fifty? Hanging in there somehow at EMI, still laughing at some cunt of a radio DJ's jokes as he tries to sell him on playing some disgraceful pop record. And here was the thing: no one bought records any more anyway. Rearranging the deckchairs on the *Titanic*? Fuck that – these cunts were trying to sell champagne at Belsen. Truffles at Auschwitz. No one cared. No one had any fucking money and – besides – they could get it all for free with the click of a mouse. How well he remembered those downloading conversations around the turn of the century: *'People are always going to want the whole album . . . you want the artwork and the packaging.'* Yeah, right, mate. Then you wake up five years later to find yourself starring in some horrible version of the fucking *Matrix*: a plug in the back of your dome and the machines are all talking to each other all round the world, giving each other all your hard work for free. For fuck all. You suggested paying for music to anyone under seventeen and they looked at you like you were fucking nuts. Quite right too, Stelfox reflects. The market did what it did. Don't come crying about it. All those clowns still running around trying to sell ten thousand albums forgot a powerful fundamental: *free is a pretty big fucking incentive*.

So no cunt bought records any more.

Except for his. It was too, too good.

Sipping, shuddering, he hits 'PLAY' and Jesus' face begins talking again, this time from a slightly smaller plasma screen suspended above the marble island in the middle of the kitchen, still answering the question 'Why do you want to be on the show?'

'. . . the reason I came back down here – well, got sent back down to tell you the truth, it wasn't exactly a comfortable ride the last time round – was to try and, you know, lead, inspire, help people, but that's pretty hard to do these days and –'

Yeah, Stelfox is thinking. This could definitely work. On a couple of levels this could work. He wouldn't want this indie *freak* – he is now disdainfully eyeing Jesus' Folk Implosion T-shirt – doing anything mental like actually *winning* the fucking show of course. But he could definitely fulfil a role.

Stelfox already knows who he wants to win this season. However, the show needed certain narrative strands, arcs, in order to work properly: triumph over adversity, comic relief, crap like that. It was constructed as carefully, plotted as finely, as a Hollywood blockbuster. The public, the *cunts* to use the technical term, sat out there and wondered how they pulled the rabbits out of the hat. All those A&R guys he used to work with, still, like the great man said, throwing darts at a fucking board.

Stelfox doesn't throw darts at a board any more.

He bets on sure things.

Freeze-frame on Jesus' face, looking right at the camera for a moment. Those eyes. Stelfox finds he cannot hold that gaze too long, even in two-dimensional form. Something about it bothers him.

Goodness. That was it.

The cunt was *riddled* with goodness.

3

N THE CONDITIONED AIR OF THE LIVE ROOM OF THE
studio off Ventura Boulevard, Herb Stutz – on
the sofa in chinos, Ralph Lauren shirt and Rolex
GMT – is listening to Pavement's 'Summer Babe'
while Jesus – stretched out on the floor in Levi's, Slint T-shirt
and plastic Casio – sings along softly, his eyes closed. The track
ends, leaving the air in front of the speakers shimmering, for JC
had the volume chest-suckingly loud, and there is silence for a
moment before Herb leans forward.

'Son,' he says, 'are you out of your fucking mind?'

'How can you not like that song, man?' Jesus says.

'Have you ever watched the goddamn show?'

'Ah . . .'

'How far you think you're gonna get with this kind of art-
rock, lo-fi bullshit? I mean, how many people do you think have
ever heard of this fucking band?'

'What's that got to do with anything?' Jesus asks, genuinely
confused.

'We gotta find material people know. That they like.'

'People like cheese straws. People like SUVs. People like the fucking show! We can't be trusting people, Herb.' Through the glass window to the control room the camera crew are filming, getting some shots of the mentoring process to cut into the show.

'Anyway, forget it,' Herb says. 'We'd never get it by Steven.'

'I thought we got to pick what songs I do?'

Herb laughing.

'Shit,' Jesus says. 'Well, what does he like?'

'Ballads. Steven likes ballads.'

'Oh, fuck all that.'

'We don't have to go totally down that route,' Herb says, moving over to the wall of black hi-fi equipment where he unplugs JC's iPod and plugs in his own. 'Reason he wants you on the show, other than . . . well, one of the reasons he wants you on the show is to do something rockier, something a little different.'

'Right, so how about –'

'I said a *little* different, kid. You ain't gonna be dusting off no fucking Sex Pistols B-sides so you might as well forget all that shit right now. We need something that rocks, that makes a statement about who you are, but something with a *monster fucking tune*.' Jesus smiles. It was kind of funny to know that people still talked like this. 'A song that millions of people will know. Not some dipshit indie nonsense that fourteen weirdos in the East Village are gonna love. Here, lemme play ya some stuff I figure is more in the ballpark . . .'

Jesus has spent worse hours – in prisons, hospitals, welfare offices – but not many. Herb plays 'Since You Been Gone' by Rainbow (*'Ahhh no, man! I fucking hate Ritchie Blackmore!'*), he plays 'Keep on Lovin' You' (*'Speedwagon? Are you fucking insane?'*), and he plays 'More Than a Feeling' (Jesus, grudgingly,

'It's a cool song, but come on, man. So obvious. Why don't I just sing 'My Country 'Tis of Thee?'). And so on and so on.

Much later Herb plays 'Don't Wanna Miss a Thing'.

'Fuck, Herb. If we're gonna do Aerosmith can't we at least do some *early* Aerosmith? Something off *Toys in the Attic* maybe?'

'You keep saying the wrong words, son. "Cool." "Early." "So obvious." You know who the core audience for the show is? Mom and Pop in Oklahoma and little kids. And lemme tell ya something, *'Mom and Pop and the little kids don't give a good fuck about cool and early or about shit being so fucking obvious!'* Herb sits back, frazzled. The balls on this kid. Who was he to –

Jesus sighs. 'Look, Herb, we can crack this. What we need is something cool and hip that makes a statement about "who I am", whatever the fuck that means, but which also sold millions of copies and every person sitting in front of a TV set will have heard of.'

'Oh yeah,' Herb says. 'Let's just draw up that list. I think I got the back of a fucking matchbook in my pocket.'

Silence for a while. Then Jesus starts grinning. He gets up, heads over to the stereo, plugging his iPod back in and wheeling the dial. Three minutes and thirty-nine seconds later Herb is smiling too.

'Huh?' Jesus says.

'Yeah. Maybe,' Herb says, chuckling. 'If we can get it by Steven.'

4

EEK TWO, THE SATURDAY AFTER LABOR DAY, THE number-one TV show in America going live. The menagerie all had tickets and here they were in the bleachers, wedged in among the great mass of Midwesterners who made up the studio audience, many of them wearing T-shirts and baseball caps with the names of the other studios whose tours they had undertaken earlier that day, making the most of their time in LA. The warm-up guy was finishing his act now, the theme music starting up, Jesus, sweating in the wings, cradling his guitar.

It had been a traumatic week, the first rehearsal week. When Jesus heard the studio orchestra playing his number for the first time he'd calmly taken his guitar off, leaned it feeding back against his amp, and walked off towards the dressing room. 'WILL SOMEONE PLEASE TURN THAT FUCKING GUITAR DOWN?!' Barry the conductor screamed, not for the first time.

Herb came shouldering into the dressing room after him. 'What the fuck is it now?'

'What the fuck, Herb? What's with all those strings and fucking keyboards? There's none of that shit on the record.'

'Come on, kid, we gotta sweeten it up some.'

'Why?'

'Listen.' Herb came over, closing the door behind him. 'We got twenty-eight of the best studio musicians in the country waiting around out there, some of 'em on double scale, and I have to take time out to argue with you about arrangements? Just do the fucking song, OK?'

'Uh-uh.'

'Oh man. If Steven gets word of this you are out of here so fucking fast.'

'There's guitar, bass and drums on the track. That's all it needs. Can't I just use my own guys? I could get Kris and Morgan up here and we could –'

'Are you fucking insane?' Herb splutters. 'You're pissing Barry off by the fucking minute, you want to change the arrangement and now you want your own fucking dipshit band up there with you? Get your fucking ass back up there and do the number as –'

'He keeps telling me to turn my guitar down. That guy Barry.'

'Listen, Mom and Pop in –'

'AHHGGH! If I hear about Mom and Pop in Oklahoma one more time, Herb!'

Herb sighed and leaned against the wall. This fucking kid. Week two and he'd given Herb more grief than he'd had in two seasons. But there was something . . . yeah, it was fair to say Herb liked the little fucker. The door opened and the inevitable girl with headphones and clipboard appeared. 'Herb, they need you guys out there. Now.'

'Yeah, yeah,' Herb said. 'Look,' he said, turning to JC as the door closed behind her, 'I'll talk to Barry and get the arrangement stripped back some, OK? But there's no way you're gonna get your own band up there. And watch it with the volume, huh? Lay off that overdrive pedal. This ain't CBGB's.'

'Thanks, Herb.'

'Yeah, yeah.'

Stelfox had surprised Herb by acceding to his suggestion for JC's opening number so readily. It was, in truth, exactly the kind of music Steven hated. But Stelfox, a great studier of demographic breakdowns, of audience composition surveys, of Nielsen ratings, had his reasons. He had a hunch. If he was wrong, well, he'd kick that ragged madman's indie ass out of here quick-style.

'PLEASE!' The warm-up guy's voice booms out of the studio speakers. 'A HUGE ROUND OF APPLAUSE for your host *KEVIN LEARY*!'

'Oh man,' Morgan whispers to Kris up in the bleachers, 'this is some showbiz shit right here.'

An explosion of light as Leary comes bounding down the neon staircase to crazy applause. 'Thank you, thank you,' he says as the whoops and cheers die down. 'Well, here we are again! Twelve hopefuls over the next ten weeks with you, the public, choosing who goes and who stays. But you will, of course, be receiving some expert guidance along the way from our panel of judges. Time to meet the judges?' Whoops and cheers. 'Shall we bring them out? Ladies and gentlemen, Miss Darcy DeAngelo!'

DeAngelo coming out, gold dress, hair flowing, plump, perfect teeth reflecting the insane wattage of lighting pouring down. 'Darcy, how you been?'

'Well, Kevin . . .'

'Damn,' Morgan whispers. 'How long does this shit go on for?'

'Shh,' Becky says.

Darcy babbles for a while and then Stutz comes out and babbles for a while and then Leary is saying, '. . . and the man they all dread, the most feared Englishman in the Western world, more acid than an acid bath, *Mr Steven Stelfox!*'

The audience goes nuts as Stelfox — black suit and black open-necked shirt — takes measured strides onto the stage, nodding almost shyly at the applause, generally doing a perfect impression of a reasonable human being. 'Steven,' Leary says, holding the mike out to him centre stage as the cheering fades away, 'looking forward to this season?'

'Very much so, Kevin.'

Stelfox is certainly looking forward to the coming season considerably more than Leary, whose attempted salary renegotiations had been terminated by Stelfox just a few days earlier with the words: *'Listen, you little cunt, we're not paying you a red fucking cent more and if you don't like it why don't you fuck off back to stand-up comedy and presenting some fucking breakfast show on Radio Arkansas or wherever the fuck you came from.'*

But Leary is a pro — he's managing to look at Stelfox with unadorned respect and affection as he says, 'There'll be some great acts, some not so great, and I'm sure some will be downright awful! We'll have a few surprises along the way, as I think you'll see from the first number tonight, and, at the end of the day, as always, it'll be you, the public, who decides.' He manages to say 'the public' as though they were the most precious words known to him.

'Thank you, Steven! The man himself!'

Stelfox walks off to take his seat at the long, logo-festooned desk with DeAngelo and Stutz.

'And so,' Leary continues, turning to the audience, 'without further ado, to open tonight's show, a guy who's already been causing some controversy – from New York City, it's Jesus!' The audience screaming as the house lights go down ('Oh fuck,' from Becky. 'Man, I'm gonna shit in my pants,' from Kris) and there is just black darkness for a second, then an icy, underwater blue light fades up along with a familiar, rippling guitar riff. 'No fucking way,' Kris says immediately as the stage lights come up full, the bass and drums rolling in softly, JC stepping to the mike and singing *'Come as you are . . .'* as spontaneous applause and whoops break out.

The audience clapping along, cheering as the first verse rolls on, the judges watching, scribbling notes, Herb nodding along proudly, Darcy grinning as always, even Stelfox smiling as, at 1.23 exactly, the song reaches the first chorus proper and Jesus, with the slightest grin as he thinks about Barry the conductor behind him, raises his foot over his forbidden overdrive pedal. The pedal is a vintage Ibanez Tube Screamer from 1984, one of the few items to have escaped the pawn store in recent weeks. It has the sacred D-9 chip in the circuit board, and its volume has been preset to maximum. Jesus' battered sneaker presses the metal pad down as he scrubs his plectrum all the way along the strings from bridge to nut and the Tube Screamer does what it does: it fills the studio with the sound of a 747 with a pair of cruise missiles strapped to it coming screaming down onto the tarmac. Jesus screaming now too, swearing that he don't have a gun as he *leans* into Cobain's guitar break, just a variant on the melody really, turning round to face the orchestra, urging the song forward. Barry's back is towards Jesus as he waves his baton in a braking fashion, trying to slow the tempo, but the drummer's into it, he and Jesus exchanging a grin as one lays into the hi-hat harder and harder, the other wringing the notes out of the guitar, close to his amp now, which is breaking up, on the verge of feeding back, the rest of the orchestra confused and panicking, trying to run with this altered script.

Barely a couple of minutes after that and Jesus is standing facing the judges, sweating a little as the applause dies down. It's been confused applause for sure: some sections of the audience – the menagerie included of course – going unreservedly nuts while others, the older, theme-park shirt-wearing contingents, are still scrubbing their pinkies in their ears, shaking their heads and shouting 'What?' at their neighbours.

'Boy, was that loud!' Darcy begins. Herb is giving Jesus a thumbs up with both hands.

'So,' Stelfox begins. 'Nirvana? I think that's a first for the show . . . and hopefully a last.'

'Oh, get outta here, Steven!' Herb responds. 'Kid nailed it.'

'It's . . .' Stelfox tails off, seemingly lost for words. 'The whole grunge thing, I mean, really, who cares?'

'Hey,' Herb counters. 'That's a great song. That album sold, like twenty million copies, you're not telling me no one cares?'

'Yeah, about twenty years ago it sold millions. The song's not terrible,' Stelfox allows, 'and I think there's a decent version to be done of it. But that wasn't it.'

'Ah,' Jesus says. 'What didn't you like about it?'

'Too sloppy. Too amateur hour. I mean, the whole thing sped up about halfway through!'

'Hey – all rock and roll speeds up,' Jesus says, as though any moron knew this to be true.

'Darcy?' Stelfox asks.

'I think you've got an amazing presence about you,' she begins, 'you play amazing guitar, but your material isn't really my kind of thing. So I'm afraid, for me, it's a pass. Sorry.'

'Hey, don't worry about it,' Jesus says over some sympathetic oohs and aahs from the audience.

'Well, we know where Herb stands,' Stelfox says, 'so I guess it's down to me whether we put you to the public vote or not.' He pauses dramatically, tapping his pen on his pad. Jesus standing there, nonchalant, his weight on one foot, the unplugged Gibson dangling by his side. 'Against my better judgement,' Stelfox begins, 'I'm going to put you through to next week. But —' whooping and cheering — 'but, and I can't stress this enough, you'll have to be a lot more discerning about your song choices and arrangements if you're going to progress very far in this show.'

Herb laughs. 'You try talking to this kid!'

'Have you any idea,' Stelfox says, turning back to Jesus, 'how much experience this guy has?' He jabs his pen in Herb's direction. 'How many multi-platinum artists he's worked with? If you want to stand a chance against the calibre of talent we have here, you'll really need to start listening to your mentor.'

'Hey,' Jesus says, 'I like Herb. He's a cool guy but . . . neh.'

The audience cracks up as Herb shrugs in what-can-you-do? fashion.

5

HIS SHOW AND THE EVENTS LEADING UP TO IT establish a pattern for the following weeks: Jesus and Herb scream at each other for a day or two about which song he's going to do before they manage to reach a compromise. (In weeks three and four he plays Blur's 'Song 2' and a lead-guitar-sodden version of Prince's 'Purple Rain', mining the thin seam of songs deemed commercially acceptable by Herb – or, rather, by Stelfox – and 'cool' enough for Jesus to countenance, who goes on lobbying futilely for tracks by everyone from Sebadoh to Joy Division.) Once the song has been agreed then the arguments about arrangements and orchestration begin with Barry, who has quickly grown to loathe Jesus with an unreserved passion. On each show there is then a face-off between Jesus and Stelfox with Herb in JC's corner and Darcy as a floating voter. So far, so scripted: Stelfox had decreed that Jesus is not allowed to face the public vote until week five, which is the first show after ABN will receive solid Neilsen ratings data for the first month of the new season. The boss is keen to test his theory, his hunch.

In the meantime Jesus is becoming, well . . . a celebrity.

The catcalls and high fives in the street increasing.

The well-wishers stopping by the table when they're all sitting poolside at the Chateau.

The steady stream of autograph hunters when they go out to the movies, or to eat, or to take a stroll at night.

Stelfox is in his office when Samathan Jansen knocks at the door, the sheaf of new ratings data tucked under her arm.

'Well?' he says.

'It's off the fucking scale, Steven. I mean, I didn't think the show could get much bigger,' she says, handing him the graphs and stats. 'We're up nearly three points on this time last season. It's incredible. They're screaming with joy down in the advertising department.'

'You know, Sam,' Stelfox says, yawning and swinging his two-thousand-dollar Lobb shoes up onto the desk as he stretches out to savour those sweet, sweet figures, 'it actually almost gets boring being so fucking right all the time.'

'What I don't get,' Sam says, flopping down on the colossal leather sofa in the corner, underneath a quadruple platinum sales disc for an album by an act called Songbirds, a girl group she knows Steven was involved with back in the nineties, when she was still at Stanford, 'is who are we picking up? I mean our stats were already off the chart for last season.'

'It's obvious,' Stelfox says, tossing the Neilsens aside, 'and, by the way, tell Al I want a bunch of new demographics commissioned to confirm this. Just think. Who *wasn't* watching the show until now?'

'Eskimos?' she says. 'Itinerant gypsies? Amazonian tribespeople?'

'The fucking indie kids,' Stelfox says, grinning. 'All those dickless, vegetarian, too-cool-for-school *cunts* who'd rather have raped a fucking Alsatian dog than watch the show? Well, they're watching it now. Why wouldn't they? There's one of their own on there . . .'

6

SHOW FIVE, THE SHOW WHERE ALL CONTESTANTS must perform a Beatles song of their choosing, is where it all comes off the rails.

Darcy and Stelfox are unconvinced by Jesus' version of 'Come Together'. (It had been a long, heated argument with Herb about why he couldn't do 'Helter Skelter'.) The other offering considered to be the weakest that night is Ryan Crane's NutraSweet take on 'With a Little Help from My Friends', which is pronounced too bland and artificial even for Stelfox's tastes. As Stelfox had outlined in his pre-show run-through with the judges, Jesus and Ryan would be put to the public vote. He was confident enough in his theory after the Neilsens that Crane would be the one going home.

Crane and Jesus, standing in front of the judges now, criminals in the dock as their cases are discussed, the usual banalities like 'presence', 'star quality', 'originality' and 'impact' getting thrown around between Stelfox, Darcy and Stutz. 'Well, I think you're both fantastic performers but the thing I'd like to know,' Darcy says, looking up at the two contestants, 'is why do you want this? How badly do you want it? Do you want to go all the way?'

'Uh, all the way where?' Jesus says.

'Darcy,' Crane says, cutting him off, 'I give one hundred and ten per cent every time out there.' He points dramatically towards the sacred space of the stage behind him. 'I believe God chooses our paths for us and –'

'Well,' Stelfox says, cutting in, 'I think you'll find Jesus here probably believes that too . . .' A few giggles from the audience.

'Ah, no. Not at all,' Jesus cuts in. 'Matter of fact, God hates that kind of nonsense.'

'Excuse me?' Crane says, turning to look at JC for the first time.

Oh God, don't get into this, Becky thinks, sitting there in the bleachers. *Not now. On live TV.*

'That whole idea of preordained destiny, the hand-of-God-guiding-you bull— ah, rubbish. It gets used by everyone from serial killers to tyrants and dictators. God gave you the whole free-will thing, so you know, do what thou will and all that.'

'Oh, so we can just do what we like?' Crane says.

'Well, up to a point. I mean, you need to be remember the one big rule.'

'And what's that?'

'Just . . . be nice.'

'You know,' Crane says, his jaw set as he turns fully to face Jesus, 'speaking as a Roman Catholic I find you using the stage name Jesus –'

'Catholic, huh?' Jesus says, the only person in the studio whose pulse is still completely normal at this point. 'How about that Pope of yours? You know he refused to sign a UN declaration acknowledging the rights of homosexuals and the disabled? The dude's practically a Holocaust denier too. He –'

Panic in the control room now. Harry the director screaming into earpieces – 'Get them offa this! Christ!'

Gasps from the studio audience as Stelfox tries to regain control. 'Right, guys, that's enough. I think –'

'The . . . the Holy Father –' Crane is trying to say as Jesus keeps on going with the chapter and verse about the Pope.

'– punished known paedophiles in the Catholic Church by sentencing them to a "period of penitence". I mean, he didn't like *fire* them or anything. Hell, half the time they'd get moved to other parishes where they could just start again! But then this is the same Pope who had the giant, hairy balls to go to Africa and tell them that using condoms could actually *increase* the spread of Aids –'

'How dare you –' Crane, going red-faced now.

All across America people reaching for their telephones, fury going long distance, the ABN switchboard lighting up like the Fourth of July.

'To get back to the music –' Darcy is saying.

'– member of the Hitler Youth. An anti-Semitic, homo-phobic –' Jesus is saying.

'I FIND YOUR REMARKS TOTALLY OFFENSIVE!' Crane finally explodes.

'Hey, then forgive me,' Jesus says as they cut to a commercial. 'You're the Christian.'

7

AY CLANCY IS A BIG MAN. SIX FOUR, A FORMER varsity linebacker, Clancy was born of good Catholic stock and went the traditional route: prep school, Princeton, ABN, becoming President of Standards and Practices by the age of thirty-two. It is a position he has held for nearly twenty years. In those twenty years as one of the most senior executives at ABN there has not been a live television exchange that has angered him as much as the one he has just witnessed.

'THIS IS SUPPOSED TO BE A GODDAMNED LIGHT-ENTERTAINMENT SHOW!' Clancy screams, pacing behind his desk, Stelfox, Jansen and Harry sitting across from him. 'WHAT THE FUCK IS GOING ON THAT THERE'S THESE COCKSUCKERS ARGUING ABOUT RELIGION ON THERE?'

'I . . . it just got out of hand so quickly. I'm sorry but live TV, sometimes —' Harry is saying.

'Mr Clancy, sir, the contestants are told —' Sam begins.

'I MEAN, WHAT WERE YOU THINKING, HAVING

A KID LIKE THIS ON THE SHOW?'

'Oh, please stop shouting,' Stelfox says. 'You're giving me a bloody headache.'

Clancy looks at him, astonished, and takes a moment to gather himself. 'Now you listen to me,' he begins slowly, 'who the fuck do you think you're talking to? You fucking arrogant English son of a bitch. That kid is off the show.'

'What's the big deal?' Stelfox says, looking around, genuinely struggling to get his English, atheist head around the American hot-button response to all things religious.

'The big deal? That little bastard just insulted the Holy Father live on TV and you're asking me what's the big deal?'

'Christ, who cares?'

'Mr Stelfox,' Clancy says, collecting himself, becoming formal, 'this is not a debate. I will not risk the potential offence caused to our viewers and stockholders by having that kid on the show. He's gone. Next week.'

'You know what percentage of the public vote he got tonight?' Stelfox says. 'Ninety-two. Guys, have we ever had someone take that kind of vote share this early in the season?'

Harry and Samantha both shake their heads.

'You're not listening to me,' Clancy says.

'Finally, something we agree on,' Stelfox says. 'Look, this kid is pushing our stats through the roof. Advertising revenue is up over 10 per cent already. He stays on.'

Clancy, looking at Stelfox with arctic fury now, gripping the edge of his desk. 'Who the fuck do you think –' he begins.

'Oh, fuck off, Ray,' Stelfox says.

Jansen closes her eyes.

'What did you just say to me?'

'I said fuck off,' Stelfox says, raising himself up out of the chair now. 'But perhaps I should amplify that – FUCK OFF,

YOU CUNT! YOU FAT, STUPID, *OLD* CUNT! ARE YOU OUT OF YOUR FUCKING MIND?!' Stelfox starts big and steps it up, his mega-fury quickly making Clancy's outburst sound like a three-year-old in the supermarket. *'LET ME SPELL IT OUT FOR YOU: I OWN THIS FUCKING SHOW! MY CONTRACT IS UP AT THE END OF THIS SEASON AND IF YOU SAY ONE MORE FUCKING WORD TO ME – JUST ONE – I AM WALKING ACROSS THE ROAD AND TAKING THE WHOLE FUCKING THING TO NBC OR FOX AND YOU CAN WALK UPSTAIRS TO FRED'S OFFICE AND EXPLAIN TO HIM HOW YOU JUST LOST THE NUMBER-ONE-RATED TV SHOW IN AMERICA!'*

Italics, upper case, bold, underlined: all of these combined cannot do justice to the ferocity of this outburst.

Humming silence as Stelfox sits back down, completely calm now. Harry and Sam stare at him open-mouthed.

'Oh I'll be talking to Fred about this, you conceited little motherfucker,' Clancy says, trembling.

The next day, in a Heads of Department lunch meeting (sushi, catered) in Fred's basketball-court-sized office on the seventh floor, Ray Clancy is saying, 'It's outrageous, Fred. You know what that Limey piece of shit called me? I mean, I know their numbers are good, but Jesus Christ, the Holy Father? Sometimes there's more important things in life than ratings. Am I right?'

Old Fred, nodding and chewing.

Later that evening, in the best booth at Dan Tana's, front room, corner, left-hand wall, Steven Stelfox, over a two-hundred-dollar bottle of red wine and a rare New York strip steak, is saying, 'I'll give the little bastard a slap, keep him in line. But

Fred, with this kid, three million dollars for a thirty-second ad spot during the finale? Totally achievable. Bigger than the fucking Super Bowl.'

Old Fred, nodding and chewing.

From the front cover of the following week's *Variety*:

RELIGION ROW PROPELS *AMERICAN POP STAR* TO RECORD VIEWING FIGURES!

From page 3 of the same edition:

CLANCY OUT AT ABN!

It was confirmed on Monday that ABN's long-serving S&P President will be leaving the network to pursue other opportunities. 'We wish Ray every success in the future', says ABN Chairman Fred Goodman.

A few days later Herb and Jesus get ushered into Stelfox's office: gold discs, chrome and leather, oatmeal carpeting and three advertising executives hunkered round the boss's desk. Stelfox claps his hands together. 'Hey! It's Jesus – the indie kid!' He cries to laughter from the ad people. Jesus smiles tolerantly. It is the first time he has been asked in for a one-on-one with the great man. 'Give us a minute, guys,' Stelfox says to the trio of suits.

'I loved your Prince cover last week,' one of them, a girl, says to Jesus as she leaves.

'Herb, Jesus, take a seat,' Stelfox says as the door closes. 'Well, we came out of this OK. Thank fuck. Actually did me a favour in terms of getting rid of that fucking fossil Clancy. And a little controversy never hurt anything, but listen – I will not tolerate the show being used a platform for your half-arsed views on whatever. Save the Whale, the fucking Pope, God, whatever.'

'I told him,' Herb says.

'But what am I meant to say?' Jesus says. 'Some guy comes out with –'

'Listen, mate,' Stelfox says, cutting him off, 'here's what you do. You stand there and smile your pretty smile and bat those big blue eyes and say "God bless America" and sing your little song and shake your tush for the people at home and you *shut the fuck up with your two cents.'*

Jesus sighs and runs his eyes over the gold discs on the wall. 'Wow,' he says. 'You sure have been involved in a lot of lame-assed music, huh?'

Stelfox laughs at the audacity. 'Look, cunt,' he says, 'what you don't know about music would need its own fucking series. So go back to the hotel – and by the way, why am I looking at a fucking room-service bill from the Chateau for over ten thousand dollars?'

'Ah,' Jesus says.

'You're taking the fucking piss. In the unlikely event I pick up your recording contract at the end of the season I'm deducting every shrimp fucking cocktail and Bloody Mary from your advance. So, go back to the hotel and listen to your fucking B-sides, jerk off to Tom Verlaine's fucking guitar solos, piss and moan to your loser friends about the state of the world, do whatever the fuck freaks like you do in lieu of a life, and then show up for rehearsals with a fucking big smile on your face and without a thought in your head. Or you will be off this show so fucking fast you won't fucking believe it.' Stelfox pauses, then, as an afterthought, adds, 'You fucking cunt.'

'Uh. I thought the public had to vote me off?'

Stelfox laughs, harder this time, his head thrown back to display gleaming, perfect teeth; one of the first things he'd had done when he moved out here and started making some unreal money, instead of the real stuff he'd been making back in London. 'Christ,' Stelfox says, 'you're thirty-fucking-one too. You don't even have the excuse of youth. The public? Those *animals*? Do me a fucking favour. Look, I like the indie shtick, OK? The whole "I mean it, man" crap? It's working, it's adding viewers. The unwashed fuckwits who weren't watching the show? They're watching it now. Cos of you. But get with the programme and keep your half-baked opinions on world events to yourself. Keep your mouth shut during the interview stuff or you're gone. With me?'

'Sure,' Jesus says, smiling pleasantly.

'We hear you,' Herb says, standing to leave, Jesus doing likewise.

'Good. Thanks, Herb. Actually, you can go. I just want a quick word with our saviour here.'

'OK . . .' Herb says as Jesus lowers himself back into the chair.

When the door has closed behind Herb, Stelfox comes around the desk, perches on the edge of it and says, 'So let's talk seriously.'

'Uh, about what?'

'About you. What do you want out of all this?'

'Ah . . . a way to help people? To try and show them a better way to live?'

'Yeah, yeah.' Stelfox waves a hand airily. 'Hug a whale, save the fucking tofu forests, I get it. I mean, what do you want out of this musically? *Financially.*' To Stelfox these were, of course, the same thing.

'Ah, I guess maybe to make a record with my band again. Kris and Morgan? Get out on the road and play a few shows.'

'Fuck me,' Stelfox says. 'Listen – fuck all that. Would I make
a record with your poxy band after all this? Probably. If I had
to then, yeah, we could make some lame dipshit indie record
and probably go gold just on the back of the show. You could
tour and play to a couple of thousand cunts in major cities.
Or . . .'

'Or?'

'You go solo, dump the clowns and we do a record of cover
versions. I pick the songs and you listen to me on the marketing
and promotion and we make twenty or thirty *million fucking
dollars*. Look, think about it. You want to go off and help
penniless spastics, yeah?'

'Well, that's not how I'd –'

'Whatever. Go my way on this and you'll have enough dough
to open all the fucking soup kitchens you want.'

'Right. But, er, aren't you already worth like three hundred
million?' Herb had mentioned this figure.

'Four hundred,' Stelfox corrects him.

'So what's the difference?'

'Excuse me?' Stelfox – genuinely confused.

'What's the difference between four hundred million and
four hundred and thirty million?'

Stelfox looks at him like he's insane. 'Thirty million dollars,'
he says.

8

HE WEEKS PASSING, THE WEATHER, EVEN HERE IN LA, growing crisper as November runs out and suddenly Christmas is on the horizon, his birthday coming up.

Through the fall and into winter – the ratings rising and headlines accumulating as one by one the hopefuls slip away: Harmonix are voted off following a badly essayed hip-hop-tinged version of Cyndi Lauper's 'Time After Time'. Laydeez Night go out when one of them goes 'ghetto' on Stelfox during a frank exchange of views regarding their cover of Beyoncé's 'Crazy In Love'.

Out there in America, there are three distinct camps voting for Jesus. The indie kids, who are watching and voting despite themselves, knowing the show is a pile of garbage that represents everything they hate but buying into the relationship Stelfox has masterfully crafted between himself and Jesus, that he personally hates the kind of music Jesus represents and everything he stands for. Then there's the ordinary viewers, who care less about the songs Jesus is performing but who are loving the tension, the fights between Stelfox and this straggly, scruffy lunatic who thinks he's the son of God. Then there's the gay vote, a huge and loyal block who steamed in en masse after the Pope/Aids/homosexuality incident.

Every day at the Chateau Marmont messages are piling up in JC's pigeonhole: soft-drinks companies, guitar manufacturers, clothing companies, airlines, candy-bar people . . . all wanting him to lend his name to their products. TV shows, magazines, newspapers and websites all clamouring for interviews. Piles of screenplays for his consideration. Agents and management companies are sending over fruit baskets and magnums of champagne, which prompts Kris to say at one point, 'Man, can't they send something useful? Like socks or something?'

'Whoa, dude,' Morgan says. 'You wanted a platform? We got one now, baby.'

Sunday brunch with the menagerie by the pool has become a tradition. In the first few weeks they'd go out and find a diner somewhere – Miles and Danny were big fans of Ray's Drive-In just along the road on Sunset – but recently it has become nigh on impossible to leave the sanctuary of the hotel: the fans and the haters. The handshakes and extended camera phones and the insults and catcalls.

'Yeah,' Morgan says, shaking ketchup onto a Denver omelette, 'what exactly is the plan? Two months of this shit now. You're famous enough we could start getting some decent gigs. Get out there and start playing ourselves again.'

'Is this,' Pete begins carefully, 'because you know they won't let you guys play with him on the show?'

'Shit, I don't care about that,' Morgan says. 'Think I want to be on the stupid fucking show?'

'I think you could bottle it,' Becky says.

'Fuck you,' Morgan says.

'Look,' Jesus says, digging through his oatmeal, looking for a blueberry, 'I just need to hang in there a little longer.' He sits back, putting the spoon down, popping that soft blueberry against the roof of his mouth and thinking, *Dad, you do good work*. He looks around the table at everyone. 'I had, like, a vision the other night . . .' he says, embarrassed at how lame it sounds.

'Man,' Morgan groans. 'What – a vision that told you to stay on the show as long as you can so you can kick it at the Chateau and get recognised in the street? Yeah, that's real visionary.'

'What's your problem, man?' Kris says.

'Nothing. Fuck!' Morgs throws his serviette down and pushes away from the table. 'Since when couldn't you say shit around the big pop star?'

'Frag!' Bob says, annoyed.

The night before, sleeping on some cushions in the corner of the big bedroom, Kris's snoring coming from the chaise longue, Becky and the kids in the bed, he'd heard the *pssschhtttt* of a bottle being opened and had rolled over to see Him crouching there in the amber half-light of the minibar, a frosty Coke in His hand.

'Hi, Dad,' Jesus said, his voice thick with sleep.

'Ten dollars for a fucking soda?' God whispered, coming over and sinking into an easy chair by his son's makeshift bed. 'World's off its tits.' He was wearing golfing gear: chinos, polo shirt, his old sweat-stained visor.

'How you been?' Jesus asked, propping himself up on an elbow, the only light in the room the soft blue pool glow coming in through the drapes from the patio.

'Can't complain, son, shot a seventy-three the other day.'

'Wow.'

'Yeah, not bad at my age, huh?' God took a long pull on the Coke and let out a satisfied burp.

'So,' Jesus said, 'what do you think?'

'Well,' God said, looking around the dark room at the sleeping figures, 'it's probably not the way I'd have gone. But, at the same time, I guess you had to adapt. You're closer than you think, you know.'

'Huh?'

'I know you're hating this whole thing, and shit, I can see why. I mean, those Harmonix guys doing that Beatles medley the other week? Shit. You should have seen John.'

'I bet.'

'And if I hear one more of those little cocksuckers thanking me or mentioning my fucking name . . . Anyway, you're on the right track, son. Hang in there. Cos you're gonna need money. Ten dollars for a fucking soda? Everything's money down here. Not crazy money, by the way. But a chunk.'

'Dad, please, less of the cryptic. What do I need this money for?'

'It's a *vision*. Needs to be cryptic. Think wide-open spaces.'

'Wide-open spaces?'

'Think – *if you build it, they will come*.'

'Aw, get fucked, Dad. That movie sucked.'

God laughing, 'It sure did, didn't it? Right, look, I got to run. I was thinking about appearing in a tub of ice cream or a rock or something in Mexico or Ireland or somewhere on my way back up. Fuck with the goddamn Catholics. Always a hoot.'

'Wide-open spaces, huh?'

'Yep.' God drained the Coke and set the bottle down. 'C'mere, you little bastard.' God roughly scrubbed His son's hair as He pulled him in for a hug, kissing the top of his head and getting in a quick, playful punch on the kid's arm too, Jesus foot flailing out from under the blankets, trying to kick his dad in the nuts. Boy he missed roughhousing with the old man. (*'Never trust a father and son who don't try and kick the shit out of each other for fun now and then,'* his dad had told him once.) 'Shh,' God said. 'Quit fucking around. People trying to sleep. OK, I'll see you, son. Get back to sleep. And be nice, OK?'

'Yeah, yeah.'

'Oh, you got any grass?'

'Ah, in the ashtray there.'

God fished the long, half-smoked Thai stick out of the ashtray and ran it under His nose. 'Sweet,' He said. 'Later, son.'

'Bye.'

God floated up into the ceiling and vanished and Jesus rolled over and went back to sleep.

Jesus sits back, stirring his coffee, and looks around the table, all of them staring at him.

'Wide-open spaces?' Becky says. 'What does that mean?'

'Fucked if I know,' Jesus says. 'These things usually become clearer later. You know, you see something and it makes you think "oh, right".'

'Ah, JC,' Claude says. 'Does God really curse like that?'

9

EEK ELEVEN, THE PENULTIMATE SHOW, JUST THREE acts left and only one is outperforming Jesus with the public.

Jennifer Benz – America's sweetheart.

Mentored by Stelfox himself, Jennifer has floated through the competition, propelled effortlessly forward by her tumbling blonde hair, her curves, her alabaster teeth, her tastefully revealing outfits (a length of brown thigh here, firm tanned cleavage there) and a succession of perfectly executed ballads.

Carey.

Houston.

Dion.

Stelfox's holy trinity.

As JC saw it – and this is someone who can find something to like in just about anyone – the only problem with Jennifer was that she made a Playboy bunny look like a model of feminist assertiveness. Her parents – a living, breathing Ralph Lauren ad – shepherded her everywhere and Jesus didn't think he'd once heard her answer a question directed at her. In wardrobe (a department that had long given up trying to do anything with Jesus) it would be: *'Jennifer, you want to wear the cream gown with the aqua brocade?' 'No,'* Jennifer's mom would say, *'the champagne with the ivory trim.'* Or in catering: *'Some potatoes?' 'Just salad,'* Dad would reply.

'Poor bitch isn't a daughter so much as a racehorse,' Becky said.

Garry MacDonald's still in there too. The big kid's not getting the freak vote predicted by Kris so much as the sympathy vote: every week in the early stages of the season a segment of the show was devoted to telling a little of each performer's backstory and Garry's – with the clapboard house in New Orleans, the little brothers and sisters, the struggling welfare mom – had proved compelling. (Especially when set against the Republican Party recruiting film that told the story of life with the Benzes: the impeccably dressed family touring the leafy grounds of their Westchester home, standing on the slopes at Aspen, playing volleyball on the beach at Malibu, 'we're very fortunate people etc.', and which served a different viewer function: *'Aspirational,'* Stelfox said. 'Give the cunts at home something to make them feel better about themselves and also something to look up to.') Garry had a sweet, shy presence and great pipes; a big, strong soul voice, bell-clear and nimble in the upper registers in an Aaron Neville kind of way, though Jesus and the guys lamented the choice of material Darcy DeAngelo was feeding the kid. Stelfox-friendly ballads and saccharine pop songs. 'Man,' Morgan said one week, watching Garry tremble through 'Money's Too Tight to Mention' (many of his numbers obviously being lamely chosen to tie into his domestic situation), 'you'd love to hear this kid cut loose on something with some fucking balls, huh?'

'Tonight, only three remain.' The announcer's voice, solemn

as it thunders through the Burbank studio, sombre as it comes out of TV speakers across the country. 'Tonight it's time for you to decide who the finalists will be. Tonight, live from Hollywood, California, it's . . . *American Pop Star*!'

Boy, Jesus thinks, coming down the narrow backstage hallway – threading between the hurrying technicians, being careful to keep the neck of his guitar up and out of the way so it won't get knocked and detuned, a little five-watt Fender practice amp in his other hand – listening to the guy's voice coming out of the speakers mounted all along the walls, you'd think he was announcing the end of the goddamn world.

'Hey, shouldn't you be in make-up?' a passing headset and clipboard says to him.

'Yeah, yeah.'

He reaches the end, makes a left and knocks on the blue door. 'Come in,' a muffled voice says.

Jesus ducks into the dressing room to see the family MacDonald getting ready to take their leave: Mom and all those little brothers and sisters. 'Hey, Garry, what's up?'

'Hi, JC. This is my family.'

'Pleased to meet you, kids . . . Mrs MacDonald,' Jesus, grinning at the kids, shaking hands with Garry's mom, who takes his hand suspiciously.

'So you the one thinks he's the son of God?'

'Ah, yes, ma'am.'

'Son – you for real?'

'Afraid so.'

She holds his eyes for a moment. 'Mmm-hmmm.' Then, turning back to Garry, kissing him on the cheek, she says, 'Good luck tonight, son. You just do your best now.'

'Yeah, Momma.'

'And don't be eating all them sandwiches, you hear?' She

gestures to the tray of cold cuts on the counter. 'Just cos they here don' mean you have to eat 'em all.'

'Yeah, Momma.'

'Well, all right then.'

She ushers the kids out, Jesus closing the door behind them and saying to Garry, 'Look, man, would you help me out with something tonight?'

Jesus runs through the song, his guitar plugged into the little practice amp.

'Man, I don't know, JC,' Garry says. 'We ain't meant to do nothing like that. We could get in trouble.'

'What trouble? Come on, what's the worst could happen?'

'Get thrown off the show. I know you don't care, but I need this, man.'

'They can't throw us off live on air for something like this. Trust me – the folks at home will love it. You need to do something like this. What's up – you don't like the song?'

'I love the song, man. I been wanting to do something more like that. Darcy won't let me.'

'Darcy. Fuck Darcy. Come on, dude, this'll give people a chance to see you really cutting loose on something good for a change.'

'Shit, I dunno, man.'

'Garry, trust me.' Garry looking into those big, luminous eyes.

'Five minutes until showtime . . .' The voice coming metallic through the speaker on the wall. *'Would all contestants . . .'*

Something in the man's eyes, Garry thinks. He'd heard about the phrase 'leadership qualities' one time. On a form at school, before graduation, that you had to fill in so they could figure out what job you might be best at. They'd told Garry 'auto mechanic'. Garry hated cars. But JC, standing right here, one foot up on his little amp, grinning at you like nothing bad could ever happen so long as you stuck with him . . . Garry believing it too.

'Shit, OK, man.'

'Attaboy. What verse?' Jesus handing him the sheaf of lyrics he's scribbled down.

'Second one?'

'That's what I was thinking,' Jesus says, turning the volume on the guitar up with his right pinkie. 'OK, quick let's run through it.'

Garry kicked the evening off with a horrific version of 'An Innocent Man' by Billy Joel, a song chosen by Darcy as being representative of his demeanour and underdog status on the show but which was, as Morgan pointed out, 'just representative of a song that really sucks fucking ass'. Jennifer Benz, sparkling sequinned in the spotlight, is on now doing a *huge* arrangement of 'Don't Stop Believing'. Garry and Jesus watching from the wings, close to a hundred million viewers watching at home, one of the biggest TV audiences in recent American history.

Tonight is a theme night. They'd had one a few shows back (Motown) but tonight's is broader, looser: 'Classic American Artists'. Well, 'Classic American Artists' as defined by Steven Stelfox. Jesus had frowned his way down the short, one-page list, his tone of voice hopping between disbelief and outrage – 'Michael Jackson . . . Billy Joel . . . *Journey*? You gotta be fucking kidding me, Herb?' – until, and almost at the last name on it, he'd started nodding. One name he could run with. 'And it can't be no obscure, early-album track,' Herb reminded him.

Benz is bowing now as the strings scrape and whirl to a crescendo, the studio audience erupting into applause, screams and whistles.

'How about that?' Kevin Leary is yelling as he bounds onto the stage. Benz flounces by Jesus and Garry, a light sheen of sweat on her brow and a 'follow that' look on her face, and into the arms of her parents behind them. 'You stumbled a little on the bridge,' Jesus hears her father say to her, then he is tuning back into Leary saying, '. . . he's caused some controversy on this show, but a lot of you love him because he's still here, it's –'

'Meet you in the middle, baby,' Jesus whispers to Garry, giving him a quick pat on the back as he runs out into the spotlight and the applause.

'And what you got for us tonight?' Leary has his arm around Jesus, buddy-style.

'Well, Kevin, I guess you could say it's kind of the, uh, the unofficial American national anthem . . .'

'Mysterious as ever. Ladies and gentlemen, let's hear it for Jes—'

Before Leary can even get the name out, before his hand is even off his shoulder, JC's running back towards the orchestra, pumped up, actually looking forward to playing with the house band on this one because, for once, the song suits, fucking *needs*, a full arrangement, three guitars, piano, organ and everything from glockenspiel to goddamn triangle. So pumped up he's jumping onto the drum riser, cutting off an astonished, enraged Barry who just stands there, baton poised, as Jesus screams *'ONE TWO THREE FOUR!'* into the drummer's face and, incredibly, the whole orchestra gets it and crashes in as one right on the 'FOUR!' – a massive *WHUMP* of sound – Jesus twanging that Duane Eddy guitar riff over the top of everything before he turns and leaps ten feet in the air, scissor-kicking back over the head of the piano player as the audience screams and flashbulbs pop in the photography pit, grabbing the image that will be in every single newspaper the following day – Jesus in mid-air scissor-kick, the piano player open-mouthed and looking up at him – and Jesus somehow making it to the mike just as the band launches into a soaring, deafening 'Born to Run', hitting the opening line right on cue, singing that line about how, by day, folks sweat it out on them streets, as the studio audience spontaneously rises to its feet, people yelling out, punching the air, people at home yelling at friends and family to get in here and see this pure untrammelled energy blasting out of the set, Herb Stutz watching with pride, Darcy with her hand over her mouth, Steven Stelfox feeling something odd, something he does not quite understand, the hairs on the back of his neck and along his arms puckering up, Jesus finishing the first chorus to wild singalong recognition, running back again, pumping the guitar riff wildly at the orchestra, many of them grinning now, caught up in it too, taking it much faster than the sheet music dictates, Barry's baton an insane blur, no choice now but to go with it as Jesus turns to the wings and gives the nod, the roar of applause somehow intensifying as Garry runs out into the middle of the stage, grabbing the mike off the stand and asking a girl called Wendy to let him in, singing about how he wants to be her friend, as Stelfox's eyebrows soar up towards his hairline, Jesus dampening the strings on the Gibson down with the flat of his right hand, reining it in a little, the orchestra following him down, Jesus conducting now, not Barry, letting Garry's voice soar clear over everything, Garry throwing his head back roaring, the studio audience screaming along with him, Garry's mom and brothers and sisters bursting with pride in the wings, Jennifer Benz's father's face a scowling mask of fury behind them, Jesus already soaking in sweat as he throws the guitar around his back and takes the mike from Garry for the middle eight, all the cameras following him down onto one knee as he half speaks the lines about girls combing their hair in rear-view mirrors and boys trying to look so hard, Jesus timing it perfectly, singing about that everlasting kiss just as, all at once, he gets the mike back onto the stand and swings the guitar up as they crash into the instrumental section, the kid from the orchestra getting that frenzied bass solo just right, Jesus and Garry dancing together in the middle of the stage, like Clarence and the Boss, Garry banging on a tambourine he's picked up, both of their faces washed in the wild transport of joy, utterly lost in music, and then the stuttering breakdown, notes falling, descending down fretboards till they hit that open E, Jesus leaping up on top of the grand piano, grinding out that big E forever, scrubbing it at the seventh fret before screaming 'ONE TWO THREE FOUR' again and scissor-kicking back off the piano as Garry makes it to the mike in time to testify that the highways are indeed littered with heroes who are broken, Jesus, making it in time to lean in and take the next line, and then they're both trading lines right to the end, the orchestra pummelling the climax, Garry with his arm around Jesus' shoulder as together they scream the chorus right into the ground, both of them pouring sweat in the spotlight, Jesus holding the guitar up high now as he scrubs out the final chord, then turning and locking eyes with the drummer before he leaps five feet in the air, landing back on his feet exactly as they crash out the final beat and as the entire studio audience and millions of folks at home all go absolutely nuts.

Maybe only four people in America not feeling it: the family Benz and Steven Stelfox.

10

'HAT THE FUCK DID YOU THINK YOU WERE DOING?!'

They're in the green room, down a corridor off the main sound stage, and the people out in the corridor – the family Benz, the family MacDonald, Becky, Morgan and Kris, all being kept at a distance from the door by a knot of clipboards and headsets – can hear the muffled roar.

'THIS IS MY SHOW! MY FUCKING SHOW! YOU LITTLE COCKSUCKER! AND STAND UP WHEN I'M FUCKING TALKING TO YOU!'

They're off air for two hours, during which time America will be voting, the lines closing just twenty minutes before they're due to go back on. Jesus, sweating, wrung out (man, how *did* Bruce do that shit every night on a forty-date tour?), is stretched out on the floor, as is his custom. Garry MacDonald sits on the edge of a chair, looking down, nervously twisting a plastic Evian bottle in his hands. Sam Jansen and Trellick hang back while Stelfox rants.

'Oh, calm down, man,' Jesus says. 'What's the big deal? We kicked ass and people felt it.'

Stelfox somehow resists the urge to run forward and boot Jesus full force in the face.

Jansen shakes her head. 'By performing an unauthorised duet and giving yourselves an unfair advantage over another contestant you violated the terms of your contract and we are perfectly entitled to disqualify you from the show. No matter what the public vote says.'

'Oh shit, man,' Garry says. 'I knew it.'

'Are you fucking insane?' Stelfox says. It takes everyone a moment to realise he is talking to Jansen. 'Kick them both off? We've got the final next week, you retarded fucking bitch – what's that going to be? A five-minute show where we tell everyone "Hey, here's Jennifer Benz. She's the winner. Thank you and good-fucking-night"? Use your fucking so-called Ivy League brain.'

'Hey,' Jesus says, 'there's no need to speak to her like that, man.'

'Listen to me, you fucking piece of shit,' Stelfox says, turning on Jesus now. 'Here's what's going to happen. Lardass here –' he indicates Garry – 'is finished. Out. Tonight. We're going to say he chose to run on during your number and what could you do? Nothing.'

'Bullshit,' Jesus says. 'All my idea.'

'I don't give a fuck. He carries the can and goes home tonight and you go into the final with Jennifer next week with a big fucking smile on your face. Play ball or you're finished. I'll make sure no record company ever signs you and the only TV appearance you'll ever make again will be when your fucking suicide is on the news.'

Jesus laughs. '"You'll never work in this town again"?'

'Abso-fucking-lutely.'

'Neh,' Jesus says.

'What?'

'Nope, that – Garry, can I get a sip of that water, man? Thanks – ain't gonna work. What else you got?'

Stelfox and Trellick look at him, sitting up on the floor now, cross-legged, sipping Evian.

'Well, how about this,' Trellick says. 'We sue you for breach of contract, for every single penny of that hotel bill – which is now into six figures by the way – for damages to the show if the final is affected in any way whatsoever, for loss of advertising revenue –'

'We're talking about *tens of millions* of fucking dollars here, you lowlife indie cocksucker,' Stelfox cuts in. 'And that's ju—'

'OK,' Jesus shrugs. 'Do what you need to do.'

Sue him, Stelfox and Trellick are both thinking. For what? A collection of vintage T-shirts?

'Unauthorised, excessive hotel charges,' Trellick continues. '*Fraudulent* hotel charges. Which the show refuses to pay. The hotel sues you and you go to jail, my friend.'

'So I go to jail. Fine.'

Stelfox feels his shoulders give. He sits down, rubbing his temples. How to negotiate with someone who will not be intimidated? Who simply does not care?

There is sharp knocking at the door. 'Come,' Stelfox shouts. The door opens – hubbub outside audible, Benz's father shouting '*This is outrageous!*' – and assistant producer Jamie enters, holding some papers. 'We're getting record calls. Phone lines are melting down.'

'What's it looking like?' Stelfox asks.

'It's looking like "Who the fuck is Jennifer Benz?" The boys here are coasting it, SS.'

'FUCK!' Stelfox screams. He had it all planned – her number-one single, the Christmas album, Jennifer soft focus in Santa hat on the cover. A little cleavage. Silence in the green room for a moment, then Stelfox runs his hands through his hair, takes a deep breath, looks at his watch and says, 'Right. Here's what's going to happen when we go back on . . .'

11

HIRTY MINUTES LATER, THE THREE OF THEM, JC, Garry and Jennifer Benz, standing on their podiums amid the cheering of the studio audience as the lights go up. Kevin Leary walks in front of them and across to the judges saying, 'What a night! What a night! I don't think we've seen anything like this before, huh, Steven?'

'No, Kevin,' Stelfox says. 'It's . . .' He shakes his head, trying to appear lost for words. Darcy and Stutz watch him solemnly, both having been instructed to 'keep your fucking mouths shut'.

'Two of you,' Stelfox continues very seriously, looking over at Jesus and Garry, who are trying their best to look contrite, more successfully in Garry's case than in JC's, 'decided to take this show into your own hands and performed an unauthorised duet.' Clapping and cheering from the audience, which Stelfox ignores. 'Which . . . which may have been very enjoyable for some people in the audience but which put Jennifer at a clear disadvantage in terms of the impact she could make on the viewers at home.' Some clapping and cheering from the loyal

Jennifer fans in the audience. 'That's why this week I feel I have to take a completely unprecedented step in the history of the show and . . .' he pauses, getting into it now, '. . . declare the results of this week's phone vote null and void.'

Gasps and shouts from the audience. Boos and catcalls. People at home are shouting at their TV sets.

'Now, Steven,' Leary interjects as scripted (hurriedly scripted, in the stage-right hallway about fifteen minutes ago) over the gasping and shouting, 'there's gonna be a lot of people watching at home who spent money calling in who feel –'

'Quite right, Kevin, I'm coming to that. I just want to assure our viewers that next week's phone vote will be free, *and* they'll get a chance to do it all over again because, for the first time in the history of *American Pop Star* . . .' he looks around, shakes his head as though he can't believe what he's about to say, '. . . we're going to carry all three acts on into the final.'

Insane applause and cheering breaks out.

'And the person with the biggest percentage of the public vote will win. But, *but*,' raising his voice over the audience, 'I feel I need to say something to you guys,' Stelfox continues, looking at Jesus and Garry. 'We absolutely will not tolerate any further behaviour like tonight. This is a live show and as such it is open to forms of abuse should people choose to do so. The rules we have were put in place so that everyone gets a fair chance to present themselves in the best possible light. Do we understand each other?'

Leary has walked back towards the contestants, between Jesus and Garry, holding his mike out, the moment where they both, as scripted, mumble apologies and promises.

'Yeah,' Garry says. 'Sorry, Steven. Sorry, Jennifer.'

Then something very definitely unscripted happens.

Jesus reaches out and takes the mike from Leary. There is

resistance, he has to tug a little, and fear in Leary's eyes, as Jesus steps down from his podium and says, 'Ah, that's right, Garry. I'd just like to apologise to Jennifer too. Sorry, Jen, we didn't mean any disrespect.'

Stelfox, Jansen, Harry up in the director's booth, everyone on the production staff, nervous as long as Jesus has that mike in his hand, going out live to almost a hundred million people. (Nielsen data would later reveal it was a little more than that. Almost 34 per cent of the American population were watching.) But the audience is clapping as Benz sweetly bats her eyelashes at JC and Stelfox is thinking, *not bad, this could actually work*.

He thinks this for precisely two seconds.

The time it takes Jesus to step past Leary – who is reaching out to take the mike back, smiling – and say, 'I'd also like to take a moment to apologise personally . . .'

'Oh fuck, no,' Sam Jansen says as she turns from the wings and starts *running* for the control booth.

According to ABN corporate policy, only two people have the authority to terminate a live broadcast as it is actually happening: the producer – in this case Stelfox – or the executive in charge of the show on behalf of the network: Jansen, who is now running full tilt down the backstage hallway. The next three minutes of live television would lead to serious questions about that policy being asked all across America, from dive bars to the Supreme Court.

'To apologise not only to Jennifer, but, ah, which camera are we on?' He moves to the rim of the stage, only a few feet from the audience, looking right into camera 2, with its bright red light glowing steady, sending him out there into all those living rooms. 'But to apologise to America . . .'

'OK, thank you. I think that's –' Stelfox says.

'Lemme tell you about this guy,' Jesus says, moving over

towards Stelfox, the cameras, the heads of the audience turning to follow him.

Jansen, careering round a corner now, hearing Jesus' calm, slow voice coming out of the speakers all along the backstage hallway.

'You know what this guy thinks of you? You, the people out there at home, watching this show? He thinks you're pond life. Morons. Just . . . the dumbest pack of retards ever. Good for paying money every week to call these stupid numbers and to buy all these . . . these products,' JC slaps a hand at one of the logos festooning the judges' desk, 'and to buy the lame records he puts out at the end and to –'

In the control booth, Harry panicking, the director looking for direction. Was this part of the plan? 'Just . . . um, stay with him,' he says. They still had over two minutes of airtime until the next scheduled commercial break: an eternity in live TV.

Jansen rounds the last corner and BANG! She runs straight into Big Bob, her head smacking square into that massive chest, like a quarterback going full pelt into the biggest guy in the defensive line. Everything goes black, Jansen unaware of the light pressure on her ankles as Bob gently, carefully (he doesn't want to hurt the lady any more than necessary) pulls her into an empty dressing room and closes the door behind them.

'I mean, you're the kind of guy,' Jesus continues, perching up on the desk close to Stelfox now, 'the kind of horrible bully who's somehow wound up running the world, huh, little man? Feeding people a bunch of crap and claiming you're just giving them what they want? You give little kids a bunch of candy and they'll keep asking for more even with the teeth falling out of their goddamn heads.'

Some of the cameramen, grinning, pulling focus a little, wanting to get the best possible reaction shots of Stelfox for this one. Stelfox goes to speak . . . and finds he cannot. He is staring into those blue eyes and discovers that words will not come. A luminous corona of light seems to be surrounding Jesus; a humming is filling Stelfox's ears, drowning out the screaming in his earpiece. He just stares, entranced, as Jesus turns back to camera, saying, 'Anyway, enough about that. I don't think I'll have very long here, so I just wanted to say, you've got to rethink this whole thing down here. The whole religion thing especially. Have you any idea how much you're pissing God off? You got people killing one another based on their faith. You got pro-lifers killing doctors – and, man, pro-lifers, I gotta tell you, He *really* hates you guys – you got these idiots on TV taking money off people in God's name. Do you think God wants a red cent out of you? The pollution, the obsession with money, all the crap you put yourselves through every day to make money to buy all this stuff that nobody needs? You . . . you've allowed it to get to a point where there's bankers making hundred-million-dollar bonuses and people are sleeping in cardboard and eating pet food. Are you all nuts, man? You got a significant portion of the world believing it's OK to cover women head to foot in black sacks and to hang and stone gay people, and another significant chunk worshipping a clown in Rome who – fact – helped cover up child abuse. He's in the Vatican. He should be in a goddamn penitentiary!'

In the audience Morgan, Kris and Becky watch with open mouths. The first time they have ever seen Jesus get mad, like he's been saving it all his life for this moment. Becky looks around at the rest of the audience; they're gawping, slack-jawed, hypnotised almost, that corona of light seeming to fill the studio now too, bathing everyone, drawing them in . . .

'And then, right here in America, you got the country with the biggest number of people who profess to be Christians in any First World nation *letting all this shit happen*! I mean, what do you think He's thinking about all this? You've got a planet that you've been on for all of five minutes and you've turned it into a human toilet. You've got . . .'

Outside the studio Saturday-night America is reacting in all its huge variety.

TV sets being shut off.

People cheering.

Children being ushered out of rooms.

Telephones getting picked up.

Emails and blogs being furiously typed.

People shouting 'Go back to fucking Russia!'

People clapping and whistling and saying 'Go on, man!'

People fumbling for the 'RECORD' button on their TV.

There are some at home – like Stelfox, like the studio audience – who are staring at the set mesmerised, near catatonic, seeming to see that shimmering, pulsating light bleaching out everything around and behind JC as he moves closer into the camera now, filling screens from Denver to Detroit, Florida to Seattle. Finally doing it. Teaching, leading, inspiring. Enraging some too, yeah, but you can't have it all.

'. . . Christians against Gays, Christians against Abortion, Christians against Socialism, Christians for Guns, Christians for Nuclear Weapons. I mean, I didn't make that one up! What happened to your sense of *community*? Don't you get it? BE FUCKING NICE!' He is right at the front of the stage now, looking directly into the camera.

'Anyway, I'm about done here. If anyone out there is interested in trying to live their life a different way, a way where you don't have to screw people over, where you don't have to get up at five in the morning and spend half the day stuck on some train or in your car, where you don't just see your kids for a couple of hours a day and then turn round years later and wonder why you can't relate to them, where your daily routine doesn't have to involve taking a few years off the life expectancy of the planet, then come and find me. It'll be in all the papers. Thanks for listening. Goodnight.'

He drops the mike onto the floor – a thud, a squawk of feedback – and walks off the set.

That squawk of feedback snaps Stelfox out of his trance and he looks up, seeing the set as if for the first time that night: the empty podium where Jesus was. Benz and Big Garry standing there, open-mouthed. Stutz and DeAngelo looking at him, the audience weirdly silent as suddenly the floor manager yells 'THAT'S COMMERCIALS! WE'RE OUT!' and a clipboard and headset girl is tugging at Stelfox's elbow and then all hell is breaking loose.

12

ESUS SPENDS THE NEXT FOUR DAYS STRAIGHT – THE rest of the first week of December – in the bungalow at the Chateau: giving interviews and having his photograph taken for any publication that will pay for the privilege. There are a lot of takers: everything from the *Enquirer* to *Harper's* to *Celebrity Lifestyle*. He is on the front cover of every English-speaking newspaper in the Western world. In four days he earns nearly a million dollars in fees.

On day three Steven Stelfox arrives at the Chateau; his chauffeur-driven black Cadillac Escalade SUV squeaking regal up the tiled forecourt.

'Hey there,' Jesus says as Stelfox takes a seat in the lounge, across the coffee table from Jesus and Morgan, looking around distastefully at the mess; room-service trays, underwear hanging on the radiators. There are what appear to be a couple of old winos passed out on the patio. 'Ah, what the fuck's going on with those tramps?' Stelfox asks.

'Oh, that's just Gus and Dotty. They're friends of mine.'

'Right. Figures. So, let's get down to it. Who'd have believed it – you're the biggest star the show's produced. Fuck it – you're probably the biggest name in America right now. I'm going to exercise my option to sign your record and publishing deals.'

'What's that worth?' Morgan asks.

'Ah, and who the fuck are you?' Stelfox responds.

'Listen –' Morgan begins, getting up from his chair.

'Easy, Morgs,' JC says. 'This is Morgan. He's the drummer in my band.'

'Oh, the *drummer*?' Stelfox says, flattening a hand on his chest in 'excuse-me' fashion, making the words sound like 'the emperor'. 'I'm sorry. I had no idea. Please, do go on. Tell me, what kinds of drumsticks do you use? What kind of miking set-up do you favour on your kit? What, actually hang on, just fuck off, would you?'

'*Motherfucker!*' Morgan says, getting up again.

'Ah, Morgan,' Jesus says, placing a hand on his arm, 'maybe you should go get a drink or something. It's cool, man. I'll handle this.'

'Don't sign anything, man,' Morgan says, over his shoulder as he leaves.

'So, how much?' Jesus asks.

'A million dollars for your publishing and a million for your record contract. A third of each payable on signature, a third on delivery of the album and a third on release.'

'Yeah. OK,' Jesus says.

Stelfox takes a moment to adjust. Not the kind of negotiation he's used to. 'We'll make the record here in LA, I'll pick the songs of course, and, also needless to say, the closest your drummer friend and the rest of your so-called "band" are gonna get to the record is when they come by to deliver pizza.'

'No,' Jesus says.

'How's that?'

'No. I'm gonna use the guys and we'll make the record ourselves in our own studio. Otherwise no deal.'

'You're aware there's a clause in the contract you signed for the show prohibiting you from recording for any other labels?'

'Um, well, if you say so.'

'So what will you do?'

'Not record any music?'

Stelfox thinks. *Doable. It's all fucking doable. As long as you got a couple of singles to sell the album who really gave a fuck what else was on the poxy record? Have Trellick bury a phrase deep in the contract about the label having permission to remix certain tracks as they see fit. Remixing was a pretty broad remit. Just take the vocal into a real studio with a real producer and reconstruct the track so normal people would like it. Yeah, it could be done.*

Stelfox appears to think for a long time before slowly beginning to nod his head. 'I'll agree to that if you'll agree to include two cover versions of my choosing on the record.'

Jesus thinks. *What the hell. Record 'em so badly he can't do anything with them.*

'Yeah. OK. Deal.'

'OK, we'll be in touch.'

They shake hands, Stelfox removing his sunglasses for the first time during the meeting. Jesus seeing those bats falling into the blackness of his pupils; sparks of fire dancing there too. Stelfox, in his turn, feels the goodness. Riddled with it.

Jesus tells Morgan and Kris.

'Wow,' Kris says. 'So, basically, we get a third of this two million dollars right now, whatever happens?'

'Yep,' JC says.

'That's great!'

'Mmmm,' Morgan says. 'You boys know how much that works out to?'

They look at him.

'Exactly six hundred and sixty-six thousand dollars.'

'Whoa,' Jesus says. 'Six-six-six. Freaky, huh?'

'Mmmm,' Morgan says.

While Jesus goes on smiling for the camera by the pool and answering questions like 'Who is the real Jesus?' everyone gets their shit packed up and Kris buys new transport: a spacious luxury minibus, with aircraft seats, frosty A/C, DVD player and powerful stereo. On the Thursday following JC's final show the menagerie saddles up and hits the road, a chunk of their new fortune going towards settling the room-service tab at the Chateau Marmont and leaving a hefty tip for the staff. (Who have treated the menagerie righteously throughout, even asking some movie producer who complained about Gus being passed out by the pool to leave. *Two places everyone gets treated the same*, Jesus reflected, *Heaven and really, really good hotels*.) 'Man,' Kris says as their tyres squeak down the hotel's tiled driveway towards Sunset Strip, 'it is hard to leave this place.'

The season finale of *American Pop Star* airs that Saturday without its biggest star. A record number of viewers still tunes in to see, in a shock upset, Garry triumphing over Jennifer Benz (largely due to his revelatory performance with Jesus the week before) but, given the events of the previous week, the show is described as 'one of the biggest anticlimaxes in television history. Literally *Hamlet* without the Prince.' Jesus is happy for Garry and what the money will mean to his family, finding himself chuckling at the thought of Stelfox smashing his office up as he shreds the marketing plans for Jennifer's Christmas album. Meanwhile they're heading back east, Los Angeles disappearing behind them under its sweating dome of smog, Kris at the wheel, singing along to Willie Nelson's 'On the Road Again' on that fine new sound system as they head towards Arizona, looking for those wide-open spaces.

'Hey,' Morgan says. 'What's the last words you want to hear after you've sucked Willie Nelson's dick?'

'Dunno,' Kris says over his shoulder, eyes on the road.

'I'm not Willie Nelson,' Morgan says.

Part Five

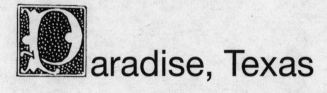aradise, Texas

'There is a growing feeling that perhaps Texas is really another country, a place where the skies, the disasters, the diamonds, the politicians, the women, the fortunes, the football players and the murders are all bigger than anywhere else.'

Pete Hamill

'*in't that something? Heck of a view now, ain't she?'* These had been the realtor's words as they'd stood on this outcrop of rocks looking down the valley nearly a year ago. Even then, on that December morning, it had indeed been something. Now, in the rippling heat of an early-September afternoon, it was . . . well.

'Shit, Dad,' Jesus said, raising his beer to the valley. 'You sure can put a thing together.' The beer was cold, metallic on his throat. He relit the joint – man, this crop, their first, was, well, nothing on the weed in Heaven of course, but still, it was 'the nuts', as Morgan had put it – pulled his hat down over his eyes and lay back on the rock, thinking. Like Dad always said, if you're in the office all the time, you're just firefighting. You needed to get out regularly, clear your head, or rather fuzz it up a little, and let the ideas flow. This promontory where he lay looking west was where JC came to do just that.

Collard Creek wound its way downstream away from him, all the way to the wetlands that marked the western end of their land, nearly three miles away. The banks of the creek were dotted with juniper, scrub oak, live oak, mesquite and pinyon pine. Good hunting down there in the woods towards the wetlands – whitetail deer, scaled quail, waterfowl, the odd feral hog and wild turkey too. (Claude had shown them how you could catch the turkeys and now they had a little pen of them over near the farm itself. 'Good eating,' Claude had promised, proving himself right when he roasted one of those big boys whole in an oven he dug in the ground and they ate it out under the stars with a few potatoes he'd thrown in with the bird.)

Over to his left, forming the southern boundary of the property, was what little Miles had imaginatively christened 'Big Lake', shaped like a crooked arm, over two miles long and about a quarter-mile across at the widest point, blazing silver beneath the afternoon sun, the trophy bass and the fat catfish circling in the cooler depths. Big Bob and Morgan – keen fishermen – often heading over early in the mornings with their rods, reels and bait. Big Lake was big enough to waterski on too, though JC had yet to try it. But you'd hear Becky with Pete or Kris some afternoons, one of the guys driving the little speedboat while she shrieked with laughter behind it, her cries and the buzz of the engine carrying far across the still air.

To his right, north, lay a high ridge of pine-fringed mountains, cut through by the road that eventually took you up to Bruntsville, their nearest town, five miles away, or onto the interstate, where you could turn left and head all the way to Austin, a good day's drive away. Now and again you'd see cars come a little way down that hillside and pull over, then there'd be the glinting of sunlight off highly polished glass: the long-lensed cameras of the press, the binoculars of the occasional tourist or curious local, trying to get a glimpse of the freaks at play. Nestling all along the foothills of the ridge were the houses the new people were building, all in various stages of construction, the faint sound of hammering and the knifing buzz saws carrying up to here. A couple of these new places gave right onto the other lake, Little Lake.

JC rolled over onto his stomach, the sun hot on his back, the flat rock warm on his forearms as he propped himself to look back east – across the roof of the big ranch house, mostly occupied by themselves, what they'd come to jokingly call the 'original settlers', and, next to it, the first couple of houses they'd built under Pete's guidance, fairly rickety affairs to be sure, but watertight and windproof, with solar panels glinting all over them – towards the farm which lay about half a mile away. It was all activity over there; people going back and forth, wheelbarrows, crystal arcs of water sparkling from hoses and sprinklers. Behind the farm, towering over it, the two big wind turbines, gently turning even in this light breeze.

Claude was nervous, coming into this, but man, the kid had done a job of work here. Back at the beginning of the year, in the late winter and early spring, Claude working fifteen-hour days, planning, planting, getting everyone to help with the digging and composting. (The soil wasn't bad for the region, Claude had said, but he'd still insisted they truck in tens of thousands of dollars' worth of high-grade compost.) And now here was the result of all that work, bursting up out of the ground in bold blocks of colour: green rows of sugar snap and lima. Southern peas and Swiss chard. Yellow splashes from the fat squashes, the flowers of the zucchini plants and the succulent peppers. The red of the tomatoes and chillies.

Their first harvest.

He sat back up, draining that beer, the gold can crumpling up pleasingly in his hand, and burped happily, sitting here just about slap bang in the middle of it all: two and a half thousand

acres, almost four square miles, of Texas Hill Country just off
the Edwards Prairie savannah. All theirs bought and paid for,
Jack Berry at Berry and Franklin cutting them what he called
a 'sweet, sweet deal' – six hundred dollars an acre with the
crumbling old five-bedroom, timber-frame ranch house thrown
in.

Fish in the lakes, animals in the woods and about every
vegetable you could think of coming up through the dirt over
there. Fuck, man, it *was* a sweet deal.

His reverie is interrupted by the high-pitched growl of an
engine. Jesus sits up and sees Kris coming up the dusty hillside
towards him on the green dirt bike, the one on which Kris had
painted 'EAT MY BALLS' across the petrol tank. He ramps
up over the edge of the hill, kills the engine and lays the bike
down on its side, walking the last few yards so as not to shower
JC in dust.

'Hey, man,' Kris says, easing himself down onto the rock next
to Jesus. Man, Fat Kris was nearly no more. He must have lost
thirty pounds over the summer, miles away from junk food,
working in the dirt with Claude, or in among all the timber
with Pete, eating right and swimming every morning.

'Hey, big fella,' JC says, passing him the jay. 'How's tricks?'

'Got some new arrivals down there.' Kris nods north towards
where the private road down the mountain terminates at the
gates onto the estate itself.

'Oh yeah? Where from?'

'Uh, family from Detroit, I think.'

'Few more from the Motor City, huh?' They've had several
arrivals from Detroit. Place was on its knees. Goddamn shame,
Jesus thought. It was a good rock-and-roll town. MC5, Stooges.
White Stripes. Bunch of righteous techo stuff too.

'Yeah, well, Becky's dealing with it but you'd better come

down. They want to talk to you. Mr Detroit's got handguns and stuff.'

'Oh man, not again.'

It had happened a bunch of times already, people wanting to come out here and live in total peace and harmony with a fucking Magnum under their pillow. Some Americans, man, naked without that piece.

'Hey, JC!'

'Big guy!'

'Hey, you wanna play some touch football later?'

He smiles and waves and returns the odd high five as he follows Kris across the dusty courtyard, kids running around. Saturday morning. Man, every day felt like Saturday morning and every night felt like Friday night. Jesus hears a snare-drum fill clattering across on the breeze: Morgan, down there in the studio they're building, tinkering with the kit, not happy with the drum sound he's been getting. They hadn't gone *too* nuts buying guitars and stuff – Kris got a new Fender Precision bass and JC treated himself to a gorgeous off-white 1960 Les Paul Junior: double cutaway, à la Johnny Thunders. They've been working hard at demoing tracks for JC's album. (Not without pressure and disagreement. For the past six months Stelfox and JC had been locked in argument over what the two contractual cover versions should be. Stelfox had flown in by chopper to hear work in progress back in July and had basically told them to make the vocals louder, cut all the guitar solos and get to all the choruses faster. Then he'd choppered straight back out with a remark about why was JC living in a hippy cesspit when he had millions of dollars in the bank.)

'Hey, Becks,' Jesus says, taking in the scene as he arrives at the main gate: Becky, her back to him, arms folded (a bad sign)

looking good in cut-off denim pants and an olive-green combat
vest, talking to a little white guy with glasses and a Tigers
baseball cap. Mr Detroit, JC guesses. His family, an even tinier
wife and two kids – boy and a girl, around ten or eleven – are
clustered behind him and the little girl squeaks with delight
when Jesus appears. 'He looks different from on TV,' she
whispers to her brother. The whole family seem to straighten up
when Jesus appears, smiling at him. *Fame, fame fatal fame*, Jesus
thinks. *It can play hideous tricks on the brain*.

'Hi, folks, what's the problem?'

'The problem,' Becky says, 'is that Terence here has a gun in
his luggage.'

'Just give it to them,' the wife hisses.

'Sorry, buddy, no weapons,' Jesus says.

'But, I just saw a guy walking by over there with a rifle.'

'Yeah, we got rifles here for hunting,' Jesus goes on. 'Which
you're welcome to use as and when you want to go hunting. But
we don't allow personal firearms.'

'I . . . but it was expensive. What'll happen to it?'

'I already told you –' Becky begins, near boiling point now.

'It's cool, Becks,' JC says, planting a hand softly on her
shoulder. 'I got this one. We'll keep it safely stored and if you
ever want to leave you can have it back.'

'We should just dump the lot of them in the goddamn lake,'
Becky says.

'Do I get a receipt?' the guy, Terence, asks.

'Ah, that's not really how we do things around here . . .' Jesus
laughs.

'Terence,' the wife hisses.

'OK, OK. I . . .' He goes into his rucksack and digs out an
ugly-looking black revolver. 'I didn't mean to cause trouble. I
just, I didn't know what to expect here. You know?'

Kris takes the gun as Jesus ushers them through the gate. 'You haven't caused any trouble, Terence, come on in. Hi, kids, ma'am. I'm Jesus, most people call me JC.'

'Oh, we know who you are!' the wife laughs, girlishly, thrilled. 'I'm Teresa Brokaw. This is Sean and Clare.'

'You sure put that Stelfox guy in his place,' little Clare says.

'Ah, he's not so bad.' (Jesus is capable of lying.)

The family Brokaw follow JC and Becks into the compound, taking it all in, their necks craning around, the air tangy with the smell of grilling meat, music drifting from somewhere – hard funk, George Clinton or something – and the sound of hammering and sawing.

'If you're hungry,' JC is saying, pointing over to the ten-foot-long grill, 'we got some barbecue burning right over there. Sleeping-wise, you'll find cots in those Quonset huts down along that path there, by the woods,' Jesus points off down a wooden walkway. 'That's where we put new folks at first. There's showers and toilets and whatnot down there too. Or you're welcome to pitch a tent about anywhere you like. And, well, that's about it for now, guys. We can go over the other stuff later. You wanna soda or something? Beers?' They have arrived at the shaded porch off the main house. Bob is playing racing cars with Miles on the deck.

'Yeah, thanks,' Terence Brokaw says. 'I . . . I guess I didn't know what to expect. I mean, I'd read about it, but . . . it's kinda like being at a rock festival, huh?'

'Yeah, maybe,' Jesus says, digging in a cooler, coming up with some icy beers and a couple of sodas for the kids. 'But without the two-hundred-dollar tickets, fifteen-dollar burgers and lame corporate rock. Cheers.' They touch cans and sit down on the wooden steps.

'A regular utopia, huh?' Teresa says, taking her sunglasses

off.

Jesus groans. 'Please don't call it that. It's *not* a utopia.'

'What would you call it?'

'Just . . . a community maybe. In the sense of what that used to mean.'

They nod, sipping their beers, looking uphill towards the farm.

'How many people live here?' the little girl asks.

'Maybe a couple of hundred now, Clare. Families, individuals. What have you.'

'Wow, they're big. Those wind turbines, huh?' Terence says, gesturing with his beer.

'Yeah.' Jesus follows his admiring gaze towards the pair of glinting propellers. 'We got a fella in from the Horse Hollow Wind Energy Center, over in Taylor and Nolan County? I say "we", old Pete over here was the one who took care of it. Hey, Pete,' Jesus calls to Pete, who is standing over some blueprints spread out on a bench in the sun. 'These are the Brokaws from Detroit.'

'Hey there,' Pete says, coming over, offering his hand.

'Anyway,' Jesus goes on, 'Pete got this fella in and he laid out how we could do it all, even sourced those bad boys second-hand for us. Cleaned us out of the best part of half a million bucks for the pair, but they generate, what, Pete?

'Nearly a million kilowatts per annum. What with the solar panels for the hot water 'n' all we are just about totally energy self-sufficient, baby.'

'Yeah, when they work,' Becks says.

'Yeah, they were a pain in the ass at first,' Pete says. 'Not storing up energy properly, not turning over when they should have been. In the end the guy put a couple of little digital video cameras up there on top of them, to monitor the props 24/7, find out when they were turning over. They record right onto hard drives in the base of the turbines.'

'Sure, we've had some teething problems,' Jesus allows. 'Old Becks here is kind of a glass half-empty kinda chick.'

'Get bent. Someone's gotta be practical around here,' Becks says.

'So when,' Terence says, wiping beer foam from his top lip, 'when do you have like services and stuff?'

'Services?' JC says.

'Yeah, like church and prayer and whatnot.'

Jesus and Becky both laugh.

'Dude,' Becky says, 'you have most definitely come to the wrong place for that.'

2

'T'S JUST . . . I DON'T LIKE IT ONE BIT. YOU
understand what I'm saying, don't you, Ike?'

'Mmm. I can see you're concerned, Pastor,'
Ike says, trying to sound non-committal.

Sheriff Ike Sturges leans back in his chair, the old wood
giving a good squeak as he brings his feet up onto the desk,
resting his coffee mug on his belly. In his in-tray lay the pending
crimes of the town of Bruntsville, Pell County: traffic citations,
a couple of public drunkenness things, a few domestic
disturbances. Business as usual. Old Ike hasn't had a major
crime in his little town in fifteen years (that rape, still kept him
up nights, God help him) and that's just the way Ike likes it.
Now here's Charlie Glass, Pastor Charlie Glass if you please
(and Charlie pleases, boy does Charlie please), in here wanting
to start something. Start what exactly? Ike wonders, scratching
his silvery beard, wishing he could smoke, but knowing how
the Pastor feels about that.

'The thing is, Charlie, I'm not sure quite what you want me
to do here.'

Pastor Glass sighs. He takes his spectacles off – not the kind of spectacles you'd expect on a church fellow, Ike thinks. Expensive designer things, with some kind of logo and yellow-tinted glass – and begins polishing them with his tie as he speaks slowly, as though Ike were some kind of buffoon. 'Have you read some of this man's pronouncements?' He slides the glasses back on and taps a finger on the copy of the *New York Times* he's spread on Ike's desk. A photo of Jesus on there, taken during his big speech on the show. 'He believes he is Our Lord. Son of God. Here to save us all. I mean, the open blasphemy of it. You know, if he were a Muslim going around claiming to be Muhammad someone would probably have chopped his head off by now.'

'Well, thank the Lord we're not Muslims, Charlie, huh?' Trying to keep it light. 'You want some more coffee there? Another piece of cake?' He gets up and crosses to the coffee pot on the other side of his office. Through the glass window, out in the main station, he can see Diane typing away, talking to Chip and Burt, his two deputies, the three of them laughing about something.

'No, thank you,' Glass says, speaking over his shoulder. 'And one could argue that at least religion is still central to Muslim lives. The thought of goodness knows what going on down there, just five miles from where our children go to school, where our wives shop . . .'

'Far as I can tell, Charlie, there's nothing going on but some farming. They got a hell of a crop coming considering they only been since January 'a' all.'

'So you've been down there?'

'Sure. I swung by a couple of times.' Ike, settling back down now with his refilled mug.

Pastor Glass looks at him expectantly. Ike has to laugh. 'And nothing, Pastor. Just a bunch of folks going about their business on their own private property, as is their enshrined constitutional right.'

Goddamn it, man, Ike thinks. *Live and let live, huh? Ain't we supposed to be Christians here?*

'Did you meet him?' Glass asks.

'The Jesus fellow? Yeah. Friendly, polite. Maybe a little, uh, out there. But no more so than half the kids you meet these days. Times change, you know?'

'Can you think of anything that's changed for the better recently, Sheriff?'

'Pastor, if you're so concerned about their presence in the area all I can suggest is that you take a ride out there and see for yourself. How about that?' Ike sits forward and clasps his hands together, hoping to signify that they are about done.

'I might just do that. Well,' Glass gets up, smiling stiffly, unfolding his long, skinny frame from the chair, 'thank you for your time. I just wanted to . . . air my concerns. You understand?'

'Oh, I understand, Pastor.' Ike standing up to shake now.

'Give my best to Marjorie, won't you? And I'm sure I'll see you both in church this Sunday.'

'That you will. Oh, don't forget your newspaper.' He holds it towards Glass, his hand on the doorknob.

'You keep it. For your personal edification.'

'Why thank you, Pastor. You have a good day now.'

Ike sits back down and dabs at the last few crumbs of cake while he watches the man nod his way through the little station and out into the sunshine. Ike pegs the *New York Times* into the wastebasket.

Pastor Charlie Glass. Ike remembers his dad, Pastor Willard Glass. When you get towards sixty, Ike realises, you remember everyone's dad in a place like this. Ike wonders if Charlie knows anything about his dad's rap sheet, still in a Manila file somewhere in back here. Back in about '86, when little Charlie was still in high school, old Willard had been pulled over for a speeding violation, out near the state line. He had a fifteen-year-old black girl in the car with him, a girl he was giving, in his words, 'a ride' and 'some guidance' to. Let off with a caution, the whole thing smoothed over by Chief Graham, Ike's predecessor. Ike had been a deputy then. '*Yeah*,' he remembers Jimmy Krebb the arresting officer saying at the time '*looked to me like the Pastor was planning to "guide" that little nigger girl good and proper.*'

That was something that had changed for the better – folks didn't say things like that any more. Not around Ike if they had any sense.

A quick rap on the glass and Chip was coming in with some paperwork for him to sign. 'And what was troubling the good Pastor?' Chip asks. 'Not a thing, Chip,' Ike says, signing away. 'Not a thing. Now, is there any of my wife's crumb cake left out there or have you vultures had the goddamn lot?'

3

 EOPLE HADN'T COME AS QUICKLY AS THEY'D thought they would. Nor as many. Sure there had been a flurry of interest early on, in the weeks after Jesus had left the show in such a blur of publicity, but a lot of those early arrivals had been, well, JC would never use words like 'freaks' or 'freeloaders' (though Morgan and Becky would), but they hadn't exactly been . . . committed. And when they realised they'd be spending the cold winter nights in those draughty Quonset huts (rented from a firm outside Austin), that they'd be expected to pitch in with digging and preparing hard ground, and that when they weren't doing that they'd be helping build the houses they were to live in, a lot of them simply got back in their cars, or onto their motorcycles, or threw their packs over their backs, and disappeared back up that hillside.

Pete and Claude had been the key to the whole thing getting off the ground at all. Working with an architect from Bruntsville, Pete had drawn up plans for simple wood-framed two- and three-bedroom homes, lodges really. They'd got Harry

Pitts in, the local builder recommended by Jack Berry, and he and his crew had put up the first couple, by which point Pete had learned enough to be able to manage the building work himself, guiding Morgan and Kris and Jesus and a few of the other early arrivals as the first few cabins went up around the old ranch house. At this point – back in March – there were maybe thirty people here, including the original menagerie, and work went slow. When they weren't building they worked for Claude, digging beds and boxing them in with old railway sleepers they'd found on the property, down near the wetlands, raising them up off the ground to thwart the night crawlers who came scuttling out when the sun went down, hungry for their greens. (Good bait for those trophy bass though. Everything in its turn.)

Then, in the spring, when the weather improved, a steady trickle of people began to arrive. Before long there were a few dozen of them here.

What kind of people were they? What kind of people would throw up their old lives – jobs and homes and friends – to live in a valley in the middle of Texas with a guitar player who claimed to be the son of God? Well, as you'd expect, some were hippies, just looking, itching, for a way to drop off the radar. Some were clearly damaged people, the kind of people who didn't have jobs, homes or families to throw up in the first place. Some were clearly just curious or awestruck – fans of the show, dying to get a chance to hang with JC in person. It didn't matter. No one was turned away, although a few – surprisingly few – were asked to leave. (Refusal to help with the work, a couple of incidents of women being harassed.)

Now and again, as the whole thing grew, they'd have to have meetings about stuff. Like his dad, JC *hated* meetings and it fell to Becky to organise and run these gatherings, which were held in the old barn, everyone sitting around on bales or on the ground while topics were thrown around.

The meeting in progress this morning was a fairly typical affair: the Traums, Marty and Angelina, the old hippy couple who lived in a huge tepee (a 'yurt' they called it) that they'd pitched way off near Big Lake, had complained that they kept on being woken early by the splashing and shouting of the kids who'd come down to dive and swim off the old wooden dock a couple hundred yards from their place. It was decided that, well, kids would be kids and they couldn't really dismantle and move the lake so if it bothered them that much then a bunch of them would help the Traums move their yurt further off away from the lake. Mary Schetterling, a very serious-minded thirty-something vegetarian from San Francisco, had renewed her motion – to an audible groan from JC – to try and grow a certain type of beansprout in great quantity, a process which would require the building of a dedicated polytunnel, and which Claude felt was not worth the resources required. Once again the decision was referred to Claude who shook his head and bobbed a thumb down towards the ground. Mary was consoled by being told that Claude would help her build a small polytunnel out back of her cabin so she could grow a personal supply of the precious vegetable.

Many of those who came were initially surprised at the degree to which JC was a hands-off kind of guy. He rarely spoke in the meetings. He never made big speeches or gave anything in the way of spiritual guidance. Most people, in their early days here, would at some point approach him with a question, religious, philosophical or otherwise, and would come away bewildered at the inevitable 'Ah, um, gee. Wow. Who knows?' response they received. ('Damn,' JC said to the guys, 'I feel like Dylan in the sixties.')

'OK,' Becky is saying, wrapping the meeting up. 'Now remember, we're into the fall now and soon it's gonna be winter. For most of you it'll be the first one you'll have had here. It gets cold at nights, so if anyone's worried that their place isn't going to be warm enough, especially any of you with young kids, please talk to Pete or someone and they'll see about getting you properly winterised. Those of you in tents – Marty, Angelina, I know you guys are OK in that bitching yurt – some of you might want to think about moving up closer to the main ranch house or into one of the huts at some point in the next few weeks, because, trust me, come November, it *will* be cold. OK, any more questions?' Jesus, already getting to his feet, levering himself up by leaning heavily on Morgan's shoulder, when Julia Bell puts her hand up. Julia is a big, butch old lesbian from New York City who arrived with her partner Amanda back in the early summer.

'Jules?' Becky says.

'Ah, sorry to bring this up, but Guff still hasn't cleared up that area out back of his cabin. Despite –'

'Now hang on a minute . . .' Guff Rennet says, getting to his feet.

Ah shit, Jesus thinks, lowering himself back down. The fucking Rennet brothers. Few were asked to leave, true, but some were constantly walking the line. Like the Rennets. Their crew was comprised of brothers Guff, Pat and Deek and their wives and various children. They were swarthy Midwesterners who'd arrived back in August and they constantly seemed to be getting into something with someone. They were rough-and-ready kind of survivalist types who'd had to be relieved of a couple of rifles (one semi-auto) and a handgun when they arrived: just the kind of people who honestly weren't great neighbours. However, at one of the several meetings they'd had to discuss the problem of the Rennet clan, it had been Jesus who'd argued that they should stay. They did work hard (Guff, Deek and Pat had single-handedly built their own cabins down in the treeline near Little Lake, next to Julia's) and the kids were great. 'Besides,' Jesus said, 'not everyone who shows up here is going to fit our idea of the perfect citizen. We gotta teach folk by example. Not just kick 'em out.' But the Rennets weren't the neatest people in the world and over the last couple of months their back and front yards had gradually become littered with engine parts, old appliances, broken toys and the like. Julia had complained a few times and at the last meeting Guff had grudgingly agreed to undertake a clean-up.

'Just a goddamn minute,' Guff says, standing up now and glaring over at Julia. 'We cleaned up all that stuff you were talking about.'

'No you haven't!' Julia says from her sitting position. Julia could be kind of a pain in the ass too, though, if you asked some people. 'That rusted-out old car with no wheels is still sitting –'

'We're fixing that up!' Deek says, looking up to Guff who nods slowly.

'It was agreed,' Julia says, 'that anything like that should be stored in the garage rather than lying in your yard like, like –'

'How we s'pose to move it before we fix it up, Jul-ee-ah?' Guff says.

'That's not the point. I –'

'OK, guys,' Becky cuts in. 'Deek, you can use the 4×4 and tow the car up to the garage and work on it there, OK?'

'Ah shit,' Guff says. 'That means we gotta haul ass all the way up there whenever we want to work on it? Where I come from folks have cars blocked up in their yards all the time.'

'Well,' Jesus says, getting to his feet, dusting the knees of his jeans off and speaking for the first time in the meeting, 'like they say, we're not in Kansas any more, Guff. We done here?' He's itching to get back down to the studio with the guys, play around on that new Junior, get back into that song they were working on.

The meeting breaks up with mutterings from the Rennets and a triumphant flouncing out from Julia and Amanda. JC, Kris, Morgan, Claude and Pete are drifting out towards the sunshine when Becky says, 'Hang on, you guys, we need to go over some stuff.' Groans as they drift back towards the big trestle table Becks has already seated herself at the head of. Just as they're settling down Guff Rennet strides up.

'I ain't happy about this,' he says. 'That old truck ain't hurting no one.'

Becky speaks without looking up from her papers. 'Just take the 4×4 and move it. Please, Guff?'

'Taking orders from those fucking dykes.'

'Hey!' Jesus says, standing up. 'Cut that shit out.'

Guff Rennet is a big guy: six four, around 220. Even after JC stands up Guff still has a couple of inches on him. 'Listen, buddy, just do like Becks says, huh?' JC says. Guff bristles, staring him down for a long few seconds, but feeling JC's presence, those eyes.

'I ain't happy about this,' Guff repeats, before turning and stomping off.

'Shit, that asshole gets on my nerves,' Morgan says,

'Amen,' Becky adds. 'Now. Money.'

'Oh man.' JC's head thunks onto the table. 'Come on, Becks, can't we do this another time? I wanna go play –'

'Hey, will you stop making me feel like Old Ma Boring just because someone's got to make sure this place doesn't fall apart?'

Becky says, flattening open her ledger. 'Now, listen up, we got a little over half a million dollars left in the bank.'

'So happy days,' Morgan says.

'Yeah, right,' Becks says flatly. 'We got state property taxes due end of the month. Repair bill for that plumbing thang. Pete's put in a request for more timber. The schoolhouse is gonna take more than we figured to get finished in time for winter –' They were building a classroom for the kids. The tutors who came out from Bruntsville and the surrounding area to teach the kids held classes here in the barn, which had been fine since May, but come November . . .

Becky goes on, breaking it all down, while Jesus tunes out. Truth is, he hates thinking about all this stuff. It worked like this – people who came along and lived in tents or in the Quonset huts for a while and then decided they wanted to stay on could buy the materials to build a home at cost. Labour wasn't a problem as there were always plenty of bodies to pitch in. At the same time, folks who wanted to stay and who didn't have enough money were generally lent the materials anyway. They were almost self-sufficient in energy now and all their food came from the estate, except beef which they'd struck a deal for with the farmers' market in Bruntsville. But a property this big needed a lot of maintenance, some of it specialised, or requiring hiring machinery they didn't have, and that cost money. There was outlay for toiletries, dry goods, the cooking items they couldn't grow (oil, spices, rice and the like) and luxuries like liquor and so forth (Claude reckoned the grapes would be good for wine from next year). In terms of income there was the money JC earned for giving the odd interview (although he'd turned down millions of dollars in potential fees for advertising products) and there would be the next chunk of his recording and publishing advances when they finally finished the album. (Or, more accurately, when Stelfox accepted the album.)

'Bottom line,' Becky is saying now, 'it costs nearly thirty thousand dollars a month to keep this show on the road. That's without factoring in our generous policy on repeatedly loaning building materials to those who can't afford them and without allowing for any major disasters like that leak we had in the water tank or, say, some weather damage. On that basis you could confidently say we'll be good for another year at least. Now, there's gonna be some income from the farm, thanks to Claude, selling off our excess crops, but I'm not sure exactly how much that's gonna be . . .'

'OK,' JC says, 'so I'll do some press or something. We can invite some of those stupid magazines to do a bunch of "At Home With" type crap. And –'

'Ah, excuse me for interrupting, Mr Celebrity-At-Home-With,' Pete butts in, 'but I wouldn't be too sure your fee's gonna be as high for that stuff as it was a year ago.'

'Huh?' Jesus says.

'He's right,' Becky says. 'You're old news now. America's got new idiots to play with. The new series is starting.'

'Damn,' Jesus says. 'Am I, like, over?'

'Washed up, baby,' Morgan laughs.

'Shit.'

'OK, all I'm saying is can we all get our thinking caps on?' Becky says. 'Ways to reduce costs and increase income. It ain't rocket science.'

'What would I know?' Jesus says, still sulking. 'I'm a has-been.'

'Come on,' Kris says. 'Let's go up the studio.'

'Uh-uh,' Claude butts in. 'First you and the has-been owe me a shift up on the farm.'

'Oh man,' Jesus says.

'Self-sufficiency costs,' Becks says. 'And this is where you start paying.'

'In weeding,' Claude adds, slapping him on the back.

'Oh man,' Jesus repeats.

4

O MUSIC IN PASTOR CHARLIE GLASS'S CLEAN American car. The stereo still has that transparent piece of film covering its aqua-green facia. He turns it on occasionally when he's up on the high mountain pass – like today – when he can get WKLM Broadcasting out of El Paso, his cousin the Reverend William Lomax's *Old Testament Radio Hour*. He likes to hear Willie wrangling with the sinners who call in, mostly troubled housewives worried about their children, stuff like that. Willie occasionally has Charlie on as a guest and, boy, is that fun. The feeling of power as that big transmitter blasts your voice all over the state, getting to shout down the callers, girls thinking about having abortions, young men struggling with their 'sexuality' and the like.

'*And . . . and I don't know all what, Reverend. At this bar she goes to with all the young folks,*' this housewife's voice is saying, crackly over the FM.

'Sinners,' the Reverend responds simply.

'*Lord, I know it, Reverend.*'

'*Do you read the scripture to your daughter, ma'am?*'

'*I . . . she's seventeen. She won't listen to –*'

'*Listen to me now – your daughter will be forever lost unto sin,*' Willie thunders, '*unless she repents now! The Good Book says . . .*'

Pastor Glass, smiling as listens to his cousin shouting the woman down. Good preparation, he feels, for what he is soon to face, turning off the 184 now, making a right across the macadam and onto the leafy, narrow two-lane blacktop that leads south-east down through the mountain, pulling the shade down to keep the mid-morning sun from burning through the trees into his eyes.

'*I'm sorry, I been weak. I failed her,*' the woman sobs.

Weakness. They're surrounded by it. Like that old fool Sheriff. Smiling and nodding and eating his fucking crumb cake and basically saying to him – to *him*, to Pastor Charles Glass! – go fuck yourself. Well, they'll see about that, he thinks, making a left off the blacktop now, down onto the gravelly single-track lane, past the old sign that has been there since it was the Hausman place, the one that said 'PRIVATE ROAD'. Below it, idiotically, in jaunty white paint someone has daubed 'ALL WELCOME!' He slows and pulls out to pass two people walking hand in hand along the side of the road, their backs to him. A boy and a girl, the girl wearing cut-off denim shorts, so cut-off he can see the gooseflesh white of her buttocks where her tanned legs stop, just below the jagged material.

The Pastor glances back in the rear-view mirror to catch a glimpse at her front, oh yeah, like he thought; her breasts swinging in that tight vest top, the deep V of brown cleavage, the guy laughing at something she's saying, the two of them later, or earlier, coiled together on a filthy mattress, her on top of him, grinding, or him behind her pushing her face hard down into the mattress, the Pastor taking the man's place as he . . .

The Pastor shakes his head violently from side to side, like someone trying to wake up from a terrible dream, and accelerates away, the couple dwindling in his rear-view mirror. He speaks out loud, talking over the radio in the empty car, 'Protect me, Father. Keep me from Satan's power,' the words seeming to work, his head clearing and the sick pulse in his groin fading as, up ahead, he sees the wooden gate barring the road and he pulls up and pushes the button on the intercom.

'I'm not too sure where he is, Father,' Pete is soon telling him, up at the farmhouse.

'Pastor.'

'Shoot, sorry. Pastor. I think he was up on the farm. Was it something specific? I *love* your sunglasses by the way. Very chic.'

'Just a neighbourly call.' The Pastor smiles stiffly at the thin, simpering young man in a purple tank top.

'Well, why don't I see if I can go find him? Have a seat on the porch here. Missing you already,' Pete trills as he trots off around the corner.

The Pastor takes a seat on the porch, near a huge, bearded guy in a filthy combat jacket who is sitting on the deck shelling peas into a big colander; music – rock and roll – and cooking smells drift out from the kitchen behind him. 'Morning,' the Pastor says.

'Frag,' Bob twitches. 'Frag,' gesturing at the sunshine.

A homo and a retard, the Pastor thinks, smiling back at Bob, brushing a piece of lint from his trousers.

'Hey there,' a woman's voice comes from the kitchen, 'how we coming on with them peas?' Her voice growing louder as the question progressed, the woman herself appearing in the doorway now. She was in her forties, the Pastor guessed, and deeply unattractive: heavyset, with short cropped hair, work jeans and stout motorcycle boots. The simpleton held the colander up to her. 'Thanks, Bob,' she says, looking the Pastor's way as she turns to go back inside.

'Good morning,' the Pastor says.

'Oh, hi, Father,' Julia says. He lets it go. 'Are you . . . is someone taking care of you?'

'Indeed they are,' the Pastor replies, maintaining his smile in the manner of someone holding their breath while wading through a rank, gaseous swamp.

'Can I get you anything? Coffee? Soda?'

'Why no. Thank you all the same.'

He watches her walk back into the kitchen, across the room to the range, where another woman – smaller, slighter, similarly dressed – is stirring a large cooking pot. The fat one slips an arm around the cooking woman as she hands her the colander and kisses her on the cheek. The Pastor turns back towards the cool October sunshine.

A homo, a retard and a pair of goddamned dykes. Batting three for three he just has time to think as the fag comes back around the corner, trailing in his wake an unkempt blond-haired man who the Pastor recognises from his newspaper article and his Internet browsing.

'Found him!' the homosexual trills as they come up onto the porch, the Pastor rising, still managing that smile, as the blond-haired man sticks his hand out and says, 'Hi. I'm JC. What's up, man?'

'There's still a lot to do, Pastor, but we're making a good start. Should hold up to about thirty kids. This'll all be finished by Christmas, Pete reckons.' They are walking through the half-built schoolroom, JC giving the good Pastor the tour. An autumn breeze blows through the milky polythene covering the spaces in the timber walls where the windows have yet to be put in. Their footsteps echo hollow in the empty room, JC's battered Converse with 'Modest Mouse' written on them, the Pastor's six-hundred-dollar alligator-skin loafers. Planks of wood, leaning up against work tables, grey electrical wiring spilling out of tears and gouges in the drywall. Cans of paint and bags of cement.

'Pete?' the Pastor asks.

'Our carpenter. The fellow who showed you in? We picked Pete up way back in, um, Kansas, I think. He's HIV-positive and some of your fellow, ah, believers weren't acting too Christian.' Pastor Glass nods, inwardly shuddering remembering that handshake, fearing that this goddamn smile may soon break his face. 'Anyway,' Jesus is saying, 'you come through here . . .' the Pastor following him out and along a narrow jerry-built hallway, 'and this corridor – we added this ourselves by the way – connects back to the main house. We got a couple of offices in here . . .' They pause to look in: a desk with a glowing PC on it, used mainly by Becky, a couple of tattered old fly posters on the wall (Morrissey, Shellac) and there, in the corner, where the Pastor was staring, the gun cupboard: stout oak with wire-mesh screens, the heavy black metal of the rifles visible through the mesh.

'I see,' the Pastor says, stepping into the room, 'that for all the talk of peace and love you maintain an armoury?'

What's so funny about peace, love and understanding? JC thinks, following him in. 'It's not exactly an armoury, Pastor. We got the rifles for hunting and the handguns and whatnot . . .' Jesus points down, leading the Pastor's gaze to the bottom shelf of the cabinet, where over a dozen pistols were haphazardly stacked. The Pastor, a keen weapons aficionado, recognises most of them: Sig Sauers, Smith & Wessons and Glocks. Revolvers and semi-automatics. 9mms and .38s, Saturday Night Specials and an eight-hundred-dollar German Walther. The semi-automatic assault rifle they took off the Rennet brothers is in there too, along with boxes of various calibres of ammunition. 'Well, people just keep showing up with 'em. We confiscate them, no one's allowed on the property with a personal weapon, and when – if – they leave they can have them back. They're kept under lock and key at all times. It's just . . .' Jesus tails off, looking at the ugly pile of black and chrome metal. 'Why? You know? Why the fuck? Excuse my language.'

'We have the constitutional right to defend ourselves,' the Pastor says. 'And, as I'm sure you know, the Good Book teaches us the same. "*Keep the munition, watch the way, make thy loins strong and fortify –*"'

'Yeah, yeah, "fortify thy power mightily".' JC says, finishing the quotation for him. 'Nahum 2, verse 1.'

'You know the Old Testament well, my so—'

'But Nahum? Really? Come on, Pastor. A couple of thousand out of nearly a million words and the goddamn NRA retards pick 'em out and use 'em to justify keeping themselves armed to the titties forever. Meanwhile thousands of kids die in gun-related accidental deaths every fucking year. Excuse my French. Anyhoo, moving along . . .'

The Pastor takes a moment before he follows, keeping his anger in check. Casting another glance over that gun cupboard.

'And back where we started.' The Pastor catches up as JC strolls back into the kitchen. The two dykes at the stove, a couple of sweating young men washing at the sink, a few kids running around. There is a sweet herbal smell over and above the cooking and the Pastor notices that one of the young men at the sink is openly smoking a marijuana cigarette. 'JAYYYSUZZZZ!' a little girl shrieks delightedly, running full tilt at him. Matilda, Guff Rennet's daughter, eight or nine years old. Jesus scoops the kid up and whirls her around while she howls delightedly. He throws her onto the floor and rips her T-shirt up, burying his face in her brown belly and blowing raspberries into her while she screams with laughter. The Pastor watches uncomfortably, his hands thrumming in his pockets. 'You got kids, Pastor?' Jesus is asking him from the floor.

'MORE!' the kid shrieks.

'Two,' the Pastor replies.

'Fun, ain't they?' Jesus says.

'Indeed,' the Pastor says, looking away. Here, JC knew at once, was a man who had never roughhoused with his children. Who had never thrown them on their backs and buried his face in their flesh. A man whose own father would probably have been more likely to run naked down Main Street than to have interacted physically with his children. Someone who was nothing less than emotionally crippled. 'Is that,' the Pastor says, 'is she your daughter?'

'Hell no,' Jesus says. 'This is Matilda. Say hi to the Pastor, Matty.'

'NO!' Matty screams. Children – their instinctive talent for sensing those talentless with children.

'You got time to stay for lunch, Pastor? What we having today, girls?'

'Vegetable curry,' Julia says over her shoulder.

'I'm afraid not,' the Pastor replies.

Guff Rennet strides in. It is not a happy stride. 'Hi, Guff,' Jesus says. 'This is Pastor Glass. Pastor, Guff Rennet –'

'Oh yeah, all happy goddamn campers in here, huh?' Guff

cuts in, seeing Julia and Amanda and JC all together in the kitchen. 'Matty, c'mon. We're outta here.'

'We're playing!' Matty says, hiding behind JC's leg.

'You going up to Bruntsville?' JC says.

'We're going home. For good,' Guff says.

Little Matty starts to cry.

'Look, man, come on. So we had –' JC says.

'Matty, get your ass over here now!' Guff says, ignoring him.

Crying, doing that slow kid-crying walk, Matty reluctantly makes her way across the room towards her father. Jesus fights the urge to give the kid a hug, tell her it'll be OK. 'Guff,' he says instead, 'we can work this out, can't we?'

'Get fucked, you freak,' Guff says. 'My brothers gonna stay on a while, get that pickup sold, get some of their shit straightened out. But we're outta here.' He throws his crying daughter over his shoulder and stomps on out.

Silence for a moment. Julia stirs that curry. The Pastor clears his throat. Jesus sighs. 'See, Pastor. Hardly a utopia now, is it?'

'Mmmm,' the Pastor says.

'Well, come on then,' Jesus says. 'I'll give you a tour of the farm before you go.'

5

HEY COME WALKING ALONG A RIDGE UP ABOVE THE farm, looking down over the main house with its many extensions and outbuildings, Jesus explaining about their plans to extend it further in the spring, talking about their wind power and solar panels and everything.

'You seem to be well organised in practical terms,' the Pastor says. 'It's more the spiritual side of matters that prompted my, as I say, long-overdue visit.'

'Spiritual, Pastor?'

'You've shown me your wind turbines and your farm, your houses and your solar panels, your water tanks and your schoolhouse. But where –' he stops and turns to JC – 'where is your church?'

'Come on, Pastor,' Jesus says, absent-mindedly toying with a sprig of rosemary he's picked out the ground. 'No disrespect, I'm sure you're, ah, really into, ah, whatever it is you do, but what do I, what do we, want with a church?'

'Salvation, my son.'

Jesus laughs. 'Do you really think – and excuse my language in advance – that God gives a squirt of piss if you worship Him or not? I mean, it's like the Rolling Stones, OK? The Rolling Stones. On a Stones tour there are *hundreds* of people on the road: truck drivers, set designers, carpenters, electricians, caterers, guitar technicians, production people, personal assistants, humpers, teamsters, sound and lighting guys. Do you think Mick Jagger gives a shit whether or not the dude who helped carry a speaker onto the stage in Philadelphia, or the guy who picked up litter in London after the show, do you think Mick cares what that guy thinks about him?'

'I . . . to say that is to try and make a mockery of everything I believe in.'

'So if you believe a bunch of shit people aren't allowed to mock it?'

'One must respect the beliefs of others.'

'Why?'

'Why?'

'Yeah. Why should I respect your bunch of shit? Because you say so? Come on, if you really believe it what do you care what I think?'

'The atheist –' the Pastor begins.

'Are you outta your mind?' Jesus cuts back in. 'Of course I'm not an atheist. I have kissed the face of God, Pastor. And –'

'Blasphemy.'

'– and lemme tell you, He'd kick your ass clean across the room for half the crap you believe.'

'What "crap" would that be?' The Pastor getting close to it now, his temper slipping.

'You know what I like to do for fun sometimes, Pastor?' Jesus steps towards the man, controlling his own temper too now, the Pastor smelling something sweet and herbal from JC's clothes.

'Flip that FM radio dial and listen in to some of the religious stations around here. Man, are there a lot of them, huh? You think I don't know who you are?' JC steps even closer to the Pastor, who suddenly feels himself caught in the force field of a much greater personality. 'I heard you on that asshole Lomax's show, coming down on gays, calling for violence on abortionists, arguing against abortion even in the case of rape? All that retarded stuff. What are you thinking, dude? Are you out of your mind? Don't you know God loves fags? You gotta get off of all of this hate- and fear-mongering shit, because you are going to go straight to Hell, buddy. You know what that little bastard does with people like you down there? False prophets and religious hypocrites? Dude, you will wind up pedalling a ten-foot-long, cast-iron, barbed-wire-spiked dildo into your own ass for all fucking eternity.'

'You . . .' the Pastor is saying, words choking in his throat, the rage coming thick now.

'And, trust me, that is not just a baroque image, Pastor. That's the truth. I've seen it.'

'You have built nothing but a palace of sin here.'

'Yeah, well, feel free to take your miserable, hateful, repressed, vengeful, merciless, Christian-rock-listening, homophobic, sexist fucking ass out of it any time you like.'

The Pastor finds himself breaking the law within seconds of leaving the estate – guilty of using a cellular telephone while in control of a motor vehicle. Scrolling through his address book with a trembling thumb he comes to the number for his cousin Daniel.

Fuck Sheriff Ike.

6

HE FEDERAL BUREAU OF INVESTIGATION ALREADY had a file on Jesus. A celebrity with extreme left-wing views? One who denounced America on live television and then set up his own alternative lifestyle community in the Texan wilderness? Come on, of course there's going to be a file.

In the great, bygone days of J. Edgar Hoover this file would have consisted of several fat Manila folders crammed with transcripts of wiretaps, with glossy, blurry 10×8 black-and-white photographs taken with long-lensed cameras and with inky carbon copies of field agents' reports. Today it consisted of a single digital file on the central server at the Langley Field HQ in Virginia, accessible to any agent anywhere in the country who had the requisite security clearance.

Special Agent Melanie Bruckheimer, at her desk in the FBI's Austin Field Office, finishes taking the call from a Texas ranger named Daniel Glass, taps in her security password and brings the file up on her screen. She pops several documents open; JPEGs and Word documents; a potted biography and personal history, photographs of Jesus on the set of *American Pop Star* and walking down Melrose in LA. There is a 'known associates' file, with photographs of Kris laughing by the pool at the Chateau, Bob scowling from an NYPD mugshot. Then there are the aerial photographs of the Bruntsville estate, taken during several flyovers during the course of the summer. It is these photographs that most interest her. She opens up an email to her friend Gerry Cauldwell at the Bureau of Alcohol, Tobacco and Firearms over in Houston, and attaches one of the aerial photographs. She types 'Call me' into the body of the email and then, into the 'Subject' box, she types the words 'BRUNTSVILLE COMPOUND'.

She is the first person to call it that.

7

IVEN THE CORRECT ENVIRONMENT CERTAIN TYPES of marijuana will, as God intended, grow freely with very little tending. A low-maintenance plant. Their patch was on a plateau of high ground down towards the southern boundary. Sheltered from the wind by surrounding rocks, south-facing and bathed in the warm Texan sunshine for most of the day, it was a fifteen-minute walk from the main centre of the camp: a nice walk too, following the creek for part of the way, then turning uphill through a grove of live oaks, the trees almost bare now in the last days of October.

'October, the trees are stripped bare . . .' Jesus sings again as he and Morgan walk along, canvas sacks thrown over their backs.

'Man, I hate U2,' Morgan says. 'I'm gonna have that in my goddamn head the rest of the day.'

'See,' JC says, 'it's a good song.'

'And talk about a Messiah complex. That's your guy.'

'Damn, Morgs. You're a real indie kid sometimes, you know that?'

'*I'm* an indie kid? Who's the motherfucker owns the complete works of The Field Mice?'

'Good band, man,' Jesus says as they come through the space between the rocks and into the little clearing, the marijuana patch spread out before them, about thirty square yards of plants, yellowing now in the cold. 'OK, I'll start on the left, you take the right and I'll meet you in the middle.'

'Are we doing this because of that preacher asshole the other day?' The lazy drone of a light aircraft carried down to them on the breeze, the small propeller airplane moving slowly across the sky above them, casting shadows across the wetlands.

'Well,' Jesus says, bending and picking, taking only the greenish leaves that are worth drying out, 'let's just say I thought it'd be a good idea to, ah, tidy up some . . .'

8

OUSTON, THE CONDITIONED AIR AND GREEN FERNS (remarkably similar in outline to the marijuana plant), the credenzas and grey honeycomb cubicles of the BATF. Special Agent Gerry Cauldwell, twenty-eight and eager, in the conference room with his boss, Section Chief Don Gerber, forty-three and sceptical. Sceptical but interested, as he passes aerial photographs and field reports from one hand to the other, chewing now and then on the stem of his black, half-moon spectacles.

'And what started all this rolling?' Gerber asks.

'Some pastor reported it to a cousin of his in the Texas Rangers. Ranger passed it on to Mel Bruckheimer at Austin FBI. Mel rang me on the gun stuff. I got the Pastor's statement in here.' He rooted through his file and passed over three pages of stapled A4.

'What's with this Pastor? He got an axe to grind? Something personal?'

'Other than the fact that he's a man of the Church and you

got some long-haired guitar player running around his patch claiming he's the son of God?'

'Mmmm,' Gerber says, reading, nibbling on that stem. 'And the cousin? The ranger?'

'Good record.'

Gerber whistles. 'Lotta stuff in here ... *"drug use ... cache of semi-automatic weapons . . . inappropriate behaviour with children"*?'

'See, that's what I'm thinking, if we –'

'Not much for us here really though, Gerry. On the gun stuff? A dozen or so semi-automatic pistols, an assault weapon or two, some hunting rifles. Christ, half the basements and rec rooms in Texas are better armed than that. The guy's hardly fucking Rambo.'

'Yeah, but they're not his. It's unlawful possession.'

'Technically, yeah, but –'

'I know what you're saying, boss, but listen, the FBI have been keeping a loose eye on this guy. He's made a bunch of public pronouncements in favour of legalising marijuana, talked openly about using it, and if you look here on the aerial shots –' Cauldwell leaned across the table and pointed with his pen – 'they've indicated what might be a possible marijuana patch. Now, none of this interests the Feds too much, but they do want to take a look at the child-abuse claims. So, I was thinking –'

'A multi-agency effort?'

'You got it.'

'Bring the DEA in on the drug stuff, the Feds on the kids and we take the guns?' Gerber says, leaning back.

'Pretty much.'

'And the Texas Rangers – they're gonna want their piece of all this too.'

'Yeah, I figured that.'

'Mmm.' Gerber sits back, swinging his loafers up onto the table, crossing the ankles. 'I think the FBI would want some more substance on the alleged child-abuse stuff. But . . .'

He weighed it up. He had a bright, ambitious twenty-eight-year-old special agent sitting across the walnut table from him, itching to make a name for himself. You didn't do that by the routine stuff; enforcing the Contraband Cigarette Act, busting trucks coming across the border from Juarez with a few hundred cases of Camels. So, Don was wary of his subordinate's interest in this business, yes, but, at the same time, there were the BATF budget hearings coming up in Washington, where Congressmen looking to save a buck would once again be questioning the agency's usefulness. A high-profile case involving a celebrity, guns and drugs? A celebrity who was outspokenly pro-drugs, pro-abortion, anti-nuclear, anti-Church? Who, from what Don was reading here, had pretty much made it a point of honour to insult and defame just about everything America stood for. Might not play too badly with the public at all. Plus, making it a multi-agency effort would – as the kid here had foreseen – mean that the burden of responsibility was spread around. True, they would have to share credit too but, hey, that was rock and roll, as his son was fond of saying.

'What kind of people are they in this compound?'

'Women and children, maybe a hundred men. Communal living. You know, religious lunatics probably.'

In weighing up the pros and cons here, Don Gerber, a sports nut, was also mindful of his stats. In the last three years the BATF had used its SWAT teams 578 times, largely against drug dealers, and had seized around fifteen hundred illegal weapons in the process. In all those hundreds of raids they had come up against gunfire only twice, resulting in three fatalities:

all on the sides of the drug dealers. Hell, in the past decade
they'd only lost one agent in the line, some asshole in California
who blew himself up disabling fireworks. When people saw
heavy force coming down at them – those guys in the black
jumpsuits and combat boots, toting their M16s – nine point nine
times out of ten they just gave it up. Threw down and assumed
the position. The way this looked, a bunch of stoners with access
to maybe twenty weapons, none of them, from what they knew,
even fully automatic? Well. A cakewalk is what it looked like.
In and out. Easy money.

'OK,' Don said finally, swinging his feet back down. 'Get
onto the DEA and keep talking to the FBI. Like I say, I think
they'll want more juice on these child-abuse allegations but . . .
I guess I can take this upstairs to Sam.'

'You da man, boss,' Cauldwell said, slapping his file on the
table.

Politics. Money. Ambition. Public relations. Ego.

The usual reasons stuff got done.

9

ILL YOU KIDS SHUT THE FUCK UP?!' GUFF YELLS,
sticking his head into the doorway that connects
the two bedrooms they've taken at this piece-
of-shit motel; the kids in one room, him and
Carol in the other. Two fucking TVs on, the kids yelling and
her hairdryer coming from the bathroom. Can't hear yourself
fucking think, he thinks as he tears open his third beer. Two
days driving and they were hardly out of Texas. Was gonna be
a long fucking trip, with the kids pissing and moaning about
how they wanted to go back the whole time. His own fucking
kids – fonder of that asshole than their own . . . expensive trip
too, with all the gas and everything, for what had amounted to
a long vacation. A fucking working vacation at that. At least
they'd given him the money back that they'd spent on building
materials. That cocksucker. Talking to him as though he were
a fuck –

'Guff!' Carol's voice, screeching over the hairdryer.

'What?'

'There's someone at the door!'

Sweet Jesus.

He throws the door open, beer in hand, expecting the manager or some neighbour about the TV volume, and sees instead suits, ties, white shirts, an ID in a plastic wallet held towards him, the guy behind the ID saying 'Mr Rennet?', that particular appellation usually a bad sign for Guff.

'Yeah?' he says, trying for a mix of indignant aggression and uncertainty.

'FBI.'

10

ETTING COLDER NIGHTS, SHERIFF IKE THINKS AS HE crosses Main Street, pulling the brim of his hat down into the wind. He was to pick up some creamed corn on his way home, his son and daughter-in-law coming round for dinner. Hopping up onto the sidewalk and about to enter the A&P he notices the car parked about thirty yards up the street in front of Franklin Hardware: a boxy new sedan, spotlessly clean, Austin plates. He notices the driver too: a young fella, sunglasses in place at 5 p.m. on this winter evening, dark suit and tie. As Ike holds the glass door open for Mary Flanders coming out (*'Why thank chew, Sheriff'*, *'Not a problem, Mary'*), he sees a second young man coming out of the hardware store: sunglasses in place, dark suit and tie, purposeful, entitled stride. Ike pretends to read the little postcards stuck in the window of the A&P (*'Cleaner available'*, *'Good home wanted for cats'*) while the car drives carefully off down Main, taking the road up and out of town, towards the mountain pass, observing the speed limit at all times.

Ike walks the thirty or so paces across to Franklin's and wanders on in.

'Evening, Rick.'

'Howdy, Sheriff. You just missed some of your fellow lawmen.'

'I saw. What did those FBI fellas want? If you don't mind me asking.'

'Now how d'you know they were FBI?'

'Shoot, might as well have had a neon sign on that car.'

'Well, they were asking about them hippies over at the old Hausman estate, where that fella who was on the TV is? Askin' 'bout their account. Don't know how they even knew those folks had an account.'

'I guess cos they're the FBI, Rick. And what were they asking about it?'

'Oh, had they made any unusual purchases. Ammonia. Nails. Certain kinds of detergents. Stuff like that . . .'

'Is that right?'

'Yep. You know, I'd have thought they'd come see you first if they had business in town. Professional courtesy 'n' all.'

'Ah, I guess they're busy fellas. Tell you what, gimme a bar of that peanut brittle you got by the register there and I'll be on my way.' The Sheriff, rooting through his change, squinting at the copper and silver in the murky light of the dusty old store.

'No charge, Ike. You have a nice evening now. Give my best to Marge.'

'Much obliged.'

'You think them hippies been up to no good? Couple of the boys were hunting up there. Told me they saw some of 'em skinny-dipping out on the lake.' Rick laughed a scratchy old laugh, like a beat-up car trying to start.

'Hell, lake's on their property 'n' all. Ain't no law against that. G'night, Rick.'

An uneasy Sheriff Ike – crunching his peanut brittle as he walks back towards the A&P, looking east along the road towards the mountains, the moon in the sky now at the same time as the sun – thinking about that car, about ammonia and nails, and about the telephone repair van Chip said he'd seen parked up all day the day before last, out by the wires on the 112, the road that ran parallel to the southern boundary of the old Hausman estate.

11

NTER-AGENCY MEETING AT THE BATF'S PLACE, silver pots of coffee and plates of pastries on the side, jugs of ice-water and files on the table and, projected on the big whiteboard that took up most of one wall, a high-res aerial shot of what was now, officially, the Bruntsville Compound. Projected beside this, smaller, was a grainy close-up of a smaller part of the estate, what looked to be an enclosed, rocky escarpment, the blurred figures of two men visible at its edges.

Eight people gathered around that table, six men and two women. Representing the BATF were Gerry Cauldwell, Don Gerber and Agent Bryan Brent from their Special Weapons and Tactics Division. Representing the FBI were Melanie Bruckheimer and her boss, Section Chief Stanley Tąwse. Over from the Drug Enforcement Agency in San Antonio were Connor Rifkind and Shirley Blass, and over there in the corner, eating his Danish and feeling out of place among all the government badges, was Captain Craig Kinman of the Texas Rangers.

This thing was moving now; the new intelligence coupled with the positive response Don's boss, BATF Bureau Chief Sam Rodman, had received to the mooted raid in Washington ('This man,' Barbara Muller, the Attorney General, had said to Rodman, 'seems to me to be deeply anti-American at the very least') had seen to that.

'Shirley, Connor,' Don was saying, very much the man in charge here (it was the BATF's party for the time being), 'why don't one of you guys fill, ah, fill us in on the DEA's take on what we're seeing in that, in the smaller image up there?'

'Yeah,' Rifkind said, moving to the whiteboard, picking up the pointer. 'This was taken last week on a flyover. It's a secluded area to the southern end of the property. Definitely a marijuana patch we think. A hundred square yards. Mature plants. You'd get a decent-sized crop from there, something in the region of fifty to sixty kilos –'

'Is it arguable –' Tawse cuts in, 'sorry, Connor – but is it arguable from a legal standpoint that this volume could be considered for personal use?'

'Sixty keys?' Shirley Blass replies. 'Not for the amount of people living there. Not unless it was personal use over the next couple of years.'

'So there's intent to distribute there?' Cauldwell says.

'Correct,' Rifkind says. 'From these images we can't determine what type of plants they're growing, but there's a good chance it's a hydroponic varietal. One of these new super-weeds you've been hearing so much about, ladies and gentlemen.'

'Thanks, Connor,' Don says. 'And I believe the FBI have some breaking news for us too?'

'Yeah,' Tawse says, reaching for the nearest coffee pot. 'Go ahead, Mel.'

'We tracked down and questioned a family who surveillance said had recently departed the Bruntsville Compound.' Melanie Bruckheimer, standing and passing around copies of the statement, shoving them along and across the lacquered walnut conference table that was bought and paid for by the citizens of the United States. 'The Rennets. They stayed at the compound for nearly three months before deciding to leave. Field unit detained them at a motel on the Oklahoma/Texas border. The father, a Mr Guff Rennet, alleges that one of the reasons for their departure was what he felt was inappropriate behaviour on the part of this Jesus character toward his eight-year-old daughter.'

'What does the daughter say?' Don, not looking up from the statement.

'We haven't questioned her properly yet,' Bruckheimer replies. 'We're bringing them here to meet with a child psychologist.'

'The other question that needs to be asked,' Tawse says, 'is what's going on with all these kids – and from what we can gather there's maybe fifty or sixty of them – being out of the school system and holed up in a private compound like this?'

'Exactly,' Gerry Cauldwell says. 'Our feeling is that in PR terms this is an easy sell. A religious nut who's made explicit anti-American statements, who's holed up in some jerry-built private compound with lots of children and a cache of weapons, and who we now know to be cultivating drugs on the property?'

'On the weapons front – do we know anything definite there?' Tawse asks.

'Bryan?' Don Gerber gestures to Bryan Brent from SWAT.

'I interviewed this Pastor Glass who made the initial allegations and who claims to have seen this "armoury". He seems to know his guns. From what I could establish from showing him photographs, they've got at least half a dozen high-calibre hunting rifles in there, some with telescopic sights, maybe a dozen pistols – some semi-autos, some large calibre too: nines and forty-fives – a few revolvers and, most worryingly, a couple of assault rifles, AR-15s, which, as you know, are the civilian equivalent of our M16 –'

'It's very possible that these have been converted to full automatic fire,' Gerry cuts in.

'Yeah, many of the street-level AR-15s we seize have been converted in that way,' Brent allows. 'But I couldn't say for sure based on what the Pastor was able to tell me. What is certain though . . . you got about twenty pieces in there, lot of semi-automatics . . . depending on their ammunition situation they could, you know, they could give you some trouble with these weapons.'

'I'm getting the sense that the BATF is already leaning in a certain direction here . . .' Tawse says, looking at Gerber, almost smiling.

'Well, Stan,' Don Gerber replies, 'given the size and layout of the property – I mean, we're talking about a couple of thousand acres here – the scattered nature of where people are living, where the drugs are, where the weapons are . . . the scenario of knocking on the front door and going through the motions with a routine search warrant would give ample time for some kind of cover-up or disposal operation. And, as you know, statistically we have an excellent track record on performing these kinds of raids.'

'I have to say,' Rifkind says, 'from a DEA perspective, we would definitely favour the element of surprise here.'

'So what are you thinking, tactically speaking?' Tawse asks, blowing on that coffee.

'Three teams,' Brent says, getting up and going to the board with his pointer. 'The first one in position here, on the south-west border, who would come in through the woods here and take the marijuana patch here.' That pointer clicking against the board every time he says the word 'here'. 'The second team coming in through the wire near to the main entrance here and proceeding straight to the main house to seize the weapons, and a third team in reserve, to be dropped in by helicopter here if needed – in the middle of the property to the back of the main house. Fifty or sixty men in total. Texas National Guard would supply us with Black Hawks and maybe a tank or two for backup.'

'Mmmm. Pretty fucking ballsy considering the number of women and children in there . . .' Tawse says.

'You know,' Don Gerber says, 'I really don't anticipate a single shot being fired . . .'

'Yeah,' Tawse concedes, 'I hear you, Don. But you're coming from a point of view of taking down drug dealers: people who know they've done bad and who know when they're outgunned. You can predict how people like that are going to behave in a given situation. These guys –' he picks up a glossy photograph, taken at long range, showing Jesus, Morgan and Pete laughing at something – 'in their minds they're just innocently going about their business. You're less certain what they're liable to do when they see black jumpsuits coming out of the woods at them.'

'Are you saying the FBI would favour a less . . . direct approach?' Cauldwell asks.

'No,' Tawse says, 'not necessarily. A raid might well be the right tactic. I'm just . . . making a point, guys.'

'Duly noted,' Gerber says.

'And in terms of time frame?' Blass from DEA asks.

'Agent Brent's already got his squad in training at Fort Rigg,' Gerber says.

'We're just sixty miles south of Bruntsville,' Brent nods. 'We should be ready to roll in three to four weeks.'

Dates, strategies, tactics. Logistics and practicalities. Not a whole lot on ethics or morality. Once things got rolling, stuff like '*Why* are we doing this?' tended to take a back seat to '*How* are we going to do this?'

It would be noted later – at the internal inquiry, at the trial – that in this meeting the FBI's Stanley Tawse had raised 'concerns' about how the 'compound inhabitants' were likely to react to the 'potential use of deadly force'. It would be noted, but it would still not be enough to save his job.

12

OBBY DENVER'S BAR-B-Q CHICKEN AND RIBS IS A fifteen-restaurant chain with outlets across central Texas. Founded by the IRS-troubled country singer in the late 1980s, they specialise in 'honest Lone Star State cooking': whole chickens and blackened slabs of pork baby back ribs slathered in dark barbecue sauce; collard greens, black-eyed peas and pretty good cornbread. Low lighting, piped country and western and comfy faux-leather banquettes. Licensed too. The branch situated just off the 122 between the estate and Brunstville was a favourite with Miles and Danny and it was here that JC brought everyone for a Thanksgiving-dinner treat.

Seated all along both sides of one of the long wooden tables in the back, near the restrooms: Becky, Miles and Danny. Morgan, Kris and Big Bob. Gus and Dotty. Claude and Pete, Julia and Amanda, and, in the middle leaning back against the wall, hands behind his head, a grin on his face, his third beer starting to get good to him as he listens to Becky trying to make a dumb-assed speech over Morgan and Kris's heckling, Jesus Christ.

That's right, there are thirteen of them present.

'Will you assholes shut up?' Becky says.

'Man, in front of her kids too,' Morgan says.

'Terrible,' Kris says, shaking his head, Miles and Danny giggling.

'All I'm trying to say,' Becky raises her glass of beer again, 'is that I think, given how well the harvest has gone, couple of deals we've been able to do on selling some stuff on, and thanks to Claude on all that . . .'

Claude grins shyly.

'. . . well, financially, it looks like we're going to be in a much better position that I originally thought. So, everyone, well done.'

Whistles and cheering and the clacking of beer mugs as the food arrives – *'Who wanted the spicy chicken?'* – and everyone starts digging into those steaming baked potatoes, glistening mounds of slaw and beans, everyone talking over each other, happy and excited as they pass those plates around.

Jesus stops with a forkful of emerald-green collards halfway to his mouth and looks around the table: the guy with HIV laughing with the dirt-poor farm boy, the lesbians and the broken Vietnam vet, the ancient alcoholics all scrubbed up for their night out, the ex-hooker, ex-junkie single mom passing plates down to her kids, the ex-fat guy and the black drummer. The poor, the pissed-on, the off-the-radar, non-taxpaying dreck. Other than his dewy-eyed, Springsteenesque belief in the potency, the primacy of rock and roll, JC is not a sentimental man, but, at this moment, as he looks from face to face, as in a made-for-TV movie, the light seems to get softer, the film slowing down, a gentle tinkling of piano fading up on the soundtrack. All his people right here right now.

To bring hope unto the hopeless.

Just as he allows himself a smile at this thought, he glances around, across the restaurant, and sees a middle-aged couple. The man has been looking their way but his head dips back down towards his food as Jesus looks over, the guy's mouth still working, muttering something, shaking his head as he cuts his steak. A couple of tables away from the couple is a group of four younger guys, one of them whispering something to his buddy, the buddy grinning as he looks their way, Jesus following the guy's gaze and realising he's looking at Julia tenderly wiping something off Amanda's face, the two women in their big boots and work denims and short hair, that look saying all the usual things it said to a bunch of young guys with mullets and metal T-shirts and cap-sleeved denim, Jesus depressingly understanding what the guy's commentary probably consists of, Jesus thinking all of this through in a couple of seconds, all of it coming right on the back of *'to bring hope unto the hopeless',* and triggering a second, ancillary thought lower down in his brain, a darker thought, shadowing, stalking the first one: *This will end.* To live in peace, love and understanding with your friends? To work a little and blow some grass and drink beer and hang out and be happy? Surely this will not be allowed to continue?

A squeaky voice next to him and a little fist banging into his thigh brings him back. 'Ow! Miles, what's up, buddy?'

'I said – we know something you don't know!'

'Oh yeah?'

'Yeah,' Danny says, leaning in over his brother. 'We do!'

'It's your birthday soon . . .' little Miles whispers, grinning to bust the goddamn band.

'Miles,' Becky warns from along the table, that mother hearing in full effect.

Jesus laughs and looks along at Becky. 'No surprises, OK, Becks?' he says. No surprises. He meant it too. He'd be thirty-three this December 25. Thirty-three didn't work out too well for him the last time around.

Danny and Miles both giggling their asses off now. 'Oh you think that's funny, huh?' Jesus says, grabbing Miles round the thigh, digging his thumb right into the muscle there, the kid laughing hysterically, squeaking with delight, trying to say 'No! No!' The unforced, genuine laughter of children, spontaneous as sneezing: truly the music of God. Jesus playing that music for all it's worth, tickling and jabbing at the boy, grabbing him into a headlock and nuzzling his rough stubble into the soft flesh of his neck, Danny punching at Jesus' arm, trying to get in there, wanting his piece of the action, Jesus flicking an arm out at Danny, getting the odd playful tickle in under his guard, the boys' cries competing with the piped Kenny Rogers music, drawing more glances from the other diners.

'Ah, 'scuse me, Jesus?' He looks up, the howling Miles practically stretched across his lap by this time, and sees first the butt of the pistol in the black, leather holster, the golden badge on the chest, the silvery beard above it. 'Sorry to interrupt your dinner, but could I have a minute of your time?'

'Sure, Sheriff.'

They take their drinks to the bar, the glances from the diners emboldening into actual stares as Jesus, in faded jeans, Converse and tattered Melvins T-shirt follows the Sheriff across the room.

'What fresh hell is this then?' Pete says to Becky as they watch Jesus and the Sheriff take up position at the bar, both men drinking beers – JC a glass filled from the table pitcher, Ike a long-necked Bud – and leaning easily against the mahogany.

'Who knows?' Becky sighs, patting Bob's forearm reassuringly, Bob having automatically tensed up some as soon as something unexpected intrudes on the boss.

'Yeah, we need nails from time to time,' Jesus is saying across the room, raising a palm to Bob to let him know all is well. 'But ammonia? What do they think we're up to out there?'

'I think they think you're making bombs.' The Sheriff keeps his voice down and his eyes on Jesus.

'Bombs?' Jesus says it like it is the strangest word he's ever heard. Just lets it hang there. 'I mean, *bombs*? Hell, why would they even think that?'

'Well –' Ike takes a long pull on his beer – 'you know the FBI. Since events up in New York City some years back, the damn Patriot Act and all, I sometimes think 'less you got the Stars and Stripes flying in your front yard and your family reciting the Pledge of Allegiance before dinner every night, they figure you *got* to be up to something.' Ike shakes his head, traces a bead of beer running down the neck of his bottle with his fingernail. 'And don't forget, son, some people probably struggle to get a handle on why you're doing the things you do. See, I'm a Christian myself. The wife and I go to church every Sunday, rain or shine. And, just between the two of us –' Ike leans in conspiratorially – 'I don't think you're any more the Son of God than I'm Columbo. The thing is . . . most young folks who make a pile of money on a TV show and get their picture in all the papers they want the easy way. They can't get to Los Angeles fast enough. Buy themselves a mansion and hang out in nightclubs or what have you. From what I can gather you *left* Los Angeles, bought a broken-down old ranch way out here in the back of beyond and declared open house for about any misfit that finds their way to your door. Don't seem like the easy way to me. So I figure you must have a good reason for going the hard way.'

'Well, Sheriff,' Jesus smiles, 'sometimes the hard way is the hard way for a reason.'

Ike nods and rests his elbows on the bar, moving closer to

Jesus. 'But, just seeing as we're talking here, tell me, son, have you pissed anyone off lately? I mean, more than usual?'

'Ah, we had a family leave, but that's happened before. Uh . . . oh, wait. I had kind of an, um, set-to, with that Pastor guy a few weeks back.'

'Pastor Glass? Charlie Glass?'

'Uh, yeah. That's him. He a friend of yours, Sheriff?'

'No. But he's not someone you'd want as an enemy.'

'Hell, I ain't got no enemies, have I?' They both laugh at this. Jesus sighs and looks into his glass. 'You say you're a Christian, Sheriff, but you're not like the Pastor.'

'Well, a lot of folks like to overcomplicate things now, don't they? I ain't too bright so I try and keep it pretty simple myself: do unto others. That kinda thing.'

'Man, you'd get on with my dad, Sheriff.'

Ike laughs and looks over at their table, Miles and Danny chasing each other around now. 'You folks having a good time?'

'Always,' JC says. 'Happy Thanksgiving, Sheriff.'

'And to you, son,' Ike says as they touch beers, the neck of the Bud clacking against the frosted glass of Jesus' mug.

Exactly as this is happening, as beer touches beer, the word comes down from Washington, from the Attorney General's office, to Tom Hawkes, Director of the BATF, and then from Tom's office down to Don Gerber's office. And Don finds the word to be good. As does Gerry Cauldwell, who places the call to Special Agent Bryan Brent at Fort Rigg, who also finds the word good.

Two weeks' time: Saturday December 8.

Brent walks out onto the porch of the officers' mess, into the cold Texas night, and looks out over the assault course, listening to the shouts and cries of his men as they go through their paces, practising forced entry, scaling razor-wire fences, finding cover in open fields. The pleasing crunch of heavy combat boots on the canopy of pine needles carries across to him in the gathering dusk.

13

NCREDIBLE THAT SUCH A DAY HAD THE TEMERITY TO even begin, that the sun would even dare to rise upon the elements that were locking into place below it, elements that one of the defence attorneys would later argue constituted 'a perfect storm'.

Unusually, JC had risen early that December morning, Morgan and Bob having finally convinced him to come with them to try and tempt some of the really big catfish out of the pool up at the head of Big Lake. They'd set off in the old jeep just before dawn, the only light from the main house the glow of red, yellow and blue bulbs from the big Christmas tree in the hall (yeah, JC hated making a fuss over his birthday but you had to play ball for the kids), JC rubbing his eyes in the back seat of the jeep and fumbling with the cap for the flask of coffee Morgan had brought. Jesus had slept badly – a low, light drowse he kept waking up from, being pulled up out of shallow sleep by a far-off growling noise, like something was out there deep in the woods, circling.

At 7.22 a.m., just as Special Agent Enrico Pelo of the BATF's

SWAT team cut through the old, rusting barbed wire on the southern perimeter (his twenty-four-year-old heart pumping, having to stop himself from grinning, alive with the excitement that, after nearly two years on the squad, he was finally not only going in on a live raid, he was in the lead team), JC, Morgs and Bob were dropping their lines into the cold dark water about a mile and a half from the main house.

Becky and the boys were sleeping late, the door to Miles and Danny's bedroom left open a little, because Miles didn't like the dark, he liked the soft light of the big Christmas tree in the hall falling across his bed, reminding him that Santa was just around the corner.

The Rennet brothers were up early too that day, down at the makeshift garage, where they'd finally towed that pickup. Deek had got a new transmission and they figured if they got it in by late morning then Deek would drive the truck over to Austin with Pat following in his Dodge. They'd sell it for a nice profit and be back with the extra Christmas money by nightfall. Pat zippered up his overalls in the headlights, shivering and yawning, while Deek rooted around on the floor of the pickup for the wrench, shoving the big old Remington .306 along the back seat. They always brought the hunting rifle with them when they came down here to work: you never knew what edible wildlife you'd run into on the way back.

The coolest heads far away.

Young excitable men in combat gear ready to see action.

Children sleeping in a wood-frame house.

A couple of good old boys with last night's beer still thick in their veins and a high-powered rifle by their side.

'A perfect storm' indeed.

Pelo lagging just behind team leader Sergeant Anthony Berkowitz as they come through the woods, fifteen of them spread out, dressed in black camo, M16s cocked and locked and carried combat-ready. 9mm pistols on their hips, flash grenades on their belts, all of it bought and paid for by the US taxpayer, taxpayers like the ones they are advancing on now, brown leaves and tiny branches crushing softly underfoot, Pelo and the others stopping in their tracks just short of the edge of the treeline and dropping down as the Sarge raises a clenched, gloved fist silently in the air. Something up ahead, light and noise a few hundred yards away across the open ground. Pelo checks his watch – it has taken them just over ten minutes to cover the half-mile through the woods. Right on schedule. The B team should be in position by the wire near the main gates now.

'*Motherfucker*,' Pat Rennet says from under the truck as, with a final grunt, he wrenches the bolt off the casing and takes out the old trans. He passes it up to Deek who bends over to examine it in the headlight. 'Yeah,' Deek says, 'shot to hell all right.'

'Gimme that rag down, will ya?' his brother says. 'Fucken oil everywhere.' Deek moves around the front of the pickup to grab a rag from the box by the passenger-side front wheel and stops as he glances off into the dark woods.

'Shit,' Deek Rennet whispers.

A couple of miles away Morgan says, laughing, 'And remember that time, that dressing room in Denver? Where some filthy, nasty motherfucker had taken a shit in the goddamn shower stall?'

'Oh man,' Jesus says, laughing too. 'And the promoter thought it was one of us?'

'Who were we playing with that night? Scud Mountain Boys?'

'Nah. Wasn't it Slint?'

'Slint, that's right.'

'Frag,' Bob says softly, holding a finger to his lips, nodding towards the water.

'Sorry, Bob,' Jesus whispers.

'Shit,' Morgan says, quietening down too, 'don't you miss touring, man?'

'We'll get back to it,' Jesus says. 'We'll get back to it. Here, pass that coffee over, Morgs . . .'

Becky yawns and rolls over in her sleep, dozing but knowing it's getting to the time when the boys will be awake, one part of her mother-hearing already tuned towards them. She loves this time of the morning now, because she knows that it wasn't always this way. A few years back, before she met JC and the guys, when she was still drinking and hitting the pipe, some days she'd come round on the kitchen floor with Danny slapping her awake and Miles looking on, scared and nervous, like he thought she'd died. She'd nearly lost them, the boys. The thought of them winding up state-raised is still enough to flash a cold sweat over her and to remind her just how much she values this – waking up fresh and clean and sober and there for them. She eyes the clock by the bed: 7.33. She has some banking stuff to do up in Bruntsville this morning and then she's going Christmas shopping with Pete and Claude. Cold out there. Ten more minutes. Her foot finds a warm spot.

'Where?' Pat elbowing forward under the truck, his head and shoulders coming out by the tyre, Deek crouched down out of the headlight beam, pointing towards the woods.

'There,' Deek says.

Both brothers straining in the half-light, scanning the treeline. 'Probably just a fucken deer,' Pat whispers.

'Wasn't no deer.'

'Who the hell is gonna be out in th—' Pat snaps the word off as he sees a black shape moving fast, darting between two trees, something glinting in its hand. 'Fuck,' he hisses. *Fuck*. Get, get the –'

'Way ahead of you, brother,' Deek says, reappearing at Pat's elbow now, the big Remington cradled in his arms, the bolt going back with an oily clack as he chambers a round and starts moving towards the door.

'Careful,' Pat says. 'Shit. There's lots of 'em!' Another shape moving in the darkness.

'Hunting rifle,' the Sarge whispers back.

'I got a shot,' Pelo tells the Sarge as he looks at Deek Rennet's head in the cross hairs of his infrared scope.

'Do not fire unless fired upon,' the Sarge whispers. 'Robertson, see if you can get up around there and come in behind –'

'HEY!' Deek's voice booms out. 'Whoever the fuck you are, come on outta those trees right now!'

'Shit,' the Sarge whispers. Split second: take them out but give away surprise with several hundred yards to go to the main compound? Fall back into the woods and tell the B team to go in first? Abort?

'Fire a warning shot,' Pat whispers to Deek.

Deek tilts the rifle at the treetops and – *BOOM!* – The high-calibre weapon shatters the dawn silence and all hell breaks loose.

A barrage of automatic fire blazes from the woods, *tearing* into the cinder-block garage, sending Deek scrambling backwards behind the truck, Pat rolling out from under it as lead whips a few feet above their heads, ding ding dinging through the truck they had about finished fixing up.

'JESUS CHRIST!' Pat yells.

'What the fuck is that?' Jesus says, he and Morgan standing up as one. Bob is already whipping past them, sprinting through the trees for the jeep, knowing exactly what a dozen or so M16s firing together sounds like.

Becky leaping out of bed and heading for the boys' room.

Claude looking up from the row of winter squashes he is tending up on the farm.

People waking up all over, in their cabins, Quonset huts and yurts.

'Come on!' Deek says, taking his brother by the elbow, the Rennet brothers coming barrelling out of the back door and down a little hill, under cover now and sprinting for the main house as, behind them, bullets tear the garage to pieces.

'Get to the fucking gunroom!' Deek yells at Pat, a few years younger and already a few yards ahead of him, before he turns, crouches and caps off a round in the vague direction of the woods.

'Raven, this is Falcon,' Berkowitz is screaming into his radio, concussion in his ears, cordite in his nostrils. 'We are under fire! Repeat, we are under fire! Move in! Move in!'

A Bradley tank – a fucking *tank* – crashing through the fencing a few hundred yards north of the main house now, SWAT troopers pouring in behind it, throwing themselves onto their bellies, seeking cover as an astonished Claude watches from the farm.

JC and Morgan holding on tight as Bob takes the muddy potholed track at sixty miles per, the shots they've been hearing muffled now by the roar of the engine, audible again in the tiny gaps of silence when Bob drops down to shift gear, a deer leaping out of their way, the farmhouse out of sight, just over the next hill.

Berkowitz's A team coming up the path from the south, running hard, bringing a second front down on the farmhouse. A sleepy teenage boy wandering out of one of the Quonset huts into their path, getting a rifle butt in the stomach and his face forced down into the dirt and told to stay there.

Deek and Pat Rennet in the gunroom, Deek smashing the window with the barrel and levelling the Remington at one of the black figures elbowing his way along the muddy bank near the main gate, Pat behind him working a crowbar into the metal doors of the gun cabinet. 'Hurry the fuck up!' Deek screams. 'There's hundreds of them!'

'Sir! Weapon at two o'clock!' a trooper says, seeing the long barrel from behind the Bradley just as Deek's finger tightens on the trigger. Deek squeezes a shot off, missing the guy, and, half a second later, half a dozen M16s start emptying in the direction of the gunroom, 5.56mm rounds shredding through the wooden house, slamming into the big cinder blocks.

Becky screaming, Miles crying, as she gets the boys under their bed. 'Stay here!' she says and starts crawling towards the gunfire.

'Mommy! Mommy!'

Claude running full tilt down the path towards the troopers, pitchfork still in hand, shouting 'Hey! Hey! What the fuck! What the fuck!' above the gunfire and the diesel roar of the Bradley. He is less than a hundred yards from the troopers when one of them sees that pitchfork, just seeing a guy running towards him with a 'long rifle-like shape' in his hands (the words he will use later, at the trial), and he raises his M16 and puts a short burst through Claude's chest, Claude dead before he hits the ground, three holes the size of oranges across his lungs.

Berkowitz on the radio again: 'Multiple shooters! Send Eagles! Repeat, send Eagles!'

The jeep coming skidding around the final bend: JC's and Morgan's jaws dropping as they see the battlefield ahead of them; the tank manoeuvring clumsily in front of the farmhouse, skeins of silver-blue gunsmoke drifting on the pale morning air, the crackle of automatic weapons, the thud, thud, thud of rounds hitting the wooden structure.

'What the fuck?' Jesus is saying as Bob floors it, doing eighty straight downhill now.

Becky crawling into the gunroom just as Pat Rennet tears the door off the gun cabinet, Deek behind him capping off with the Remington, working the bolt and just holding it above his head to fire.

'WHAT THE FUCK ARE YOU DOING?!' Becky screams.

Pat, ignoring her, pulling out their confiscated AR-15, setting it to 'semi-auto' with trembling hands. Becky hears something smashing beside her head and just has time to register that a bullet has gone through the glass door of the office a couple of feet to her right, before she throws herself at Pat, grabbing the gun. 'Put that down! *You're going to get us all fucking killed!'*

'Lady, we are being attacked!' Rennet yells as they tussle over the rifle.

'Gimme the fucking gun!' Becky screams.

Pat tugs the gun away and smacks Becky sharply in the face with the butt, breaking her nose, sending her sprawling in broken glass and shell casings. He throws himself against the wall by the window, yelling 'YEE-HAW! GET SOME!' and cutting loose as the air fills with an ominous shuck and thump.

Jesus, Morgan and Bob piling out of the jeep and throwing themselves onto the ground as, all at once, they see Becky come stumbling out of the back door, blood streaming down her face while, with an explosion of noise, two helicopter gunships clatter over the roof of the farmhouse, each one bristling with ordinance.

Surreal, Jesus thinks. *This is just surreal.*

He grabs Becky. 'Becks! What the f—' shouting over the chopper blades, the gunfire, the roar of the tank.

'The Rennets,' she says nasally, pinching the bridge of her nose. 'The gun cabinet. They –'

Right then a guy they don't even know, who JC vaguely recognises as someone who arrived a couple of weeks ago, comes running out of the house with a rifle in his arms and starts firing at the helicopters, blazing away in open view. He goes down in a hail of bullets from the nearest chopper as the two ugly, black beasts dip their noses towards the ground and then scatter away across the fields, the backdraught nearly knocking them off their feet. A SWAT trooper comes tearing around the corner and is levelling his rifle when there's a staccato burst of gunfire right behind them and the trooper goes down. They turn to see Pat Rennet disappearing back into an upstairs window.

'Oh no, oh fuck fuck fuck,' Jesus is saying, and now there's a roaring noise, a searing heat, the clanking of metal and the Bradley comes around the corner, a jet of flame from its turret licking along the side of a wall, the wooden farmhouse going up like tinder.

'The boys!' Becky screams. Morgan is huddling down against the concrete base of the water tower, his head in his hands, crying.

'WHAT ARE YOU DOING!' Jesus screams at the tank, stepping towards it, his arms extended, as bullets whip all around them. In response to JC's advance the machine gun mounted to the right of the Bradley's flame-thrower begins to swivel around towards them.

No, Big Bob thinks. *Way wrong time*.

He knows well his friend's insistence on reason, his near inexhaustible willingness to meet hatred and malevolence with love and understanding. But Bob knows what happens in firefights, those pockets of hell where men switch off things like reason and understanding and plug straight into the reptilian core. No mistake – these people mean to kill them. Just as the tank's machine gun – Bob recognises it as a 7.62mm – opens up, taking fist-sized bites out of the concrete wall of the rec room behind them, Bob *throws* himself into JC and Becky, driving both of them down beside Morgan, into the drainage ditch that runs along the wall of the house, JC's head piling into the breeze-block lower wall, knocking him out cold, Bob pushing Becky down on top of him, cramming those he loves into that safe space down behind the water tower.

It is Bob's moment now.

In many senses his whole life has been but a prelude to this moment.

The whumping chopper blades, the stinging clouds of cordite, the rattle of the M16s, the smell of fire, the screaming of the terrified and the wounded.

Home again.

Bob: moving eerily fast now for a man of sixty, throwing himself into a low run, quickly getting inside the tank's range, the coaxial machine gun unable to follow him, Bob's mind slipping so fast into old patterns, looking for defilades, working out fields of fire, escape routes, instinctively hugging the building, the building hot, burning inside, as an automatic rifle opens up somewhere nearby and he throws himself headlong into the drainage ditch, pulling the body of the dead trooper Pat Rennet shot into the ditch with him and snapping the strap on the guy's M16 off, pulling extra clips out of the guy's webbing belt. Bob grabs a peek above the ridge and sees two SWAT troopers running towards him, one reloading, one already aiming at him. Bob firing two short, controlled bursts from his shoulder and both guys going down, Bob not watching them fall, already heading back the way he came.

Bob throwing himself through the ragged, shot-out window frame, cutting himself up pretty good and landing on his ass in the back hallway that connects the main house with the schoolroom, hot as hell in here and someone screaming, heavy footsteps coming towards him through the smoke and flames: Pat Rennet running along holding a shotgun now, working the pump, screaming 'YEAH! YEAH!', his eyes glittering, crazed, combat-fried, a look Bob last saw beside some river near the Cambodian border nearly forty years ago. Bob crouches and shoots him straight through the face from about fifty feet, a crimson spray and Pat vanishing.

Into a low run again, bullets ripping through the wood just above him, down towards the big hall where he can see the Christmas tree – a thirty-foot-high blaze, Bob's eyebrows and beard crackling and singeing even at this distance – a body on the floor in front of him and, with a sick lurch, Bob realises it is Pete, his eyes open, his neck hanging open too, just a slash of meat. 'Frag,' he says tenderly, closing his eyes and then tearing off Pete's white T-shirt, ripping it in half right down the front. Rolling sideways into a bathroom Bob sees Kris; in a corner, trembling, shaking, his left hand pressed to his right shoulder, moaning in pain, blood streaming thick between his fingers, Bob checking the wound quickly, telling Kris 'Frag', meaning 'stay here' as he dunks the T-shirt into the toilet bowl, soaking it, and ties it around his head. Glancing left he sees orange and red blips whipping noiselessly past the window and just has time to think, *tracer, they're firing tracer rounds into a wooden building full of women and children,* before he's rolling sideways back into the corridor on his belly, a SWAT uniform appearing in front of him and Bob shooting him twice right in the chest, a fast double-tap, then crawling over the body – the guy's speaking, trying to say something to Bob through a gurgle of blood – heading for the doorway to the burning hall.

JC comes round to the sound of a rifle cracking close to his right ear, firing several shots in quick succession, the concussion deafening him. To his left he sees Morgan and Becky, Morgan holding her tightly while she cries and struggles, trying to run out into the whipping storm of bullets, saying something over and over again that JC cannot hear but that he knows is *'the boys, the boys'*. He turns to his right and sees the long rifle barrel protruding from the window just a foot or so from his shoulder, Deek Rennet behind it pumping the trigger, a terrible snarl across his face. *Should have listened to the guys and kicked them out of here. I'm sorry.* There is a pause in the firing and the rifle tilting upwards as Deek goes to slam another magazine in there and Jesus jumps across and grabs the barrel, pulling it down and away from Deek, clean through the broken window. Jesus hefts the rifle up and tosses it out into the open. He falls back down into the ditch in time to see that Deek is shouting at him through the window as he reaches behind his back and pulls out a chrome pistol. *Becky. Should have listened to Becky and dumped all those guns in the lake. I'm sorry.* Deek pulls the slide back on the pistol and levels it at Jesus and then there is an explosion of gunfire somewhere behind and above them and Deek Rennet's body simply seems to vaporise in a pink mist as the helicopter gunship roars straight overhead, its minigun still firing, a rainbow of burning tracer tearing up the building and arcing over the roof and off into the Texan sky, the big wind turbines turning over impassively behind it all.

Bob reaches the doorway leading into the main hall. It's just an inferno in there, burning timbers falling, the Christmas tree over on its side, flames from floor to ceiling. *Fuck it.* Into the inferno, no time to crawl or take any kind of cover, just a full-tilt sprint, clutching the wet T-shirt to his face, feeling the flesh on the back of his hands burning off, barrelling straight through, crying out as he feels one, two, three bullets hit his left side – thigh, abdomen, biceps – hoping he'll have enough strength to make it, coming smashing through the door and throwing himself onto the floor, the smoke so thick, visibility just a couple of feet, Bob crawling forward, pulling himself with his elbows, his left leg numb now, blood filling his boot as he sees them: Miles and Danny, still under the bed, good little boys doing just what their mom told them to do, Danny crying, cradling his little brother who lolls unconscious against his shoulder, his lips blue against his milk-white face as Bob gathers them to him, the bedclothes above them smoking hot now too.

Not much time. On so many levels, not much time.

The wall with the window, but the window is melting, just a furnace. Forget it.

No way back across the hall either, barely made it through the first time.

The back wall of the bedroom, wooden, giving out onto the yard.

Bob levels the M16 and empties the mag into the wall, vaguely hoping there's no one he cares for standing on the other side. Schlocks another mag in there and empties it too, then another, Bob putting nearly a hundred rounds through the wooden wall, close grouping at point-blank range. Searing pain all up his left side, fluid, blood, sloshing in his lungs now as he picks up the boys and gets to his feet, mostly using his right leg, the left about gone. He runs at the wall and leaps, turning around in mid-air as he reaches it, Danny screaming 'Mommy!' Bob screaming too as he slams his right shoulder and back into the shredded, smoking timber, all six and a half feet and 230 pounds of him hitting it with everything he has.

Outside Morgan and Becky look on, stunned, as a few yards away the back wall of the house seems to *explode* outwards and Bob comes flying through clutching the boys to his chest.

The surreal sensation of going from a black, hellish, boiling room into bright clear sunshine in a split second, Bob still clutching the kids as he falls through six feet of cold winter air, breaking his hip as they land on the concrete path, Miles cutting his forehead open but waking up, coughing and retching, the kids struggling to get up and away but Bob still holding them tight to him, knowing the firefight is still raging. Then he hears Becky, crying as she crawls towards them, and he lets go.

JC's face appears above him, luminous, as a black helicopter banks across the blue sky behind him. Bob tries to speak but tastes thick, coppery blood in his throat. JC is stroking his face tenderly, pushing the hair out of Bob's eyes. He's smiling. Becky's face dips into the picture too, she's crying and saying something as she bends to kiss him, but Bob can't really hear anything any more, just a whooshing sound in his ears, like when you put a seashell to your ear when you were a little kid and they told you it was the sea you could hear. The helicopter banks back overhead again, lower now, starting to blot out the sun behind JC, its blades looking like they're in slow motion. Bob feeling cold, like he heard so many guys say they felt back in the day. Bob needs to speak, has something he needs to say to JC, a word that needs to be dredged up through the blood and lead and pain in his chest. His lips are moving, his top teeth touching his bottom lip as he searches for the fricative. Jesus leans in close to him, his pale blue eyes calm and clean amid this hell.

'Fr . . .' Bob says with great effort. Jesus, taking his hand now.

'Fr . . .' Jesus kissing him softly on the lips, getting some blood on his face.

'*Friend*,' Bob says for the first time in thirty-eight years.

For the last time too.

As the light starts to fade, as the cold he's feeling starts to thaw, getting replaced by a warm glow Bob's never heard about, as he starts to feel every atom in his body coming apart, he sees the single tear going down JC's right cheek and a rifle barrel appearing at his left temple as the black shapes of SWAT troopers loom behind him. The last thing Bob sees as he dies is Jesus putting his hands up in the air.

Part Six

ftermath

'I am for the death penalty. Anyone who commits terrible acts must get a fitting punishment. That way he learns the lesson for the next time.'

Britney Spears

1

E WAS TRYING TO WRITE A SONG IN HIS HEAD, ONE he'd been working on for months. He had an opening line – *'I know you won't be coming back again, sketch a smiling face in the misted windowpane'* – and he could hear how he wanted the first part of the chord sequence to go – A maj to C-sharp min to F-sharp maj, kind of like Wire's 'Outdoor Miner' – but he couldn't quite hear where it should go after that. Up a step to B and start again? Or resolve to E for kind of a chorus? Difficult without a guitar in your hands, but he'd heard of songwriters who wrote whole things in their heads and then got them down when they next picked up an instrument.

He sat up in his bunk and looked out through the tiny, barred window: spring was officially upon the land but still the battleship skies, grey upon grey, even the clouds grey, the sun invisible, a sharp wind keening across Polk County, keening through the razor-wire fence in the distance, slapping at the sentries in the tower, rattling against the big metal sign over the entrance gate, a sign that JC could only see the back of, but he knew the front read: 'ALLAN B. POLUNSKY UNIT' (*operated by the Texas Department of Criminal Justice*').

This was the penultimate stop in the system: a couple of dozen dirty grey buildings set in 470 fenced, heavily guarded acres.

He yawned and dropped down off the top bunk onto the cement floor. He had the cell to himself. They all did on this block. Pity, he'd been looking forward to a little company, but apparently, one of the guards had told him with a savage grin, a lot of guys lose it on this wing. JC would hear them at nights, crying or talking to themselves, most of them talking to God or their mothers.

With a bare toe (they only gave you plastic slippers in here and he hated the way they felt against his skin) he moved some of the newspapers around, drifts of them, covering the floor of the cell. Man, the newspaper coverage the past few months. He couldn't believe it, especially the first few weeks: 'COP KILLER!' 'CULT LEADER IN SHOOTOUT!' '14 DEAD IN CULT SIEGE!' 'MESSIAH OR MURDERER?' '*AMERICAN POP STAR* FINALIST IN MASSACRE!' 'ALLEGED CHILD ABUSE!' 'GUN RUNNER!' 'DRUG DEALER!' And so on. He'd rarely read past the first paragraph of any of these articles. They all said pretty much the same thing:

The musician and self-proclaimed 'Son of God', 32, shot to fame last year on the ABN talent show *American Pop Star*. He went on to open a so-called utopian commune in central Texas with his earnings from the show – estimated to be in excess of two million dollars. Officers from a combined BATF, FBI and DEA taskforce raided the compound near Bruntsville, Texas, on December 8 following increasing concerns about drug production, a cache of automatic weapons and, more recently, fears that child abuse was taking place within its walls. They were met with deadly force and the ensuing shoot-out claimed the lives of six officers and eight cult members while 18 others, including several children, were left wounded.

Then there was the photo – the same one used again and again – a blurry, pixelated shot of Jesus holding up the rifle he'd just taken off of Deek Rennet, caught for a split second on a camera mounted on that helicopter, caught hefting it up to throw it away. Not that anyone at the trial believed that, of course. The ballistics expert the prosecution brought in had tied the bullets taken from two dead troopers to that rifle and had expertly argued that the shots had come from exactly where JC was standing.

'Literally a smoking gun,' the prosecutor had said.

'Oh man,' Jesus had said.

Regardless of the fact that not one child who came out of the estate confirmed the abuse allegations the damage was done: child abuse, drug dealing (JC had freely admitted they'd grown marijuana, but argued that it was solely for personal use. The judge had refused to believe such quantities could possibly be just for personal consumption and had let the dealing charge stand) and the murder of six federal officers. It had taken the Texan jury just four hours to convict him on the drugs and murder charges. Capital murder too. 'The murder of a public servant in the line of duty.'

The reason JC kept all these newspapers in his cell wasn't so he could go over all the details of the trial in the hope of mounting an appeal or something. (Even though many of the 'quality' papers – the *Washington Post,* the *New York Times* and the *Guardian* and the *Independent* over in England – had started running stories questioning the motives and strategy of the government agencies, with some writers beginning to allege that they alone were responsible for the tragic events of December 8.) No, it was because of all the photos of his friends that were in there: Becky being led handcuffed from the estate, a good shot of Morgan onstage a few years back, grinning as he smashes a cymbal. (Where was that goddamn gig? JC wonders.) A photo of Kris talking to Jesus by the pool in LA. One of Bob as a young man in full combat rig, standing with arms folded in front of a helicopter somewhere. Even a photo of old Gus and Dotty, who'd died in their sleep in their bed, the smoke pouring in under their door failing to wake them before it dragged them under. A photo of Steven Stelfox accompanied a couple of the articles, interviews Stelfox had given where he denounced Jesus as 'a deluded, warped individual' and promised the public that, 'out of respect for those who died', the music JC and the guys had recorded would 'never see the light of day'.

One good thing: over the course of the trial he'd managed to convince everyone that he alone was responsible for the events, that Becky, Kris and Morgan had been under his 'considerable personal magnetism', as their lawyers put it, and consequently not responsible for their actions. Of course it had taken some effort, and a lot of back-channel dealing through the lawyers, to get Becky, Kris and Morgan to go along with this. Kris had still ended up getting sentenced to six months for contempt of court after he called the judge a 'fucken right-wing Nazi asshole scumbag'. He was doing his time at another jail, somewhere north of here. Jesus hoped he was well and had healed up OK. That bullet in his shoulder. Hoped he could play again. More oddly, Morgan had sold his story about his time in 'the cult' to a supermarket tabloid, making out that he'd been 'inducted', brainwashed and all this stuff. Man, that was funny. Jesus hoped old Morgs had got a load of money and that, wherever he was, he was happy too. Maybe going up to the B would be better than dropping it down to E . . .

'Hey there.'

Jesus looked up from the newsprint. It was Tommy, the guard who'd been mean to him when he got here – who'd told him about guys losing it with a wicked grin – like all the guards had, believing all the stuff they'd read in the papers. Tommy was real nice to JC now. Most of them were. You're around the guy long enough . . .

'How you doing?'

'Good, Tommy. What's up, man? Did your little girl get over that chickenpox?'

'I believe she's on the mend now, yeah. Uh, you got a visitor.'

'Visitor? I wasn't down for any, was I?'

'Nope. Bit last minute. Irregular and all but the Governor decided to let it go, seeing as . . . you know?'

'Wow. Who is it? Nah, don't tell me. I could use a surprise.'

Manacled and down the antiseptic hallway to the visiting room. The door opening and Jesus grinning instantly as she runs up to him, arms flung wide.

'Becky,' he says.

2

REATED ME LIKE A CRIMINAL. PUT ME THROUGH all kinds of interviews. The boys too – child psychologists and God knows what all else, trying about everything they could think of to get them to say something bad had happened to them. Sons of bitches. Three months they were away from me, in a home at first and then with a foster family. Danny said the home was awful but the foster people were nice. I mean . . . all those years when I was drinking and drugging and I managed to hang onto the boys and then, when you're clean and sober and working hard and living right, they come in and just . . . your own government. You know?'

'Yeah. I know.' Jesus smiles. Becky tries to, looking at him in that orange jumpsuit through her tears and red-rimmed eyes. She blows her nose into a paper towel again.

'I'm gonna go see Kris next week.'

'Yeah? Tell the big guy I said hi. Damn, he did such a good job losing all that weight. I hope he ain't piling it back on.'

'I'd have gone sooner, but it's a bit of a trip and I've been short on gas money. You know all our assets are still frozen?'

'Yeah. Listen, Becky, you know how Morgan sold his story to –'

'That piece of shit. If I –'

'Why don't you do the same thing?'

'Are you nuts? That scum –'

'Seriously. See what you can get. If you need money, get some money out of it.'

'What and have them distort it all so you come out of it looking like some fucking madman and –'

'Becky – who cares? It's just some bunch of shit in a newspaper. Don't be hard on Morgan. He must've needed the cash. Listen – no, Becky, listen to me. I want you to get hold of him somehow and –'

'There's no way I'm ever speaking to –'

'Get hold of him and tell him that I said we're cool and that I love him. Promise me, Becks.'

'Fuck, I . . . OK. I promise.'

'Good girl.'

A pause, Becky shredding that paper towel, not looking at him as she speaks. 'Tell me something, JC. How come you and I never got together?'

'Huh?'

'You never made a pass at me.'

'Well, we're friends.'

'Come on. Even early on, when we hardly knew each other, you never made a move.'

'Well, you weren't in great shape then. And, the thing is, Becks, I liked you too much. You know?' He smiles at her. 'And it was always going to end something like this. It wouldn't have been fair of me to get us involved. There were the boys to think about too. It'd be harder on them if we'd been –'

'You think this isn't gonna be hard on them anyway?'

'What have you told them?'

'I haven't said much to Miles. He just thinks you're going away. But Danny . . . Danny's old enough to read the papers. He knows. He hasn't said anything about it. But he knows. They're outside.'

'Outside? Why didn't you bring them in?'

'The whole time I've known you I don't think I've ever had more than five minutes when it was just the two of us. Can't a girl get some quality time?'

They hold hands and sit quietly side by side on the bench, Tommy the guard keeping a discreet distance on the other side of the room, reading his paper under the big clock in a metal grille. The minutes ticking past, nearly done. He can feel Becky beside him taking quick breaths, steeling herself, holding his hand a little tighter, working up to it. They're done with the catching up and the small talk. They're all caught up. Time for the big talk.

'Aren't you scared?' Becky asks finally, her voice a tiny whisper.

'No, Becks.'

'But, what, what if it's, I . . .' her tears starting.

'Shhh, come on now.'

'Oh God, *I just can't stand to think of them hurting you*!' She breaks down properly, falling into his lap, her shoulders heaving with racking sobs. He folds himself around her, stroking her wet face, his blond hair tumbling down over her, Becky drinking in his smell, trying to inhale him right down into the centre of her being, to keep a piece of him there forever. JC waits until she's got it under control a little and then lifts her up to face him, her raw eyes and slick cheeks beautiful to him even under those cold fluorescent strip lights.

'Listen, Becky, in the second it happens everything that is me will be flashing across the universe and I'll be home.'

'Oh God, I so want that to be true.'

'Shit, girl,' Jesus says, laughing. 'It's a good thing for you Dad doesn't give a fuck about who believes in Him or not.'

'Five more minutes, folks,' Tommy says softly.

'OK, OK, OK,' Becky dries her eyes and blows her nose one more time. 'I'll go get them. Look, let's . . .'

'Yeah, we'll keep it light.'

3

ATER THAT NIGHT THEY COME TO HIS CELL, TOMMY
and the younger guard, Phil, Jesus thinks. Phil is
holding a pad and pen. 'What's up, guys?' Jesus
asks.

'Ah,' Tommy says. 'We need to get your order. For your, uh,
meal.'

'Oh, right.' He nods, knowing this is difficult for them,
wanting to make it easier. 'You know, fellas, I don't need anything. Why don't I just order the maximum amount of food I'm
allowed – pizza, chicken, whatever – and maybe someone could
just take it out and give it to the first homeless people they find?'

Tommy and Phil, looking at him. 'Honestly?' Tommy says.
'I don't think they'll allow that.'

'Right.' He thinks for a long time, scratching his chin. 'In that
case . . . could I have baba ganoush?'

'Excuse me?' Phil says.

Jesus repeats it. Phil just looks at Tommy, none the wiser.

'I'll spell it,' Jesus says. 'It's B-A-B-A G-A . . .'

'"*Babaganoush*"?' Phil repeats, writing it down slowly.

'That's the one. It's kind of a Middle Eastern thing fellas. With some pitta bread and maybe some olives? That would be great.'

'Shit, I ain't never heard of that before,' Phil says. 'Most fellas up in here, you know, it's fried chicken or burgers or whatever.'

'Yeah? Can a lot of them, you know, still eat at that point?' JC asks, genuinely interested, leaning easily against the bars, talking to them like this was all something relating to somebody else. Just a subject for discussion. *Shit*, Tommy thinks. *This is either the coolest motherfucker I have ever fucking seen in my life or else he's in total denial and when he realises what is going down he is going to freak the fuck out.* Tommy hopes not. Hopes JC can meet it with the same dignity he's shown so far.

'Shit, they try,' Phil says. 'I once saw a guy, child-murderer son of a bitch too, ordering –'

Tommy shoots him a look and the kid shuts up. But JC is smiling, listening, and says, 'No, go on, man. I wanna hear. It's OK, Tommy.'

Tommy nods and Phil goes on. 'Right, well, this guy, right, he orders medium-rare steak with A1 Sauce, fried chicken breasts and thighs, BBQ ribs, French fries, onion rings, bacon, fried potatoes with onions, sliced tomatoes, salad with ranch dressing, *two* goddamn hamburgers, peach pie, milk, coffee *and* some iced tea.' Phil's laughing, Tommy shaking his head, smiling.

'Shit,' JC says, laughing along.

'Well, he got about halfway through that lot and then – woosh! Was like a goddamn fountain coming out.'

'Still,' Tommy says, trying to get off it, 'this Middle Eastern thing of yours . . . doesn't sound like a whole lot of food to me. You sure there's nothing else you want, son?'

'You know, Tommy, there is one other thing I'd really like . . .'

4

HE FOLLOWING AFTERNOON THE SUN IS SHINING. The first week of April, the first real spring day Texas has seen this year. Just JC and two different guards – Alan and Herman – sitting around in a different cell in a different prison, the third one he's been in over the course of the last four months. They'd made the forty-mile trip first thing that morning, JC handcuffed in the armoured bus, looking out another tiny barred window at a square of dirty sky that lightened over the course of the ninety-minute drive. He could see why they did it the way they did it: new people around. People who hadn't got to know you at all.

This is Huntsville.

The oldest prison in the state, built in 1849.

The last stop in the Texan justice system.

There is a big, square patch of sunlight on the cement floor between Jesus and the guards. Somehow old Tommy had come through for him. He must have had a connection over here or something, and Jesus has his bare feet up on the table, noodling around on a cheap, old acoustic guitar. He'd asked if he could be left alone with it for a while, to try and finish his song, but they'd said no on account of the strings. 'Fella could put them to improper use if he had a mind to. Cheat the taxpayer out of what he feels he's entitled to,' Herman had said.

The baba ganoush had proved more problematic than the guitar. It was beyond the repertoire of the Huntsville kitchen and they hadn't been able to find anywhere within twenty miles that did it. So JC had asked the guards what they'd like to eat. They'd demurred of course but Jesus figured that seeing as they were good Texan boys a little barbecue wouldn't hurt, and he'd asked for a big bucket of chicken and ribs with all the sides and fixings.

'You sure you don't want none of this?' one of them is asking, helping himself to another piece of chicken. JC shakes his head, smiling, and says, 'Hey, you boys know this one?' He strums an urgent, staccato A, all on the downbeat and goes into Springsteen's 'Johnny 99', the two guards listening, serviettes tucked into the collars of their uniforms, eating their barbecue and having a little private concert put on for them. Man, JC is enjoying playing the guitar again after all these months. It's a cheap, shitty mail-order guitar to be sure, strings way high up off the fretboard ('*Camper's guitar*', Kris would have said. '*You could pitch a goddamn tent under the strings.*' Never did get his Martin back from that pawn store in Democracy. He hopes someone got some use out of it), but playable if you don't try anything fancy, and there's a nice echo in here off the stone walls. Funny thing, guitar playing – if you don't do it for a long time it gets so your body physically misses the experience. Jesus sings that last line, the one about letting 'em shave off your hair and putting you on that execution line, letting the final chord ring out for a bit before dampening it down with the flat of his hand. Alan and Herman, both looking at him, barbecue sauce glistening on their lips.

'Shit,' Alan says after a moment.

A soft cough behind Jesus, the sound of a key going into a lock, and he turns around to see the Warden standing there, flanked by two more guards and another man carrying a bag who JC figures has to be the doctor. The Chaplain too.

'It's time,' the Warden says.

5

IX O'CLOCK.

The last room.

The Death House.

Smaller and more crowded than he imagined as he follows the Warden in. Maybe ten foot by twelve, smaller than the cell they just left, and right there in the middle, taking up the whole room: the gurney. It's big: silver metal with white foam pads and thick brown leather straps with silver buckles. There are five men standing around the gurney, a couple of them looking towards Jesus, some averting their eyes, looking at the floor, or fiddling with the buckles. Jesus realising that each of them is manning a part of the gurney that will relate to a part of his body: legs, arms, head. All the Huntsville staff hoping the same thing they always hoped on these days: that the guy wouldn't resist and that everything would go smoothly.

The Warden takes his place at the head of his team and the man next to him – an old, powerfully built guy in his late fifties with silver hair – says to JC, 'Son, I need you to hop up here with your head at this end and your feet down there.'

'Sure,' JC says.

Most of the men in this room have taken part in over a hundred executions. They have seen men crying. Men babbling and singing songs. They have seen men twitching uncontrollably. Men whose hearts have been pounding so hard you can see them beating against their shirts. They've never seen one this calm. It takes them just thirty seconds to strap him in, his arms extended out to each side of him, reminding him of striking a similar posture on that hill a couple of lifetimes ago. Well, JC thinks, at least we're lying down on foam pads this time. Progress of a kind, even if the nature of the offence remains the same. Atavism, he thinks. 'Thank you,' he says to the last man as he finishes strapping his left leg in. The guard manages the tiniest of smiles, the most imperceptible of bows as he follows his colleagues out of the room. The guy will remember Jesus thanking him for tying him to the execution gurney for the rest of his life.

The men who tied him down leaving the room now as two others enter, each quickly taking one of his arms and swabbing the inside of his wrists with rubbing alcohol. Medics. JC has, as a couple of junkies have had occasion to tell him, 'good ropes' and it only takes them a couple of minutes to hook the two IV lines up, one into each arm, the clear plastic tubes running along the gurney, down across the floor and disappearing into the wall to his right. There is a mirrored panel in the wall above where the IV lines disappear and Jesus pictures the poor guy sitting in there, flexing his fingers, getting ready to push the plungers on those syringes. Would his hands tremble? Jesus wonders. Or was it just another day in the corps? It is difficult for him to move his head too much but he turns fractionally in the direction of the mirrored window and smiles softly, hoping to reassure whoever is in there that he feels no animosity towards them. Like Dylan said – only a pawn in the game. Like those troopers, killing and dying in the cold Texas mud.

Now he turns to look straight ahead, looking through the gunsight of his feet, through heavy Perspex windows to where people are beginning to file into the viewing room. 'Ah, Warden,' Jesus says. It is only JC, the Warden and the Chaplain in the room now. 'Am I allowed to ask who's in there?'

'The wives and parents of three of the troopers who died, members of the press and a couple of people from the FBI and the BATF,' the Warden says softly.

Jesus watches as they take their seats, a few of them pulling their chairs right up against the glass. The journalists have notepads out. One of the women – a pretty, young blonde girl – is staring straight at him, her features just a snarl of hatred. An older couple are crying, cradling each other. At the back, in neat dark suits and ties, stern expressions on their faces, Jesus sees Stan Tawse and Don Gerber and remembers their testimony from the trial. Their phrases like 'reason to believe', 'probable cause' and 'necessary force'. Now the Warden speaks, his voice louder and more formal than it was a moment before as he asks, 'Do you have any last words you wish to say?'

JC sees that a boom microphone is lowering from the ceiling. He sees the clock on the wall: 6.11. Hardly more than ten minutes since they came in. He thinks for a long time, about injustice, cruelty and the almighty dollar. About hypocrisy and power ballads. About ego, ambition and politics. The usual reasons stuff got done down here. Jesus looks at the glass, at the hateful, grieving faces, and speaks softly towards the microphone. 'When the truth of all this comes out none of you should be too hard on yourselves. You . . . I mean, the Bible's mostly a crock, but there's no other way to say this, folks . . . you know

not what you did. Just try and remember,' he smiles, '*be nice*.'
He looks at the Warden and nods.

The Warden looks towards the mirrored panel and removes
his spectacles.

The signal.

Behind the mirror, the first plunger going down, the Sodium
Pentothal flowing through the clear tubing towards JC's left
wrist. As the powerful sedative hits him he is reminded of the
very few times he tried heroin. Once in a motel room in . . . San
Francisco was it? At that place where all the bands stay. The
Phoenix? Him and some bass player slumped in the shower
stall, how the bass player had said that if God had made
anything better than heroin then he'd kept it for Himself and JC
thinking about how there was maybe something in that but that
ultimately it was wrong because heroin was basically morphine
and was intended for pain relief and why would you need pain
relief in a place where there was no pain? But then again, just
because you didn't need something wasn't any kind of argument
against wanting to alter your consciousness anyway and who
was it that said that maybe God left certain drugs on the planet
as a way of accelerating our evolution and maybe we can go to
the moon and shards of millions of other conversations he'd had
in his time down here ebbing through his brain as his body
prepared for shutdown. More plungers going down now, firing
the two remaining compounds in the three-drug cocktail
towards his right wrist: first the chromium bromide, a muscle
relaxant that will cause his lungs and diaphragm to collapse, and
then, finally, the potassium chloride, the drug that will stop his
heart. And here it comes, not the cliché about heading into the
light and floating above his body and seeing all the people in the
room below him. Just the sense of . . . hang on. Hang on a
goddamn minute now, this *hurt*.

Holy shit – *this hurt*. Even through the heavy wash of sedatives he can feel the bromide corroding into his lungs, his heart, his spleen. Everything collapsing, liquefying from within, like his whole body is suddenly a vessel of bile. Acid. It's like having blistering acid pumped into every crevice of your insides. He tries to scream but can't, still conscious enough to experience all this agony but too far down the well of sedation to do anything: like having the worst, most lucid nightmare possible, where you can see the room around you but cannot snap awake. He feels something come loose in his stomach, things collapsing, falling in on themselves. And suddenly, despite all he knows, he wants so very badly to live, to hang on to a shred of life. The blinding glare of the lights, the Warden's inclined head, the black microphone like a terrible insect, trying to scream again but feeling blood and liquefied tissue hacking up into his windpipe, inhaling his own collapsing lungs and such terrible, terrible pain and then, suddenly, he's dissolving into a billion atoms, every single one of them a tiny him and . . .

6

THE BILLION TINY PARTS OF HIM TWINKLING THROUGH TIME AND space and then, with the sensation of coalescence, of iron filings gathering towards a magnet, of everything coming back together, of coming round after being briefly knocked out, he is screaming as he falls into the arms of his father, who is saying, 'Easy, son, I got you,' Dad having to raise his voice a little over the clapping and cheering and whistling.

'Fuck!' JC says. 'Shit.'

'Welcome home, kid,' Dad is saying in his ear, hugging him tightly while behind Him the clapping and cheering and whistling goes on. They're in the big conference room. It's decked out for a party. Jesus – breathing hard, sweating, like waking from a terrible nightmare – can see Jeannie and Lance and Jimi and Peter and Andrew and all the saints and a bunch of the others, and right there, in the middle of them, are Pete and Claude and Bob and they're all wearing fucking *togas* of all things.

'Ow,' Jesus says, rubbing his chest, 'that *hurt*, man.'

'Oh shut your pie-hole,' God says, affectionately slapping his cheek. 'Lethal injection's a walk in the park. Shit, you're lucky you weren't in Virginia or Alabama. They still use the chair there. Lemme tell ya – that'll put hairs on your balls. Listen to you whining about a little jab. How about your buddy here? The big guy took three fucking rounds in his ass and he still walked in here like a man . . .'

'Ah, give the kid a break,' Big Bob says, coming forward now.

Around this time, less than thirty seconds after his arrival in Heaven, the mortuary assistant in Huntsville is walking into the prison morgue, a piece of paper in his hand, JC's death certificate. On the certificate, under 'CAUSE OF DEATH', are the words 'State Certified Legal Execution'. The mortuary assistant Jim Baker – a man who will spend much of the next few weeks being interviewed by police and reporters – places a hand on the metal drawer and pulls it out towards him, finding nothing where he expected to find the three-day-old body of Jesus Christ, thirty-three once again at the time of death.

'Bob,' JC says, embracing him. 'What's with the toga, dude?'

'Listen to Mr State Penitentiary 1982!' Lance shrieks, plucking distastefully at JC's prison jumpsuit.

'Thought we'd go toga for your welcome-back party,' God says, handing Jesus a big white sheet. He pulls the jumpsuit off, starts putting the toga on, people whistling.

'Yeah, I like it, man,' Bob says, touching his robe. 'All those years in combat gear down there . . .'

So funny, so great, to hear Bob talking normally, in full sentences.

'Right, fanny-baws, get yer laughing gear round this,' Andrew says, cracking the cork out of a bottle of pre-war champagne. There are lots of them, Jesus sees, stacked in big silver bowls overflowing with ice on the long trestle table at the top of the conference room. A good-looking buffet laid out too; cold cuts, a huge salmon with slivers of cucumber sliced to look like scales placed all over it and lots of fruit; melons and mangoes and pineapples and peaches. Right in the middle of the table there's a huge copper bowl filled with what looks like strawberry punch. Shit, the fruit in Heaven. Oh man.

'So – what's happening?' JC asks.

'Well, first,' God says, exhaling, passing His son the mammoth blunt he's just lit, Andrew passing him an icy glass of that good champagne, 'we're gonna get loaded.'

'Yeah?' Jesus says as music starts up. He can see Peter on the decks in the corner, dropping hip-hop.

The party starts kicking off, the music getting louder, people dancing as Pete comes over and they embrace. 'I was going nuts watching your trial,' Pete says.

'Yeah, how about that?' Jesus says.

'No,' Pete says. 'What I mean is – I can't believe none of you idiots remembered.'

'Remembered what?'

Pete tells him. Jesus slaps his forehead and then he's fighting his way through the crush of well-wishers towards God. 'Here, Dad, hold the fort. I got something I need to do down there. I'll be back in, like, five seconds our time.' Jesus looks to his wrist for a watch, but it isn't there. 'Hey, how long's it been down there since I came back?'

God wedges the blunt in His mouth and a champagne bottle under His right armpit as He looks at the Timex on His wrist. 'Uh, you been back a minute or two . . . I dunno. Maybe a few weeks?'

'Shit. Yeah, I'll be right back.'

'Don't be long,' God says.

Everybody slapping him on the back as he threads his way through the crowd, some chick pinching his ass. He sees two pairs of feet sticking out from under one of the buffet tables and lifts the cloth as he walks by: old Gus and Dotty, passed right out, surrounded by a drift of empty champagne bottles. Must've started early.

7

MALL-TOWN OHIO, THE DAWN STREET EMPTY SAVE for two kids on their bicycles, fishing rods tucked under their arms. Their chatter dries up as they self-consciously watch the stranger in the big funny gown approaching them.

'Hey, guys,' Jesus says. 'Is this the right street for the Anderson house?'

'Uh, who?' one of the kids says.

'The Andersons? Old couple but they got some boys living with them right now.' One of the kids is eyeing JC up, thinking something over. 'Miles and Danny?' JC says. 'Danny's about your age.'

'Oh, Danny?' one of them says. 'Yeah, mister, it's the third house on the left down there. One with the red truck in front.'

'Thanks, man,' JC says. 'Later, kids.'

'Hey, mister,' the quiet boy says, causing Jesus to turn around. 'Are you on TV?'

'Ah, I used to be,' Jesus grins.

The two boys will also spend much time being interviewed by the media over the coming weeks.

And then Danny is rubbing his eyes as he wakes up, saying 'Mom?' instinctively as his vision clears and he sees Jesus sitting on the end of his bed. Danny's mouth forms a tiny 'O'.

'Hi, buddy,' Jesus whispers. He's already seen the newspapers on the kitchen table downstairs: his face on every one.

Danny can't speak.

'It's OK, Danny, nothing to be scared of.'

'I'm not scared,' Danny says.

Jesus gives it a moment, just sitting there quietly, smiling, before he asks, 'How you been, kid?'

'OK, I guess.'

'Yeah? How's school?'

'We got a strict teacher, Mrs Douglas.'

'She busting your balls, huh?'

Stirring now in the bed on the other side of the small room, then something small and warm and sleepy is suddenly at JC's elbow. 'Uncky Jesus?' little Miles says. JC lifts the boy up onto his knee. 'You're wearing a dress!' Miles says.

'Ah, kind of. It's called a toga. It's a party I'm at. I just popped out to say hi to you guys.'

'But you're dead,' Miles says matter-of-factly.

'Miles!' Danny says.

'Sorry,' Miles says, sensing he might have caused offence. 'I, I mean you . . . you don't live any more.'

Jesus laughs at the euphemism. 'That's right. Well, I don't live down here any more. I live back in Heaven. Like your home is here with Mom and Grandpa and Grandma now. How you all getting along?'

'Grandpa takes us bowling!' Miles says.

'And buys us candy all the time,' Danny adds. 'Too much, Mom says.'

'How is your mom?'

The boys look at each other. 'She cries a lot,' Danny says.

'All the time,' Miles adds, nodding.

'Is that a fact?' Jesus says. 'Well, let's see what we can do about that . . .'

Children accept the very strange more easily than adults do and, of course, Becky's first instinct is to scream. He presses a hand gently across her mouth. 'Shh, Becks, it's OK. It's OK. It's me.' She's breathing very rapidly, sleepy eyes wide open now as she presses herself into the corner of the little single bed in what Jesus guesses is the bedroom she grew up in. There's discoloured patches of wallpaper with four holes at the corners where posters once hung. A stack of posters on the floor, one for the first Hole record on top, a pile of old photographs and CDs next to it. Lemonheads, Smashing Pumpkins, Mudhoney. She's been going through her old stuff. *Sign of depression*, JC thinks.

'Becks,' he whispers, 'I'm gonna take my hand off, OK? There's nothing to be scared of, OK, baby? Trust me.' He slowly takes his hand away.

'I'm dreaming,' she says.

JC shakes his head. 'It's me. Here . . .' He takes her hand and lays it on his chest. She feels warm skin through thin cotton, the slow flex of his heartbeat.

'How?' Becky says.

'Ah, technically? It's complicated. Don't fully understand it myself. How you been, Becks?' He strokes her face, smiling.

'I . . . not great.' She manages a weak smile. 'I been so close to drinking again.' She's right on the verge of tears. Jesus nods. 'I haven't but . . . it's just, for a couple of years there, when we were all together, doing stuff, I don't just mean since the show and all that, I mean before that, back in New York? I felt, it felt like I –'

'Like you had a purpose?'

She nods, a tear falling now.

'You still do.' He moves in close, taking her face in his hands. 'I got something to help you. A job.'

'A job?' she says, wiping away that tear.

'Yeah, I saw Pete and –'

'Pete?'

'Back home? You know . . .' He nods skywards. 'Anyway, Becks, you remember back on the ranch when we had the wind turbines put in? Remember there were a few problems and the guy from the company wanted to monitor exactly when the props were turning over, when they were storing up power? Remember? Pete was dealing with it.'

'Yeah.' Becky thinking, her mind turning over slowly, like one of those props on a still summer day, remembering that morning, her and Pete and the guy from the company standing around the base of that huge thing. The guy, he installed a –

'You got it,' JC says as her face breaks into a grin.

'Shit, I'm a fucking moron,' Becky says. 'How could I not have –'

'Hey, don't beat yourself up,' JC says. 'It's been a traumatic few months. You'd have remembered eventually. Now, you haven't been to see Morgs yet, have you?

'No, I . . .'

'Shit, come on. You promised me. He knows he did wrong with that story thing but, like I told you, probably wasn't thinking too clear. Needed cash or whatever.'

'Yeah, like I couldn't use a few bucks,' Becky says, gesturing at her teenage room.

'Get over it, Becks. *Forgive him.* I have. Shit – nothing to forgive. Get together with Morgan, tell him you've seen me –'

'He'll never believe this.'

'I could only come see one of you. You needed it more. Tell him you've seen me and you guys break the fuck in there if you have to, but get on it. It'll be worth a lot of money too . . .'

'I'm dreaming,' Becks says again.

'Well,' Jesus says, 'get your sweet cheeks on over there and we'll find out . . .'

8

ACK IN HEAVEN AND THE PARTY DID INDEED GO ON and on till the break of dawn. And you best believe that no one throws a party like God. That great, brimming bronze bowlful of strawberry punch? Laced with a kind of all-natural super-strength MDMA from the Boss's personal stash. It blasted you to the fucking moon within thirty minutes, kept you there for six straight hours and involved no comedown whatsoever. It was so good that God had indeed kept it for Himself. They danced on tabletops, they drained the bar (which was, of course, instantly, magically, restocked. No one makes dawn runs to dubious all-night liquor stores in Heaven), they sang themselves hoarse – Jesus at one point being carried around the room during the Roses' 'I Am the Resurrection' – and they all took turns in corners and on sofas telling each other how much they loved one another.

Sometime around daybreak JC finds himself stretched out on a beanbag talking about the meaning of life with a mad, totally random old group: Big Bob, John Belushi, Gandhi, a cab driver called Max, the former British Prime Minister Neville Chamberlain, Abe Lincoln, a couple of the Brontë sisters (wild, wild chicks, man) and Dean Martin. Martin is telling a story about some orgy he'd been to once and Chamberlain, who isn't handling the strawberry punch too good, is saying, 'I feel rather, um, *sideways* at the moment –' when God comes over and takes His son by elbow.

'Got a minute?'

They stumble off down the hall towards God's office, daylight streaming in through the cracks in the drapes as they pass a couple rolling around on a chaise longue.

'Guys,' God says, 'get a room.'

Jesus flops down in one of the easy chairs facing God's desk, yawning, beat but happy, as God goes into the little cocktail cabinet behind His chair and brings out the good Scotch. The *very* good Scotch, JC sees. Bottled in 1889.

'What's up, Dad?'

'I thought we'd have a little nightcap and catch up on recent events,' God says, handing JC a crystal tumbler of the centuries-old malt. He helps Himself to an enormous Cohiba, takes a seat next to His son, and thumbs the remote control. The bank of screens on the wall lights up and they settle back to watch selected news footage from earth, where, of course, some thirty years have passed since they got the party started last night.

His legend had really kicked up a gear with the disappearance of his body from the Huntsville morgue. Conspiracy theories a gogo. Internet meltdown. All that shit.

Then there were the guys.

Becks and Morgan had broken into the abandoned, burned-out ranch near Bruntsville and gotten the hard-drive recorder from the base of one of the big wind turbines. The hard-drive recorder that was linked to the digital camera on top of the turbine. The camera that had, like Pete thought, been pointing the right way, at the back of the house, giving a wide, high master shot of the whole fucking mess. The footage was clear, sharp and unarguable: the helicopter gunship strafing the compound, the huge sizzling rounds tearing the building apart, JC clearly visible as he disarmed Rennet and threw the rifle away, the tank opening up with its flame-thrower, spraying fire into a timber structure where women and children were hiding. That was the bit that every news service in the world played over and over again, usually followed by the clip of the BATF and FBI directors being interviewed in the wake of the atrocity, Stanley Tawse from the FBI saying, 'Categorically, we did not use unreasonable force.' Don Gerber from BATF saying, 'We did not burn that building down.'

Gerber resigned first.

Tawse soon after, later committing suicide.

The Attorney General was fired and then subjected to prosecution for her role in green-lighting the disaster.

Then the footage of Becky, Morgs and Kris on the interview circuit, on chat shows, news programmes, *Breakfast with America*. The best-seller Becky wrote about her life with JC.

People wearing the T-shirts saying 'BE NICE!'. Bumper stickers saying the same thing.

Steven Stelfox's U-turn was breathtaking in its audacity; he posthumously released the demos they'd recorded in Texas, calling Jesus a 'modern American folk hero', saying how he'd always, deep down, believed in his innocence and greatness. He called the album *The Vindication* and it spent thirty-two weeks at number one, going on to sell fifteen million copies in the United States, several million more around the world, becoming one of the biggest selling records of all time, earning Stelfox a fortune to complement the one he already had.

Then God saying 'Shit, look at this!' as he freezes the frame and zooms in on a shot of a heaving Times Square, getting closer on an overweight woman making her way through the lunchtime rush. Closer on her face, Jesus not quite understanding what he's so excited about until he sees it dangling from a chain around her neck.

A silver syringe.

'Oh shit, you gotta be kidding me . . .' JC says.

Then they're both howling with laughter, slapping their thighs and falling about on the floor and gasping for air as the door opens behind them and Lance comes in with a sheaf of papers. 'Ah, fuck,' God says, wiping a tear. 'That's too good. Man, I almost wish they had electrocuted you. Bitch would have a fucking chair around her neck.'

'Gee, thanks, Dad.'

'What are you hets cackling about?'

'Ah, human stuff. They sure do love to worship, don't they? Thanks, Lance,' God says, taking the papers.

'The overnight numbers,' Lance says, God already expertly sifting through the figures. 'You'll be happy. The kid done good. Right, boys. I am off to bed. Alone sadly.'

'Later, dude,' JC says as Lance shuts the double doors behind him.

God is indeed happy. A sports nut, He loves his stats. 'Well then,' He says, 'we are up on admissions by 22.8 per cent on the previous half-day.' The half-day referring to approximately twenty-eight years on earth, of course. 'Peter's estimating we'll increase that by another 7 to 8 per cent in the coming twenty-four hours. Looks like the SOBs are actually playing nicer . . .'

'Well, good to know it wasn't a total waste of time.'

'Hell no, son.' God looks at His watch. 'Is it too early to . . . nah, fuck it, let's give the little prick a call.'

Jeannie has the day off to recover from the party, like the rest of His outer office, so God dials the three digits Himself, the huge videoconferencing screen lighting up as soon as He taps the last '6'. A few rings then a bleary-eyed Satan answers. He's in a kimono, sitting on the edge of his bed. 'Morning, scumbag!' God says brightly. 'Didn't wake you, did we?'

'Fuck you,' Satan says. There's something in the bed behind him, a horse or something. 'The fuck you want at this time?'

'Sin never sleeps, pal. How's your numbers looking?'

'Ah, get fucked,' Satan says, yawning.

'Cos from where I'm sitting you gotta be down, down, down, buddy . . .'

'Yeah, yeah. Laugh it up, fucko. This shit ain't over. It's a marathon, not a sprint. I'm going back to bed. Why don't you two go fuck each other and I'll see you in Hell?'

'Aw, come on, don't be like that,' God says, 'Come up for dinner tonight?'

'Maybe,' Satan says. 'I'll call you. Now fuck off.'

The screen goes black. 'Ah,' God says, rubbing his hands together merrily, 'it's the little things that get you through.'

'Right, Dad, I'm gonna hit the hay.'

'Yeah, get some rest. Your buddies will be here soon.'

Shit, of course – Becky, Morgs, Kris. All in their sixties now. They'd be here by the time he woke up.

'Night, Dad. You should turn in too, you know.'

'Yeah, won't be long. Goodnight, son.'

God smiles as He watches His boy shuffle off to bed and then He takes His drink and cigar across to the French windows behind His desk, overlooking the emerald orchard where the souls of toddlers and tiny babies play. He watches them gurgle and gambol in the morning light, squeaking with delight among the flowers. Many of them had met violent deaths;

burned alive in house fires, beaten until their delicate spines broke or their chests caved in, drowned in dun canals, in rivers the colour of lead, strangled with bunched, tattooed fingers. Some gassed in ovens and others sundered with machetes or shot with automatic weapons at close range. All perfect and unscarred here of course. The infants are the luckiest ones really; the ones who get to grow up in Heaven, who will never know anything else. Why do babies on earth cry? The thought causes God to remember a line from John Updike, whose work He's been enjoying very much recently. (Nice guy. Decent, honest golfer too. The kind of fellow who won't take a gimme if he thinks there's a chance he'd miss it.) He thinks of the line now as He stands in the dawn sun savouring the last drop of that good Scotch, the last couple of inches of the Cuban:

As souls must cry when they awaken in tiny babies and find themselves far from heaven.

Literature. Now that was some good shit.
He was glad they'd come up with that.